HERMSPRONG

Priestley Riots →

    series of disturbances during which
loyalist "Church-+-King" mobs
attacked + destroyed the chapels
+ properties of local Dissenters, as
well as prominent members of the
Lunar society. Violent expression of
loyalist support in opposition to
parliamentary campaigns of

Protestant Dissenters for political +
religious reform. Wider anti-
revolutionary activism in response to
French Revolution.
(14 July 1791; military restored order
17 July 1791 [they attacked Bastille
banquet + spread out — 4 Dissenting
chapels destroyed 127 homes attacked])

Joseph Priestley — most prominent; had
house + chapel destroyed.

Anglican officials may have been
responsible for directing + coordinating attack.

(4 of 50 men
convicted)

HERMSPRONG;
or MAN AS HE IS NOT

ROBERT BAGE

edited by Pamela Perkins

broadview literary texts

National Library of Canada Cataloguing in Publication Data

Bage, Robert, 1728-1801
  Hermsprong; or, Man as he is not

(Broadview literary texts)
Includes bibliographical references.
ISBN 1-55111-279-5

I. Perkins, Pamela Ann. II. Title. III. Title: Man as he is not.
IV. Series.

PR4049.B5H4 2002   823'.6   C2001-903863-1

Broadview Press Ltd. is an independent, international publishing house, incorporated in 1985

North America
Post Office Box 1243, Peterborough, Ontario, Canada K9J 7H5
3576 California Road, Orchard Park, NY 14127
Tel: (705) 743-8990; Fax: (705) 743-8353;
e-mail: customerservice@broadviewpress.com

United Kingdom:
Thomas Lyster, Ltd.,
Unit 9, Ormskirk Industrial Park, Old Boundary Way, Burscough Rd,
Ormskirk, Lancashire L39 2YW Tel: (1695) 575112; Fax: (1695) 570120;
E-Mail: books@tlyster.co.uk

Australia:
St. Clair Press, P.O. Box 287, Rozelle, NSW 2039
Tel: (02) 818-1942; Fax: (02) 418-1923

www.broadviewpress.com

Broadview Press gratefully acknowledges the financial support of the Book Publishing Industry Development Program, Ministry of Canadian Heritage, Government of Canada.

Typesetting and assembly: True to Type Inc., Mississauga, Canada.
PRINTED IN CANADA

This book has been printed on 100% post consumer waste paper, certified Eco-logo and processed chlorine free.

Contents

Acknowledgements

In preparing this edition, I have consulted earlier editions of *Hermsprong* by Stuart Tave and Peter Faulkner; I have learned a great deal from their scholarship, and I would like to acknowledge a general debt to their work in addition to the specific debts that I have noted in the introduction and the text of the novel. I am also grateful to the Birmingham Public Library for arranging to have Bage's letters to William Hutton microfilmed for me and for allowing me to quote from them. Finally, I would like to thank George Toles and Cliff Eyland for reading and commenting on a draft of the introduction and Lea Stirling for her help with the translation of the Latin epigraph.

Introduction

Hermsprong is "a very ugly name," a young woman says dubiously after first meeting the eponymous hero of Robert Bage's 1796 novel (89); other characters agree, mangling the pronunciation and forming dark suspicions about the mysterious origins and intentions of the outspoken, intensely radical, and oddly-named young man who suddenly appears in their Cornish village. Readers today, hearing the title of the novel, are likely to find the name just as strange and off-putting as do Bage's characters, as *Hermsprong* is not a book that has ever received much attention. That neglect might initially seem easy enough to understand. A novel defending the new, radical philosophies of 1790s England, by an author whose other books are even more obscure, might not, after all, appear to have much to offer readers more than two centuries later. Yet however much it has tended to be overlooked, *Hermsprong* continues to charm many of those who do read it, and for reasons that might not be expected of a book that focuses on two-hundred-year-old political controversies. Peter Faulkner, who edited the novel in the 1980s, called it "one of the liveliest and most entertaining political novels in English" (vii); Stuart Tave, another of Bage's very few twentieth-century editors, praises the book's "active play of mind, and its likable and equable manner" (12). Lively, entertaining, likable, and equable — these are adjectives that might not immediately spring to mind when one thinks of political fiction, but they are entirely appropriate to *Hermsprong*, a book that focuses as much on the pleasures offered by clever, witty debate as it does on the ideas developed in such conversation. Indeed, Bage not only presents his ideas with wit and tolerant good-humour, but suggests that these are the deeper values underlying his characters' calls for specific reforms. While the details of 1790s politics might not be a matter of pressing interest to most twenty-first century readers, what *Hermsprong* offers is more than a program for late-eighteenth-century reformers; more generally, it suggests that wit, tolerance, and the free play of intelligence are not merely tools for political change, but the human qualities that any political system worth endorsing must foster.

Good-humoured tolerance is not, perhaps, the first quality one thinks of in connection with political reformers of any sort, then or now, and a brief overview of Bage's life around the time that *Hermsprong* was written might lead one to expect to find more anger than humour in the novel. The 1790s were not an easy time for Bage, a provincial paper manufacturer who had earned a moderately comfortable living from his business on the outskirts of Birmingham since the 1750s. He had suffered serious financial losses in the late 1770s, and by the mid 90s, when he was in his late sixties, his livelihood seemed threatened again by rising wages, rising costs, and falling profits.[1] Nor were his troubles limited to business. His youngest son had died in 1793, a loss that apparently contributed to his decision to move from the tiny village where he had spent his entire adult life to the nearby town of Tamworth. His strongly-held political views were increasingly unfashionable, even dangerous; Bage's long-time friend and business associate, William Hutton (1723-1815), had lost property to looting and fire in the Birmingham Church-and-King riots of July 1791, and matters did not improve much in the following years. Shortly after the riots, Bage wrote that "in every company I have had the misfortune to go into, my ears have been insulted with the bigotry of fifty years back;"[2] later, in a 1793 letter to Hutton, he reported bitterly that "I abstain from all society, because respect for my moral principles is scarce sufficient to preserve me from insult on account of my political —" (106). His uneasiness about speaking his mind seems justified, as in 1796, two speakers from the radical London Corresponding Society were arrested and put on trial in Birmingham after holding a public meeting to call for annual Parliaments and universal suffrage.[3] Under such circumstances, it would not be surprising to find in *Hermsprong* something along the lines of the bleak view of society provided by Bage's younger contemporary William Godwin (1756-1836) in his extravagantly pessimistic *Caleb Williams* (1794), one of the most influential political novels of the era. Yet as critical as it is of existing British society, *Hermsprong* differs from the work of God-

---

1 Bage had invested in some ironworks which had gone bankrupt; he alludes to this loss in the preface of *Mount Henneth*, his first novel. For a more detailed discussion of this episode, see Hutton (Appendix A) and Faulkner, *Robert Bage*, 18.

2 Robert Bage's letters are owned by the Birmingham City Archives, in the Birmingham Central Library (catalogued as Robert Bage's Letter Book 486802 IIR 29), and are quoted by permission; this quotation appears on page 76 of the manuscript. All further citations from the letters will refer to this manuscript and will be by page number in the body of the text.

3 The activities of the Society in Birmingham are recorded in Mary Thale's *Selections from the Papers of the London Corresponding Society*.

win and of most of the other radicals in almost every respect other than its reformist politics. Amused and urbane, *Hermsprong* offers a quirkily optimistic vision of late eighteenth-century Britain in which social and political corruption can be vanquished by little more than common sense, good will, and good-humoured mockery.

★★★★

If *Hermsprong* is, in some ways, out of step with the more gloomily pessimistic visions of other political novels of the 1790s, Bage's location and generation both help to account for some of those differences. Although his work is always grouped with that of the so-called Jacobin novelists — that is, those who were inspired by the French Revolution to explore both the possibility of and the need for political and social reform — he was not part of the Jacobin literary and social circle, which included writers such as Godwin, Mary Wollstonecraft (1759-97), and Mary Hays (c.1760-1843).[1] For one thing, Bage (who was born on or before February 26, 1728[2]), was closer in age to the great comic novelists of mid-century — Henry Fielding (1709-61), Laurence Sterne (1713-68), and Tobias Smollett (1721-71) — than to his fellow Jacobins. More importantly, he was never part of their urban

---

1 The Jacobins were the most radical group of French Revolutionaries; their name was given to a loosely associated group of English writers — which included Thomas Holcroft, Helen Maria Williams and Elizabeth Inchbald, along with Wollstonecraft, Godwin, and Hays — by their conservative opponents. It was inaccurate, as none of those writers supported the Jacobin agenda of Robespierre and Danton, and most were sympathetic to the political ideas of the moderately Republican Girondins, who were defeated and executed by the Jacobins in a development that deeply shook revolutionary sympathies in England. See Gary Kelly's *English Jacobin Novel* for a full discussion of the topic; Marilyn Butler also provides a survey of the works of these writers in *Jane Austen and the War of Ideas*. Eleanor Ty has discussed radical women writers of the era in *Unsex'd Revolutionaries* (1993) and Claudia Johnson provides an excellent study of the debates between Burke, in particular, and the radicals in her *Equivocal Beings*.

2 This is the date of his baptism (see Faulkner, *Robert Bage*, 33-34, 157), although Hutton gives 29 February as his date of birth in his obituary. Bage himself claims in a letter to Hutton dated 11 March 1800 that "This day I am seventy" (243) and he seems to have told Godwin, in 1797, that he was then 67.

literary world. A native of Derbyshire, where his father had run a paper mill in the small town of Darley, Bage spent most of his life in Elford, a village near Birmingham where he established his own paper mill following his marriage in 1751. His fellow novelists thought his literary achievement in such a milieu both striking and noteworthy. Years afterward William Godwin reported, as a surprising curiosity, that Bage had "very seldom" travelled more than fifty miles from his village, had never spent "more than a week at a time" in London, and was thus "a memorable instance ... of great intellectual refinement, attained in the bosom of rusticity" (Paul, 1: 264). Sir Walter Scott (1771-1832), in his biographical introduction to Bage's fiction, commented rather proudly that Bage was "[o]ne of that class of men occurring in Britain alone, who unite successfully the cultivation of letters with those mechanical pursuits which, upon the continent, are considered as incompatible with the character of an author" (276). In a far more hostile manner, John Gibson Lockhart (1794-1854), in his review article on Scott's s *Lives of the Novelists* (1826), sneered at the idea that "the son of a miller, and himself a paper-maker in a little country town" would think himself able "to paint the manners of English gentlemen and ladies" (367). Bage was not unaware of the kind of reactions that a writer who was also a tradesman might provoke; he demurely replies to anticipated objections by "Messieurs, the Reviewers" in his preface to *Mount Henneth* (see Appendix B.3). It is precisely the self-consciously genteel distaste for trade exemplified by Scott and Lockhart that Bage is mocking in *Hermsprong* as he makes foolish Sir Philip as desperately ashamed of his successful tradesman father as he is proud of the bloodthirsty aristocrats from whom his mother is descended.[1]

As such satiric touches make clear, Bage's isolation from the London literary world did not mean that Bage himself was an unsophisticated or uneducated rustic; on the contrary, the edge of condescension present even in Godwin's sympathetic commentary seems all the more unjustified if one turns to other accounts of Bage, who was apparently devoted to literary and scientific pursuits throughout his life. According to a memoir by William Hutton, who had known him from boyhood, Bage had been something of a child prodigy and, by the time he was seven, was "the wonder of

---

1 Bage also features a merchant hero in *Barham Downs* and sympathetic merchant characters in all of his novels.

the neighbourhood" because of his progress in Latin. Later, he mastered Italian, French and music without formal instruction, and "being inclined ... to learn the abstruse branches of mathematics" when he was in his late twenties, he hired a teacher in Birmingham to instruct him. Hutton, who attended some of the lessons, claimed that within a month Bage "was able to teach his master" (478; see Appendix A.2).

Whereas Scott and Godwin present Bage, a provincial intellectual, as something of a curiosity, Hutton stresses that his friend was able to develop a lively and full intellectual life in the provinces, a matter which perhaps seems more plausible to twenty-first-century readers, familiar with the subsequent development of the industrial Midlands, than it did in the London-centred world of Bage's contemporaries. Birmingham had doubled in population during Bage's adult life, and by the time of his death in 1801, it had been transformed from the comparatively isolated city of his boyhood to a hub of the industrial revolution, a transformation resulting as much from intellectual as economic activity. Bage's novels indicate his regional pride; in *Man as he Is* (1792), the hero visits Birmingham, a city the narrator describes as

> a place scarcely more distinguished for useful and ornamental manufacture, than for gentlemen who excel in natural philosophy, in mechanics, and in chemistry. One of these has a manufactory at a small distance from the town, scarce better known in England, than in France and Italy, Holland, Germany, and Russia, or wherever commerce has displayed the British flag. (2: 216)

In this reference to the distinguished gentlemen of Birmingham, Bage probably had in mind some of the members of what was in fact one of the most important intellectual circles of the era. The Birmingham Lunar Society (so-called from its practice of meeting monthly on the first Monday after the full moon) was a group of men with wide-ranging scientific, political, literary and artistic interests. Members included the manufacturer Josiah Wedgwood (1730-95); the educational theorist Richard Lovell Edgeworth (1744-1817); James Watt (1736-1819), inventor of the steam engine; Joseph Priestley (1733-1804), the scientist who first identified oxygen; the industrialist Matthew Boulton (1728-1809); and the poet and scientist Erasmus Darwin (1731-1802), perhaps most famous today for being the grandfather of Charles Darwin, but then known for such work as his long erotic/comic poem *The Loves of the Plants* (1789), written to illustrate the Linnaean system of botany.[1] These men, all more or less free-thinking in politics and religion by the standards of the day, were vitally important to Midlands intellectual life — as well, of course, to Midlands life in general, as they helped to establish the new industrial economy that was, in the next century, to transform the region. Bage's connection with the group is admittedly tangential at best; indeed, according to Peter Faulkner, "there is no evidence that Bage knew of the Lunar Society as such," even though he was acquainted with at least some of its members (17). He was a "very particular friend" of Erasmus Darwin, whom he had known for more than forty years at the time of Godwin's 1797 visit (Paul 1: 262), and it is quite possible that he had met Priestley, who was a close associate of William Hutton. At the very least, he knew Priestley's work; he told Hutton that he enjoyed reading Priestley "on any subject except theology" (Birmingham ms. 486802 IIR 29, 106).

However limited Bage's personal connection with the Lunar Society, the intellectual tone of the group was evidently congenial to his interests, as the sort of non-conforming scepticism generally associated with the Midlands philosophers was a stance which he endorses explicitly in his letters and implicitly throughout his fiction. Bage himself seems to have been something of a freethinker, as in both his novels and his letters he expresses considerable sympathy for religious as well as political dissenters, including his good friend Hutton. His own religious affiliations are unclear; Sir Walter Scott, judging by both the sympathy with which Bage treats Quaker characters and the style of Bage's letters, assumes that Bage was raised in the Quaker faith, but it is evident that he was not a practicing Quaker as an adult. (Hutton says carefully that Bage "though barely a Christian, [was] yet one of the best" [479].) Whatever Bage's own faith, however, there is no doubt that he was deeply sceptical of the civic and social power of the Church of England, seeing that power as matter for far more serious criticism than any of its religious dogmas. His admirable characters repeatedly challenge church-and-king pieties, and while they do so in the name of tolerance of all faiths, Bage's less than reverential treatment of the established religion was one of the matters that got him into trouble almost from the beginning of his literary career. In 1784, *The Monthly Review* warned in an otherwise very favourable review that

---

1   See R.E. Schofield's *Lunar Society of Birmingham* for a history of the group and its impact on British scientific and cultural life.

Bage's "levity ... hath a strong cast of irreligion" (see Appendix B.1). Years later, Sir Walter Scott went much further, and torn between delight in Bage's prose and stern disapproval of his principles, he reluctantly concluded that despite the praiseworthy sympathy with Quakers, Bage had by adulthood "reasoned himself into an infidel" (283).

Fascinated as he might have been by contemporary religious and philosophical debates, and able as he was as a student of languages and mathematics, Bage was nonetheless never more than moderately successful as a businessman. William Hutton, who had, "from a very small beginning" attained "a state of affluence and respectability" in Birmingham society, recalled that in their childhood, Bage had "moved in a sphere more elevated than I," but that situation didn't last (Saintsbury in Scott 276, Hutton 478). Bage's letters indicate that Hutton was the more powerful figure in their business association, and in a letter to Hutton's daughter Catherine, printed by Sir Walter Scott, one of Bage's sons readily admitted that their fathers' "success in life was very different," in part because Bage "never had a strong passion for wealth" (Scott 282).[1] This is not to say that Bage was a failure as a manufacturer; Hutton estimated that his custom alone had brought Bage an average of £500 per annum in the years after 1756 (479), and while he apparently bought all of Bage's paper from 1761 on, Bage did have other business interests. Nonetheless, the heavy losses from the collapse of the ironworks in which he had invested were a major setback in Bage's career — so major that Hutton, Godwin, and Scott (the main contemporary sources for biographical information) all agree that Bage initially turned to novel writing in order to distract his mind from the severity of his financial problems in the early 1780s.

Nor were these investment losses Bage's only business difficulty. His letters to Hutton from the late 1780s on, witty and good-humoured as they generally are, reiterate the difficulties to which he is being driven by excises, high costs and wages, and low prices. In a 1795 letter he writes despairingly, "Everything looks black and malignant upon me. Men clamouring for wages which I cannot give — women

---

1 Bage had three children, all sons. According to Scott, "one ... died as he was approaching manhood, to the severe affliction of his father. Charles, the eldest son, settled at Shrewsbury, where he was the proprietor of a very extensive cotton manufactory. He died in 1822, at the age of seventy. Edward, the younger son, was apprenticed to a surgeon and apothecary at Tamworth, where he afterwards followed his profession. He died many years before his brother" (281-82).

threatening to pull down my mill — rags raised by freight and insurance — excise officers depriving me of paper! .... Am I to hang myself?" (Birmingham ms. 486802 IIR 29, 154). His gloom during these years was, again judging by his letters, increased by a political atmosphere that he found inimical to both his business interests and his own political views. Scott, who had no sympathy with the attacks on church and king in either the fiction or the letters,[1] thought that Bage's views "of state affairs were perhaps a little biassed [sic] by the frequent visits of the excisemen, who levied taxes on his commodities, for the purpose of maintaining a war which he disapproved of" (283). Yet he is somewhat unfair to Bage in implying that it was mainly personal interest and resentment at what he found to be excessive and even harassing visits by excisemen that made him dislike the government. Strikingly, Scott avoids even mentioning the Birmingham riots, an event which, it is clear from Bage's letters, added greatly to Bage's distaste for the political views shaping government policy during the last decade of his life.

These riots, to which Bage refers in *Hermsprong*, were probably the most significant outbreaks of counter-revolutionary violence in Britain and were sparked by a dinner given to commemorate the fall of the Bastille. They were not limited to demonstrations against the dinner itself, however, and they spilled over into general attacks on religious as well as political dissenters. Joseph Priestley's house and both of Birmingham's Unitarian meeting houses were burned, as was Hutton's country house (his town house was looted but not burned). Hutton, who was invited to but did not attend the Bastille Day dinner, seems in fact to have been marked out as a target, presumably because of his prominence as a Dissenter; Catherine Hutton recalled years afterward that

> A farmer's wife, who lived at the distance of a mile and a half, dressed herself in her holiday clothes, and came in her dung cart, with a party of her friends, to enjoy the spectacle of a house in a blaze; and appeared in some confusion when she found we were yet in possession of it, and she was obliged to explain the motive of her visit. (Beale 75)

The riots speedily degenerated into simple, terrifyingly uncontrolled mob violence — Hutton later claimed bitterly that his property was burned and he was driven from the city "by people who would have

---

1 Scott prints substantial excerpts from the letters in his article, but he is not always accurate in his transcriptions.

sold their king for a jug of ale, and demolished the Church for a bottle of gin" (qtd. Beale 70) — but Bage, like many other radicals,
blamed the reactionary social climate for inflaming old prejudices,
setting the rioters in motion, and then doing nothing to check them
until too late. While his own property was not endangered by the
riots, his satiric allusion to them in *Hermsprong* is shaped by some
direct experience. It was to Bage that Hutton and his family turned
for aid when they fled Birmingham; as Hutton later gratefully
recalled, Bage not only paid their bills when they turned up penni-
less at the local inn but refused to take any repayment and scolded
them for not coming to his house (479). That giving such aid
required, in the uncertain temper of the times, not just generosity but
courage as well is indicated by the contrast between Bage's behaviour
and that of the neighbour who refused to help Hutton's son salvage
some property from the smoldering ruins of their house, or that of
the proprietor of their original retreat, who hastily asked the Huttons
to leave (Beale 75-88). As a reformer and a freethinker, hoping for
change but tolerant of dissenting opinions, Bage could not have
found much to console him for his business problems in the unsettled political mood of the last decade of his life.

★★★★

After Robert Bage died on September 1, 1801, it was Hutton
who wrote the most important of his obituaries, and given their
long friendship, it is not surprising that Hutton chose to focus on
Bage's personal qualities, recalling his "generous cast of mind" and
his "*honour* and peaceable temper" (479; see Appendix A.2). Yet as it
was Bage's work as an author that earned him this relatively long
obituary in a national magazine, it is perhaps a little odd that Hutton says so little about his friend's six novels. Part of the reason for
that might be that even though Bage had been moderately successful during his lifetime, by the beginning of the nineteenth century
his fiction was already beginning to fall out of fashion, largely
because a changing social and cultural climate had made the novels'
political content unappealing. In her prefatory remarks on Bage in
her 1810 collection of English fiction, Anna Laetitia Barbauld
(1743-1825) — a liberal thinker who was shortly afterwards
attacked in the press for her own satire of English society in her
poem *Eighteen Hundred and Eleven* — observed rather austerely that
Hermsprong "is democratical in its tendency" and hence has fallen
out of favour with readers (ii). Sixteen years later, the sternly Tory

John Gibson Lockhart went even farther in his otherwise very favourable *Quarterly Review* article on *Lives of the Novelists*, scolding Sir Walter Scott (Lockhart's father-in-law) for rescuing Bage's novels "from an oblivion which we cannot help thinking they merited," as they recall the excesses of the Revolutionary era and are a "vehicle of all the anti-social, anti-moral, and anti-religious theories that were then too much in vogue among the half-educated classes" (367). Scott himself felt obliged to warn his readers against what he saw as Bage's dangerous "speculative errors" and "to point out the sophistry on which ... [Bage's principles] are founded" (290).

This caution, thought necessary even by an admirer such as Scott, contrasts vividly with the enthusiasm of the reviewer who, in 1782, proclaimed that Bage's "whole design is to infuse into the heart, the most engaging examples, the principles of honour and truth, social love, and general benevolence" (*Monthly Review* 66: 130). Nonetheless, it is true that even in the more relaxed 1780s, some reviewers were a little dubious about Bage's freethinking, and there is no doubt that the social and political changes between the 1780s and 1820s were so great as to make it not altogether surprising that a writer who, in 1782, could be admired for his solid morality might be seen as a dangerously radical figure by the 1820s. What is noteworthy about the nineteenth-century reception of Bage's fiction is not that its politics troubled later writers such as Scott and Barbauld, but that they thought it merited reprinting and critical attention anyway. Bage was not one of the many novelists who win some measure of critical respect during their own lifetimes only to vanish entirely from literary history as soon as the taste that briefly brought them into fashion changes. Despite Lockhart's irritated regret that a novelist as politically unsound as Bage had not been allowed to fade from memory, and despite their own reservations, both Scott and Barbauld felt obliged to include him in their collections of what they saw as the best of English fiction. They were prepared, in other words, to agree tacitly with those reviewers of the 1780s and 90s who ranked Bage with Smollett and Sterne rather than with the anonymous mass of his fellow Minerva Press novelists,[1] a judgment which might seem

---

1   Minerva Press, which published Bage's last two novels, unabashedly catered to popular tastes and while financially very successful, it did not tend to print authors with any serious claims to literary merit. When Dorothy Blakey calls Bage "undoubtedly the most distinguished novelist ever connected with the Minerva Press" (62), she is stating a simple fact, not indulging in hyperbolic praise of an underrated novelist.

almost as eccentric to twenty-first century readers, for whom Bage is hardly a household name, as it did to Lockhart.

Bage is, after all, something of a literary oddity, combining the unconventional comic outlook of such older contemporaries as Smollett and Sterne with the political radicalism of the younger novelists of the 1790s with whom he is more usually grouped. As such, he is a figure who slips between the cracks in literary history. Arguably, he is also unusual in that, as a middle-aged businessman, he began novel writing at all. There were novelists among the Birmingham intellectuals, but they tended to be the daughters of prominent men — Maria Edgeworth (1767-1849), most notably, but also Catherine Hutton (1756-1846), the serious-minded daughter of William Hutton, who, leaving history and politics to her father, wrote several novels in the early years of the nineteenth century.[1] Novels were still a slightly disreputable genre at the end of the eighteenth century and the early years of the nineteenth, as Jane Austen's (1775-1817) famous defence of them in *Northanger Abbey* (1818) suggests. They were by then, according to all the clichés, almost exclusively the preserve of talentless hacks and of silly, half-educated women who poured out trite love stories by the score, and after the admirable work of the great mid-century male novelists — Fielding, Smollett, Sterne and Samuel Richardson (1689-1761) — the genre was supposedly sinking into irreversible decay.[2] Bage himself seems to have had mixed feelings about

---

1 Although entirely forgotten today, Hutton was fairly prolific — she published a dozen books and sixty periodical essays — and moderately successful. In one of her letters, she commented that she found Jane Austen's "pictures of common life, [to be] something like mine, but much more varied; and her character is either something like mine, or what I would wish mine to be" (qtd. Beale 183).

2 This version of the history of the novel, which assumes a sudden falling off between the mid-eighteenth century and the age of Scott, was repeated in many critical histories up through the 1970s, although most twentieth-century critics would cite Austen, not Scott, as the significant early-nineteenth-century innovator. More recent histories, especially those shaped by feminist and cultural theories, have, however, challenged this construction of the history of the novel. In particular, Claudia Johnson (in *Equivocal Beings*) and Clifford Siskin (in *The Work of Writing*) have provided insightful arguments about the cultural impetus (both in the nineteenth and the twentieth centuries) for devaluing the type of fiction being written in the 1780s and 90s and preferring the very different types of writing offered by Scott or Austen.

authorship; in a letter to Hutton, he says in reference to *Man as he Is* that he has "taken great pains, and sunk money to Lane [his publisher] in the price, not to be known any more as a novel writer — The title of my last I even concealed from my sons" (100). (Admittedly, this deprecatory attitude did not prevent Bage from telling Hutton about his earlier novels before they came out and from asking for reports on any reviews of *Man as he Is* — but only if they were positive [Birmingham ms. 486802 IIR 29, 28, 100].) Such scepticism about the worth of fiction persisted beyond Bage's lifetime, and even as late as 1814 — at the moment that Walter Scott was almost single-handedly bringing new critical respectability to the genre — the critic William Hazlitt was proclaiming in an article in in *The Edinburgh Review* that the age of the novel was over.[1]

Bage was flippant about the genre in general as well as about his own novels in particular. He had no need to explain the "nature of the work" he claimed in his preface to *Mount Henneth* (1782), "for novels have all one nature." Critics might complain about the sameness of the plots, but they have no one but themselves to blame if they choose to read them, as their reviews are unnecessary: "Books of this class are printed, published, bought, read, and deposited in the lumber garret, three months before the Reviewers say a syllable of the matter" (1: iii, vii; see appendix B.3). When, in *Hermsprong*, poor Mr. Woodcock desperately seeks to supplement his income by literary pursuits, he cannot bring himself even to consider switching from his unsalable sermons to something that is "now pretty generally considered as the lowest of all human productions," despite his publisher's assurance that he might have some success "in the novel line" (114). Mr. Woodcock's publisher notwithstanding, if the novel as a genre tended to lack artistic respectability, that failing was not balanced by any guarantee of commercial success. Popular as they were, novels were not an easy way to make money, as many disillusioned novelists make clear. Years after the fact, the mid-century writer Jean Marishall (fl. 1766-89) recalled with dry irony the jarring injury to her pride when, expecting to be able to earn hundreds of guineas by dashing off

---

1   This argument appears in an overview of the history of the novel with which Hazlitt opens a review of Burney's *Wanderer*. Not everybody was immediately inclined to see Scott as successfully reanimating the genre; one reviewer, reporting gossip that Scott was indeed the mysterious author of *Waverley*, wondered rather grumpily why a man of Scott's reputation would stoop to write a mere novel.

three or four novels a year for eager booksellers, she was offered five guineas for the copyright of her first book. Matters didn't change much for first-time, unknown novelists in the following years. Nearly three quarters of a century later, the Edinburgh literary hostess Eliza Fletcher (1770-1858) indignantly described her daughter's foray into publication, in which she earned exactly ten pounds for her three-volume novel.[1]

Yet if fiction didn't offer Bage much in the way of respectability or extra money, what it did offer was a loose, flexible genre that provided him with the opportunity to explore what were obviously his very eclectic political and social interests in an accessible, popular medium. In doing so, Bage can in some ways be seen as looking back to the novel of mid-century, writing in the tradition of a number of works in which unstructured, episodic plots are the vehicle for wide-ranging social commentary and satire. In many cases, the only narrative continuity in these works comes from the perspective offered by a central, more or less passive, figure who observes the action — sometimes a figure as conventional as a traveller, at other times more unusual onlookers, such as the lapdog that narrates Francis Coventry's *Pompey the Little* (1751) or the guinea coin that narrates Charles Johnstone's *Chrysal* (1760).[2] Bage avoids such narrative gimmicks, but as he includes long inset narratives by minor or secondary characters, he ensures that his own novels are no less wide-ranging and episodic. The result is that even though his central narrative never strays from the basic sentimental plot of young English ladies and gentlemen falling politely and suitably in

---

1 Marishall 2:154, Fletcher, f90v. "[S]o much for a Lady's authorship!" Fletcher concludes. The novel was *Concealment* (1837), published in London by Bentley, and the author was Fletcher's youngest daughter Mary (later Richardson). (No author is given in the British Library catalogue entry for the book.) This is not to deny, of course, that there were spectacular success stories, and even an unknown with a promising manuscript could do fairly well — as did, for example, Susan Ferrier, with her £150 for *Marriage* and Jane Austen with the £140 she cleared on *Sense and Sensibility*. Yet Austen sold the manuscript of *Susan*, the early version of *Northanger Abbey*, for only £10. Bage himself received £30 for his first novel (Blakey 74).

2 Other examples of this genre include *Adventures of a Banknote* (1770-71) and *Adventure of a Corkscrew* (1775), in which a libertine, whose spirit has been confined in a corkscrew as punishment for his excesses, is the narrator.

love, his novels still manage to feature such wildly, comically implausible figures as a beautiful, aristocratic Transylvanian refugee whose dialogue is a pastiche of the political writing of Edmund Burke (1729-97) (*Man as he Is*); a French marquis who wanders with imperturbably urbane interest from battlefields in America to an Ottoman prison (*The Fair Syrian* [1787]); and a wild-eyed scientist who wants to electrify his gardens to improve the crops and who advocates the use of balloons for air war against France (*James Wallace* [1788]).

Bage owes a considerable debt to mid-century novelists in his comic characters and episodes as well as in this loose structure. Sometimes, that debt is very general, as it is in his setpiece scenes of virtue in distress which might be taken from any sentimental novel, although even there, Bage often gives a twist of his own. When Hermsprong, for example, is faced with that most familiar of eighteenth-century sentimental tableaux, a poor but virtuous family transfixed by despair as debt collectors raid their house, his initial response to their picturesque helplessness is a startlingly unsentimental but practical-minded regret that their "weakness" — and even "total imbecility" — prevents them from taking a single step to help themselves (283). At other points, the debt seems more specific. An elderly farmer who loses everything to debt, is pressed into the army, and eventually comes back weak and ill after years of service only to find his children dead and his grandchildren helpless orphans, appears in both Bage's s *Fair Syrian*, and (rather more famously) Henry Mackenzie's *Man of Feeling* (1771). There are also elements of Sterne's style and techniques in the novels,[1] and Tobias Smollett seems to have been a particularly strong influence. *Man as he Is*, for example, might owe something to *Humphry Clinker* (1771) in its Winifred Fluellen, a comic Welshwoman with a tendency to lapse into malapropisms (although comic Welsh characters do appear in a number of eighteenth-century novels). More glaring, and more generally noticed, is an episode in *James Wallace* in which the hero serves the woman he loves as a footman, an incident which, in the words of one contemporary critic, is "so nearly copied from the *Roderick Random* [1748] of our incomparable

---

1 Wayne C. Booth sees Bage as one of the few successful eighteenth-century imitators of Sterne's narrative method; see *The Rhetoric of Fiction*, 234-40, for Booth's discussion of Sterne imitations in eighteenth-century literature. Faulkner also points out examples of Bage's debt to Sterne in his edition of *Hermsprong*.

Smollett, as to displease by a too close imitation" (*Critical Review* 76).[1]

Yet if Bage looks back to an earlier generation of writers in plot and tone, as well as in his flippancy about fiction as a genre, the pervasive political flavour he gives his comic narratives, especially *Man as he Is* and *Hermsprong*, is entirely typical of the 1790s. By that point, novelists were using fiction for far more specific polemical ends than their predecessors had tended to do. William Godwin, explaining (perhaps somewhat defensively) in the preface to *Caleb Williams* why he had chosen to follow up his massive philosophical tract *Political Justice* (1793) with a novel, observes that many who will not pick up a work of philosophy will read fiction: the genre is thus a means of diffusing new ideas under the guise of entertainment. This idea soon became a commonplace, and in 1797, the *Monthly Magazine* was listing Bage and Holcroft among the "philosophical" authors who "have probably diffused more liberal, and more just moral ideas, than could, in the same space of time, have been inculcated upon the public by a thousand sermons, or by as many dry political disquisitions" (qtd Tave 5). The dissatisfied lady Bage quotes (or more probably invents) in the preface of *Man as he Is* (see Appendix B.3) is perfectly correct in observing that Bage's fiction tends to be careless about plots and to avoid detailed character studies, but in the novel of ideas, that Bage, like Godwin, is writing, those are minor flaws. The main interest in the books lies in the clash of political and social philosophies among the central figures, and it is this play with ideas that leads Bage to be classified today with the 1790s Jacobin writers rather than with the earlier novelists such as Smollett with whom he also has such marked affinities.

★★★★

The most obvious of the ways in which Bage manifests his Jacobin sympathies is probably, for readers today, in his treatment of women and sexuality. While predictably deprecating or condescending comments about women readers occur in all of Bage's

---

1   This comment appears in *The Critical Review*, which had been edited by "our incomparable Smollett." However, loyalty to their founder didn't make them unfair in their criticism; Marilyn Butler, writing in 1975, also thought that "a hero driven by necessity to become a footman is too memorable a feature to be used more than once" (76).

novels,[1] he was also sufficiently liberal in his attitudes towards female sexuality to seriously discomfit Sir Walter Scott, who wrote in some alarm that Bage's principles "would open a door to the most unbounded licentiousness" (287). Readers who turn from Scott to Bage expecting, on the basis of that comment, something along the lines of Choderlos de Laclos' *Liaisons Dangereuses* (1782) would, however, be very disappointed. Scott's dismay seems to arise simply from the fact that secondary characters in Bage's novels survive to make happy marriages after seduction (*Mount Henneth, Barham Downs* [1784]) and rape (*Mount Henneth*) — both of which tend to be fatal in the more typical eighteenth-century sentimental novel, or at the very least to cause irreparable and unending suffering.[2] Scott seemed particularly alarmed by what he saw as Bage's dangerously lax treatment of the seduced heroine of *Barham Downs*, who initially and very bitterly repents her seduction but then simply gets on with her life, happily marrying a man who knows her story and believes that her difficulties have made her a stronger character. Scott, deeply shocked, admits that seduced women might, on occasion deserve compassion, but then observes severely that with that compassion "there must be, not penitence and reformation alone, but humiliation and abasement" (287). Yet where Scott saw dangerously old-fashioned immorality, Bage's readers today are more likely to find a refreshingly modern, commonsensical tolerance. While Bage's novels do have their share of typically eighteenth-century sentimental virgins, brimming with timid innocence, they also feature an array of virtuous but knowing hero-

---

1   The stereotypical female reader, according to fiction of the time, was frivolous, conventional, and looking only for trivial amusement. Kate Flint's *Woman Reader 1837-1914*, although focusing on a later era, begins with a brief survey of eighteenth-century clichés about the topic; see, in particular, pp. 24-25.

2   The seduction in *Mount Henneth* is entirely off-stage; the girl in question, a precocious adolescent, is the schoolmate of one of the heroines. The rape victim is a major figure in an inset story and the mother of one of the heroines; Bage includes a dialogue in which she horrifies her future husband by assuming, on the basis of the English novels she has read (she is an East Indian), that she is dishonoured and unfit to marry him. He admits that his countrymen express such ideas in novels but hopes "for the honour of the human intellect" that few actually believe them (1: 234). Kitty Ross, in *Barham Downs*, conventionally enough falls victim to a smooth-talking wounded soldier.

ines who are easily able to defend themselves against would-be seducers — characters whom J.M.S. Tompkins describes as "militant Clarissas [who] defend themselves with sarcastic and resolved vigour" (202). In Bage's world, ingenues escape sexual danger not by tears, sighs, and faints, but by threatening a brothel keeper with prosecution ((*Mount Henneth*), by pushing a would-be seducer into a pond and nearly drowning him (*The Fair Syrian*), or simply by laughing off an attempt at seduction, as does Miss Fluart in *Hermsprong*. As Tompkins' comment suggests, Bage offers his readers conventional sentimental entertainment with a decidedly 1790s twist.[1]

Yet what Miss Fluart and her predecessors in the earlier novels embody is as much an amused, tolerant pragmatism about human nature in general as it is a specifically Jacobin feminism. Indeed, Bage's amusement at human foibles is decidedly at odds with the dominant tone of the work of many of the other novelists with whom he is associated. Jacobin philosophy — at least as presented by William Godwin, the dominant political theorist of the group — was optimistic, looking forward to a steady improvement for humanity, even if that improvement was deferred until the distant future. Yet the novels, usually purporting to show things as they were at the troubled end of the eighteenth century, tend to be thoroughly pessimistic, especially in their treatment of women's issues. Mary Hays, Mary Wollstonecraft, and Helen Maria Williams (1762-1827) all show women's lives shattered by a social system that thwarts women in their efforts at physical, mental, and moral development. Their world view tends to be fundamentally tragic, unlike Bage's amused exploration of human imperfection. In Bage's world, the villains are no match for the virtuous characters, and where they are not finally converted — as is *Hermsprong*'s Lord Grondale — they are ineffectual in a manner that is usually more dangerous to themselves than to their victims. The would-be seducer Sir Everard Moreton (*James Wallace*), for example, not only fails in his attempt to carry off the sweet, hapless, and rather dim-witted orphan who has caught his eye; he also accidentally injures a close friend who interferes and then botches an attempt to shoot himself in a moment of suicidal penitence. The aristocratic soldier who

---

1 I have developed some of these ideas about Bage's attitudes towards women elsewhere; see "Playfulness of the Pen: Robert Bage and the Politics of Comedy," *Journal of Narrative Technique*, Vol 26: 1 (Winter, 1996) 30-47.

seduces and abandons naive Kitty Ross in *Barham Downs* is selfish and callous, but he lacks the sort of destructive power that other seducers of sentimental fiction, whether radical or conservative, tend to have, mainly because after her initial shocked self-reproach, Kitty herself is able to accept the idea that a mistake of judgment, even one that her society deems catastrophic, does not destroy her identity at a single blow.

This attitude is somewhat different even from that of the Jacobin novelist with whom Bage's fiction has the most affinities, Thomas Holcroft (1745-1809). Those affinities are easy enough to see; in particular, the eponymous heroine of Holcroft's best-known novel, *Anna St. Ives* (1792), has a number of points in common with witty and strong-minded heroines such as Kitty Ross or Miss Fluart. When abducted and threatened with rape by the villain, Anna is able to defeat him without too much trouble. Both her energy of mind — a much-admired characteristic in Jacobin fiction, and one that Hermsprong shocks Mr. Sumelin by attributing to women — and her energy of body, as she proves herself remarkably adept at scaling walls, reduces poor Sir Coke Clifton from a would-be Lovelace to a comically inept swaggerer somewhat in the fashion of Sir Edward Denham in Jane Austen's fragmentary *Sanditon*. (Sir Edward, having read "more sentimental Novels than agreed with him" decides to seduce an orphaned ingenue, who knows perfectly well what he was about and has "not the least intention of being seduced" [Austen 6: 404-05]). Yet while Anna shares the pragmatic ability to take care of herself displayed by Bage's threatened or penitent heroines, those heroines lack Anna's verbosely humourless high-mindedness. Holcroft's world is one in which living is a philosophical exercise and pleasure a matter of moral calculus. (Anna decides, for example, after an elaborate chain of reasoning, that there is more social utility in following her heart and marrying her father's gentlemanly gardener than in making a conventionally "good" match with the handsome, wealthy and titled Sir Coke.) Bage's characters tend to be much more tolerant of whims, passions, and imperfection. However much even Hermsprong, perhaps the most thoroughly humourless and political-minded of Bage's heroes, might delight in challenging Caroline Campinet to follow reason rather than social convention in her relationships, he remains, after all, convinced that there are aspects of human interaction that are not subject to rational calculation. As Glen observes of Hermsprong when he hears that Caroline has returned to her father, "he was the perfect philosopher" in his words, but his obvious dismay "proved him 'no philosopher at heart'" (322). For Hermsprong, unlike Anna St. Ives, love is not, even in theory, a simple matter of rationally weighing options and then choosing the partner who will serve the highest social good.

If Bage's plot lacks the strict social utilitarianism that Holcroft, at his most politically programmatic, seems to envision, Bage also lacks the angry despair at things as they are that marks the more familiar Jacobin feminism of writers such as Wollstonecraft and Hays. Trapped by both male desire and social conventions, the heroines of their novels live in a nightmarish world in which women have no freedom to direct their own lives. Caroline Campinet, trapped between paternal power and her own desires, might seem to face a similarly impossible dilemma, but she differs from the heroines of more tragic radical fiction in several ways besides her ability to achieve a happy ending. For one thing, sweetly dutiful as she is, she is nonetheless able to formulate and assert her own feminist views without being destroyed by other characters' attacks on or manipulation of them. In her rejection of Hermsprong's flattery and in her insistence that "virtues have their limits" (268), to be determined by reason alone, she sounds more like Mary Wollstonecraft herself than like Wollstonecraft's victimized heroines, and while she is distressed by her father's arbitrary cruelty, she is also, finally, driven by it to rebel and escape his coercion. (As Bage repeatedly links Grondale's attitude to that of the absolute Bourbon monarchs, it is possible to read a light political allusion into Caroline's eventual desperate rebellion.) It is also worth noting that even though Hermsprong angrily dismisses her return to her father as a craven retreat into conventional and mistaken pieties, Miss Campinet finally takes Hermsprong on her terms, not his. She will not, in other words, let even Hermsprong coerce her into violating her own sense of integrity, even in the name of personal freedom. As she writes, in her dignified response to Hermsprong's reproving letter, "[h]owever wrong I may have been, I have at least the merit of having been governed by your own first principle of action; I have done what I thought to be right" (330). One should not, of course, make too much of this point, as that integrity involves an abject submission to paternal authority, something that all the rest of the right-thinking characters attack vigorously. Yet these attacks point to yet another difference between Caroline and more typical sentimental heroines, as they imply that Caroline is trapped not by a tragically and inescapably destructive society, but only by her own mistaken political views. What Caroline believes to be natural virtue — filial obedience — is, both Hermsprong and Miss Fluart insist, merely socially imposed custom, which Caroline has both the right and the ability to violate if she chooses. What William Blake called "mind-forg'd manacles" are thus mere illusions that ought to disappear the instant they are recognized as such, an idea that in some ways inverts the message of almost every Jacobin novelist except Holcroft. While novelists such as Godwin and Wollstonecraft are prepared to admit that social constraints are artificial, they nonetheless show those constraints as being so powerful that attempts to escape them are almost as self-destructive as passive acceptance of tyranny.

While this sense of the ease with which social constraints can be shattered is of course the source of much of Bage's comedy, it also leads to what some readers have found the greatest weakness in his fiction in general and *Hermsprong* in particular: sunny endings in which characters eventually win true love without having to sacrifice worldly prosperity. Several critics, including Marilyn Butler and Mona Scheuermann,[1] have regretted Bage's tendency to back away from the more radical implications of his characters' ideas in the fairy-tale implausibility of *Hermsprong*'s happy ending, and there is no doubt that Caroline, in particular, is in this respect little different from the typical sentimental heroine who loves, suffers, and then wins her happy ending by patiently virtuous endurance. It is also an implausibly thorough happy ending, as Hermsprong turns out to have not only the attractions of the unconventional outsider, but also the solid, insider advantages of title, estate, and fortune, ensuring that Caroline doesn't have to choose between love and money. Indeed, despite his "exotic" education and his taste for the works of Thomas Paine (1737-1809), Hermsprong even reveals a solidly British faith in the virtues of proper social subordination as he encourages striking miners to demonstrate proper loyalty to their king — an episode so out of tune with other scenes in the book that Stuart Tave calls it "a curious incident" and "something of a surprise." Tave explains the passage by pointing out that as unlikely a speech as it is from "a youth trained among savages" it is entirely reasonable coming from

---

1 Butler criticizes what she sees as Bage's failure to maintain either his "irony" or his "intellectual daring" to the end of the novel (84); Scheuermann argues that Bage begins by making "many basic criticisms of his society," but then retreats and "arrives[s] at his happy ending by ignoring the larger issues he has raised" (225-26).

a middle-class, property-owning reformer such as Bage, especially as its assumptions are in fact not all that different from those underlying the notorious pamphlet by Richard Price that provoked Edmund Burke to write his *Reflections on the Revolution in France* (9). Even so, Butler might not be alone among modern readers in wishing that Bage had at least had the literary courage to let Hermsprong end, as he began, as a nameless and iconoclastic wanderer.

Such regrets should not, however, distract one from the more innovative aspects of the plot, built around the comic secondary characters, Glen and Miss Fluart, who swerve just enough from literary conventionality to unsettle the otherwise almost outrageously conventional conclusion of the novel. Neither Glen nor Miss Fluart is entirely original, of course. Glen, the clever, rootless picaro figure, has ancestors throughout seventeenth- and eighteenth-century fiction, and if sweet Miss Campinet recalls aspects of Richardson's long-suffering Clarissa, Miss Fluart owes something to tart, outspoken Anna Howe — although Anna Howe is never given the opportunity to help Clarissa by such unladylike tactics as skillfully seducing her father into a proposal of marriage or pulling a pistol on her oppressors. Nor do Caroline's gentle rebukes have anything like the effect of Clarissa's lengthy and careful arguments with Anna. On the contrary: like Caroline Thurl in *James Wallace* (who explains, at length, why a friend is justified in falling in love with her footman rather than with Miss Thurl's rich and well-meaning but boorish brother) or Rebecca Carlill in *Man as he Is* (who sharply rebukes her friend's suitor for his libertine behaviour), Maria Fluart is a character who voices unconventional attitudes that the main heroine might be expected to feel but cannot be permitted to express within the boundaries of normal eighteenth-century feminine propriety. As such, she dominates the action in a way in which Caroline, the nominal heroine, never does.

This dominance is partly, of course, a result of the almost inescapable literary advantages that a witty heroine has over a sweet, more quietly decorous friend: Beatrice is more memorable than Hero in Shakespeare's *Much Ado About Nothing*, and readers of *Pride and Prejudice* invariably prefer Elizabeth to Jane Bennet. Yet by the end of their stories, these wits usually come to share at least some of the demure self-control of their modest friends. Beatrice's final words are "stopped" with a kiss; the newly-engaged Elizabeth checks her witty impulses because Darcy has yet "to learn to be laught at" (2: 371). Even the fiercely sharp-tongued Anna Howe finally subsides into dutiful marriage with the unexcitingly worthy

Mr. Hickman. Miss Fluart, however, is not absorbed into the tidy silence of the conventional marriage plot. Refusing to "buy herself a master," she sets up an establishment of her own and continues, "once a day," to quarrel with Hermsprong "about *le bon ton, et le bel usage* ... calls him savage; [and] abuses his antediluvian ideas" (338). As she insists she will not marry until she can find another "savage like himself," and since, as the novel's subtitle points out, Hermsprong is an example of "man as he is not," Bage leaves little reason to think that Miss Fluart is likely to join Beatrice, Elizabeth, and Anna in being silenced by a kiss.

This mildly unconventional twist to the very conventional pairing of sweet and witty heroines is especially noteworthy because of the ways in which Bage aligns Miss Fluart with Hermsprong and Glen, the novel's other outspoken freethinkers. Neither her decision to remain unmarried nor her feminist ideas leave her, like a Wollstonecraft or Hays heroine, a lonely voice in the wilderness that is eighteenth-century England and vulnerable because of that isolation. Admittedly, part of what links these three characters is the fact that they are all, to some degree, outsiders to begin with — Miss Fluart as a woman, Glen as the illegitimate son of a man who grudgingly accepts only minimal parental responsibility, and Hermsprong, at least initially, as a nameless wanderer. Moreover, all are literally or figuratively orphans: as Glen, the only one of the three with a living parent, proclaims at the opening of the novel, "alas! I am the son of nobody" (58). Yet in a world in which literal and figurative filial duty — not only to one's father, but to institutions such as the church, the monarchy, and the aristocracy — is repeatedly and insistently invoked by such unsympathetic figures as Lord Grondale and Dr. Blick, the orphaned, outsider state of these characters reinforces their wider sense of freedom from arbitrary authority and links Miss Fluart's lively, proto-feminist assertiveness to Hermsprong's more soberly reasoned insistence upon political and personal independence, rather than leaving it as the disregarded protest of an isolated character.[1] Such connections are particu-

---

1 Such anti-patriarchal rhetoric is particularly appropriate from the American-born Hermsprong. In *Prodigals and Pilgrims*, Jay Fliegalman has analysed the ways in which American Revolutionary and early Federalist discourse was shaped by a rejection of metaphors linking government and paternalism, and as his study shows, Hermsprong and Miss Fluart's arguments against Caroline's submission to Lord Grondale parallel those used to justify American rebellion against British "paternal" government.

larly worth emphasizing, given that the novel ends with Caroline reasserting her abject sense of filial duty and winning her independence by submission, not revolt, and with Hermsprong, the most overtly radical figure, being absorbed back into literary convention and the landed gentry, making it the radical man, not the witty woman, who is in this case silenced by the tidiness of literary marriage. Yet by leaving Miss Fluart, at least, still quarrelsome and independent, and by emphasising the continuity between her ideas and Hermsprong's, Bage avoids complete subsidence into literary and social conformity.

Bage thus provides a sharp counterbalance to the fairy-tale marriage plot in Miss Fluart's more pragmatic decision to remain single; he also balances the conventionality of Hermsprong's return to land and family against the fate of Glen, another wandering orphan. The figure of the orphan appears frequently in eighteenth-century fiction, usually with the character in question searching for and ultimately finding home, family, and a stable place in society. As Hermsprong, like more familiar figures such as Tom Jones or Roderick Random, eventually proclaims and reclaims his family name and estates, he is thus following a pattern as comfortably familiar as that of Miss Campinet, as she marries and lives happily ever after with the handsome young man she wants, rather than with the foolish rich one her father proposes. The result, just as with the conventional marriage plot, is a retreat into established social order and interdependence, rather than the independence that Hermsprong has been preaching throughout the book. Yet it is a social order which, as closely as it resembles the one in place at the beginning of the novel, still has at least one important difference: it has room for both Miss Fluart, an unmarried, independent woman, and Glen, who, unlike Hermsprong, does remain legally "nameless" and attached to his society by ties of friendship rather than by patrimony and landed inheritance. One of Bage's original reviewers, who found Glen's narrative an awkward false start, complained that Glen "appears at the beginning intended for the hero, but the level of his importance subsides with the continuation of the narrative, and at last evaporates into air — into 'thin air'" (*Monthly Review* 21 n.s.: 21; see Appendix B.2). Yet this shadowy double of the central hero does become significant again at the conclusion of the novel, as he reappears to wrap up the fates of every character "above the degree of a candle snuffer" — except himself. He remains an orphan, an observer, an outsider, whose unassimilated presence, like that of Miss Fluart, stands out sharply against the tidy fictionality of the central Hermsprong / Caroline plot. Jocular references to his name-less, genderless Editor only emphasise his refusal to tie up all the loose ends in his own story and increase the force of the contrast between the main and secondary characters. Unlike more tradi-tional romantic comedies — including Bage's earlier novels, which tend to conclude in a flurry of matchmaking in which all the major as well as the secondary characters are paired off — *Hermsprong* ends with a vision of social integration which includes, but signif-icantly is not limited to, marriage and the reestablishment of the rightful and benevolent head of a landed estate. This might not be the sort of radical re-imagining of society that *Hermsprong* toys with earlier in the novel, but it is one that, in its droll, self-consciously pragmatic tip of the hat to readers' expectations of happily-ever-after romance, fits far more comfortably with Bage's amused accep-tance of imperfection than would either Godwinian tragedy or Holcroft's rather pallidly redemptive Utopianism.

★★★★★

While Bage's feminism and political radicalism, however quali-fied both qualities might be, have attracted a lot of attention, then and now, his novels also reveal a number of other interests typical of his age. Most important among them, in any discussion of his fic-tion centring on *Hermsprong*, is an ongoing fascination with Amer-ica, which was, to say the least, a topical subject in the early 1780s when Bage began his career. Indeed, according to Robert Heilman, whose 1937 work remains the fullest study of the subject, any men-tion of things American seems to have been a selling point in British fiction of the last quarter of the eighteenth century, no doubt in part for the obvious political reasons. It is difficult to over-estimate the shock to British public opinion caused by the Ameri-can Revolution — first of all because British soldiers were fighting people whom many in England saw as their countrymen, and sec-ondly because they were defeated. Bage's opinion on the war is suggested by numerous passages in his fiction; in *The Fair Syrian*, for example, a young Englishman realizes that his father was right to dissuade him from taking arms against the Americans. "I thought myself a patriot," he writes in a penitent letter to his father,

> I pressed forward to the service of my country. Alas! Experience,
> Reflection, and Observation, have taught me, I could not have served it
> worse. Fatal to half the world would have been the hour in which we

had enslaved America. — Most fatal to ourselves. Happy, that the nature of the country, the independent spirit of the greater part of its inhabitants, and our unsettled councils, have combined to render the design, if it was design, abortive. (1: 23)

A passage from *Mount Henneth*, reprinted approvingly in the *Monthly Review*, mocks the debate about American taxation in a thinly disguised allegorical dialogue between Carthage and its colonies in the Hesperides. The colonies of course end by refusing the Carthagenian demand for taxes and so, as the narrator dryly observes, "Carthage sent out fleets and armies, and spent as much of her own money in five years, as she had expected to get of her colonies in one hundred!" (see Appendix B.1).

In this interest in America, Bage fits in not just with the central group of Jacobin novelists but also with a wider circle of late-eighteenth century English novelists who used American settings — and particularly American revolutionary settings — to explore issues of British domestic morality. While it would be wildly inaccurate to suggest that there was any sort of consensus about America in this fiction, and while the more conservative novelists often present American culture as being at best the work of vulgar malcontents and at worst as something approaching the demonic,[1] novelists who were dubious about the justice of the British cause in the American revolution tended to create innocent but noble minded Anglo-American characters who slash through the corruptions of European society. As such, these characters offer British readers not just a vision of life in a new and exotic land, but, more significantly, they are like Hermsprong often either implicitly or explicitly presented as possessors of simple virtues which, while they have been lost to an increasingly rich and luxury-minded England, might yet be regained, as the Americans themselves demonstrate. America, in other words, becomes not just a literal refuge from the corrupt old world but, more generally, a discursive figure representing the possibility of European renovation and reconstruction.

---

1 See, for example, Henry Pye's *The Democrat* (1796), in which "the seeds of Republicanism sown among the French army" (1: 12) in America are responsible for havoc in Europe, or Charles Lucas' *Infernal Quixote* (1801), in which the anti-hero and his emigrant friends are massacred by hostile Natives.

This motif was not confined to fiction, and in creating Hermsprong, Bage might have drawn upon any of several non-fictional or quasi-fictional innocent Americans who appeared in books published in Britain in the 1780s and early 90s. J. Hector St. John de Crèvecoeur's popular and successful *Letters of an American Farmer* (1782), for example, depicts the Franco-American narrator as a diffident, simple man, worried about making a fool of himself in his correspondence with his educated and urbane English friend, but nonetheless a man whose shrewd, practical wisdom can offer his English readers a model of natural life and independence. Of course, as many critics have observed, the version of America offered by Crèvecoeur (1735-1813) is based heavily on transplanted European myths; Susan Manning, for example, points out the ways in which Crèvecoeur's supposedly simple, unmediated observations about America are built on a long tradition of European literary pastoralism.[1] That no doubt explains in part its appeal to European audiences, as what they are being offered is less an entirely new world than it is a blank space in which they can imagine restarting, rather than abandoning, European society.[2] Crèvecoeur himself hints at this in his mildly paradoxical definition of an American as being simultaneously brand new and ancient. What is an American? he asks rhetorically at one point in his letters, then replies that he is "a new man who acts upon new principles ... [who] ... must therefore entertain new ideas" (44). Yet at the same time he is someone who will restore "the ancient dignity of our species." What Crèvecoeur offers, at least in the early letters (the final ones are much darker in tone), is a version of American simplicity which echoes deep rooted myths of honest English yeomanry, with Americans reclaiming qualities which had supposedly thrived in an age before the corruptions of vice and luxury sapped the British character.

This concept of the Euro-American was not unique to Crèvecoeur, and in his creation of Hermsprong, Bage could have turned to other "real-life" models of innocent Americans who are living reproofs to the corrupt Europeans they meet. The nameless recipi-

---

1 See Manning's introduction to her edition of the *Letters from an American Farmer*, especially xv-xxvii.

2 Edward Said has discussed the use of the imaginative space given European writers by the vast colonial empires in *Culture and Imperialism*. The issues in this fiction are somewhat different from the ones Said discusses, but his arguments have influenced my approach to these novels.

ent and Editor of letters about Kentucky by the American adventurer Gilbert Imlay (c.1754–1828?) thinks it self-evident that "A man who had lived until he was more than five-and-twenty years old, in the back parts of America" must possess "that simplicity of manners natural to a people in a state of innocence" (i);[1] Mary Wollstonecraft, in her early days with Imlay, agreed, describing him to her sisters in terms which might apply equally well to Hermsprong. "Having ... been brought up in the interiour [sic] parts of America," she writes, "he is a most natural, unaffected creature" (Wardle 251). The hint of America as Eden latent in the phrasing of Imlay's Editor picks up on motifs implicit in Crèvecoeur's early letters, but both Imlay and the Editor take the argument a step farther than does Crèvecoeur. Far from their innocence making them childlike or culturally fragile, as supposedly "primitive" peoples are often represented as being in English writing of this era,[2] Americans' artless simplicity leaves them, according to the Editor, "better calculated than ourselves to judge of our manners" (v–vi), and the book as a whole presents Imlay as a kindly but judgmental friend to the English. Unlike Crèvecoeur, but very like Hermsprong, Imlay doesn't merely teach by artless example; he actively harangues and exhorts, creating for English consumption an American who is culturally innocent but nonetheless sufficiently experienced to be shrewdly aware of the rhetorical power of that innocence and to be able to offer it up for European admiration. What Imlay tacitly proposes as the fundamental marker of American culture is the possession of an innocence able to grasp fully and then reject old world corruption: precisely the qualities that, a few years later, Bage was to associate with his virtuous, simple, but highly rational Hermsprong.

The society that produced these innocent Americans was at least as attractive to eighteenth-century audiences as were the

---

1 The Editor might of course be nothing more than a convenient fiction; there is no indication in the text as to the possible identity of the recipient who, like Crèvecoeur's English friend, solicits, collects, and publishes the letters.

2 "Innocent" cultures are almost always shown as being on the verge of decay or corruption, a motif particularly obvious in much of the writing about the Scottish Highlands from this era. For a discussion of British ambivalence about colonized, "primitive" peoples at a slightly later period — they are admirable in their simplicity, but offer little of value to English culture — see V.G. Kiernan's s *Lords of Humankind*.

individuals themselves, even if descriptions of it often seem to belong in the genre of fantasy rather than that of travel literature. Imlay's Kentucky today seems at best a mildly implausible world, as, with minimal effort, settlers there find everything they could possibly want in Europe without any of the old world tyranny and corruption they might want to avoid. Yet implausible or not to twenty-first century readers, it was a vision that appealed tremendously to contemporaries; Coleridge's and Southey's pantisocratic fantasies, which were influenced by Imlay, are only the most famous example of schemes for blissful colonies of radical emigrants.[1] One anonymous emigrant, probably writing in the early 1790s, took it for granted that there would be numerous groups of "men of from 600 to 6000£ fortune ... in a great degree known and attached to each other [who] ... are almost universally opponents of the present government in England, as being inconsistent with the principles of liberty" and who would therefore be candidates for group emigration of the sort imagined by the pantisocrats (*Extract of a Letter* 2). Potential emigrants were apparently not restrained by any serious worries about the hardships of frontier life. Mr Woodcock's plaintive doubts about his fitness for pioneering might seem eminently reasonable to today's readers of *Hermsprong,* but Bage was, if anything, moderate in his vision of what his characters might expect if they colonized Hermsprong's undeveloped American acres, as one can see by comparing his work to that of his younger contemporary Frances Jacson (1754–1842). Her 1797 novel *Disobedience* portrays 1790s Kentucky as a golden dream world of airy, comfortable log cabins inhabited by settlers whose lives are a pastoral fantasia of light work alternating with such simple, "rational" pleasures as listening "to the modulated buffoonery of the mocking bird, or dancing on the chequered turf to the sound of the pipe or the flute" (4: 202–03).[2] Holcroft's Frank Henley also dreams about

---

1 See Richard Holmes' *Coleridge: Early Visions* for a discussion of Coleridge's debts to contemporary writing on America in his development of pantisocracy. David John Jeremy, in his edition of a 1796 travel journal by the dissenter Henry Wansey, also includes a detailed discussion of an attempt to set up a Utopian society in America by a number of emigrants, including Joseph Priestley's son and Mary Wollstonecraft's brother Charles.

2 Jacson is following Imlay's language closely — "modulated buffoonery of the mockingbird" is his phrase (139) — but the picture as a whole is far more evocative of pastoral fantasy than his.

emigration to a free and rational America, where he "may aid the struggles of liberty, may freely publish all which the efforts of liberty can teach me, and at the same time may form a society of savages, who seem in consequence of their very ignorance to have a less quantity of error, and therefore to be less liable to repel truth" (292). In effect, what the anonymous emigrants want, what Jacson's characters find, and what Frank Henley imagines is exactly what Hermsprong proposes to develop as he invites all his friends — from the adventurous picaro Glen and the sophisticated Miss Fluart to the elderly, delicate Mrs. Garnet — to join him in creating Utopia on the Potomac.

The main difference between Bage and novelists such as Jacson is that in *Hermsprong*, at least, emigration from England is never more than a possibility (at least for the younger generation) and ultimately becomes unnecessary. Instead of creating characters who despair of old world life and are driven to leave their country, Bage explores the extent to which the freedom associated with literary Americans such as the semi-fictionalized American farmer, the non-fictional Imlay, and the fictional Hermsprong, might be emulated by their British counterparts. Crèvecoeur and Imlay imply an absolute divide between inhabitants of the old world and the new, one which can be bridged only by emigration; Imlay, indeed, goes farther, suggesting that it will take years before emigrants are "impressed with [the] characters of [their] new State" and able to become free-thinking Americans like him (190). Yet in *Hermsprong*, Bage creates a character whose "Americanness" lies not so much in his living in America as in the attitudes with which he approaches Britain. In doing so, he offers a version of American culture which explores the possibility of reforming Britain rather than simply retreating from it, as Imlay rather gloomily implies virtuous Americans must. Bage's Hermsprong is thus presented as a character whose cultural allegiance is more a matter of what he is not — to borrow the phrasing of the subtitle — than of what he is. When Bage has Hermsprong describe his own and his parents' lives in America, he does so by making clear that he is not, even while living in the backwoods of Michigan, culturally identical with the Native Americans among whom he is raised, any more than, when in England, he shares a culture with the decadent Britons among whom he lives.

If there is a single key difference between Britons and Americans in Bage's novel, it is that in America there is ample space, both physical and mental, to resist the limiting effects of public censure or

disapproval, so that Americans, like Hermsprong, are not con-
strained by the English "polite hatred for opinion" (328). When
Hermsprong plans to return to America, his inability to endure
being "fettered and cramped throughout the whole circle of
thought" is a consideration at least as important as his "sixty thousand acres of uncleared land upon the Potowmac" (327, 329). Yet
the freethinking independence embodied by Hermsprong is not,
the novel insists, available only to Americans, despite the advantages
given them by their space — evidently not, as it is presented and
recommended in an English novel. The foreignness and oddity of
Hermsprong, which either delight or infuriate those he meets in
England, are undoubtedly presented as arising from his upbringing
in America, but he expects the English around him to be able to
become no less free-thinking, and, at the end of the book, he is able
to settle down with a happily like-minded group of people in England. Even while Bage shows an American as the source of fresh
ideas and impulses in a corrupt, stagnating society, the novel thus
makes clear that the vision he is offering is one which can be transplanted to England — is in fact in some ways a vision of a more
properly English society.[1] Emigration, finally, is unnecessary to reap
the cultural values which Hermsprong embodies. Like Crèvecoeur's American, Hermsprong is both a new type of man, riveting
the English by his oddity, and someone who offers a vision of an
older England, one existing before free thought and independence
were smoothed away by habits of politeness and luxury.[2] Bage
shows him as being, in effect, a better Englishman for being born
in America and as being non-English mainly inasmuch as his origins enable him to bring a frisson of novelty to supposedly tradi-
tional values and thereby spark reformation in England — or at
least in a few regenerate Englishmen and women.

---

1 Compare Tave on this point. He argues that the novel's key term for
   Hermsprong is not "savage" but "gentleman," emphasizing the fundamentally English qualities underlying the oddity of this "American" character
   (10).
2 The idea that smooth politeness is incompatible with independence also
   appears in British criticism of the French from this era — most famously,
   perhaps, in Sterne's *Sentimental Journey*, as Yorick compares the French
   character to a coin worn smooth by handling. Gerald Newman sees such
   imagery as indicative of what he argues is the Francophobia underlying
   the English patriotism of bourgeois radicals such as Bage (see *The Rise of
   English Nationalism* 148ff).

This discourse of Anglo-American life is not the only aspect of European writing about America which Bage explores; indeed, there are two distinct traditions which Bage draws upon in *Hermsprong*. It is Imlay's and (to some extent) Crèvecoeur's celebratory accounts of new world innocence and simplicity that lie behind Hermsprong's plans to start a new life with a small circle of friends on the banks of the "Powtomac." Yet in his inset account of Hermsprong's parents and childhood, Bage is drawing upon a somewhat different tradition, that of Enlightenment speculation about what Native Americans, as opposed to Anglo-Americans, might represent for a European observer. If Bage owes the footman plot in *James Wallace* to Smollett, critics have argued that he is no less indebted to *L'Ingénu* (1767), a philosophical fable by Voltaire (1694-1778) for the plot device of the European, born and raised among the American Indians, landing in the old world and being shocked by its corruption. Hermsprong is of course anything but ingenuous; his criticism of British society is based on principled objections rather than the bewildered, innocent literal-mindedness which, at least at the beginning of his stay in France, marks Voltaire's protagonist (see Appendix C.2). Yet the device of an outsider revealing the limitations of European civilization, which in the French tradition goes at least as far back as Montesquieu's *Lettres Persanes* (1721) and the translation of Marana's *Turkish Spy* (1684-86), takes on a slightly different charge when, as with both Voltaire and Bage, the outsider is associated with the American Indians.

There is a wide and extensive Enlightenment literature about the Native Americans, and it is of course possible to find flatly contradictory accounts of them. There is, unsurprisingly, an array of negative stereotypes, mainly focusing on what was supposedly characteristic Native violence and vengefulness. Yet such shuddering accounts of new world barbarity are balanced by writing that moves to the opposite extreme: celebrations of the noble savage in which the high-mindedness of Indians soars far above the sordidness of contemporary Europeans and merits enthusiastic comparison with the most virtuous of Romans or Spartans. They are, in account after account, presented as being nobly disdainful of European guile and deceit and incorruptible in their simplicity, values with which they shame those Europeans who are able to recognize the hypocrisy of their own culture by the force of the contrast. (For an example of such writing, see the excerpt from Lahontan in

Appendix C.2.) The attractions of Native culture for those who had lived in it was also a matter of fascinated discussion in eighteenth-century literature, as European writers speculated, often somewhat anxiously, about why what critics today call "transcultured" individuals might actually find something to prefer in Native life. William Smith, as he observed the reluctance of some eighteenth-century white captives to leave their Indian villages, wrote uneasily that for the "honor of humanity, we would suppose those persons to have been of the lowest rank" (29; see Appendix C.1). Bage also makes Hermsprong insist that, on balance, he prefers European life. Yet even so, Hermsprong's initial experience of Europe produces such "a great decrease of plumpness and animal spirits" (254) that, in order to preserve his health, his mother is forced to agree to let him wander through Europe much in the way that he was used to wandering around America. Bage implies that the excesses and luxuries of European culture are, to someone shaped by the sort of healthfully simple life of a Native American community, almost literally deadly. In doing so, he focuses attention on what was, for the European writers who created the idea of the noble savage, one of the most attractive qualities of what they saw as Native American life: the indifference to the sophisticated, decadent pleasures of an economy catering to an expanding luxury market.

Simplicity, of course, was one of the cultural and stylistic values of later eighteenth-century literature.[1] Excessively ornamented speech or writing was denounced as decadent or corrupt, just as was luxury in one's surroundings or ostentation in dress — precisely because such luxurious ornamentation was becoming more and more common and obtainable. It is this idealization of simplicity that underlies Hermsprong's repeated references to himself as being "born a savage" (139). According to his system of values, one eats only when hungry and only until hunger has been satisfied; one walks if one wishes to travel, and one uses words to express, not conceal, one's opinions. Yet Hermsprong, like the Ingenu, is not simply a "savage"; both either have or acquire European learning. Voltaire's sharpest attacks on European society come after the Ingenu has honed his debating skills and his knowledge while imprisoned with a Jansenist philosopher, while Hermsprong ex-

---

1 The dangers of luxury was a theme which preoccupied eighteenth-century writers; for the fullest discussion of this topic, see John Sekora's study *Luxury: The Concept in Western Thought, Eden to Smollett.*

plains that his father had taken care to give him "a taste, at least, of the less useful but more ornamental parts of knowledge" (252). The result is that both transcend the position of naive outsider commentators and are shown as being able to value and evaluate their own "primitivism" to a degree which more unproblematic "savages" — noble or otherwise — are not. Their simplicity, in other words, is simultaneously and rather paradoxically both natural and a matter of intellectual choice.

There is thus a considerable degree of irony in Hermsprong's description of himself as a savage; it would be more accurate to say that he embodies a sophisticated culture's idea of wise primitivism, especially as it is very clear that Bage was not attempting any sort of realistic ethnographic account of Native Americans in his presentation of Hermsprong's upbringing and influences: Bage's Indians are a thoroughly literary construct. As (most recently) Peter Faulkner and Stuart Tave have pointed out, Lontac's discussion with Hermsprong's mother, the most extended picture of Native life in the novel, owes a great deal more to Benjamin Franklin (1706-90) than to any Native American. More generally, the whole presentation of the lives of Hermsprong and his family in the forests beyond Michillimakinac is a fantasy, as Bage would have had to be very well aware. In choosing to set his inset tale near Michillimakinac and among the Nawdoessie Indians, it seems probable that Bage was influenced by Jonathan Carver's very popular *Travels in North America* (1778), which deals with exactly that area. He might also have read, among other eighteenth-century works on the old Northwest, *A Concise Account of North America* (1765) by Robert Rogers, who had been governor of Michillimakinac; John Long's *Voyages and Travels of an Indian Interpreter and Trader* (1791); or, going back earlier in the century, Pierre de Charlevoix's account of a journey through Michillimakinac in the early 1720s (*Journal of a Voyage to North-America*, 2 vols. London, 1761). Alexander Henry, who survived the capture of Michillimakinac during the Pontiac uprising of 1763 and who was subsequently adopted by local Indians, offers in his *Travels and Adventures in Canada and the Indian Territories* (1809) what is probably the most vivid account of life among Native Americans at that time and in that area, but it was not published until after Bage's death. Even so, there was enough discussion of the Indian wars in the eighteenth-century British press to make it clear that the western frontier was not, in the 1760s and 70s, an easy place to live. Whatever Bage might have read on the subject, in other words, would have made it amply clear that the picture of the infant Hermsprong and his wealthy, convent-bred French mother travelling to Michigan and settling happily among the Nawdoessie "with our European servants, our books, our music, our instruments of drawing" (249) was a pleasant fantasy of European pastoralism, not a reflection of North American frontier life. The point is not that Bage is inaccurate, of course, but rather that he didn't have the slightest interest in giving any sort of realistic picture of Europeans among the Nawdoessie, despite his use of actual place and tribal names in his novel.

This might be obvious, but it is still worth emphasising that Bage chooses to explore a very European concept of simplicity and innocence by imagining an Anglo-American raised in an equally European, entirely literary version of a Native American community. Hermsprong, although he might call himself an American or a savage, is not in any way an attempt by an eighteenth-century Englishman to create an historically accurate picture of a contemporary, post-independence American. (Indeed, given Bage's attempt to portray revolutionary attitudes in America in *The Fair Syrian*, the almost complete avoidance of any discussion of American nationality in *Hermsprong* is striking.) Instead, as Bage displaces Hermsprong's solid, Enlightenment rationality onto a thoroughly literary version of America, he is quietly suggesting that England is unable to sustain or reproduce the most admirable of its own values. In seeing Hermsprong, so very much the embodiment of familiar European Enlightenment values, as almost terrifyingly foreign, the novel's English characters are thus demonstrating how far they have strayed from what, in Bage's view, are the most admirable aspects of their own culture and how very difficult it will be to reestablish those values in the corrupt world of Blicks and Grondales that is later 1790s England. As Bage shows Hermsprong turning into a model of the open-minded and open-handed English landowner in the midst of that world, he seems, in fact, to be offering his readers a pretty English fantasia to counterpoint his earlier, and ultimately no less implausible, American fantasy of elegant European pleasures transplanted to the free, noble and independent world that is eighteenth-century Michillimakinac.

★★★★

If Bage's America is a deliberate hodge-podge of European literary fantasies, his England is a lively blend of everything eighteenth-century satirists were most inclined to attack. Populated by venal, tyrannical aristocrats, dim-witted, selfish squires, blatantly exploitative churchmen, cheerily corrupt lawyers, and grimly determined husband-hunters who turn into shrewishly domineering wives, the England portrayed in *Hermsprong* would be nightmarish were it not for the urbane comedy with which it is described. Comic or not, however, Bage's fiction uses the contrast between Hermsprong's "American" simplicity and Grondale's matter-of-factly corrupt self-indulgence to launch a thorough attack on what the book suggests is the dangerously irresponsible behaviour of the money-mad English ruling classes. As in Jane Austen's novels, Bage's characters are almost invariably described in terms of their income, although the disparities are rather more striking than in Austen's world, ranging as they do from Caroline Campinet's gigantic prospective inheritance of between "two or three hundred thousand" pounds (294) and Sir Philip Chestrum's £15,000 a year to the £45 per year that Mr. Woodcock scrapes in from his two curacies or the annuity of £80 that Grooby reluctantly allows Glen. It is almost impossible to give contemporary equivalents for eighteenth-century British money,[1] but equivalents are a relatively minor issue in any case. What the novel insists upon most strongly is the misery and injustice of a system in which Mr. Wigley can face absolute ruin for a debt of less than what Sir John Wing gambles away in a single night, according to Miss Fluart (Sir John does

---

1   In recent years, multiplying by forty or fifty to obtain a rough contemporary equivalent has been suggested, but given the very different purchasing power of money in eighteenth-century England, any conversion into contemporary currency is at best approximate and at worst misleading. A better method of getting a sense of values at the time is to see what sort of lifestyles were obtainable with varying levels of income. For an excellent discussion of this subject, see Copeland's *Women Writing about Money*. Where the fortune is in capital, rather than in rents from land, as women's often were, annual revenues would be usually figured at 4%-5% of the total, depending upon how the money was invested. Miss Campinet, if she were to inherit a quarter of a million pounds, would thus have an annual income of between £10,000 and £12,500. Miss Fluart, with her far more modest £20,000 (£10,000 less than Emma, the richest of Austen's major heroines), would have an income of £800 to £1000. For comparison, the four Dashwood women in *Sense and Sensibility* have £10,000 among them or (at the 5% rate used throughout the novel) £500 a year, a little more than Austen, her sister, and her mother had following the death of Austen's father. By any reckoning, the Grondales and Chestrums are thus very rich indeed.

not contradict her), and considerably less than a tenth of what the hapless Sir Philip loses on his first encounter with Grondale's rapacious gambler friends. This insistence upon the idea that the English measure of a person's value is a very literal matter of pounds, shillings, and pence gives a particularly sharp edge to the scene in which Mr. Sumelin tells his wife, with dry irony, that the high cost of female slaves versus male slaves in Ottoman Turkey raises "the honour of your sex" (206). What Bage offers his readers is a world in which characters boast about their own English liberty and shudder at the supposedly savage Americans or barbaric Turks, even while reducing almost all their own institutions — marriage, the church, the law — to a matter of buying and selling and ignoring the helplessness of those without money in the face of such corrupt institutions.

It should come as no surprise to a twenty-first-century readership raised on Foucault — or for that matter, to an eighteenth-century readership with even a passing familiarity with Godwin — that law and organized religion might be seen as repressive institutions. If John Gibson Lockhart and Sir Walter Scott panicked at the dangerous unwholesomeness of a novelist who dared attack church and state, readers today might be more inclined to complain about the overfamiliarity of such satiric targets. Yet Bage slides away from what is by now the familiar Jacobin gloom about the overwhelming power of these institutions; what seems to interest him more is the bumblingly comic incompetence of their representatives. Mr. Corrow the lawyer, eager though he is to do Lord Grondale's bidding, can manage nothing better as a charge against Hermsprong than that he can "almost prove" that Hermsprong has read *The Rights of Man* and that "he has lent it to one friend," which, as Corrow observes hopefully, "is circulation, though to no great extent" (289). Slightly later, Corrow is gloomily at a loss for a legal justification for detaining Miss Fluart against her will, however certain Dr. Blick is that there must be "a legal and justifiable cause" for arresting somebody who "has crossed [Lord Grondale's] inclinations" (299). Hermsprong's appearance in court, which concludes with a triumphantly Godwinian affirmation of the irresistible force of truth, makes nonsense of the villains' inept efforts to pin charges of sedition and disaffection on him — something which, in the increasingly worried years leading up to the invasion panic of 1798, was by no means an unreasonable thing to attempt. In fact, while there is no indication of any direct influence, Hermsprong's legal trouble anticipates the later, far better-known trumped-up trial in

Charles Dickens' *Tale of Two Cities* (1859), the hero of which is, like Hermsprong, a foreign wanderer who has concealed his claim to title and estates and who rouses suspicion because of his mysterious French connections and radical sympathies. Yet whereas Charles Darnay is shown as being in real danger of losing his life, even in the more moderate climate of 1770s England and for far more moderate political views (his rather temperate praise of George Washington is less extreme than many of the comments in Bage's novels), Bage turns Hermsprong's hearing into an undignified rout for the villains, who, despite believing themselves to have the full weight of the aristocracy, the church, and the law behind them, are unable even to bring their enemy to a full trial. Ultimately, then, the satire is directed more against corrupt individuals than corrupt institutions; despite the best united efforts of several unabashedly malevolent characters with all the power that wealth and social influence can give them, truth and justice triumph in Bage's world. The law, as it ought, vindicates Hermsprong rather than being used as an instrument to destroy him, as it is in the cases of other well-meaning outsiders in Jacobin fiction, such as Godwin's Caleb Williams or Wollstonecraft's Maria. Individuals might be — indeed, very often are — selfish, corrupt, and even dangerous in Bage's world, but unlike Godwin, Wollstonecraft, and other such novelists, Bage avoids extending his satire to the impersonal structures of social institutions.

This avoidance might of course say as much about the hero's superhuman virtues and his resulting invulnerability as it does about the villains' incompetence, making it somewhat misleading to read the trial scene simply as a triumphant affirmation of the basic principles of justice. It is just as possible to argue that Bage emphasizes the corruption and ineffectuality of the legal system by suggesting that it can be manipulated to ensnare, however briefly, even someone as transcendently and impossibly honourable as Hermsprong. Turning the argument around in this way also focuses attention on the character of Hermsprong, the figure against whom Bage's English characters and institutions are measured and found wanting, and whose humourless perfection is thus inescapably part of Bage's wickedly comic picture of imperfection and folly. Opinions have varied about the success of this attempt to emphasize corruption by juxtaposing it with absolute virtue, with Bage's contemporaries tending to admire the results and more recent critics being more dubious. Mary Wollstonecraft, while seeing disturbingly exotic traces of "the wild hunter" in Hermsprong, nonetheless found him "comparatively perfect, and interesting," and even the Tory *British Critic* thought the character "exceedingly well drawn" (see Appendix B.2). On the other hand, Stuart Tave, perhaps the most important of modern Bage critics, argues that *Hermsprong* has a "grand failure" in its central character, someone who has "no one to argue well the other side, disagree effectively with *him*" and who is therefore "exempted from the condition of human nature" (11).

As the subtitle — *Man as he is Not* — suggests, Bage was quite aware that for good or for bad, as far as the novel is concerned, Hermsprong is quite immune to normal human foibles — with the possible exception of the moment at which he admits that, irrational as it might be, he can't transfer his affections from the mistaken Miss Campinet to the more politically enlightened (and lively) Miss Fluart. In part, twentieth-century reservations about Hermsprong arise from a shift in taste, one that reflects the extent to which Hermsprong, a figure who brings together Enlightenment fantasies of the noble savage and the Jacobin ideal of rational virtue, is a product of the intellectual preoccupations of his era. As such, he almost certainly cannot seem plausible or fully psychologically realized to us, Wollstonecraft's enthusiasm notwithstanding. The question arising from this point is not whether Hermsprong can have the same appeal for readers today as he did for readers of the 1790s — fairly clearly, he can't — but whether, despite being so thoroughly of its time, *Hermsprong* can be anything but an historical curiosity for twenty-first century readers.

Despite the recent revival of interest in late eighteenth-century literature, Bage has not yet garnered as much attention as some of his contemporaries. Indeed, his critical fate has been almost as idiosyncratic as are his novels themselves. None of his first five books, generally well-reviewed at the time, have been brought back into print in new editions since Scott's day. (All of Bage's novels were, however, printed as Garland facsimiles in the mid-1970s.) As a result, the first four novels, in particular, have tended to be forgotten by everyone but specialists and have until very recently been almost completely ignored in general literary criticism and histories of the era.[1]

---

1 *Barham Downs*, with its merchant hero, has recently been getting some attention; Gillian Skinner has discussed it in her study of sentimentality and economics in eighteenth-century fiction (see especially 126-29). For a wider survey of economics in Bage's novels, especially in relation to his female characters, see April London's recent analysis of his work (144-53).

Man as he Is, although it has not been any more fortunate in its print history, has received a little more attention, with some readers, from Anna Laetitia Barbauld to Gary Kelly, preferring it to *Hermsprong*. With its amiably rambling plot, its sentimental, well-meaning, but thoroughly fallible hero, and its gallery of wittily entertaining secondary characters, it offers all the satiric wit of *Hermsprong* without any attempt to create an ideal figure against which to measure the wide array of more or less seriously flawed characters that populate the novel. It might thus be seen as avoiding the occasional lapses into wooden unsubtlety that Tave and others have regretted in the characterization of Hermsprong himself. It is, however, *Hermsprong* on which Bage's reputation has usually rested, as that is the only one of his books that has been readily available in the twentieth century, and while the novel has had a number of critics who have written admiringly of it, they have tended to do so with some reservations, and the book has never quite made it back into the literary canon in the way that some formerly more-or-less forgotten novels of that era (Burney's *Wanderer* [1814] for example) have recently done. In part, that might be because Bage seems sceptical about both the passionate Utopian dreams and the more dire dystopian nightmares of his more famous Jacobin contemporaries. Sir Walter Scott might fret about the possibility of Bage converting those he entertains, solemnly warning his readers that "a good jest is no argument" (290), but Stuart Tave catches Bage's tone far better in his astute observation that

> we can see in Bage a type of the reason why the revolution did not come to England: the honest and intelligent burgher who would not give up his own freedom of thought and action or the right to advocate that freedom widely; who was openly and continually critical of his country, its state and its church and its people; who insisted, above all, on the need to learn to agree to differ, to tolerate diversities and differences of opinion in all subjects because difference is a condition of human nature. The most important thing in Bage, and what he is best at, is the dialogue and the need to keep the dialogue going. (11)

Too radical for Tories such as Scott, and perhaps too conservative for the more uncompromising radicals, both among his contemporaries and today, Bage nonetheless offers his readers books that are, to quote Tave again, "subversive of prescriptive authority and of stupidity" and that value the sort of lively intelligence that "no suppressive force can contain" (12).

Literary politics aside, the tendency to overlook Bage might also reflect a more basic difficulty: that of deciding exactly what sort of writer he is. While he is a novelist who has affinities with numerous canonical figures as different from one another as Tobias Smollett and Jane Austen — as well as with less immediately familiar figures such as Thomas Love Peacock — he almost inevitably suffers by comparison with any single writer. Mr. and Mrs. Sumelin might anticipate the witty domestic dialogues between Mr. and Mrs. Bennet, as critics such as Blakey and Tave have pointed out (Blakey 64, Tave 2), but the Bennets' dialogues are more thoroughly integrated with the rest of *Pride and Prejudice* than the Sumelins' are with the central plot of *Hermsprong*. Glen might offer droll, cynical wit, but Smollett's picaros are more complex and rough-edged than he is (or, for that matter, than is James Wallace, the debts to *Roderick Random* notwithstanding). Yet reading Bage in this way, and introducing his work by comparing it with that of more familiar writers — impossible as it is to avoid doing so — inevitably misrepresents and even diminishes his appeal and his achievement. After all, a novelist who can be spoken of in connection with both Austen and Smollett is clearly offering something that neither of those authors does on her or his own, and it is Bage's comically generous eclecticism that is the source of his strengths as well as his weaknesses as a novelist. It is also perhaps for that reason that Bage has engaged the interest of critics from Sir Walter Scott to Stuart Tave, who, while ready to admit his flaws and failings, nonetheless devote their energies to bringing his work to wider critical notice. What Bage gives his readers is, as he cheerily admits in the preface of *Man as he Is*, something of a "non-descript," and that, arguably, is the great charm of his novels. Bage's fiction, quite simply, fits no single critical template; there cannot be many novels other than *Hermsprong*, that, while consistently maintaining a sharp intelligence and lively comedy, offer readers the simple, escapist pleasures of sentimental adventure, the witty realism of domestic comedy, the political engagement of 1790s radicalism, and the utopian idealism of Enlightenment dreams of the noble savage. While 1790s fiction attracted renewed and occasionally enthusiastic attention in the final years of the twentieth century, *Hermsprong* is more than an artifact of what critics are now seeing as a peculiarly interesting moment in literary history. In its eclectic intellectual interests and its combination of a clear-eyed awareness of human imperfection with what remains, despite everything, an optimistic sense of human possibility, it stretches the conventional novel in a way that remains amusing, accessible, and strikingly original (despite its many literary debts) more than two hundred years after it was first published.

Robert Bage: A Brief Chronology

1728 Born (February) in Darley, Derbyshire, the son of a paper-maker; his mother dies soon after his birth, and his father remarries.

1732 Bage's first stepmother dies (his father eventually marries twice more).

1751 Bage marries Elizabeth Woolley of Mickleover.

1752 Bage's son Charles born.

1754 Bage's son Edward born (baptized 1 January 1755).

1756 Bage and William Hutton enter business together.

1758 Bage's son John born.

1760 Bage studies mathematics with Thomas Hanson, a "celebrated" Birmingham teacher.

1761 Hutton becomes more closely involved in Bage's business, agreeing to buy all the paper that Bage produces.

1765 Around this time, Bage invests in ironworks with several others, including (according to Godwin) Erasmus Darwin.

1766 Bage sells his mills to the Earl of Donegal (for £2000), leasing them back for £46/year.

1779 Approximately the time of the failure of the ironworks, a failure that costs Bage a large sum of money — perhaps £1500, according to Hutton.

1782 *Mount Henneth* published by Thomas Lowndes, who pays £30 for the copyright.

1784 Publication of *Barham Downs*.

1787 Publication of *The Fair Syrian*.

1788 Publication of *James Wallace*.

1791 Hutton's property is looted during the Birmingham Riots in July; Bage helps him and subsequently writes bitterly about the attacks on Dissenters in his letters.

1792 *Man as he Is* published by Minerva Press.

1793 John Bage dies; Robert Bage moves from Elford to Tam-worth, although he continues to run the mill and keeps his house in Elford.

1796 Publication of *Hermsprong* (second edition 1799).

1797 William Godwin visits Bage during an excursion to the Midlands.

1801 Bage dies on 1 September.

1810 *Hermsprong* republished in Anna Laetitia Barbauld's *British Novelists*.

1824 Sir Walter Scott publishes an essay on Bage as part of his collection of biographical studies of the major British novelists.

1828 The Chiswick Press reissues *Hermsprong*, the last edition of any of Bage's novels until the twentieth century.

A Note on the Text

Hermsprong appeared in three editions during Robert Bage's lifetime: the first edition of 1796, a pirated Dublin edition of the same year, and a slightly revised second edition of 1799. I have used the first edition as my copytext, but I have incorporated 1799 corrections of spelling and punctuation, and I have also silently corrected obvious spelling errors (for example, inconsistently spelled names that have been changed in some, but not all, places in the second edition). Otherwise, I have left Bage's spelling as it appears in the original novel. I have also incorporated the two substantive changes to the 1799 edition, both of which occur in the trial scene near the end of the novel, but I have indicated the 1796 reading in notes. The only other change that I have made to the text is to regularize the use of quotation marks, especially in the case of dialogue quoted within another character's speech. Bage made some attempt to fix what seems to be the first edition's almost entirely haphazard use of quotation marks, but neither edition is entirely clear or consistent in its usage.

HERMSPRONG;

OR,

MAN AS HE IS NOT.

A NOVEL.

IN THREE VOLUMES.

BY THE AUTHOR OF MAN AS HE IS.

Nescis, insane, nescis, quantas vires virtus habeat. Quam illa ardentes amores excitaret sui, si videretur.
Maxima autem culpa in eo est, qui, et veritatem aspernatur et in fraudem obsequio impellitur.
Assentatio vitiorum adjutrix, procul amoveatur; quæ, non modò amico, sed ne libero quidem digna est.

VOL. I.

LONDON:

PRINTED FOR WILLIAM LANE,

AT THE

Minerva-Press,

LEADENHALL-STREET.

M.DCC.XCVI.

HERMSPRONG;
OR, MAN AS HE IS NOT.

ROBERT BAGE

Nescis, insane, nescis, quantas vires virtus habeat. Quam illa ardentes
amores excitaret sui, si videretur.

    Maxima autem culpa in eo est, qui, et veritatem aspernatur et in frau-
dem obseuqio impellitur.

    Assentatio vitiorum adjutrix, procul amoveatur; quae, non modo amico,
sed ne libero quidem digna est.

★★★★

You have no knowledge, madman, no knowledge of the great powers of
virtue. What ardent love she would excite if she were seen!

    The greatest of sins, however, is committed by one who both rejects the
truth and is driven by servility into deceit.

    Let flattery, the abettor of vice, be driven forth; it is unworthy of a friend,
or even of a free man.

    [Cicero; Paradoxa Stoicorum, 17; De Finibus Bonorum et Malorum,
II. 16 (52); De Amicitia, xxiv (89)]

VOLUME I

CHAPTER I

IF human nature be always the same, it cannot have changed much since Mr. Addison's time;[1] and there may still be readers who will peruse a book with more satisfaction, when they know something of its author. The question now, perhaps, would not be so much, whether he is tall or short, round faced or long; as, How does he dress? Is he a person of any fashion? What his rank? What his condition? But before I reply to these interrogatories, I must answer another species of curiosity, which may, especially after perusal, arise in the minds of some readers: Why did he write at all?

Not for fame, certainly: No, not for fame; not to instruct the good people of England; for wisdom there, is in its greatest perfection; nor is it my intention to make my readers laugh, — for these are serious times; nor weep, — for I must first weep myself, as Horace says, and Melpomene is not my favourite muse;[2] in short, I am not determined to write by any of the reasons which authors usually chuse to assign. My motive is of tolerable universality notwithstanding. Not that I want money neither; but I see those who do, — beggars of princely denomination — on thrones — on wooden legs.

Events have happened in the village which I inhabit, not known to the universe. They relate but little to myself; but that is not my fault: Had I been any thing but what I am, I would have chosen to be the principal actor. But who would change an Iota of himself? Before I begin a recital of these events, I will reply to the first class of questions, by a full and true account of my birth, parentage, and education.

---

1 Joseph Addison (1672-1719) began the first essay of *The Spectator*, a periodical he wrote with Sir Richard Steele (1672-1729), with the observation that "a Reader seldom peruses a Book with Pleasure, 'till he knows whether the Writer of it be a black or a fair Man, of a mild or cholerick Disposition, Married or a Batchelor, with other Particulars of the like nature, that conduce very much to the right understanding of an Author" (March 1, 1711).

2 Adapted from *Ars Poetica*, by the Roman poet Horace (65-68 B.C.): "If you want me to weep, you must first feel grief yourself" (1:102-03). Melpomene was the muse of tragic poetry.

But why do I talk of parentage? alas! I am the son of nobody. I was, indeed, begotten by my valiant father, Gregory Grooby, Esq. upon the body of my chaste mother, Ellen Glen. I cannot be so exact as to the time, as was the lovely Countess of Pembroke;[1] but it was a clandestine act, for which my valiant father had no canonical warrant; and for which I am to be punished with all the disabilities the prudence of our laws can provide.

There may be, especially among my fair readers, some who may object to the epithet which I have given my mother; and others may suspect that of my father not applied with the most perfect propriety: But once for all, I beg leave to give this public information: I am a person infinitely nice in matters of epithet; and that I never permit an improper one to descend from my pen, or my tongue, unless I am writing a dedication, or addressing a lord or a lady, or unless I am making love.

My mother was a blooming girl, brought up in a cottage, and knew nothing but innocence and spinning, till my valiant father undertook to be her preceptor. My maternal ancestors had, I suppose, few records, but many traditions; one of which is, that my chaste mother defended the citadel of her honour all the preceding summer, and had surrendered, at the close of it, subdued by a too tender heart, and a flowered cotton gown. On the twentieth day of her lying in, she died of kindness and caudle.[2] The young Squire had sent in a profusion of the latter, and the neighbours supplied the former; for though the matter was rather a lapse of chastity, or, as they called it, a mishap, yet, considering it was a gentleman's child, there was not much harm done.

---

1   Anne Clifford (1590-1676), whose second husband was the fourth Earl of Pembroke and whose manuscript memoirs and diaries give a vivid picture of both her own life and that of the seventeenth-century aristocracy. Tave and Faulkner suggest Bage's source for this reference might have been the entry on Anne Clifford's father, George Clifford, in the 1784 *Biographia Britannica*; a note about Anne begins "[s]he informs us, that ... she was begotton by her valiant father, and conceived with child by her worthy mother the first day of May in 1589" (qtd. Faulkner 249). A more famous literary precedent for beginning a fictional autobiography at the moment of conception is Laurence Sterne's *Life and Adventures of Tristram Shandy* (1760-67).
2   A thick gruel, mixed with wine or ale, served warm to invalids or women in childbed.

My valiant father, in the very month in which my chaste mother died, had arrived at twenty-one. His father had lain two years in the family vault. His estate was 2000l. a year. He had a pack of excellent harriers; his springing spaniels were staunch; his greyhounds the fleetest in Devonshire; his cellars were filled with October and Port; and he might have been pronounced a happy man, had the dowager lady possessed a taste as rural as his own; but they disagreed in so many points, that my father, one day, an hour after dinner, signified to her, with abundance of valour, that he should be happy to pay her a visit at her jointure house.[1]

My father must have had no small quantity of tenderness for my mother, for he remembered her several months. His housekeeper, his butler, and his coachman, were ordered to become sponsors for my faith. He kindly allowed them to give me his own Christian name; and, finally, ordered three shillings a week to be paid my great grandmother, for my maintenance, and two pounds of the best shag,[2] per annum, by way of super-remuneration.

But, alas! the old lady was almost eighty, and almost blind, and as soon as she had nursed me into rickets, withdrew from the world, and left me to the care of a great aunt, a labourer's wife, stout and hearty; under whose care I throve well, till I was ten years old. Her husband dying, she was driven, by the humanity of our poor laws, to a very distant parish,[3] and I was transferred to the care of Goody Peat, from whose hands I received victuals not too abundant; but accompanied with abundant thumps, to facilitate digestion; and pious wishes, that every mouthful might choak me. Under her care I grew lean apace, and might soon have been settled, to the satisfaction of my valiant father, to whom I was now becoming troublesome, had it not been for a meddling parson, who knew something of law, and something of gospel; and who did not find that murder, even of a bastard, was sanctified by either.

---

1   A jointure house is property reserved for the use of a widow in her lifetime, after the main property has been passed on to the next heir. Grooby is, in other words, ordering his mother — "the dowager lady" — out of his house. "October," here, is ale.
2   Rough tobacco.
3   The poor laws required parishes to care only for paupers born within their boundaries, so that those without other means of support would have to return to their birthplaces to be eligible for relief.

The doers of good in our parish, and perhaps in others, might have been divided into three classes: Those who do it for pity or for piety; those who do it for the sake of the report; and those who never do it at all. This latter class was said to be far the most numerous; but this I take to be the *scandalum humani generis*, and as deserving of the pillory as the *scandalum magnatum*,[1] at least. At the head of the second class stood my father's house; the first, far from branching out into *genera* and *species*, consisted of a single individual, namely, Parson Brown himself.

Mr. Brown was too respectable a man, too much beloved by his parish, and too able to divide it even against the Squire himself, to be quite overlooked at the hall. He was a cheerful companion also; and as he never assumed any learned airs, my valiant father was well enough pleased, upon a rainy day, to have him the companion of his pipe.

One dull day they were thus employed, when Mr. Brown, glad to embrace the opportunity, said, "I fear that sweet boy, little Greg. Glen, is not in good hands."

My valiant father had been married two years; and having begun to make boys and girls canonically, did not like to hear of any thing done in that way before the consecrated Era. He made, therefore, some slight answer, which rather irritated the parson, who being, upon proper occasions, a determined speaker, said, that when people took the trouble to beget children they ought to take the trouble to provide for them.

To this the Squire answered, "He thought he had not been deficient in that duty: Ten pounds a year was a sufficient allowance for the maintenance of a bastard."

The parson's face kindled at this expression: He told the Squire it was harsh, it was unnatural, it was inhuman. My valiant father now felt his own anger rise. On such occasions he swore. He met the parson's reproof for that indecency also; and, in short, they became so loud, that Mrs. Grooby, a most respectable woman, who

---

1 Scandalum magnatum is "[t]he former offence of making defamatory statements regarding persons of high rank, such as peers, Judges or great officers of state" (P.G. Osborn, *A Concise Law Dictionary*, 2nd ed. London, 1937, 282). It differed from most other forms of slander in that proof of damage was unnecessary for such statements to be actionable; the statute was repealed in 1887. "Scandalum humani generis" would, if there were such an offence, be the crime of making slanderous statements about the human species.

heard the altercation, but knew not the cause, thought it necessary to interfere by her presence.

On her entrance, my father found his rage subside in a moment; Mr. Brown ceased, from a motive of politeness; and to the lady's question, the Squire answered, "Pshaw! — nothing — nonsense — politics."

Mrs. Grooby retired, saying it was a privileged subject for anger. "And yet," she added, "I wonder it has not been yet fully felt, that anger renders all argument useless; for in that state of the mind, truth can neither be discovered nor perceived."

Mr. Brown felt the force of this observation; and the obvious inference was, that he was not taking the right way to the object he had in view. No; irritation was not the right way. Adulation, — but that he hated adulation, — was a surer method; and it could not be sinful, — not very sinful; if it were, would so many of his worthy brethren make it the common path to a benefice, or to a mitre.[1]

This mental soliloquy passed pretty rapidly on. At the end of it, Mr. Brown, in a softened tone of voice, said, "No, Mr. Grooby, no, you cannot think of making him a barber, — (for such a hint my father had dropt) — no, you cannot — I know your generous temper is above that. He is the prettiest boy in the parish, and resembles you so perfectly, that people would be apt to think you used him hardly. Barbers' shops, you know are receptacles of scandal."

"What the devil would you have me do with him," asked my father, "make him a parson?"

"Yes," Mr. Brown replied; "yes, Mr. Grooby, I think I would: It is an excellent thought; it may be inspiration, for any thing I know. I am positive the boy has genius. If you bring him up to the church, you may give him this living;[2] I will engage to resign whenever he claims."

"This living!" said my valiant father, and he swore too, the better to express his surprise at so extravagant a demand; "no, master parson, I'll have no bastard of mine spitting fire and brimstone at

---

1 The possession of an ecclesiastical property. A mitre, the staff carried by a bishop, is a symbol of his office.

2 The parish for which Mr. Brown is responsible and the income arising from parish tithes. At the time, landowners often had the right to appoint the incumbents of parishes on land which they owned, a privilege which could be used to provide for family members or to earn money by selling the right of succession in a parish.

me from the pulpit. No, parson, that's too much. And the consistency! He must not be a barber, because of the prate; and yet you would stick up his damned handsome face, so like my own, as you are pleased to say, in a pulpit, as a perpetual memento of my youthful indiscretions."

Mr. Brown did not gain much upon my father in this conversation; but as no time was to be lost, he sought opportunities of renewing it; and at length, peace was concluded on the following conditions; that I should be consigned over to Mr. Brown, to do with me what he pleased, except making me a parson; that during Mr. Brown's life, he should receive 50l. per annum, for my board and education; and that when he died, I should have an annuity, secured on land, of 80l. per annum, provided I left Patten-place, and did not presume to settle within forty miles of my father's residence.

In his youth, Mr. Brown had been upon the point of marriage. The lady died; and he could never replace her to his satisfaction. He was a bachelor, therefore, and considering me as deodand,[1] took me home, and became my preceptor. Mr. Brown was not a profound scholar; but he knew something of every thing. I was taught a little Latin, a little mathematics, some botany, a sprinkling of chemistry, a portion of theology, with some history; and the belles lettres came as they could.

I was yet in my seventeenth year, when Mr. Brown's only brother, a mercer, in Exeter, died. He was supposed to be rich; and might have been so, but that his wife preferred, as ladies are oft inclined to do, gentility to accumulation. She died a year before her husband, leaving one child only, a daughter, imbued with her precepts, and possessed of her inclinations. Soon after her father's death, this young lady came to her uncle's to reside; and brought with her a pretty face, soft melting eyes, and a heart that — but for her looking glass — must have burst with grief.

For she had lost not a father only, but a fortune; and with it two affluent lovers, each capable of keeping her a coach. No event is better calculated to shew young ladies the sordid nature of man. When I have enumerated her accomplishments, who would believe, that a diminution of a single cypher in her fortune — a

---

1 "[A] personal chattel which, having been the immediate occasion of the death of a human being, was given to God as an expiatory offering" (OED).

simple taking away of 0 from 5000l. — should change the hearts of men.

Brought up under a careful mother, who considered the embellishments of person, as the first great duty of woman, Miss Brown learned to dress with the most enchanting elegance, and to animate a pale cheek with the milk of roses.[1] Nor was her mind neglected: No, — it was adorned with all the literature which this learned age has produced for the service of the ladies. To the novels of the present day were added the Cassandras and Cleopatras, — the classics of a century or two preceding:[2] Besides this, she was no small proficient in music; and could actually perform several songs upon the piano forte, very much to the envy of her less accomplished companions. And must money be added to all this? Heavens! what things are men.

See then this charmer transported to Patten-place, where there was nobody to charm. She wept; it would have softened a tyger — and I was not a tyger; but I was a child, and wholly incapable of giving her the consolation she wanted. At length, indeed, I was permitted to seek crow-quills for her piano forte,[3] when her grief was softened by time. At length she accepted from my hands drawings, to work in gauze; and to complete my felicity, I was allowed to read the sublime Cassandra to her, while she worked in the summer evenings, in a little alcove, at the bottom of the garden. What draughts of love I drank! who, that had seen the soft languish of her eyes, whilst I read the sublime meltings of the soul of Oroondates — who would not have thought she had drank too?

All at once, toward the close of the year, this delirium of bliss was dissolved by an event so extraordinary — so unexpected, —

---

1 A cosmetic facial cream.
2 A reference to chivalric romances written in seventeenth-century France and usually set in a vaguely classical world. They were, for a time, immensely popular, but from the mid-eighteenth century onwards, English writers — for example, Charlotte Lennox in her *Female Quixote* (1752) — mocked them for both their length and their implausibilities. *Cassandra* (1652) and *Cleopatra* (1674) are romances by Gauthier de Costes de La Calprenède. Oroondates and Statira are lovers and central characters in *Cassandra*; Artaxerxes is Statira's brother.
3 The quills would be used to play the instrument by plucking its strings, a technique which, while used with harpsichords, would be very unusual on a pianoforte.

so impossible, — that, in short, my fair Statira was ravished from my longing eyes, by a young hero, who measured cloth in a neighbouring town. This unheard of injustice inspired me with the very soul of Artaxerxes; and I determined to pursue the detested ravisher to the extremities of the earth. It was necessary, however, to provide arms for this heroic enterprize; and I had no money. The question too, whether my princess might not have been carried away by her own consent, would sometimes arise. It occurred to me, that whenever the cloth-merchant came, they were shut up in the parlour together; and I began to doubt, whether this circumstance arose, as I had hitherto supposed, solely from the difficulty the young lady found in chusing amongst the many patterns of elegance, which, I concluded, he came to offer to her acceptance.

If this were so, what had I to do with vengeance? Nothing. But what, — since I had lost all that made it desirable, — what had I to do with life? A noble disdain of this trivial thing, called existence, took possession of me: I resolved to lay the burthen down; and was only perplexed by the mode: I knew that pistols were the fashionable instruments, but I had them not; my heroic soul disdained a halter; the brook, which ran irriguous thro' the vale of Patten-place, was a pitiful brook; it would have disgraced my cause to have been found in it; so, as it was not more than twenty miles distant, I resolved to throw myself into the ocean.

This magnanimous exploit was no sooner determined upon, than I became all eagerness for the execution. I set out the next morning, and as I walked with anger, I walked with speed. My valiant heart would scarce submit to the calls of hunger, which were strong and importunate. I had in my pocket three shillings and one penny; and becoming rather faint, I yielded to the invitation of our holy champion, St. George, who was slaying the dragon at the door of a decent fabric.[1]

I did not at this time know the turpitude of the crime I was going to commit; I did not know it was murder, and of all murders the most flagitious. I might kill another man, and repent; but I could not repent of killing myself; nor could God ever forgive me for rushing into his sacred presence without a passport.

All this I did not then know; I only knew how Cato, how

---

1 That is, a pub with the sign of St. George.

Brutus, how Sappho died,[1] and thought I was going to be great like them. Yet I had not totally forgot Mr. Brown; and toward the end of my walk, I did shed a few unheroic tears, at the thoughts of parting with him for ever, and determined to take a grateful farewell by letter, that I might not add suspense to the distress with which I was going to afflict him.

This letter was written whilst my hostess of the George was preparing the last meal I ever was to eat. It was a pathetic story of my sufferings, and of my resolution to end them.

It said, "Who would groan, and bear the pangs of despised love?"[2] and it finished with a farewell, as sad as I could find words to make it. This letter I sealed and directed; then put it in my pocket, with an intention to drop it into the post-office, at Lime,[3] through which the road to heaven, I had made choice of, lay.

Dorchester beer was written in large characters over the door of the house. I ordered a tankard; and being thirsty with my walk took off half at my first draught. I felt myself and my courage both much strengthened by the operation; and I continued it till I had swallowed three tankards. Thus armed, I paid my reckoning with great liberality, resumed my walk, and my purpose; and am of opinion, could I have reached the sea, nothing would have prevented my plunging headlong in — but the sight of it. But to my longing eyes this sight was denied.

In the remembrance of what passed this important day, I have very much failed: I know only that I waked from sleep, and found myself on a bed, in a strange room, with an elderly woman sitting by the side of it.

I was seized, on my waking, with a violent sickness; a medical gentleman came to my relief, but did not relieve me; and a certain Mrs. Garnet stood by me, with pity in her looks. In time, the fit abated; the man of medicine gave me a composing draught; and I was put to bed. I slept much and long; and awaked with no complaint but the head-ach, and a degree of nausea.

Invited to the breakfast table of Mrs. Garnet, I went down with

---

1 They all died by suicide: Cato the Younger in 46 B.C., following his defeat in battle against Julius Caesar, and Brutus in 42 B.C., after being defeated by Mark Antony in the wars following Caesar's assassination. Sappho (c.580 B.C.), who seems more appropriate to Glen's case, supposedly threw herself into the sea because of unrequited love.
2 Misquoted from *Hamlet* III.1.70-72.
3 Now Lyme Regis, a town on the Dorset coast.

great confusion of face; for I had eat of the tree of knowledge, and was ashamed.[1] My confusion was not much abated by the presence of a young lady, who could not compose her muscles to a proper expression of gravity during my examination, which was entered upon very politely, but rather too soon, by Mrs. Garnet.

Her very first question was embarrassing. "May I be permitted, young gentleman, to enquire your name?"

I blushed; I thought of my valiant father; the name of Grooby was in my head, but timidity was at my heart, and I answered, stammeringly, "Gregory Glen."

"Have you parents living?"

This was still worse; I blushed my deepest dye, though I never could well tell at what; and with some hesitation I answered, "No."

"Relations, Sir?"

"No, madam; I am under the care of the Reverend Mr. Brown of Patten-place."

"O! I have heard of him, and probably of you, Sir. Business, I presume, brought you to Lime?"

Worse and worse! I thought Mrs. Garnet very disagreeable, and the young lady very impertinent, for she broke into a titter at the question; indeed Mrs. Garnet reproved her, and said very kindly to me, "Do not let us distress you, young gentleman; I have no motive for this enquiry but your good."

I had hung down my head at the lady's last question, determined upon a sort of sullen silence; but the tone of her voice raised my eyes up to her face, and I saw in it nothing but benignity. I was emboldened by it, and said, I must own, in a perplexed strain of eloquence, "I fear, madam, — I am afraid I have been very troublesome; but indeed — indeed, Madam, — it is the first time — and I hope I shall never repeat it."

"I hope so too," she answered. "You fell into bad company?"

"No, madam? I have not so good an excuse."

"It must be some extraordinary motive, Sir, that could induce you to commit such an excess alone; but you seem an extraordinary young gentleman. May I without rudeness again ask the nature of your business here?"

"Business! madam, — I can't say I have business. To be sure, I had an intent, — a design —"

The young lady strove not to laugh.

---

1 Adapted from Genesis 3:6-12.

"Yes," Mrs. Garnet answered, "you had an intent; a strange, presumptuous, and permit me to say, wicked intent."

She then read me a long lecture on the subject of suicide; and I was astonished to find all the torments of the damned would have been my portion, for considering my life as my own property, and throwing it away, when I was weary of it.

Mrs. Garnet having concluded, Miss Bently said, with as much gravity as her roguish face could assume, "Madam, your reprehension has been too severe. You have not fully considered the importance of the cause. Do you reflect that it is love, Madam? Love, which excuses, nay sanctifies, all mad actions. Besides, the lover's leap is now so rare an occurrence, it must immortalize the man who jumps. Perhaps Mr. Glen thought of this?"

Mrs. Garnet, without noticing Miss Bently's raillery, continued thus: "When we feared your life was in danger, we searched for your pocketbook, that we might know whence you came, and advertise your friends. We found a letter to Mr. Brown; and this informed us of your purpose and its cause. I hope you now see your error?"

"Oh dear!" cries Miss Bently; "but I hope love is a better counsellor. The torch of true love is almost extinct among our present race of beaux. It wants kindling at the altar of Sappho. I hope Mr. Glen will not think of relinquishing his charming design. To be sure, I do not like death in any shape; but in a cause so important, I really think I could attend Mr. Glen, and even give him a push, if I saw his courage fail."

I ventured now, for the first time, to look up in the face of the lady who was giving me this hopeful advice. It was a lovely face; had archness in its expression, but not ill-nature; and I ventured to say, "She could not, for her heart, push me on with half the force her eyes would pull me back."

"Oh! for certain," says she, "I know my eyes have prodigious power to pull; they pulled you over a stile yesterday, with such force we feared you had broke your bones. Do you remember running, or rather staggering after a young woman whom you called your Statira. I was your Statira; I ran, however, from my Oroondates, and clambered over the stile as fast as possible. So, indeed, did you. I looked back, as Daphne did at Apollo; but my Apollo was now a dull mass of earth.[1] I feared the spirit might

---

1 Daphne, a nymph beloved by Apollo, fled from him and was turned into a laurel tree to escape his pursuit. In the original tale, it is Daphne, not Apollo, who collapses.

have taken its flight to Olympus; so I ran to acquaint Mrs. Garnet
— and —"

How long Miss Bently would have persisted in this lively persecution, or how many gods and heroes she would have called to
her aid, I know not. She was interrupted by a servant announcing
Mr. Brown. It was my revered patron, to whom Mrs. Garnet had
wrote the evening before.

To relate the remaining minutia of this affair would be equally
tedious and useless. Mr. Brown's reprehension was at once kind and
severe. He used arguments to cure my folly; Miss Bently, — eyes.
Which had the greatest effect, I dare not pronounce; but I was cured.

This affair laid the foundation of a friendship betwixt Mrs. Garnet and Mr. Brown. It was supported by kind offices and reciprocal visits. I availed myself often of it; nay even drank again of the
cup of love. I did not, however, get drunk again, nor apply to the
ocean for relief, when my dear Miss Bently gave her hand to a
merchant of Lime: It was a mania of another kind which seized my
unhappy brain: I thought God had forsaken me. This pious error
produced a vast variety of silly delusions, and cost Mr. Brown
abundant trouble to eradicate.

It had, before these events, been frequently debated to what art,
mystery, trade, or profession, I should apply, in order to acquire
some property I might call my own. Mr. Brown and myself were
agreed on the propriety of such a measure, but never on the means.
When I had recovered from my late pious disease, my friend was
advancing very fast in infirmity. He seemed to love me more, for
the trouble I had occasioned him: He seemed to lean upon me for
all the remaining comfort of his life. I would not now have left him
for any prospect of fortune; at least, I hope not; for I must own I
never was assailed by the temptation.

It was in the sixth year of that era, which I must always consider as the epocha of my folly, that I lost my benefactor. How grateful to me is his remembrance! His niece was, as she ought to be,
the heiress of his property, except his books, and the sum of 200l.
which he bequeathed to me.

I was now, by condition, to migrate, or forfeit my father's settlement. "The world was all before me, where to fix my place of
rest;"[1] so I fixed it in London; not doubting, that in so universal a

---

1 Slightly misquoted from Milton's *Paradise Lost* xii. 646-47, the point at
   which Adam and Eve are turned out of the Garden of Eden.

market for talents, mine also would find their value. I had a recommendation, from a friend of Mrs. Garnet's, to a city acquaintance; who introduced me into genteel company. I was also admitted in a compting-house; a fortnight's occupation of which convinced me that my genius was not the genius of multiplication and division. I next got an introduction to a club of literati. I drank of the waters of Helicon,[1] and produced some pieces of poetry which I thought sublime. I could not bring the booksellers to a coincidence with this opinion; and their impertinent requisitions of improvement soon rendered their society inconvenient to my feelings.

Instead of an opening for the exercise of my talents, I found one in my purse, through which had flowed, in eight little months, the sum total of my legacy: Such is the force of genteel company, genteel cloaths, and genteel reckonings. I correct myself. I had saved 50l. out of this sum, by laying it out in books, music, and mathematical instruments.

It was, however, no unfavourable circumstance, that as my purse declined, I began to call the amusements of London frivolous, and when it was exhausted, I said they were contemptible. *O rus! quando te ego aspiciam*, was oft upon my lips; and I read Thomson's seasons by way of corroborant.[2] Yet, though I sighed for the country, and detested, or said I detested the town, it was not without some violence that I prevailed upon my legs to carry me over Westminster Bridge, one fine morning in May. As I advanced, I congratulated myself on my escape; looked back and sighed; saw St. Paul's towering with majestic grandeur; became sensible I had not sufficiently examined that superb edifice; walked one hundred yards towards it; felt in my pockets; called the town a sink of iniquity; turned again, and trod, with angry strides, the road to Exeter.

At Exeter lived the banker to whom I was to apply for my annuity. Half a year was due. Thus recruited, I went forward, to see,

---

1   A mountain in Greece sacred to the Muses; in English literature, the term is usually applied to the fountains of the Helicon, the waters of which symbolize poetic inspiration.

2   Horace, *Satires* 2.6.60: "O, Countryside! when shall I see you again?" (slightly misquoted). James Thomson (1700-48), one of the best-loved of eighteenth-century poets, celebrated nature and country life in his long blank-verse poem *The Seasons* (1746).

and take leave of my kind Mrs. Garnet; for Lime was within the forbidden precincts. Alas! I saw her not: A fatal accident had involved her in the greatest grief: A vessel of Mr. Garnet's, returning from Jamaica, was wrecked on the Scilly Islands, himself on board. All was lost: No life spared, — no part of the cargo recovered. I heard, however, she was surrounded by friends; and as I was every way unable to assist her, I willingly spared to her, and to myself, the addition of grief which an interview would have produced.

This good woman had often spoke with pleasure of the village of Grondale, on the borders of Cornwall. It was her native place. I had long desired to see it; and if it answered Mrs. Garnet's description, I thought it would suit my taste as a residence. With this intention I proceeded.

Just on this side the village, I crossed a widely extended heath, called Lippen-moor. Rude, rocky, craggy, and furnishing only a fine short grass to a small number of sheep. On the edge of this moor, I was struck with a prospect the most beautiful I thought I had ever seen. It was a narrow, but fertile valley, watered by the small river Gron. The opposite bank was a gentle declivity, on which were to be seen six villages or hamlets, many agreeable houses, with woods, corn-fields, and pasture. This was a varied view of several miles in length.

Just under my feet, at the bottom of the valley, was the small clean village of Grondale, with its spire in the centre, almost hid by the lofty elms, and orchard trees, which contribute to form the singular beauty of this little spot. Up the Gron, on the right, stand the ruins of a convent,[1] many centuries the domicile of a succession of holy drones, who buzzed about, sucked the fairest flowers of the vale, and stung where they could extract no honey.

Above this ruin, on the summit of a hill, are the remains of the Castle of Grondale. One tower is left, and enough of the battlements to shew how a savage grandeur once fortified its own tyranny against the tyranny of others.

But the most pleasing of all the objects, now under my view, is a stately structure of the gothic kind, half modernized, once the seat of friendship and hospitality, — now of Lord Grondale.

---

1 In eighteenth-century usage, a "convent" could mean a religious foundation for either men or women. Bage's anti-monasticism is typical of the radical thought of his day.

When I had satiated myself with this delightful prospect, I descended to the village, where I found a spacious public house. Here I took up my abode a few days; every one of which increased my inclination to become an inhabitant. Two agreeable apartments I found at the house of a respectable widow, where I have resided five years.

By the aid of philosophy, I have got rid of ambition; and may it please Venus, I hope also of love. I amuse myself sometimes with the Georgium Sidus,[1] with my pen, my pencil, my fiddle; sometimes with shuttle-cocks and butterflies. I have nothing to do but what I like; and my principal embarrassment has been, to find what I liked to do.

But of myself I have spoke long enough; let me now speak of others; more particularly of those who have some connexion with those recent events which have induced me to write this veritable history.

CHAPTER II

OF the animated beings of the vale, high towers above the rest, in rank and wealth, the great Lord Grondale. Indeed he had been always super-eminent. In his younger years, when only Sir Henry Campinet, he was a man of the very first ton:[2] He acknowledged no superior in matters of gallantry; and had not many in the two great trades carried on at Newmarket, and in the neighbourhood of St. James's.[3]

This is a sober, a very sober age; and yet men, even great men, contrive to procure themselves the drinking diseases of older times. Upon Sir Henry the gout had spent its force at the early age of forty; and had left him a tolerable complication of diseases. On the approach to sixty, his present age, his once blooming complexion had been yellowed by jaundice, and his jolly person emaciated by some one or other of the marasmi.[4]

---

1 The planet Uranus, discovered by Sir William Herschel in 1781 and named in honour of George III.

2 Fashion; a term also used generally to refer to the aristocracy.

3 The "trades" in question would be horse-racing and gambling: Newmarket, then as now, was the site of a major racetrack, and the aristocratic men's clubs in St. James's were notorious gambling dens.

4 Any of a number of diseases causing the body to waste away.

His political career was short, and much *à-la-mode d'Angleterre*, in the 18th century. He began with opposition; but his orations not being remarkable for brilliancy or depth, his ambition could not be decently supported by flattery; and as there was no emolument, there was no stimulus for avarice. Some necessities arising, from want of success in commerce, — I mean the commerce of the great — induced him to turn his thoughts toward administration. There he was certain of reception, for he was admirably gifted. He was not addicted to scruples, and had, besides, several Cornish boroughs.[1] He accepted an office; was, like many of his predecessors, instantly illumined, and felt the error of his former perceptions.

But at court, they say, appetite grows by what it feeds on, till it becomes insatiable. Sir Henry asked, I suppose, and was denied; for there is a fatal necessity imposed upon ministers, of denying sometimes. He returned back to opposition; himself, indeed, despised by both parties, but not so his boroughs. At length the ministerial manager of that branch of traffic, bade him a barony for them; and Sir Henry Campinet was metamorphosed into Lord Grondale.

Whether this was done by writ, or by patent, I never enquired.[2] It is sufficient for me to know, I mean by their effects on the fortunate few they light upon, that they are charming things both; that they raise man far above man, and nearer to the divinity, since kings have once more become divine;[3] and enable him to look down on

---

1 Cornwall was notorious for its so-called "rotten boroughs," electoral districts which had very few voters and which were therefore effectively under the control of the local landowners. This abuse was one of the major targets of the 1832 Reform Bill.

2 Terms for the legal methods of raising a man to the peerage.

3 The divine right of Kings was a concept associated most immediately with the seventeenth-century Stuart monarchs. When James II was deposed by Parliament in 1688, it became accepted political doctrine in England, at least among the Whigs who supported the new regime, that Parliament, as well as God, made Kings. This idea was reinforced in 1714, when Parliament bypassed the closest hereditary claimants to the crown, all of whom were Catholic, and offered it to the Protestant Hanovers. Edmund Burke, himself a Whig, thus caused immense outrage when, in his *Reflections on the Revolution in France* (1791), he challenged this Whiggish interpretation of history and attacked what he claimed was the new system according to which "a King is but a man" (OUP 1993, 77).

the lesser inhabitants of this best of worlds,[1] with a due consciousness of his great superiority.

Lord Grondale had ran a long race of pleasure, and had begun to see its pains and penalties, before he thought of an heir for his illustrious house. For this laudable purpose he made choice of the younger of two sister ladies; a lovely woman, and good as beautiful; with no great fortune, and still less of fashionable propensities. This lady was mistress of Grondale Hall about eight years, and brought his lordship three children, all females; an affront Lord Grondale never could forgive. She died, — not quite of a broken heart, and not much indebted to Lord Grondale for kindness, one child only surviving her. It was her dying request to his lordship, that this daughter, Caroline, should be brought up by Mrs. Merrick, her sister, who, in order to be near Lady Grondale, had settled in a small, but elegant house, in the parish of Grondale; almost the only one, not his lordship's property. This request his kind lordship was so good as to grant; with more pleasure to himself than he chose to shew externally; for it would render his freedom more perfect; and Grondale Hall might again become the summer seat of those pleasures which Bacchus, which Venus, which Mercury, are said to preside over, if Mercury be the deity of cards and dice.[2]

But for the practice of this class of pleasures, London has such superior accommodation, that Lord Grondale was seldom at his country seat, till a long fit of gout, a consequent debility, and the advice of his physicians, sent, or more properly, exiled him thither. In a situation so forlorn, some men would have thought of a daughter, now growing into loveliness, for a companion; and of Mrs. Merrick for the superintendence of his household. But this must suppose a vast change in his lordship's manner of thinking; and it was his body, not his mind, which had undergone the change. He fixed, therefore, upon a Mrs. Stone, an officer's widow, and a person of great merit, his lordship said; and who was so good

---

1   The idea that this is the "best of all possible worlds" originates in the optimistic philosophy of Gottfried Leibnitz (1646-1716), but Bage would be alluding to a more familiar source: the savagely ironic use of the phrase by Voltaire (1694-1778) in his philosophical fable *Candide* (1759).

2   Mercury was, among other things, God of thieves and tricksters, and so by extension might be associated with gamblers.

as to condescend to take upon herself this heavy load of superintendence.

To this lady, the society of her own sex was insipid; and Grondale Hall was freed from the impertinent intrusion of dowager ladies, and ladies of rigid decorum. Instead of these, it received into its capacious bosom a few gentlemen of his lordship's acquaintance, who, when the town was empty, had the goodness to take their summer recreations at Grondale, and indulge his lordship with a taste of his once dear amusements.

CHAPTER III

THE next person upon the canvas, is Dr. Blick, rector of Grondale and Sithin; a man perfectly orthodox in matters of church and state, such as these bad times require; and, thank heaven, we have plenty of them. Dr. Blick's merit was indeed great; I cannot say it had been fully rewarded. Hitherto he had arisen in the church no higher than a poor canon, which, with the product of three livings; for he had one in commendam, scarce produced him 1000l. a year.[1] But if he joins to that merit, which now leads to honours, the agreeable art of assentation, no man knows to what dignities he may arise. Dr. Blick could not accuse himself of any neglect of this art, where the application might be useful; more especially to his patron, Lord Grondale; whose peculiar merit he conceived to be such, that even a bishopric, could he be induced to ask it for a friend, would scarce be refused him by administration. He was therefore much devoted to his lordship; and, at his express desire, had qualified for a justice of peace; in which capacity he had been of use to his lordship, in those little animosities which great men do admit to their bosoms on great occasions; such as killing a hare or partridge without due

---

1 In the Church of England, a canon is an official in one of the Cathedrals; it is a relatively low position in the church hierarchy. Church of England clergymen could hold more than one living, deputizing their parish responsibilities to an often poorly-paid curate. The phrase "in commendam" is "used of a benefice, which a bishop or other dignitary was permitted to hold along with his own preferment" (OED).

qualification, or voting against a candidate whose cause they espouse.[1]

There is a person — *vel hic vel hæc*[2] — no matter, — who does me the favour to marshall my commas and colons, — regulate my ifs and ands, — and correct my errors of orthography; who at this place surprised, and indeed vexed me, by a bolder criticism. "So far," says my critic, "you have amused yourself with drawing characters; if that be the end and intention of your book, I have nothing more to say than to advise you to study brevity and Theophrastus.[3] If your design be, as I understood it, to exhibit actions and events, I submit it to your superior judgment, if it might not be altogether as agreeable to your readers, to form for themselves the characters of your drama, from their good or evil deeds. Tell us what they do, and we shall be able to find out whether they were wise or foolish, rough or smooth, discreet or vain, or drunk or sober." To which I replied, — but whether by a kiss or a cuff, I am not at present disposed to say. It is sufficient to acknowledge, that the remark, when I had taken a proper time to digest it, had its weight, and determined me to come more immediately to the relation of those matters which induced me to add one more to the numerous list of authors.

CHAPTER IV

MRS. MERRICK, the maternal aunt of Miss Campinet, was a maiden lady, who having in her youth been deserted by her lover for a richer woman, had ever since looked upon the dark side of man, shunned his intercourse, and almost secluded herself from society. Habit, and an unbounded affection for her aunt, who well deserved it, had rendered Miss Campinet as much a recluse as

---

1 Eighteenth-century law forbade the killing of game animals by people who did not own land worth at least £100 a year or have a leasehold property worth at least £150 a year. Justices of the Peace, usually members of the local gentry or clergy, had the power to punish minor offences (for very minor offences, one justice could act on his own; in more serious cases, two, three, or four justices were required).

2 Whether male or female.

3 Theophrastus (c.372-288 B.C.) was a Greek philosopher. His *Characters*, a moral treatise consisting of sketches of various types of men, was highly regarded by eighteenth-century readers.

herself. To this young lady, therefore, books and music were neces-saries of life; to which she added drawing, and the various arts of the needle. Nature had been extremely indulgent to her, both in mind and person; if it is indulgence to give that dangerous thing called beauty, and that unprofitable quality, benevolence.

Hitherto, indeed, her beauty had bloomed to the desart air,[1] and her benevolence had been confined to the distressed and humble beings of the valley. The character of her dress, as it was little direct-ed to the gratification of vanity, was elegant simplicity; a term, which, with equal justice, might be applied to her mind.

Lord Grondale was not wholly ignorant that he had such a daughter; he even saw her sometimes; although there was, from some cause or other, a sort of repulsive power betwixt Mrs. Mer-rick and Mrs. Stone, which kept them from approaching each other. Miss Campinet's allowance, from her father, was 200l. per annum, for board and all expences. From a man of Lord Grondale's fortune, it might have been more; but his lordship had now become avaritious, and did not, beside, like to hear of any charities but his own. Mrs. Merrick's household, formed upon the interest of 7000l. could not be large. Three female servants, two male, two horses, and a chair.[2] The last, lately purchased, for the sake of fre-quent airings for Mrs. Merrick, now, unhappily, in a declining state.

CHAPTER V

IT was a fine autumnal evening, when I, the humble writer of these memoirs, returning from an afternoon's visit to the curate of Sithin, saw a sort of wild disorder in the village of Grondale, which denoted something extraordinary. I made up to the first group, mostly women. One prayed, "The Lord have mercy upon us all."

"And keep us from harm," said another; "for without his care what are we?"

---

1 Compare Thomas Gray, "Elegy written in a Country Churchyard" (1751): "Full many a flower is born to blush unseen, / And waste its sweetness on the desert air."
2 "A light vehicle drawn by one horse" (OED).

"Well," said a third, "we are all mortal, — all must die, — rich as well as poor, — all flesh is grass."[1]

"But such a good young body!" said a fourth; "we poor folk shall have a mortal miss of her: Ah, poor dear soul! we shall see her no more in a frosty morning, tripping along, to see if there was any coals to burn in the cottages, and any bread in the pantry; — but she was too good for this world."

"Pray," I asked, "who are you thus lamenting?"

"Oh dear, Mr. Glen, have not you heard?"

"No — nothing."

"Poor dear Miss Campinet!"

"What, — dead?"

"Dead! Lord help us! smashed to pieces down Lippen crag."

A cold rigor and trembling seized me; I grew sick apace; and hastening home, threw myself on my bed, in a state of mind I am utterly unable to describe.

Miss Campinet! one of the fairest — but that may be disputed, — certainly one of the best of her endearing sex. I loved her! — yes, I loved her! But if there be a spiritual affection, such was mine. I thought of her, as of an angel whom I might secretly adore; not as of a woman whom I might presume to love. Admitted sometimes to her tea-table, I was treated with the most engaging affability; sometimes her almoner, I have been obliged to repress her benevolence. With my violin, I have been permitted to accompany her at the piano forte. She has condescended to accept the loan of my books and music. I have been honoured with hers. But though thus affable, thus friendly, there was about her a dignified reserve, — a guarded propriety in her most engaging sweetness, that must have checked those vain and foolish ideas youth is so apt to form, had I been silly enough to have permitted an entrance to any such, within my bosom.

So should I have thought for ever of the amiable Miss Campinet, had this been really the fatal period of our acquaintance. But fame, as usual, had blown her trumpet with too loud a blast. Death had come near, too near, the lovely girl, but had not reached her: Down Lippen crag, she had not fallen, though within a few moments, in point of time; and a few yards, in point of space.

---

1 The phrasing here and in the preceding comments is adapted from the Litany in the Anglican Book of Common Prayer and from Isaiah 40.6.

Without an engraving, I despair of making my readers understand the ensuing description; and the patrons of this humble sort of book-making, are not sufficiently liberal to enable a poor author to gratify his readers and himself in this particular. However, when the public ask a fourth edition, I will certainly give it, with a map, at my own expence.

Mrs. Merrick and her niece, returning from their evening's airing, were pacing slowly along the edge of the moor, a thick coppice on their right, down a steep declivity, to the edge of the Gron; the servant following at some distance behind, on a young horse, but in a careless posture; when a gun was fired in the coppice, within ten yards of this horse's ear; at the same instant, a black spaniel, pursuing some birds, burst the coppice, barking, just under his nose. The horse, in an instant, threw his rider, passed the chair horse, snorting, on full gallop; but, instead of turning down the oblique road to the village, kept strait forward, along the edge of the moor. The chair horse, regardless of the reins, sprung after his fellow with all his strength. This then was the situation of the ladies: on their right, the coppice continued; a rising, but uneven ground, on their left, leading to the top of the moor; in front, and at two hundred yards distance, Lippen Crag, a rock with a perpendicular descent to the Gron, and measuring one hundred and four yards from its surface.

A well dressed young man, whom I cannot now stay to describe, was at this instant on the verge of the crag, viewing the prospect. The saddle horse, unable to stop, had taken the leap, and was dashed to atoms. The young man saw the quick approach of the ladies in the chair to the same unavoidable destiny. If ever it is allowable in sound philosophy, to suppose providence directing the actions of individuals, one may suppose it now. Great, indeed, were the chances against finding any one upon this dreary spot, and infinite against finding a man, undaunted by danger, and capable of preserving his recollection at the moment of terrible surprise. Such, however, was the person before us: He saw the imminent instant; and running to meet the horse, placed himself on the lower side; then seizing the reins, as he passed, flew along with the wild creature, who could not be suddenly stopped, turned his head toward the rising ground; and about ten yards from the brink of the crag, had by strength and agility alone, changed his direction, and forced him upwards, till he had obtained ground on which the chair stood firm. As to the poor horse, trembling and exhausted, he seemed to have as little inclination as power to move.

The stranger then turned to assist the ladies. The elder, with open eyes, which seemed not to see, might have been taken for one of Ovid's ladies, passing from life into stone.[1]

The other had fainted. The whip and reins had dropped from her lifeless hands; and death sat, or seemed to the youth to sit, on the fairest face he thought he had ever beheld. He gazed upon her with mute sorrow, trembled, perhaps for the first time, and for the first time feared death.

This sad and awful spectacle had not long occupied his attention, when the servant came up, his forehead covered with blood. The man had seen the whole; had seen that nothing but a miracle could save his mistress, and had seen that miracle performed. He was therefore well disposed to consider the person before him, as possessed of more than mortal power.

"I presume you are the ladies' servant?" said the stranger.

The man answered, "I am, Sir."

"The young lady seems in the most imminent danger; yet I thought I heard her sigh; if so, she is recoverable; assist me in getting her out of the chaise."

The man obeyed. They placed her on the rock, just covered with moss, the stranger sitting down to support her, and inclining her head upon his breast. It was not long before she opened her eyes; and their first object was the bleeding servant. Instantly they were closed again.

"Pray, don't be frightened, madam," says the man; "it is me, — your servant Philip."

"Philip!" says the young lady, again opening her eyes.

Then perceiving a man's hand and arm round her waist, "Bless me!" she cried, a faint blush tinging her cheek.

"I am your servant also," said the stranger; "be under no apprehension."

Blushing, she looked up in the stranger's face; there was nothing in it likely to inspire terror; its present expression was the softest compassion.

"Philip!" said Mrs. Merrick, beginning to recollect, "where are we? I am very sick, — come hither."

"Permit me, madam," said the stranger, to the young lady, "to

---

1 *Metamorphoses*, by the Roman poet Ovid (43 B.C.-17 A.D.) includes the story of Niobe, turned to stone by her grief for the deaths of her fourteen children.

support you a little longer, till you have more perfectly recovered your memory and strength."

"Sir," said Miss Campinet, trying to rise, "I have not the honour to know you."

"Nor I, madam, that of knowing you; I only know that I see infinite happiness in having been able to serve you."

"Oh dear! I remember now; I thought I died."

"No, madam," says Philip to Mrs. Merrick, "it was out of my power to give you the least assistance: I lay bleeding on the ground: It was that gentleman there, that gentleman; he did what I thought impossible: He saved your life and my young lady's, and, by God's blessing, did not lose his own. See, madam, how near you was to the crag."

"For God's sake!" said Mrs. Merrick, "let us get away from this horrid place; lead the horse a great way, and hold him fast."

The man did do.

"And am I, Sir," says Miss Campinet to the stranger; "am I so infinitely obliged to you?"

"If there was such a goddess as Misfortune," said the stranger, "I ought to raise an altar to her, for calling on me at such an instant."

"You are very polite, Sir," the lady answered; "my thanks and gratitude are yours. My father, I hope, — Lord Grondale —"

"It is Miss Campinet, then, to whom I have the pleasure to speak."

She bowed.

"And," continues the stranger, "she acknowledges obligation and gratitude, to such payment, what can Lord Grondale add?"

"Thanks more substantial," the lady replied.

"The most substantial good," said the stranger, "I can derive from a circumstance that might have been so deplorable, I have already, — my own pleasure, my own approbation. I am not in pursuit of fortune."

Miss Campinet looked at the gentleman with some surprise; "Can man," says she, "be too much favoured by fortune?"

"Yes, madam," the stranger answered; "much too much; England has eminent proofs. If I have learned any thing more particularly, it is a very limited adoration of this universal deity, and to pay little respect to those who have no title to respect, save from her favours."

"Such youth and such philosophy!" said the lady; "can the alliance be natural?"

"I should think it was," the stranger answered; "since it was of the sons of nature I learned it."

An exclamation of Mrs. Merrick's broke this conversation. Supported by the stranger, Miss Campinet moved towards her aunt, who complained of extreme illness. She had not advanced many steps, before, hearing a noise, she turned her head, and saw Lord Grondale's carriage; which, in an instant, came up, and from which his lordship immediately alighted.

Anger and politeness are seldom coexistent qualities, and Lord Grondale was angry. The spot on which Miss Campinet had been seated, was a very conspicuous one. Lord Grondale, who was taking his accustomed airing alone this evening, saw an unusual appearance upon it, and directing his pocket telescope to the object, saw his daughter, the daughter of Lord Grondale, leaning on the bosom of a young man. He ordered himself to be driven with all speed to the spot; and whether from a love of his daughter or his dignity; or whether from the rapidity of his driving, he found himself on his arrival, in a high degree of passion. Yet he did not knock the stranger down, — he did not. He only said, with the air of a great and angry man, "Who are you, Sir?"

The young man returned him a kind of contemptuous smile, but said nothing.

In a still more angry voice Lord Grondale repeated his question.

"I am a man, Sir," replied the stranger.

"What man, Sir?" his lordship asked.

"Not of authority," the gentleman answered; "and I rejoice at it, since the possession is so little calculated to make mankind amiable."

"My dear father!" said Miss Campinet.

Her dear father, without paying her the least attention, said, "Are you intitled, Sir, to be thus familiar with the daughter of Lord Grondale?"

"I think I am," answered the gentleman, coolly.

"Loose her, Sir," said his lordship.

"Can you stand, Miss Campinet?" the stranger asked.

"Oh yes, Sir, — yes."

He withdrew his arm; she tottered a few steps, and would have fallen, had he not again caught her.

"What is all this?" said his lordship. "Is any thing the matter, Caroline? Are you ill, or perverse? Who is this young man?"

"Dear Sir!" said Miss Campinet, "have you not heard?"

"Heard what?" said his lordship. "I have heard nothing; but I have seen — seen, Caroline, — your head resting upon this young man's bosom. Was that fit for a father to see?"

Miss Campinet could not answer; she could only blush.

"Yes, Sir," said the stranger, "most fit."

"You may think so, Sir," returned his lordship; "but I must be better acquainted with your rank and fortune before I shall."

"My fortune," answered the stranger, "kings might envy; it is equal to my desires. As to rank, — I have been taught only to distinguish men by virtue."

"Very plain and unceremonious, Sir," said his lordship. "Caroline, lean upon my arm; it is proper I should support you."

"Since, then," says the stranger, "I can no longer be of service, permit me, Miss Campinet, to wish you every possible happiness."

"I hope, Sir," she answered, "you will give me an early opportunity to thank you for —"

The gentleman bowed, and springing down the hill, leaped into the coppice, and was out of sight in an instant.

"Why this," said his frowning lordship, "this is absolute invitation, Caroline, — and before me too."

"Could I say less, Sir, to the man, who, at the risk of his own life, has just saved mine?"

"Your life!"

"Oh Sir! but for him I had been dashed to pieces. To the attitude, which so much displeased you, I was totally insensible. He thought it death."

"All this is incomprehensible."

They were obliged, however, to defer the explanation, on account of the increasing illness of Mrs. Merrick. Both the ladies, his lordship took into his own carriage, and conveyed to Mrs. Merrick's.

As to the explanation, it met his lordship soon enough. He could not absolutely deny the action to be gallant; but what young fellow would not have done the same? The eclat was great and sufficient reward. As to himself, the obligation, if there was any, was cancelled by the impertinent behaviour of the fellow, who ever he was.

"Would you believe it," said his lordship to Doctor Blick, "though I told him I was Lord Grondale, he still spoke to me with the appellation of Sir; and had the impudence to tell me he did not mind my rank."

CHAPTER VI

THE Reverend Doctor Blick seldom walked; but he rode sometimes out in his chariot; and as he was a profound antiquarian, would sometimes stop to view the remains of the castle, the convent, or a remarkable place which had much the appearance of an encampment. It was at the latter place, the day after the affair of the preceding chapter, he observed a gentleman viewing it attentively. The doctor alighted, and giving the stranger the good-morrow, said, "This place, Sir, seems to take your attention, and is indeed worthy of it. I presume you know this was once a Roman camp?"

"No, Sir," the stranger replied, "I do not know it."

"Nothing can be plainer, Sir. You see it was a square. Here must have stood the pretorium, here the augurale; that, Sir, must have been the decuman gate."[1]

"I see, indeed, ground on which these things might have been, — nothing to indicate with certainty that they were."

"I have studied the place so long, Sir, and with so much attention, that I can demonstrate it. I can tell you exactly where were the stations of the *volites*, the *hastati*, the *triarii*; their centurions and tribunes."

"They cannot arise to contradict you, Sir; nor shall I."

"I wish to convince you."

"Do not take the trouble, Sir. I have seen many places of encampment like this. Some where the Romans never were. But they shall be all Roman, to oblige you."

"You have travelled, then, I presume, Sir; but you are too young to have travelled much."

"Too young, perhaps, to have travelled to much purpose; but I have trod much ground."

"Trod, Sir! Is that term proper? I presume you did not travel on foot."[2]

"Chiefly so, Sir."

---

1 Areas in a Roman camp: the praetorium was the site of the general's tent; the augurale the place where auguries were taken, and the decuman gate, named for the tenth cohort, was either the main entrance to the camp or that placed farthest from enemy positions. The volites, hastati, and triarii were three of the four main classes of soldiers in the Roman army. They were divided according to age, experience, and property qualifications, and they would each have had a particular area of the camp for their tents.

2 In eighteenth-century England, travelling by foot would generally have been seen as an indication of either poverty or eccentricity. This idea was changing rapidly during the last years of the century; see Robin Jarvis, *Romantic Writing and Pedestrian Travel* (London: Macmillan, 1997) for a discussion of the Romantic taste for walking tours.

"On foot, Sir."

"On foot."

This was a circumstance that could not fail, in a mind like Doctor Blick's, to abate something of the respect which the gentleman's dress and manner might have produced: It did not, however, abate his curiosity.

"Pray, Sir, may I ask if you travel for profit or pleasure?"

"Not certainly for profit, if by profit you mean money."

"May I, without presumption, ask you another question?"

"Oh, Sir, — what you please. It is seldom that I have met a gentleman willing to take so much trouble about me."

"This mode of travelling, — may it be choice or economy?"

"It may be both. And your question, Sir, — may it be curiosity, or an inquisition into my purse?"

"Sir, — I — I — am — am rector of this parish — Sir,— and we think ourselves intitled, Sir, to make certain enquiries, Sir, when strangers come into it."

"And do all strangers think you entitled to information?"

"They ought."

"I fear, reverence for the clergy, — I rather mean implicit obedience, — does not stand so high now as when the castle and the convent now in view, were filled by illustrious barons and holy monks."

"A little more reverence for the clergy would be no dishonour to these times, I presume."

"They have less, in your opinion, than they merit."

"Yes, Sir, — do you say the contrary?"

"Oh, no! — I have no inclination to be libelled for heresy; Sir, I wish you a good morning."

CHAPTER VII

MRS. MERRICK had a relation at Falmouth, a cousin, whose name was Sumelin, a banker, opulent and respectable. To him, as guardian, a Mr. Fluart had confided his only child, a daughter, with a fortune of 20,000l. Miss Fluart, seven years old at her father's death, was now twenty. At sixteen she was taken from the boarding-school, — I beg pardon, — seminary;[1] and Mr. Sumelin was

---

1 "Seminary" would have been the more fashionable term. Compare Jane Austen's *Emma*, chapter 3.

much perplexed what to do with her. In his youth he had been much abroad, and had looked at men and women of great varieties of colour, modes, and manners. He had even looked at kings and queens, — at lamas, bonzes, and muftis;[1] and having compared and considered what they might, could, or should have done, with what they did, he could not always determine, whether they were delegates from heaven above, or from the earth below; or whether mankind had arrived at its ultimatum of perfection and happiness, under any church or any state, or under any alliances between them. That this is a heterodoxy most abhorred, I own; and I am sorry it should exist in any of these my people; but truth being a necessary evil in this world sometimes, a poor biographer has not the right to dispense with it, as have the distinguished personages whom I shall always look up to as my divinities here on earth. But I am making my own reflections, when I should be making Mr. Sumelin's; a man of integrity, indeed, in his dealings, but of insanity in his notions, as wisdom goes now. In short, a very odd man.

But neither Mrs. Sumelin, nor her eldest daughter, Harriet were ever charged with oddity. On the contrary, they were so extremely like ladies in general, that every man's eyes and ears may save me the trouble of drawing their portraits.

Mrs. Sumelin had seen her tenth lustrum.[2] At eighteen she was angelic; for she had a smooth white skin and 12,000l. In intellect, not super-abundant; nor was it necessary; for to the shining qualities above-mentioned, understanding may or may not be added; it is of little consequence, especially in genteel life. Its want may be copiously supplied by vanity.

Miss Sumelin, — many fathers would have doated on her, for she was a perfect copy of her mother. Fond to excess of the fine and fashionable and an adorer of sweet pretty things. It is not amongst the foibles of the dear sex that I place these propensities; for I believe it pleased God to make them a part of the constitution of their natures; and surely, in his last, best work, there could be no imperfection.

So, I fear, did not Mr. Sumelin think. Against these innocent and elegant penchants, he frequently darted his keenest arrows; but

---

1 Religious leaders in, respectively, Tibetan Buddhism, Japanese Buddhism, and Islam, especially as practised in Ottoman Turkey.
2 Five-year period; the term comes from the Roman census, which was taken every five years.

they fell dead to the ground, repelled by the panoply of this mother and daughter; and Mr. Sumelin had the satisfaction, in common with most husbands, to see these charming inclinations grow into, passions, under his reprobation.

Charlotte, the youngest daughter, was not so exact a copy of her mother; her resemblances were more to her father; and this, perhaps, was the cause why the paternal affections were rather stronger than the maternal and sisterly. Of the age of Miss Fluart, she had been mostly with her at the seminary; and I believe had imbibed a stronger affection for her than for any other human being.

For the rest, one found in the family of Mr. Sumelin, a portion of love and harmony, such as is usually given. They might, indeed, sometimes say disagreeable things to each other; but the balance of power lay, as it always ought, with the ladies; for Miss Sumelin, making it a rule never to differ from her mother when her father did, the gentleman was consequently outvoted in matters of action, and out-talked in matters of speculation; which little inconveniences he was obliged to bear as well as he was able, — and he generally bore them best at a tavern.

Poets and fabulists agree, that men are not animals very quick-sighted to their own errors; but that they are seldom blind to the errors of their wives, much beyond the honey moon. I believe Mr. Sumelin is not to be charged with any defect of vision. He saw that his own house was not such a residence for Miss Fluart, as he could entirely approve, and he determined to place her with some judicious female friend. Of these he had not a very copious list; and on scrutiny, one accident or other, too much or too little affluence, — too much or too little wisdom, — too much or too little good humour, rendered every individual not the exact person he could have wished. The highest in his estimation stood Mrs. Merrick; but she was too much a recluse. So, at length, he agreed that his ward should live half with her, and half with himself at Falmouth.

So far as it enlarged their circle of pleasures, Mrs. and Miss Sumelin liked this very well; but in the cup of enjoyment, there is usually some ill tasted ingredient or other: In the company of Miss Fluart, Miss Sumelin was less a goddess. Is there on earth one sovereign, male or female, who can bear, *equo animo*,[1] a diminution of sovereignty?

---

1   With a calm spirit.

At the time we are now writing of Miss Fluart and her friend, Charlotte Sumelin, were at Falmouth. A very regular correspondence was kept up by the fair friends during their separation. I am not allowed to oblige my readers with the whole of it; but with those letters only which have some connexion with my present purpose. A few days after her accident, Miss Campinet received the following; with it I chuse to begin.

CHAPTER VIII

MISS FLUART TO MISS CAMPINET.

I Hope, Miss Campinet, you have been fretting and fuming, though not so much as to hurt your complexion, that post after post should pass by Grondale-place, without leaving a letter from my ladyship. To how many causes can you have attributed this prodigy? Imprimis, — she is dead. Not quite so bad as that neither. Secondly, — she is married. Not quite so good as that. Thirdly, — she is eloped. A tolerable conjecture, my dear; but you have mistaken the person. Yes, we have had an elopement, sure enough; and if half the squirrels of Falmouth had died, the bustle could scarce have been greater. Poor Harriet Sumelin, the idol of her dear mother, a pattern to all the daughters of men in this town and its precincts, has so tainted her fame, that I do not believe she will be consulted this month, even about a new cap.

Mr. Sumelin's head clerk, a Mr. Fillygrove, is the author of this mass of evil; a young man with a sweet pretty face, and two well enough shaped legs. These are considered as great accomplishments by young ladies; and the contemplation of them, does probably add to the happiness of the possessors, if one may judge by Mr. Fillygrove. If this young gentleman happens to be placed over against a pier glass at dinner, if he drinks your health, his looks are directed not to you, but the glass; so, if he answers a question. Once, when he was addressed, and it became evidently necessary to direct his regards to the person he was going to answer, he intended so to do, unluckily his eye, on its road, caught the mirror, was fascinated by it, and the poor youth found it impossible to break the charm. In a walk, you see him, once a minute, bend in graceful curvature, — throw a glance at those adorable legs, — and resume his erect position with increased perpendicularity. Let us do the man justice however; he has merit in the compting-house; and his father can, if he chuses, give him two or three thousand pounds.

Miss Harriet Sumelin could not resist such weighty attractions. She was the first to feel the power of the little winged deity; but the young man, either not having received a reciprocal wound, or not having advanced in effrontery so far as to pretend to a daughter of Mr. Sumelin, a 40,000 pounder, it created a sort of an embarrassment in the poor lady, how she should give him the necessary confidence without wounding her own delicacy. Love may be, and I believe is sometimes, very ingenious; but not being able to teach ingenuity to Harriet, she was obliged to have recourse to the vulgar method of telling him all about it with her eyes. The language was intelligible enough; they soon came to a right understanding; and neither of them having the least hope of consent from the lady's father, they very rightly resolved not to ask it, and trust paternal affection for pardon. So off one night they went for Dover; intending to marry at Calais and return.

The affair was perfectly understood in the morning, by a very dutiful epistle, which Harriet had left behind her, to instruct papa and mamma; and in which, she laid the fault, if there was any fault, upon destiny; for she was sure marriages were made in heaven. We were all, that is, the ladies of the family, very much affected to be sure. Mrs. Sumelin testified her's by scolding and clamour; Charlotte, by tears, and almost by convulsions; I, by silence and meditation. Having all performed our parts a reasonable time, my guardian, who had eaten his breakfast with perfect composure, said, "Well, and for what is all this noise and pother, Mrs. Sumelin? Your daughter is gone to be married, that's all. I suppose you intended she should marry one day?"

"But to marry so much beneath her, Mr. Sumelin, — and such a coxcomb."

"As to his being a coxcomb, my dear, we must set that down as a circumstance in Harriet's favour; coxcombry being the most approved qualification of man, in the mind of woman; and as to his being beneath her, I know not what that means."

"No! Mr. Sumelin: So rich as you are, and a young lady with your daughter's accomplishments."

"As to riches, Mrs. Sumelin, they are my own, and at my own disposal. I may give Mrs. Fillygrove a large fortune, and I may not. It is true, I do not much like masses of money in the hands of fools; but she is my daughter; I shall not let her want; and her puppy husband may one day be weaned of his folly, and may make as respectable a man as his poverty of understanding will permit."

"And so you really mean to forgive them without any ado?"

"Forgive them! yes. Why, I am hardly offended."

In truth, if the old gentleman had spoke the whole truth, I believe he was rather pleased than offended.

"And you will not send after them, to stop them?" asked Mrs. Sumelin.

"No, really, I will not."

Mrs. Sumelin continuing much upon the fret, Mr. Sumelin went to the compting-house; and we saw no more of him, (a thing that happens often) till the next morning. Indeed, we scarce saw him for several days after this; for Mrs. Sumelin was always at him, with all the agreeable garrulousness of a fretful woman; and the candour of a wife, who is perfectly convinced that her husband is always wrong.

About the sixth day, Mr. Sumelin introduced to us a gentleman from France, an American born, I believe, but having property in France, had been there some years; and not liking, I suppose, the politics of that country, had been selling his property; remitting part of the produce to Mr. Sumelin, to whom he had been recommended by a house in Philadelphia, in order to have it invested in the English funds.

How shall I describe this young stranger to you, my dear? He looks like a man, I think, and yet I have seen but few men look like him. He is not an Adonis,[1] like Mr. Fillygrove; nor does he resemble that accomplished personage in dress or in manners.

The latter are, indeed, rather open and engaging, than graceful. There is an ease about him, but it is an unstudied, unimitated ease. It seems his own; and becomes him so well, that he acquires our good will, almost before he has spoke. That his conversation will support his credit with ladies in general, is more than I dare affirm. I will give you a small specimen, that you may judge for yourself. By the bye, he has a very ugly name; Hermsprong; it sounds monstrous Germanish.

Mr. Sumelin. "Have you left America long?"

Mr. Hermsprong. "About five years."

S. "Since then you have resided in France?"

H. "Properly speaking, I have not resided any where. Smitten with the love of being seen, I have shewed myself to half Europe; returning occasionally to France, as I was wanted."

---

1 In classical mythology, a famously beautiful young man, beloved by Venus.

S. "They are going on there in a strange way."

H. "Yes, strange and new. I speak of the causes which animate the French; for as to the means — the destruction of the human species — it has been a favourite mode with power of every denomination, ever since power was."[1]

S. "What are these causes you speak of?"

H. "To make mankind wiser and better."

S. "And do you approve the means?"

H. "What — all? Oh no! it is left to the loyal Englishman; and is, I am told, a new prerogative, — to approve by the lump. All! no, Sir! All the malignant, as well as the better passions, are afloat in France; and malignant actions are the consequence. Many of the acts of the assembly are acts of necessity; and some, no doubt, of folly."

"I'm sure," says Mrs. Sumelin, "if you had approved them, you must have been a strange sort of gentleman."

"Perhaps I am, madam; but will you favour me with your reasons?"

"Are not they all atheists?" the lady asked. "And have not they robbed the nobility and the parsons? and don't they hate kings?"

"There may be many such shocking creatures among the men, madam; but the ladies, I assure you, are still pious, — still loyal, — still addicted to rank and title: The English ladies can scarce be fonder of distinction. Notwithstanding their boasted principle of equality, madam, there are very few of the *better* sort of ladies in France, who would forgive a daughter who married beneath her. I am informed the English ladies, though they do love rank, are in this particular more placable."

"I fear, Sir," said Mr. Sumelin, pleasantly, "you are not well informed."

"I appeal to the ladies. You gentlemen are said at present to

---

1   The reference to "the destruction of the human species" would probably
    have been read at the time as an allusion to the Terror (1794-95),
    although Hermsprong's later reference to "the acts of the [National]
    assembly" seems to refer to a slightly earlier period of the Revolution,
    before de facto power was seized by the Committee of Public Safety.

boast of cherishing prejudices, *because* they are prejudices; ladies cannot be thus absurd."[1]

"No, faith! I will do the things what honour I can: This pitch they have not reached: They do, indeed, stick as fast by their prejudices as men can do; not for that curious reason above-mentioned, but because they like them; especially when they are founded upon their vanities."

"We are sure to have your good word," replied Mrs. Sumelin; "but I hope, Mr. — pray what is your name, Sir?"

"Hermsprong, madam."

"I hope, Mr. Humsprung, you have more sense than to believe him?"

"Oh, — I don't usually give gentlemen much credit, when they rail at the ladies; least of all on the subject we are now treating of. Could you, madam, could any mother, if she had a daughter who had unfortunately fixed her affections not quite so prudently as she ought—Could you tear her from your bosom, and give her misery, only for seeking her own happiness?"

Mrs. Sumelin seemed to sit uneasily upon her chair.

"No, madam," continued the orator, "I see an expression in your fine face, (and indeed her fine face was rather rosy) that will not permit me to suppose you can have a hard heart."

"Sir, — pray, Sir, — " said Mrs. Sumelin, "have you heard?"

"What, madam?"

"That I have a daughter so circumstanced?"

"Indeed! then I hope I am not deceived in my opinion?"

"Do you know what a wretch she has gone off with?"

"Is he a highwayman, madam?"

"No, Lord bless me! (a little peevishly;) but I wish I had never seen him. Sure, Mr. Sumelin, was bewitched when he took him into his house. He is the greatest coxcomb —"

"The charge is true, no doubt," says my guardian; "and yet the ladies never made the discovery till he was gone."

---

1 · An allusion to Burke's *Reflections*: "we [the English] are generally men of untaught feelings: ... [and], instead of casting away all our old prejudices, we cherish them to a very considerable degree, and, to take more shame to ourselves, we cherish them because they are prejudices; and the longer they have lasted, and the more generally they have prevailed, the more we cherish them" (OUP 1993, 87). The reference to "shame" is, of course, ironic in context.

A message from the compting-house called Mr. Sumelin out. "The grand disgrace," said he, as he went, "is having been my clerk."

"I should hardly think that a disgrace," said Mr. Hermsprong.

"Do you know, Sir, what a fortune Mr. Sumelin can give his daughters?"

"Oh, half a million each, I suppose."

"Lord, Sir, — you are so perverse."

"And yet I question whether some people may not think the reputation of probity, which Mr. Sumelin also possesses, is better even than that of wealth. Besides, he was not always so rich, you know. Was he so, when he was so happy as to win your affections? Oh, if a lady's love could increase as fast as a husband's wealth, how eager all married men would be to get rich."

"Sir, I don't think you talk at all to the purpose."

"I am an ignorant young man, madam, roaming up and down the world to pick up a little wisdom. I want to read hearts, especially ladies' hearts."

"Then, once for all, I tell you, Mr. Humsprug, that I wash my hands of Mrs. Fillygrove, if she be Mrs. Fillygrove, for ever."

"Suppose she should have repented her design, and stopped short of its completion?"

"But I can't suppose any such thing. And if she should, what becomes of her character? That's lost, let what will happen."

"Dear madam, you puzzle me. If your daughter is married, you disown her because she is married. This is the first case. The second is, if she is not married, you disown her, because — because she is not married."

"I can't think, Mr. Humsprug, what business you have with it, or what you can know about it, but what you have heard at Fal-mouth, where all the foul mouths in the town are open."

"I ought to ask pardon for my impertinence, and hope you will grant it, when you know that it has been my lot so far happy at least, to relieve her from a little distress at Ostend."

Our curiosity was now greatly excited; and we expressed it by silence and open mouths. Mr. Hermsprong continued.

"I imagine this was the first of Mr. Fillygrove's performances in this way; for he neither knew the expence he was likely to incur, nor the proper steps to be taken, when he was out of the British dominions. At Ostend, his money was exhausted. At one of the windows of the inn, where I was waiting for a passage, I saw a lady in tears. I presumed to enquire the cause. This was impertinent, no doubt; but I could not help it. There had been an altercation betwixt Miss Sumelin and Mr. Fillygrove; for the young man had found no better way of getting rid of his distress, than by drinking wine. She reproached, and he swore. This was their situation when I got myself introduced. I know not whether I should have got an explanation from Miss Sumelin, but the gentleman gave me one copiously. You may judge, madam, when I learned that the lady was a daughter of Mr. Sumelin of Falmouth, whom I considered, though yet unknown, except by his probity, as the first of my friends in England, the matter could not be indifferent to me. In the present state of the young lady's mind, I had no great difficulty to convince her of her error. She put herself accordingly under my protection. The young man I was under the necessity of correcting a little. I did not suffer him, however, to feel any other want than the want of common sense. He even returned to England, on board the same vessel; but left us on our landing, nor have we seen him since. Miss Sumelin had the goodness to accompany me to Falmouth; and is now, I believe, under the care of her father, who is gone to bring a repentant daughter back to the embraces of a forgiving mother."

"I assure you," says Mrs. Sumelin, "you'll not find me so forgiving neither."

"Madam, you are not acquainted with the strength of your own goodness."

This dialogue was put a stop to by Mr. Sumelin, who came to inform his lady, that her daughter was in her own apartment, hoping to see her; "and my advice, Harriet, is, that you should forgive her cordially, and at once; for I cannot turn her out of doors for an offence she has but half committed; and in my own house I desire peace."

Oh, my dear! what terrible news have I just heard. Can it be true? Can my Caroline have been so near destruction? Heaven bless her preserver, whomsoever it may be. This letter my perturbation will not permit me to finish; indeed it is long enough; too long, probably, for the state of mind in which it is likely to find you. Pray, be speedy in gratifying my impatience.

Your affectionate,

MARIA FLUART.

CHAPTER IX

MISS CAMPINET wrote to her friend as follows:

Sensible of my own deficiency, I should almost envy you your happy vivacity, my dear Maria, did it not incline too much towards satire, — and were not that satire mostly directed against a half fallen sister. But your playfulness, I know, is only of the pen, — for your heart is good and kind.

Yes, my dear, I have indeed had a most dreadful escape. I cannot think of it without terror. It is probable, nay certain almost, that I owe my preservation to that very Mr. Hermsprong, for I never before heard of the name, the subject of your last letter. For the minuter particulars, you must wait till we can make them the subject of conversation. I cannot afford an hour's absence from my dear aunt, who has been long declining, and this fright, I fear, will accelerate her last mortal hour. No one but myself, perhaps, would wish to retard it, if, as I fear it will, the small remainder of her life must be pain and sickness; but to me, you know she is of infinite importance. When I have lost her, what is to become of me? My father's house is little inviting to me, and still less proper. Lord Grondale's company when he has any, are all men; and I wish I could add, men of merit. Alas! they are men of play; for I never heard they had other occupation or amusement, if we except the pleasures of the table, where they are accustomed to sit long, and rise rather more than refreshed.

From these and other irregularities, you know my father has suffered much, and is now so much an invalid, that these parties come much seldomer than usual. When they do, they are very improper persons for me to associate with. Then, Lord Grondale has never been in the habit of tenderness to me; either, because I have not merit sufficient to engage his affection, or, as I rather chuse to flatter myself, because he has seen so little of me. Not that he does not honour me with his notice sometimes, and sometimes makes me happy by his good humour; but more commonly, he has some faults to blame, or some foibles to lash; and indeed his polite irony is very mortifying. On these accounts, my dear Maria, I am now desirous to engage your promise to be with me a few months upon the melancholy event of my dear aunt's decease, and my remove to Grondale Hall.

My aunt sends to me; I must quit my pen till to-morrow.

This morning my father called upon me, as he returned from an airing. I must relate a part of our conversation, as it gives me an opportunity to inform you of all that has since passed betwixt Mr. Hermsprong and me. After the usual questions respecting my aunt, and a minute's silence, my father abruptly says, "Caroline, when did you see your saviour?"

"My lord!" says I, with some consternation, for I was startled at the impiety, as I thought, of the question.

"Pshaw," says my father, peevishly; "I mean your knight errant; he who stopped your precipitate flight down the crag."

"I have seen him once only, my lord; a day or two after the accident. He called at my aunt's, and sent up Mr. Hermsprong's compliments, and an enquiry into our healths. I went down to thank him for my aunt and myself; and asked him if it was in my power, or — pardon me, Sir, if I presumed too far — in my father's, to serve him? He answered, he did not pretend the action laid me under the least obligation. He thought little of its merit, for it was unpremeditated. It was an impulse, — and it was irresistible."

Lord Grondale said it was a good distinction; he must profess himself of the same opinion as to its merit.

"I own, my lord, I was of a different opinion; and thought this modesty of expression rather enhanced than diminished Mr. Hermsprong's merit respecting myself; I replied to this purpose, and wished to be able to shew my gratitude."

"You must not then talk to me," he answered, "of Lord Grondale; if I must have a reward, let it be all your own."

"What cursed effrontery!" my lord exclaimed. "This was a downright declaration of love."

"I did not think so, Sir; but I remained silent, because I did not exactly know to what it tended. He explained his meaning directly. 'Your silence, Miss Campinet, (these were his exact words) accuses me of presumption; but of presumption I am no farther guilty than to wish to be allowed the pleasure of your conversation, when your doors are open to common visitors.' I then said, my aunt's indisposition prevented my seeing company at present; I feared it would end fatally; in which case I hoped for permission to reside with my father; and to him I must look up for the direction of my conduct, and the choice of my acquaintance."

"This was a proper and a pertinent reply, Caroline, if it came from your heart."

"I hope I have never given my father cause to suspect my duty and inclinations are at variance."

"The case, Caroline, is not uncommon; the generality of

daughters of the present day, may very well justify fathers in such a suspicion; but what answer did your hero return?"

"My hero! my lord."

"Well — well — Mr. Hermsprong."

"'If so, —' Mr. Hermsprong said, but checked himself, so that I cannot guess what he was then going to say. After a pause, 'I am sensible,' he said, 'your time must be now precious; if I have never the pleasure to see you again, accept my most earnest wishes for every possible felicity.' He withdrew with a haste which did not permit me to reply."

So ended my conversation with my father; and so ends all my knowledge, — perhaps for ever — of Mr. Hermsprong.

Your affectionate

CAROLINE CAMPINET.

CHAPTER X

AT the conclusion of our sixth chapter, we left Mr. Hermsprong bidding good morrow to the Reverend Dr. Blick. In the course of his morning's walk, he saw a young man taking angles with a Hadley's quadrant.[1] This was my humble self; but I hate egotism; and when I have occasion to mention this self, it shall be by the names of Gregory Glen; the first of which I derive from my god-mothers, the latter I inherit — from my mother. Mr. Hermsprong, approaching Mr. Glen, asked if he was surveying the county? To which he answered, that was beyond his abilities; this was merely a mathematical amusement. The stranger said, such amusements were to be envied.

"No," Mr. Glen replied, "your's are the amusements to be envied; if, as I suspect, you are the happy man to whom the best and fairest of her sex owes her preservation."

"Why," he replied, "if mankind is disposed to consider this as extraordinary, and to pay me for it by a larger portion of esteem, it is very well, I am willing to receive the reward, though impelled to the action by instinct, I suppose, — for I did not know the lady was the best and fairest of her sex."

---

1   An instrument primarily used to calculate location at sea by measuring the height of the sun or stars above the horizon. Invented by John Hadley (1682-1744) in 1730, it was a forerunner of the sextant.

"You refine too much, Sir," said Glen; "do you think I should have done the same?"

"I know not," he answered, "why I should suppose the contrary."

"I know," replied Glen; "terror would have deprived me of sense and motion; nor do I think I know a man on whom the suddenness of a circumstance so terrible, would not have had the same effect."

"I conceive I know many," Mr. Hermsprong said, "not indeed amongst civilized Europeans. Man may be in a situation betwixt a state of nature and extreme civilization, such that intrepidity and possession of mind, in sudden danger, may be necessary, even for existence. The Aborigines of America, when they hunt or go to war, are exposed to instant peril in many ways. They get a habit of presence of mind, and habit is nature."

"No doubt," Mr. Glen answered, "but this habit so seldom offers itself to our notice, one cannot easily conceive it."

"Oh," said Mr. Hermsprong, smiling, "you are upon your guard, I see, against the marvellous."

"No, Sir, — indeed no," replied Glen; "I assure you I have not the least suspicion, — not the least —"

"Nay, Sir, if you had, it gives me no offence. Travellers have always 'imposed upon credulity; and sensible men receive their reports now more circumspectly. I am a stranger; you know me not; I relate something that appears to you incredible; you have a right to withhold your assent, till more and better information may have convinced you. I believe I am talking to Mr. Glen."

Mr. Glen bowed his answer.

"They say here you are an intelligent man; that you are humane; honest in actions, and open in speech. All these are to my taste. I ask your friendship. If you grant it, I hope to convince you that I hold a manly freedom of thinking and speaking, amongst the most estimable qualities of man."

Was it possible to refuse a friendship so engagingly asked? No. From that hour it has been the greatest source of Mr. Glen's felicity; and you, my dear readers, owe to it this invaluable book.

CHAPTER XI

THERE was in Hermsprong a superiority in science, and an elevation of sentiment, which Glen found it impossible not to admire, and difficult not to regard with envy. This weakness vanished after some days' familiarity, and the reserve, which was its consequence, vanished after it.

Their acquaintance was not cultivated after the ordinary manner; they neither eat nor drank together; for Hermsprong's residence was an inn, and Glen boarded and lodged; and each had more taste for morning excursions, for the discovery of nature's more rare productions, plants or minerals; and especially for the reciprocal communication of mind with mind.

A sight of the encampment put Mr. Hermsprong in mind of his rencontre with Dr. Blick. Mr. Glen did not seem in the humour for panegyric; for his portrait of the Doctor was rather unfavourable. That he united pride with meanness; that he was as haughty to his inferiors, as cringing to superiors. An eternal flatterer of Lord Grondale, he did not even presume to preach against a vice, if it happened to be a vice of his patron. "And yet," said Glen, "this man is rich; has great church preferment, two good livings, and a stall;[1] keeps his chariot, and does not chuse to marry."

"I hope," said Mr. Hermsprong, "you are not now giving a general picture of the English clergy?"

"By no means," replied Mr. Glen; "as individuals, I think them generally worthy; and if you desire to see a contrast to Dr. Blick, you may find it in his curate; a man of learning; of high probity; simple in his manners; attentive to his duties; and so attached to his studies, that he may be said to be almost unacquainted with mankind. This man is married; has four daughters; and from the bountiful rector of Grondale has forty-five pounds per annum, for doing half the duties of Grondale, and the whole of Sithin, a village a mile hence, where he resides. It is true, he derives about an equal revenue from his patrimonial fortune, otherwise it would be impossible his family could be supported."

"I am as desirous to court the acquaintance of such a man," said Mr. Hermsprong, "as of avoiding the Dr. Blick's; and will take an opportunity to call on him. Or what do you say to bringing him to spend a social evening at the Golden Ball?"

To this Mr. Glen agreed; and the succeeding night was the appointed time.

---

1 A clergyman who holds a stall is a canon; see note 1, page 74.

CHAPTER XII

THE good curate willingly accepted the invitation, and was so punctual that he arrived at the Golden Ball an hour before he was expected; and before Mr. Hermsprong had returned from his afternoon's excursion. Mr. Tunny, the landlord, however, accommodated him with an easy chair in the best parlour, a pipe, and a tankard; and was, moreover, so obliging as to favour him with his own company. The Reverend Mr. Woodcock took this opportunity to enquire concerning his guest.

"Sir," said the landlord, with the air of a man who has something important to communicate, "this Mr. Hermsprong is — a — a — sort of a man — one does not often see — nor is it every man who would know what to make of him. But I have seen the world, Mr. Woodcock; I was a private in the 27th, and rose to be corporal solely by merit. I was in the hottest of the last German war.[1] Sir, I have lived upon gun-powder. My wife, the late widow Trott, preferred me to six; she knew men; and I'll be bold to say, I have not deceived her. This house is much altered since I came to it. I am sorry not to see you oftener in it, Mr. Woodcock; I have very good company. Doctor Blick has done me the honour more than once. I threw out that bow window; I set up the butts.[2] I know the world, Sir, and I know men must be attracted, Sir, my respectful service to you."

A long draught gave Mr. Woodcock an opportunity to put his landlord in mind of Mr. Hermsprong.

"I'll tell you, Sir," says Tunny; "it is by little things you know a man. That was a maxim of the king of Prussia and Marshall Keith.[3]

---

1 The last German war would have been the Seven Years War (1756-63), fought in North America and India as well as in Europe. England was allied with Prussia against (among other combatants) Austria and France.

2 Possibly targets for some sort of sport; Faulkner suggests that Tunny might also be referring to stakes marking an extension of the inn grounds.

3 Frederick the Great of Prussia (1712-86), who commanded the Prussian troops in the Seven Years War, was a sceptic who was interested in the ideas of Deists such as Voltaire — hence Tunny's later comment about his lack of religion. Francis James Edward Keith (1696-1758) was a Scottish soldier who entered the Prussian service in 1747 and was made a Field Marshall by Frederick the Great. He died at the Battle of Hochkirchen, in which the Prussians were defeated by the Austrians.

I served under Marshall Keith. He was a great commander. I was not 500 yards from him, when he fell. If he had lived I should not have been landlord of the Golden Ball at Grondale. But providence is over all: Things will be as God pleases. Marshall Keith took a liking to me. I never think of him without abundance of sorrow. So, Sir, my respectful service to you."

"Thank you, landlord; but Mr. Hermsprong."

"Why, Sir, when I think of my dear Marshall Keith, I can think of nobody else. If he had lived, things would not have been quite as they are. Not but the late king of Prussia was a good soldier too; but then he had no religion; and a soldier without religion, Mr. Woodcock, — what is he? D—n my blood, if I value any man that has no religion. The tankard stands at you, Sir. A man never fights his best that don't believe a cannon ball may carry him to heaven."

"It is a good foundation for a soldier to build upon. But we forget Mr. Hermsprong."

"Why, Sir, here he comes about ten days ago, at seventeen minutes past five in the evening; himself on foot; his servant on horseback, with his portmanteau, not coming in till eight. Now, what do you think, Mr. Woodcock, was the first thing he called for?"

"Perhaps," said the curate, "a private room for prayer and thanksgiving."

"No, Lord bless you! I never had but one guest of that stamp, and he went off with two silver spoons in his pocket. No, Sir, he called for a tub of water."

"Water!"

"Water, Sir! that's his way. He will walk you forty miles in a morning. His shoes are as soft and pliable as silk. Well, Sir, after his cold bath, he dined upon a cold round of beef; and faith, he played his part like a man. A couple of pounds vanished in a twinkling; and he seasoned them with a quart or two of good spring water. Not a drop of good liquor has he drank in my house. His servant, indeed, might have made up the deficiency a little, but he was off the next morning, and I have not seen him since. The gentleman himself took a morning's walk; and to tell you the truth, I did not much expect to see him again. However, he did return at last, and called for coffee. I observed him attentively while he eat me a twopenny loaf; for I learned to read men under Marshall Keith; and when he had finished, he did, for the first time, notice Tom Tunny, at the Golden Ball; a man that, no disgrace to Mr. Hermsprong, has conversed with as good men as himself. He talked to me about prospects and old castles, and other trifling things; it is true, he did not then know I had served under Marshall Keith. Since then, we have been better acquainted. I suppose at that time I might answer rather glum; so he ceased his questions, and demanded his bill. It came to four shillings and three-pence. So he takes out a purse; to say truth, it did not seem to want ammunition; and giving me one pound one, desired change. Then, says he, in a droll way enough; 'I have learned to divide landlords into three classes: Those who charge with primitive modesty; those who charge with the modesty of men who know the world and those who charge without any modesty at all. The first, I make it a rule to pay double; the second, according to my sense of their modesty; to the last, I pay their bills. You know the world, Mr. Tunny, and my system requires, that I should pay you three half-crowns.'[1] 'Sir,' says I, 'your servant.' For really the man's manner was so gracious and comical, that, though I thought it beneath me to take the overplus, — for, sir, I had the command of a company once on the occasion of a retreat for twenty-four hours, — yet, as this sort of humour was rather scarce, I put the affront, if it was one, quietly in my pocket. Well, Sir; he then told me he liked the country and my house; perhaps he might stay a few weeks; and as he was a stranger, and did not like daily reckonings, I must do him the favour to lock up a bank note for him in my bureau. 'Sir,' says I, 'I cannot doubt the honour of a gentleman who behaves so generously.' 'The simple language of truth,' says he, 'is the best.' Now, you know, this was not polite; but he is an odd gentleman; sometimes you would think him the politest man in the world; and at others, he minds it no more than my dragon. Have you seen my dragon, Mr. Woodcock?"

"No, really," the curate answered, "I never saw one in my life."

"Never saw a stallion in your life! Well you scholars see, or rather do not see, strange things."

The conversation was interrupted by the entrance of Mr. Hermsprong, along with Mr. Glen.

The proper civilities over, Mr. Hermsprong enquired of Mr. Woodcock what liquor he chose; to which the curate answered, Ale and a pipe were his luxuries.

"Then," said Hermsprong, "this evening they shall be mine. I wish we could make them so to honest Tom Tunny here; but, alas!

---

1   There were twelve pence in a shilling and two shillings sixpence in half a crown. Hermsprong thus pays a generous three shillings and threepence over the bill.

to him they are absolute necessaries. Mr. Glen, provide for yourself and Mr. Tunny, whose company will be an additional pleasure to us, for he knows the world, and has served under Marshall Keith."

"Sir," says the landlord, "I shall be happy to have the honour of drinking the first glass with you, you have chose to drink in my house."

"Heaven gave us wine for a cordial," Mr. Hermsprong replied, "and ale for a luxury; and I make it a point of conscience to keep them so."

"But," says our landlord, "how any gentleman can relish water, as you do, is to me surprising. Why, it has no more taste than —"

"Water," replied Mr. Hermsprong. "But salt itself will become insipid to a man who is always spreading cayenne over his tongue."

"Cayenne, Sir!" said the landlord; "zounds, I have lived upon gunpowder. Are martial spirits to be kept up by water?"

"No, certainly," Mr. Hermsprong answered; "Englishmen are lions with beer, and heroes with brandy. The field of battle is the bed of honour; and I dare say Mr. Tunny has a thousand times regretted the not lying in it with Marshall Keith."

"Curse me if I have though," says honest Thomas. "No, Sir, I have attacked a battery, and stormed a breach; I have seen death all around and about me; but to tell you a secret, the devil take me, if ever I wished him an inch nearer."

"That sentiment is so natural," said the curate; "one may rely upon the truth of it, without swearing."

"Why, as to the swearing," returned the landlord, "it's as natural to a soldier as praying to a parson; a soldier has not a bit less religion for it in his heart."

A carriage this instant stopping at the door, obliged Mr. Tunny to postpone what more he had to say in defence of swearing. It was Dr. Blick, who had taken an airing this evening as far as Sithin, to order his journeyman to double duty the next Sunday; and being informed where Mr. Woodcock was gone, was returning that way home.

When the Doctor had given his orders to the poor curate, he condescended to ask who his company were; and being informed, said, "If I could get a good tiff of punch now, I would come in for half an hour."

"As good as good rum, lemon, and sugar can make it," says Tunny.

Doctor Blick was announced by the landlord, at his entrance into the parlour.

Hermsprong had almost begun sternly to say, "By what right, Sir, do you introduce a stranger to a select company without leave," when the cast down humble look of poor Woodcock disarmed his anger, and made him forbear. He contented himself, however, with slightly rising, and sitting, down again. Glen was equally unpolite; but Tunny's bustling assiduity made it the less observable.

When the Doctor was accommodated with the easy chair, his punch, and a pipe, and no one seeming inclined to speak, "I beg," says the Doctor, "I may not interrupt the conversation."

Still silence prevailing, Mr. Tunny says, "Why, Doctor, I happened to swear a little, and Mr. Woodcock reproved me; whereas, if he had been chaplain to a regiment, he would have known that a soldier must swear; I don't see, for my part, how the service can be carried on without it."

"I do not see why," said the curate.

"Sir, I will tell you," replied the Doctor; "you cannot suppose that a clergyman can be an advocate for swearing in general; but I have heard sensible officers, both in the sea and land service say, that it supports a certain energy; and if soldiers and sailors were forbidden it, their courage would droop."

"There now," cried Tunny, with exultation, "did not I tell you? Doctor Blick has seen life. One always expects sensible observations from gentlemen that have seen life. I served under Marshall Keith, and know a thing or two. Now, here is Mr. Hermsprong has been supposing that I must be sorry that I did not fall in the field of honour with Marshall Keith; but he is confoundedly mistaken."

"Yes," said the Doctor, "it is a mistake which no man could have fallen into, who has studied human nature to any purpose. The love of life is so strong, that scarcely any calamity can weaken it."

"No," says Hermsprong; "nor in *very* civilized countries, any affection, — not even the love of heaven."

"I have been told," said Glen, "that savages are taught, and really learn to despise it."

"Sir," says the Doctor, "man cannot despise it."

"I believe," Mr. Hermsprong said, "despise is not the proper term. A savage, put to his choice, will, in all common situations, prefer life; but without dreading death with the timidity of nations, who are taught from infancy to fear it."

"Sir," replied Doctor Blick, "you may say what you please of savages; it is all nonsense. Man must fear death. It is a lesson of nature. You teach in vain, if you teach lessons contrary to nature."

"Pray, Sir," asked Hermsprong, "what is nature?"

"Ask a school boy, Sir," said the Doctor.

"It is not your rudeness," replied Hermsprong; "your imposing tone, nor airs of superior knowledge, that shall deter me from telling you, Sir, that even Doctors may make superficial distinctions. Man cannot be taught any thing contrary to nature. However he acts, he must act by nature's laws; howsoever he thinks, he must think by nature's laws."

"Sir," says the Doctor, "if I have rudeness, you have presumption. Let me ask you a simple question. Is a fever natural?"

"Most certainly. Its whole process is according to the immutable laws of nature."

"Very true; in an enlarged sense; but by natural we mean only the common course of things."

"What philosopher calls earthquakes and storms unnatural?"

"Well, Sir; but this does not prove that man can get above the fear of death."

"Will you accept, as proof, the bravery of our sailors, in the hour of battle?"

"No, Sir."

"Suicide, at least, must be proof compleat."

"No, Sir; it is lunacy."

"Alas! half the actions of our lives are lunacies, I think; and none more than those we reason ourselves into. War is lunacy, and we call in all the powers of reason to prove it wisdom. Perhaps, the fear of death itself is a lunacy; for to a reflecting mind, at least, death is not an evil."

"Death not an evil!" says the Doctor, in a tone of surprise.

"Zounds, Sir! death not an evil!" cries Tunny.

"I should suppose not," Mr. Hermsprong answered; "death is privation of sense; can any evil happen to that stone?"

This appeared to the Doctor to border on infidelity; a thing so execrable, root and branch, that it ought to be burnt out of the world by fire and faggot.

"Sir," said he, "are you an atheist? Death, privation of sensation! No, Sir; it is enlargement of sensation. It is renovation — it is the gate of life — it is a passport to eternal joys."

"Then surely," said Hermsprong, "it is not an evil."

Now the good Doctor was vexed at this; he had like to have broke his pipe; and so much the more vexed, as the fool of a landlord cried out, "But, zounds! Doctor, he has flanked you."[1]

His anger fell on poor Tunny, whom he rebuked severely, and then returned with fresh vigour to the contest.

"It must be supposed I must mean what I last said only for the good. To the wicked death surely is an evil."

"Let Tom Tunny look to that," said Hermsprong, gaily.

"Then, Sir, you think yourself the man without sin."

"Syllogistically, all men are sinners. All men who do not do what the church requires, are sinners. But all men do not do what the church requires. Then, all men are sinners."

"Sir, you have quick parts; but all the parts in the world, without faith, will not ensure salvation."

"Oh! if it depends upon faith, I have no reason to despair. At Lisbon I believed all holy catholic things; at Rome I believed in the infallibility of the tiara; and in England I believe in church and king, the first article of faith; which, if a man do not do, he cannot be saved."[2]

"Mr. Hermsprong, — that is your name, I think, — religion is not a jest."

"Well, Doctor, dispute is disagreeable; altercation pitiful. It is easy on this subject to give offence by innocent or careless expressions. I desire to give no offence; therefore beg leave to decline the subject."

"Young gentleman, I must not let you off so. It is my duty to put you right, if I find you wrong. I suspect you have imbibed some of the abominable doctrines of the French philosophers; some heretical tenets, which will plunge you into the bottomless pit."[3]

---

1 Met his attack from both sides; another of Tunny's military metaphors.
2 The tiara is an allusion to the triple crown of the Pope. The Anglican church required its members to assent to thirty-nine articles of faith, of which the first was belief in the Holy Trinity. Hermsprong's reference to "church and king" as "the first article of faith" thus implies that the rabidly patriotic conservatives are misapplying the doctrines of their supposed faith in their practice.
3 A reference to French Enlightenment philosophers such as Denis Diderot (1713-84) and Voltaire (1694-1778). These thinkers were notorious for their scepticism about traditional religious faith, although they were usually Deists who accepted the existence of a God but denied that anything could be known about him, rather than atheists. By the later 1790s, they were often blamed for preparing the way for the excesses of the French Revolution.

The Doctor now began to drink off his glasses of punch very quick; and as he had preached against infidelity but the last sabbath, he remembered much of the sermon; and, meeting with no interruption from the company, who preserved a profound silence, he preached it over again with much animation.

When he had finished, Mr. Hermsprong thanked him for the trouble he had taken, and drank his health.

"But," said the Doctor, "you say nothing to my discourse; I hope I have not preached in vain."

"In vain, I fear, to Tom Tunny here."

The Doctor looked, and, lo! the man was asleep. He was presently awaked, and received a sharp reprimand.

"Doctor," says the landlord, "I always thought a pulpit a fitter place to preach in than an alehouse; and that a man must fall asleep when he cannot keep himself awake. It is not orthodox here, to preach over our liquor. Gentlemen, my service to you. Solomon said there was a time for all things; a time to preach, and a time to let it alone;[1] and I am sure there is no better time to let it alone, than when good company meet together to be merry."

"You are beneath my notice," said the Doctor, with great dignity; "but for this young gentleman —"

"I request, Sir, you will do me the favour to consider me as beneath your notice also," said Hermsprong.

"I don't like obstinacy in a young man. You was the person who had the good luck to do a piece of service to Miss Campinet?"

No answer.

"That," continues the Doctor, "was a fortunate event for the young lady, and might have been so to you, had you thought proper to treat his lordship with proper respect."

"Sir, I have no respect for his lordship."

"No, young man; nor for any body else, I think."

"I pay it, Sir, where I owe it."

"The man will have something to do, who sets himself the task of correcting your errors."

"It is too much even for a Doctor of divinity. I ought to be grateful, however, for the intention; and to return the obligation where I can. You yourself, Sir, seem to have one small error. I recommend officiousness to your correction."

---

1 Compare Ecclesiastes 3:1.

The Doctor's face grew red with anger. In a raised tone he said, "Let me tell you, young man —"

"Stop, Sir," said Hermsprong, rising; "by what right do you presume to speak to me with the tone of a master? I owe you no obedience; and despise you for your tyrannical and contentious spirit. Mr. Tunny, let another room be prepared for Mr. Glen and I. Mr. Woodcock, when the Doctor chuses to leave a place where he had no right to intrude, we shall be glad of your company."

Mr. Hermsprong left the room as he said this, and was followed by Glen.

CHAPTER XIII

"IS this," Mr. Hermsprong asked, "a general specimen of the English clergy?"

"By no means," replied Mr. Glen; "except a certain portion of rancour against those who differ from them in religion or politics (an effect probably springing from their *l'esprit du corps*,) they are in general rather amiable than otherwise. But they are men. Sometimes, in their too earnest desire of the good things here below, they are apt to forget those above. They are wise, however; and if unfortunately they are assaulted by any violent cupidities, they commonly take the proper means of obtaining them. Doctor Blick, for example, having been seized with that capital disorder, the love of accumulation, has fulfilled himself with a prudent quantity of adulation, which has answered his purpose well; he has church preferment to near 1000l. per annum; and has not, I am told, laid aside his expectations of a bishopric."

"And is the want of this agreeable quality," asked Hermsprong, "to be assigned as the cause of Mr. Woodcock's not rising in the church?"

"Alas!" replied Glen, "not having been in the way of subjects on whom to practise, he has not taken the trouble to acquire it. Nor is this the only point of contrast betwixt himself and his reverend master. Besides, taking care not to lose any thing of his dues, by a foolish lenity, or by a love of peace, the Doctor knows it is his duty rather to govern than to teach his flock; and he governs *à la royale*, with imperious airs, and imperious commands. Woodcock, on the contrary, is one of the mildest of the sons of men. It is true, he preaches humility, but he practises it also; and takes pains, by example, as well as precept, to make his parishioners good, in all their offices, their duties, and relations. To the poor, he is indeed a blessing; for he gives comfort, when he has nothing else to give. To him they apply when sick; he gives them simple medicines; when they are in doubt, he gives them wholesome counsels. He is learned too, and liberal in his opinions; but of manners so simple, and so ignorant of fashion and folly, that to appear in the world would subject him to infinite ridicule."

"You give me," said Mr. Hermsprong, "a desire to know all that can be known of so good, and I suppose so odd a man."

"He was," says Glen, "the only child of an honest shop-keeper at Truro, who having saved some money, yielded to the instigation of his wife, who wished to see her son a gentleman. In consequence he went to Cambridge, went through his respondentia[1] with applause, and took his degrees. After this he returned home, to shew his father and mother how well they had laid their money out, and to wait promotion. This, however, never came. Instead of it, there happened a bankruptcy of a capital miner;[2] with whom Mr. Woodcock, the father, had lodged all the money he did not employ in trade. This broke the old man's heart; and after his death, his debts and effects, compared, exclusive of the money due from the miner, left a balance in his mother's favour of only 200l. A little time the widow kept on trade; but not understanding it, she had more of loss than gain. The young man then advertized for a curacy; which happened at the lucky moment, when Dr. Blick had obtained the patronage of Lord Grondale, by activity and certain skilful manoeuvres, in a contested election which, but for him, it was said, would have gone against his lordship's candidate.

"The opposite party, indeed, threatened the Doctor with a prosecution for certain matters which had only prescription to support them, not law; and which trenched a little upon moral honesty; but it soon appeared to be a hopeless business. For, besides that moral honesty is seldom applied as an agent in elections, it was found that Dr. Blick was an approved man, orthodox in church and state; such a man as these bad times want.

"The livings of Grondale and Sithin had been vacant almost a month. Lord Grondale had promised them to a Mr. Edwards, a very

---

1 Bage presumably means responsions, which are exams taken before a
   student matriculates—a term used at Oxford, but not at Cambridge.
2 That is, a mine owner or a speculator in mines. Such risky private
   deposits of savings or capital were not unusual in the eighteenth century.

worthy man. It was pity. Dr. Blick applied, and it was almost impossible not to reward such and such recent merit. Mr. Edwards was abroad, tutor to a young gentleman, but daily expected home. So Lord Grondale ventured to give the livings, and excuse it to Edwards in the best manner possible. At last it occurred to his lordship, that the promise was verbal, and made three or four years ago; and that he might easily forget it. So he forgot it.

"Dr. Blick accepted Mr. Woodcock as his curate, on the stipend of 40l. per annum, to which he afterwards generously added 5l. more, on condition of undertaking the duty of both churches,' when the Doctor happened to be absent, or indisposed; and he has been so often indisposed to the office, that it has almost wholly devolved upon the curate.

"Upon this splendid revenue, Woodcock and his mother supported existence some years, till the bankrupt's affairs were settled; and at length received 1400l. This was wealth indeed. The mother enjoyed it three years, and died. The son, after his first sorrows were over, found himself very much alone; and at length discovered that the summit of human felicity is not to be reached without a wife. But on the subject of women he was peculiarly delicate. The lady he honoured with his hand, must be as perfect as the frail state of mortality will permit. For her person, it must be genteel; she must be beautiful in face, and elegant in dress. She must be pious and charitable; well read, and well instructed in domestic affairs; moreover she must be richly endowed with all the virtues.

"Miss Dorothea Barton was the daughter of a farmer, a mile distant. Mr. Woodcock had seen her once or twice during the life his mother; but he did not then think of a wife; and, indeed, the young lady did not perfectly correspond with the beautiful idea in the parson's mind. So he thought not of her, till happening to drink tea at Mr. Snape's the miller, he met her there, and as Mrs. Snape lamented that her husband was not at home, to attend the young lady back, it became a necessary piece of gallantry in the parson, to offer himself as her escort. Miss Barton had been a virgin ten years longer than the fitness of things required, no doubt, owing to her extreme cruelty; but time disposes maidens to abate their rigour towards men. She was well read; for her brother had the goodness to bring her all the novels from the circulating library of the next market town; and she spoke of love with an enthusiasm that must have been irresistible to a man of feeling. She said it was the cordial drop of life; and she said it as she was getting over a stile. The stile was high; she was rather awkward; and there was a breeze which did not permit her petticoats the full force of gravitation. Instead of look-ing up in her beauteous face, and assisting her properly, the curate had thrown his eyes upon a sweet pretty foot, and a pillar, perhaps of the Corinthian order, which it supported. All this created a sort of confusion of idea probably in both their heads. Miss Barton said, 'O dear!' and almost tumbled into the parson's arms. What would have been the consequence, had they not opened to receive her, I cannot tell; what was the consequence, his own church bells, with-in fifteen days, proclaimed to the universe. So Mr. Woodcock got a wife; a good one; one of the notables; and as fruitful as the vine which covers the south-west end of his parsonage house. I fear, however, that this will prove a most unfortunate night."

Mr. Hermsprong was about to enquire why, when a distant noise was heard, as it should seem, of angry people. Soon after the parlour door was opened; Dr. Blick walked in hasty majesty to his carriage; saying, as he went, "I have done with you, Woodcock, — I have done with you; a parson, and tainted with principles almost republican! I have done with you; I repeat my warning; get anoth-er curacy, if you are able, in a month. I, — I foster a man whose divinity is unsound, and his loyalty questionable!"

"My opinions," answered Woodcock, "you have long known: I neither conceal them, as if they disgraced me, — nor officiously promulgate them, as if they did me honour. How is it, that borne so long, you are so enraged against them to-night?"

"If," the Doctor replied, "I have borne with them, it was out of pity to your family. I never liked them, nor you; and I don't like you the better, for taking the part of a young coxcomb against me; and telling me to my teeth, that I was wrong in argument, and rude in manner."

"I told you so," said the curate, "because it was truth; which, as you are so little able to bear, and since you have explained yourself so fully, I accept your warning, in my turn, to provide yourself, if you are able, with another curate in a month. So I wish you a good night."

The Doctor vociferated something about insolence, mounted his carriage, and was driven off.

CHAPTER XIV

THE curate, animated by the spirit which prompted the reply of the last chapter, entered to his friends; to whom he was beginning an apology for the introduction of the Doctor —

"Who, notwithstanding, introduced himself," said Glen, smiling.

"That is true," the curate replied, "but I was the cause."

"But I did not do it with malice aforethought," said Glen, taking the curate's tone and manner. "But," he continued, "how should I be angry at a thing which has exhibited my friend in a new and interesting light? I thought him almost incapable of indignation."

"I own," says the curate, "I do not love the stormy passions; and employ all my poor stock of philosophy to keep them down. But you know the proverb, Tread upon a worm, &c.[1] This night I have been less affronted in myself than in my friends, if Mr. Hermsprong will permit me to use the appellation."

Mr. Hermsprong replied, that Glen had been giving him a compendium of his history. The worthy man predominated in it. His friendship would give him pleasure.

The curate made a reply expressive of gratitude.

"Since it is so," said Mr. Hermsprong, "why should we not leap the boundaries of ceremony, the bane of true affection, — be at once old friends, and enquire what effect the quarrel of this night may have upon your happiness, Mr. Woodcock, and upon that of your family?"

"I must own," the curate replied, "we are not invulnerable to the attacks of fortune. But there are more curacies in the world; and, besides, it is not a world intended to produce flowers alone; there will be thorns intermingled. I have a very good wife, and four sweet girls. If God give them grace, they have never been in much danger from the evils of luxury in my house, nor likely to be. No matter, as Mr. Prior says, bread we shall eat, or white or brown."[2]

"And is 45l. per annum, so immense a sum," said Mr. Hermsprong,, "that it can be supplied you no other way?"

"All ways," replied Mr. Woodcock, "are interdicted to a parson, except the press; and before he attempts that, he should be persuaded that he is possessed of some kind of talent, which may prof-

---

1 According to the proverb, the worm will turn.

2 Matthew Prior (1644-1721), *Alma: or, the Progress of the Mind* (1718): "Yet let the Goddess [Fortune] smile, or frown; / Bread We shall eat, or white, or brown: / And in a Cottage, or a Court, / Drink fine Champaigne, or muddl'd Port" (3:586-89).

it his readers as well as himself; now, I have not yet persuaded myself of this."

"Have you any proof to the contrary?" asked Glen.

"I know not but I may," the curate answered; "but it is a secret which I have not trusted even to my wife. However, as it is not uncommon to keep wives ignorant of what all the world beside is acquainted with, I will venture to tell you. Once upon a time Mrs. Woodcock was patching up some matters of apparel for our young folks, when one of them, a vivacious thoughtless little thing, made a motion that utterly undid what my wife had been doing for the last hour. Now, Mrs. Woodcock is a very good woman; but she is a woman; and it is only for philosophers, and I believe, for the philosophers of past times, to bear patiently the ruin of a work almost compleated by their own labour. Mrs. Woodcock could not. First, she slapped the child, then scolded it. Next she looked at the work, sat herself down in despair, and cried. I then thought it proper to begin with a few words of comfort; but I soon found they would at present be thrown away. I ventured, however, upon a little reproof for her want of patience. "Preach patience, Mr. Woodcock," she returned, "in the pulpit; what you say there is all good and gospel, and woe be to those who offer to contradict you; but out of the pulpit, Mr. Woodcock, you know no more than other people, and perhaps not so much. I think, for my part, parsons have the faculty of not knowing most things that are useful. I wonder what their learning is good for, if they can't turn it to some profit."

"Now, I must do Mrs. Woodcock the justice to own, that this was a strain in which she does not often indulge herself: She is a good woman, but not quite so quick in comprehending the force of my arguments as I could wish. In the beginning of our marriage, I took some pains to convince her of men's natural and legal superiority. I quoted St. Paul, and quoted Juvenal.[1] She was sure St. Paul

---

1 St. Paul was often cited as justifying the subordination of women; the quotation in question might be from his first letter to the Corinthians, in which he writes that "the head of the woman is the man" and that "neither was the man created for the woman; but the woman for the man" (1 Corinthians 11:3 and 9). Juvenal's notorious sixth satire portrays massive social corruption created by domineering and uncontrollable wives. Mr. Woodcock appears to be wrong, however, in attributing the observation that concludes the paragraph to Virgil.

was not inspired when he wrote my quotation; and as to Juvenal, he was a snarling ill-natured fellow, and she durst to say, monstrous ugly. At last, as I made but an imperfect progress, I thought that domestic peace was better preserved by silence, and by overlooking small faults; for Virgil has said, the dear sex were averse to parting even with a fault, if they have had it any time in possession.

"However, if Mrs. Woodcock did not profit by my suggestions; I saw no reason why I might not by hers. 'I wonder what their learning is good for,' came across me pretty often; and the press along with it. At last I came to a resolution; and as sermons are the natural production of a parson, I set myself down to correct and new model a dozen of my own; which I sent to a bookseller in the sermon way, in London; at the same time letting him know what I expected for the copy right. This was five guineas a sermon. I received them back by the first coach, with a civil letter enough; in which he allowed this to be an age of piety; and that some sort of sermons sold very well. Mine were not of that sort. Moral practical religion was not the taste. Sermons, to succeed now, must either ascend to the heaven of heavens with Swedenborg,[1] or must pour out, with pious effusion, and in the most vituperative terms the English tongue will afford, death and damnation to the French. So far from being able to afford the price I asked, he durst not even venture to print them on his own account; but if I chose to run the risque, I might make the experiment with two or three; and he hoped he should be able to prevent its costing me above ten or twelve pounds, supposing the worst. This offer I accepted; but with injunctions of secresy; for I thought, in case the public did not chuse to read my sermons, there would be no great gratification of vanity, in owning myself the author. I did not even acquaint Mrs. Woodcock; not only because of the difficulty ladies are said to have in keeping a secret, but also, as I did not certainly know the turn her mind might take on the occasion; whether she would attribute my ill success to want of piety in the people, or want of talent in myself; and as reverence for my abilities, out of the pulpit, did not

---

1   Emmanuel Swedenborg (1688-1772) was a mystic who founded the
    New Jerusalem Church. He was briefly popular but is now best known
    to English literary history for his influence on William Blake (1756-
    1823), who mocked Swedenborg in *The Marriage of Heaven and Hell*
    (1793).

seem to be too abundant with my wife, I did not chuse to risque its diminution.

"My sermons were printed, twenty-seven copies sold; and, at the expiration of a year, my bibliopolist[1] sends me his account, balance in his favour 9l. 11s. 6d. at the same time informing me he thought I might succeed in the novel line. To me, however, this does not seem probable: A novel writer ought to be well acquainted with human life and character; I know little of either: Besides, as novels are now pretty generally considered as the lowest of all human productions, I know not whether it is for the dignity of my cloth to have any thing to do with them. However, as the press opens its mouth to swallow all things, from a primmer to an Encyclopediæ, — from Tom Thumb to Paradise Lost, — I have taken a couple of years to consider with what offerings I shall make my next approaches to it; and it is probable the affair of this night may serve to quicken my determination."

"And how," says Mr. Hermsprong, "do you think it will suit my feelings, to see the man I call my friend, reduced to write for bread; whilst I, the cause of it, have superfluity beyond my inclination to use — or abuse?"

The curate looked with a face of wonder.

"That air of surprise," said Mr. Hermsprong, "seems to check my presumption; and indeed the liberty I have taken is too great for the present state of our acquaintance. I ought first to have been more entitled to your esteem."

"Really," Mr. Woodcock replied, "I own my surprise and that I have not yet got rid of it. This mode of obligation is so uncommon in these parts."

"I hope," said Hermsprong, "we may be able soon to get rid of the word obligation so applied; with all its humiliating appendages; for the present, let us close the subject."[2]

So the rest of the evening was spent with chearfulness; the conversation turning principally on the everlasting subjects, metaphysics and politics; of the first of which man can *know* nothing,

---

1 Bookseller.
2 This comment recalls William Godwin's notorious attack on gratitude in *Political Justice*. Those with too much money, according to Godwin, were bound to help those with too little in the name of simple justice, not charity, and in such circumstances gratitude would be both demeaning and unnecessary.

— and of the last, will not. At least it is so in England, at the moment I am now writing; the order of the day, as they say in France, being determined ignorance.

"You have, no doubt, Sir, read with attention the author you now so liberally abuse?"

"I, Sir! — I read him! — No, Sir, — nor the Macintoshes, the Flowers, or the Christies; — I never read a line in any of them — nor ever will."

"It is the way, Sir, to be well informed."[1]

CHAPTER XV

MISS FLUART *to* MISS CAMPINET.

ONCE upon a time, in a fit of gravity, with which she is apt to be troubled at times, a young lady of my acquaintance asked me if I ever cried in my life? I cannot say what I told her then, but I tell her now, Yes, the very hour I was born, and several times since; once very lately, on the perusal of a letter from my Caroline. I was an orphan, you know, my dear; and my thoughts of this circumstance, when I first began to think, were, that it was a situation to be pitied, even in affluence. You are not an orphan quite; and yet I own you have a far greater claim to pity than myself. You have a distressing prospect before you, of your aunt's long illness and death; and one much worse to succeed it. I must come to help you to bear them both. To your aunt I know I shall be welcome; to his lordship I must endeavour to become so; for it is in his house principally you will want my wise advice and protection, — a house abounding in pastimes not seemly for maidens who have been taught their catechisms and their I believes.

There, — in this last half paragraph, I recognize my own stile and manner. I was not born to say grave and wise things.

I think it is now a month since the return of our fugitive; a true penitent, no doubt; humble, docile, and peculiarly obedient to papa and mamma. I know not what better proof I can give of all

---

1 Sir James Macintosh's *Vindiciae Gallicae* (1791), Benjamin Flower's *Principles of the British Constitution Explained* (1793), and Thomas Christie's *Letters on the Revolution in France* (1791) were all tracts supporting the ideas of the French revolutionaries. Macintosh, however, later changed his mind and modified his early radicalism.

this, than that for the first fortnight she was tolerably dumb. Indeed, it was not necessary for any one to talk but Mrs. Sumelin, whose collection of admonitions, to render young women prudent, is certainly inexhaustible. Oh, could I but call them to mind just at the time of need, there would not be such another discreet girl in all these parts. To Miss Harriet I should have supposed they were mother's milk, only a little sour sometimes, if one might judge by a certain odd kind of a tossing of the head, — by a sort of flashing of her fair eyes, — and by a prudent reserve, which some malevolent people might call sulkiness. Mr. Sumelin's mode is very different from his lady's. His way is, to speak his mind once for all, and have done with it.

"Enough," says he, yesterday, "and too, much of this eternal theme. If the girl had robbed a church, to have suffered this everlasting torrent of wisdom, would have been sufficient expiation of her crime."

"Nay, I'll say that for you," Mrs. Sumelin replies, "provided you can get money, and enjoy your bottle, you care not how your family goes on. If any thing had happened to me ten years since, I wonder what your daughters would have been?"

"Humph! the wisdom of women is admirable; we are for ever called upon to animadvert upon their errors, by the blundering provocation of their tongues. Charlotte has been this said ten years from under your wing; Harriet has had the full benefit of your maternal clucking; and this is its fruits."

This was too much for mortal female endurance. Mrs. Sumelin took fire, — and, oh dear! how she did blaze. But, as my guardian says, the wisdom of women is admirable; Mrs. Sumelin, in the course of rapid declamation, so far forgot things as to defend her dear Harriet from head to foot, imprudence and all.

"Then," my guardian said, as soon as he could be heard, "why do you eternally scold her for faults, if she has committed none?"

"You catch one up so, Mr. Sumelin; to be sure I did not mean to say quite that; but for your part, you take no pains to instruct your children nor never did. I don't believe you have ever said one word to Harriet about this business."

"What need? when I have a dear industrious wife who takes the department of lecturing into her own hands, and performs it so ably."

"You are enough to provoke a stone wall. I have not patience with you."

"I don't expect it, my dear. Only have goodness not to torment yourself. You were in the humour just now to think Harriet's fault a small one. With all my heart. The law does not call it an offence at all. It gives young women leave to chuse their own husbands after twenty-one; or before, provided they do not marry in England. Harriet, you see, did nothing illegal. She was going out of England, that she might not sin against the law. But the law also allows fathers to dispose of their acquired property as they please. To this inconvenience, Harriet must submit. She loves Mr. Fillygrove. I do not. To him, therefore, I shall give nothing; to her, or rather to trustees, for her, just as much as will supply her with the common comforts of life. So she will have bread to her love; and if she can get love to her bread, she may be as well off as most of her neighbours. I leave her at liberty, and I desire you, my dear, to do the same. I request your silence upon what has past for ever. Do not lay me under the necessity of imposing it upon you as a penance."

With this polite hint my guardian retired.

Mrs. Sumelin blessed herself she was not born a man; men were so positive and tyrannical. — "But this is all along of you, Harriet."

"Well," says the young lady, "do, for heaven's sake! mother, let us hear no more of it. It is enough to tire a horse. Since I have my papa's approbation —"

"Approbation!" Mrs. Sumelin cries out, "you impertinent creature! approbation!"

But I will weary you no longer, my Caroline. They went fairly to it, and Miss Harriet supported her part with spirit. Ever since, she has got up, as they say, surprisingly; and can now give her opinion on a new cap, or a man, — just as usual. For Mr. Hermsprong she seems to have a tolerable aversion. How she got it, I do not know. It may be simply his tearing her from dear Mr. Fillygrove; but there are other possibilities. Two days and two nights they travelled by sea; two days and two nights by land. Could he be playing the grave preceptor all this time? She, the humble penitent? His account is monstrous modest and respectful — and all that, but maugre. I wish I knew.

Ever your own,
MARIA FLUART.

P.S. Pray, tell my dear Mrs. Merrick I will be with her in a week; and I will make her well.

CHAPTER XVI

"I wish I knew," said the lovely Miss Fluart, at the close of her letter; and it is not impossible but I may have lovely readers, who
would like to know also; for it is certain, although Mr. Hermsprong
had told the truth, he had not told the whole truth. As I am not a
man to refuse to gratify a laudable curiosity, I will tell my fair readers all I know about it.

Mr. Hermsprong had arrived at Ostend, in his road from Sax-
ony to England. He had no sooner retired to his apartment for the
night, than he heard, in the adjoining chamber, two voices; one
soft, tremulous, and plaintive; the other rather harsh, and the tone
more like one reproving than complaining. When Mr.
Hermsprong had laid down in his bed, assisted by the silence of
the night, and perhaps by darkness, he could hear a few sentences
distinctly.

"What have you done!" says the stronger voice. "Why, what
have you done, but what every young lady of spirit ought to do,
choose a husband for yourself."

"And lost a father."

"As well lost as found, if he's as hardhearted as you think him."

"Dear Miss Wavel, how you talk? What must become of us,
if he does not forgive us! Mr. Fillygrove, you know, has nothing."

"Nothing but love, and that's worth every thing else. But what
do you talk of not being forgiven for? All the grand young ladies
run away now a days; and are always forgiven. Nay, I declare I know
two whose mothers like them the better for it. And then, Miss
Sumelin, you have not eloped for no ill, but to marry, and live
respectable in the world. If it had been for any evil, for sure it never
would have been countenanced by me. You know my character too
well for that. Every body knows me. I have lived in Falmouth from
a little child; thank God, with the best reputation; though but small
means. I might have been married more than once, but never
would, because I could not find a man that turned to God with his
whole heart. Something carnal and worldly mixed with their love.
My piety is well known, nay, I may say, it is edifying. I have scarcely missed divine service five times in twenty years. And God has
granted me my reward; patience and resignation in this life, and
assurance of a better."

"I believe you are a good woman, Miss Wavel; and but for your
advice and assistance, I never should have ventured upon such a

rash imprudent step as I have now taken. And God knows what will be the consequence here; for all Mr. Fillygrove's money, you know, is gone; and none of us know a single soul in this strange place."

"Oh, Mr. Fillygrove will find a way to get over all difficulties. Poor dear young man. To be sure it was impossible to see him going into a decline for love. You would have killed him with your cruelty, Miss Sumelin, and then have died yourself of sorrow for it."

In this strain went the dialogue on, till Mr. Hermsprong was weary of listening to it; which, indeed, he never would have done at all, but that the name of Sumelin struck his ears; and when to this was added Falmouth, he could not but suppose that the young lady was the daughter of the only man with whom he had correspondence in England; and from whom he could expect any of the kind offices of friendship; of the man to whom he was now going, and whose house he had an invitation to use as his own, so long as his pleasure or convenience would allow it.

Mr. Hermsprong also knew that his friend's family consisted of a wife and two daughters; and he thought that the daughters of a man so worthy must have some merit. From the canting piety of her companion, he concluded the young lady was betrayed; and that for her father's sake, if not her own, it might be a meritorious deed to save her. With these notions floating in his brain, he fell asleep.

In the morning, he saw in the garden of the hotel, a young man smartly dressed, with a face white as his cambric ruffles, leaning his head against the wall. This, as Mr. Hermsprong suspected, was the love-favoured Mr. Fillygrove, who had made too free with the wine of Ostend the preceding evening; wanting probably more, or other comfort than the lady had to bestow.

Mr. Hermsprong passed him with a good morrow. With more alacrity than his languid air promised, he sprung after him, with his offered hand, after the English mode.

"I am so pleased to see a countryman," says he; "would you believe it, — damme if the stupid rascals here understand a word I say."

Mr. Hermsprong, in whose esteem Mr. Fillygrove did not stand high, and his foppish dress and familiar manner were not calculated to increase it, said, but not with a tone of asperity, "If it is stupidity in these people, not to understand your language; what is it in you, not to understand theirs?"

"Oh, damme, you're peery,"[1] returns the other; "but never mind; will you assist a poor devil in the damn'dst dilemma possible? Come, you look like an honest fellow; one that would not hurt the good old cause. A lady has done me the honour to run away with me: A 50,000 pounder. But charges have run damn'd high; for I hired a whole packet from Dover, because I did not chuse the lady should be bundled up with all sorts of scrubs:[2] Now I want a parson; and how to get one, curse me if I know; and if I had one, the devil a piece of gold have I to give him; reduced down to a few shillings."

"You have bank notes, no doubt; gentlemen, on these occasions, seldom come slenderly provided."

"I had threescore guineas in my purse when I set out. How the devil would have thought I should have been stript of that in four or five days?"

"Well, Sir; you shall not want cash for any honourable design."

"Thank you, my buck.[3] Damme, I saw you was an honest fellow. But what shall we do for a parson?"

"They are to be procured here without much difficulty."

"We shall want a father too, to give her away. If you would be kind enough to do us that service too?"

"Fathers should know their daughters."

"My girl is so damned shy. However I will tell her the case, and I dare say we shall cook it."

Off ran Fillygrove, to communicate his joyful tidings to the ladies. Miss Sumelin was crying; possibly from a little sprinkling of repentance; for as the Duke Rochefoucault said, or might have said, for the remark is in his way, — we are never truly sorry for our faults till we begin to suffer for them.[4] Miss Wavel was admin-

---

1 According to the OED, "prying, inquisitive, suspicious"; Mr. Fillygrove, however, seems to mean something closer to "severe" or "critical."

2 "A mean insignificant fellow, a person of little account or low appearance" (OED).

3 A fashionable young man about town; not a complimentary term.

4 The Duc de la Rochefoucauld (1613-80) was famous for the elegant cynicism of his *Maximes* (1678). There is no exact source for this observation in his work, although its tone is very much in harmony with a number of la Rochefoucauld's maxims. Compare, for example, maxims 180 ("Our repentence is not so much regret for the wrong we have done as fear of that which might befall us") and 196 ("We easily forget our faults when they are known only to us").

istring comfort, in the awkward way of those who had no comfort to give. Fillygrove began to pour out his joy, at first, with too little connexion.

"A good honest fellow! I knew it by his face. I never was deceived in a man's face. That's he there, walking in the garden."

"What nonsense is all this?" asked Miss Harriet. "I declare, Mr. Fillygrove, I think you get sillier every day."

"Sillier! Miss Sumelin?" Now it never had occurred to Mr. Fillygrove that he could have been the subject of such an epithet. "Sillier! I wonder a person of your wisdom would think of marrying a silly fellow."

"Because," the lady answered with great quickness, "because I was as silly as himself."

This indiscretion produced a very serious quarrel; in which he told her, that if she could find the way to England, he was willing enough to go back thither without a wife. She said she would crawl thither on her hands and knees, sooner than marry a man who had used her so basely. Having said all the disagreeable things, to each other, anger could supply, love, under the mediation of Miss Wavel, took again its turn; they kissed and cried; and cried and kissed; in short, had so violent a love fit, that it was well the guardian of the young lady's honour was present in the person of Miss Wavel. At last Mr. Fillygrove came to the business which had brought him; informed Miss Sumelin of the stranger's generosity; wished she would have the goodness to go down into the garden; he was sure the gentleman would speak to her, and then she might judge for herself.

"You will go with me?" said she.

"Certainly, if you desire it, Miss; but in my opinion you will do better without me; for when a lady solicits — you know what the poet says."[1]

What the poet says, I know not; but the lady consented to go alone; and had almost passed Mr. Hermsprong upon the terrace walk unnoticed; this gentleman being at the instant in deep consideration on the means he could employ to disengage her from what he concluded was a thoughtless and childish business; a rustling awaked

---

1 Faulkner suggests an allusion to *Measure for Measure* I.iv.80–81: "when maidens sue, / Men give like gods." It is possible, however, that the empty-headed Fillygrove is merely attempting to sound sophisticated without having any specific literary work in mind.

him; from her dress, and her eyes red with recent weeping, he had no doubt who it was; and bowing with great respect, said, "Is it Miss Sumelin of Falmouth I have the pleasure to see?"

She, supposing Fillygrove had communicated her name, though angry at his indiscretion, answered in the affirmative by a courtesy and a blush.

"Is there any thing, Miss Sumelin, in which I can have the happiness to serve you in Ostend?"

Miss Sumelin thought this an odd question from a man, who, she supposed, had just been made acquainted with the nature of the service in which he was to be employed.

"Sir!" says she, with an air of some surprise.

"If Miss Sumelin will honour me with her commands, I shall be happy to shew her how much I am devoted to her service."

"Sir," says she again, "has not a gentleman — a — a young gentleman — in blue — a Mr. Fillygrove —"

"Yes, madam; but I take no commands from Mr. Fillygrove. If you will condescend to honour me, Miss Sumelin."

"But has not Mr. Fillygrove informed you, Sir, — that — that — of the cause — Sir —the cause of my leaving England."

"He has, indeed, given me very surprising and very disagreeable information."

"Really, Sir," said the lady, with a small degree of anger, "I cannot see why — to you — it should be either surprising or disagreeable."

"Is it not surprising that Miss Sumelin should have recourse to a clandestine marriage? Miss Sumelin! a lady who has only to be seen and known, to engage all hearts! Certainly any gentleman might be proud of this fair hand."

And he took this fair hand, and respectfully imprinted a kiss upon it; the lady being so astonished, or alarmed, or something, that she had not the presence of mind to withdraw it angrily, as undoubtedly most of my fair readers will think she ought.

Before I proceed, let me ask if the great question, whether it be lawful to do evil, that good may come is finally settled? I hope it is decided in the affirmative; otherwise I know not what to plead for Mr. Hermsprong in the critical case before us. He was certainly saying the thing that was not;[1] and love, which excuseth all things,

---

1   The phrase recalls the Houyhnhnms in Jonathan Swift's *Gulliver's Travels* (1726) who, having no concept of lying, can only refer to it as saying the thing that was not.

he had not; he had pity only; compassion for a respectable father, and a silly girl, who was probably running to misery for life.

"Besides," says a learned critic, whose judgment I respect, "it is a deviation from character; for the basis of Mr. Hermsprong's is simple truth."

"Yes," I answer, "to lords; but to ladies, on certain great occasions —"

But certainly Mr. Hermsprong is entitled to the praise of politeness. He told the lady she was handsome, in the most elegant way possible. If a lady is so, she seldom waits for that intelligence from man. Though not disagreeable to be told so, it is not necessary for information. If a lady is not handsome, which happened to be Miss Sumelin's case, a gentleman has it in his power to create a new existence — and such an existence! I know not but it may equal rank itself.

"If I were you," says my friendly critic, "I would not often indulge myself in digressions of this sort; they break action and interrupt dialogue. How awkward it is to suffer Mr. Hermsprong to be kissing the lady's hand, whilst you scribble two or three pages."

I wonder whether there are any ladies who can be displeased with a digression so much in favour of the lovely sex? but critics have no complaisance.

As Miss Sumelin did not withdraw her hand, it was not in the nature of things that Mr. Hermsprong should give it up; so he kept possession while they paced the terrace together. There was silence for a minute; for the gentleman did not know very well what farther to say, nor the lady to reply. At length she said, rather a little abruptly, "Pray, Sir, did you ever see me before?"

"No, madam," answered Mr. Hermsprong; "but that is my misfortune; I might have seen you before you had engaged your heart, had I earlier known its value. Your father is my friend. To your house I am now going. My name is Hermsprong, madam."

"Mr. Hermsprong! oh dear! well, I declare this is the most extraordinary thing! Yes, Sir, I know you are expected; there is no gentleman in the world my father talks of so much."

"I shall see him with double pleasure, madam, if I am so happy as to be able to do a service to his daughter."

"I believe Mr. Fillygrove is in some distress, Sir, — and —"

"On your account, Miss Sumelin, Mr. Fillygrove should be welcome to my purse, if I could forget the use he designs to make of it."

Miss Sumelin did not answer; she did not even look up.

"Pray," the gentleman asked, "in what situation is Mr. Filly-grove?"

"Sir," says the lady, blushing, "he is only my father's clerk; but I assure you, Sir, he is very accomplished."

"I am unhappily so ignorant as not to know the exact meaning of this pretty word, accomplishment."

"Oh, but you do, Sir; for you must be very accomplished yourself."

"Must I, madam? It is a most charming necessity. Pray, is it made up of honour and honesty, of learning, of knowledge, of virtue, of integrity?"

"It's made up of every thing that is elegant and genteel."

"Then I fear I have not hit upon the proper ingredients."

Mr. Fillygrove, at this instant, came dancing forward in the familiar style; a "damme, my buck," was ready to burst from his lips, when an "Oh dear, Mr. Fillygrove, do you know that this gentle-man is Mr. Hermsprong" sunk him into littleness; an effect, possi-bly, of the estimation he knew that gentleman was held in by Mr. Sumelin; or, more probably, of a certain quantity of thousands which Mr. Fillygrove himself had given him credit for in his mas-ter's books.

Mr. Fillygrove, as soon as he could speak, said, he hoped Mr. Hermsprong would pardon the familiarity he had treated him with this morning, and do them the honour to take a breakfast, which was then ready.

Mr. Hermsprong accepted the latter proposal, and had the goodness, as he led her along, to say many obliging things to Miss Sumelin, which, it is probable, she was full as much pleased with as Mr. Fillygrove, who seemed changed all at once, from the pert cox-comb to the sullen boy.

Miss Wavel was preparing the tea; Mr. Hermsprong was announced; but as this lady had not before heard him spoken of, she thought nothing more of him than that he was the good-natured gentleman Mr. Fillygrove had just become acquainted with; and she was surprised to find this young man mute, Miss Sumelin, reserved, the stranger pensive, and inattentive to the little attentions which, as dispenser of the breakfast, she had, an oppor-tunity to shew him.

Breakfast over, Mr. Hermsprong addressed Miss Sumelin, requesting she would favour him with her company in his parlour, or in the garden.

"But, pray, Sir," said Miss Wavel, "have you any thing particular to say to Miss Sumelin?"

"I have, madam," answered Hermsprong.

"But, Sir, I must beg leave to inform you, Sir, that Miss Sumelin, Sir, has put herself more peculiarly under my care, Sir, so that it is not proper any thing should be said to her, that is not said before me."

"Do you confirm this, Miss Sumelin?" asked Hermsprong.

Miss Sumelin said, with some degree of confusion, "She could not deny that she had relied very much upon Miss Wavel."

"Very well; the garden is a private one; we shall all be less liable to interruption there than here," said Hermsprong, leading Miss Sumelin; the other two condescending to follow; but in no very placid dispositions.

"I think you are very ill-treated, Mr. Fillygrove," whispered Miss Wavel.

"Yes, damme, so do I."

"You are a gentleman, as well as he: Speak your mind; and ask him, before he begins to give his impertinent advice, whether he means to oblige you, as he promised, or not."

"So I will," said Fillygrove. "So I will," advancing. "Pray, Mr. Hermsprong, — I beg to know — I desire to be informed — whether you are disposed to oblige us, as you promised this morning?"

"Certainly," Mr. Hermsprong replied, "I am disposed to oblige Miss Sumelin; but not convinced that the mode of assistance you require, would be an obligation."

"What the devil do you mean by that?"

"I mean, Sir," said Mr. Hermsprong, "that Miss Sumelin may one day think she has been too precipitate in a matter of infinite consequence; and I would save her all possible regret."

"This was treating Miss Sumelin very like a child indeed," Miss Wavel said.

"How it may appear in your eyes, madam," Mr. Hermsprong replied, "is of little consequence to me. In mine, Miss Sumelin seems to have been driven to error by the influence of passion, or by some other influence, perhaps still more malignant," looking Miss Wavel steadfastly in the face. "Miss Sumelin," he continued, "is very young, and probably has not considered the consequences of a clandestine marriage, — of offending her father, — of disgracing perhaps her family."

"Sir!" says Fillygrove, assuming a big look.

"I venture to make the supposition, Mr. Fillygrove," Mr. Hermsprong said, "because if you had just pretensions to the honour of Miss Sumelin's hand, you would have taken more honourable methods to have obtained it."

"Honourable, Sir," said Fillygrove.

"Honourable, Mr. Fillygrove," replied Mr. Hermsprong.

"This is damn'd odd usage," said the other. "Honourable!"

"Miss Sumelin, will you permit me to enquire if your father's consent has been asked?"

"No," replied Miss Wavel; "we knew it would not have been granted."

"Pray, why?" asked Mr. Hermsprong.

"Why! why, because it would not. I don't understand why gentlemen should ask questions which don't concern 'em."

"I presume," said Mr. Hermsprong, "I have the honour of speaking to some near relation of yours, Miss Sumelin?"

"What signifies it, whether I am a relation or not?"

"Miss Sumelin, is it your pleasure that my respectful questions to you should be answered by this lady?"

"Yes," replied Miss Wavel; "for she is under my care."

"To be very sincere with you, madam," Mr. Hermsprong said, "your care appears to deserve the animadversion of a court of justice; and take care it has it not."

"Me! me!" says the enraged Miss Wavel, "I defy you; it is well known that I am a person of character and piety; and, Mr. Fillygrove, if you had the spirit of a man, you would not see me insulted in this cruel manner, and all for you."

"Sir, I think this very improper treatment," said Fillygrove, "and I demand satisfaction."

"Of what sort?" asked Mr. Hermsprong, coolly.

"Of a gentleman, Sir! I don't travel without pistols."

"I think, Mr. Fillygrove," said Hermsprong, with a smile, "we had better leave this species of folly to gentlemen born; if it gets among gentlemen by assumption, where will it stop?"[1]

"That," says Miss Wavel, "is as much as to say you are no gentleman; though it's well known your father has above a hundred a-year in land."

---

1   In his dislike of the aristocratic practice of duelling (and in the opportunities he is given to demonstrate his courage in other ways), Hermsprong fits in with a range of idealized eighteenth-century heroes, from Samuel Richardson's Sir Charles Grandison to Thomas Holcroft's Frank Henley.

"Yes, Sir; do you say I'm no gentleman?" added Fillygrove.

"I allow your title, Sir, as far as your father's hundred a-year can give it you. It does not seem to be due to you by your manners, or your morals, if this enterprize is to be taken as a specimen."

"Damme if you don't say every thing you can to provoke me; and curse me if I'll bear it," said Fillygrove, advancing with an air of menace.

"Impertinence, before ladies," said Mr. Hermsprong, "does not merit a gentleman's chastisement. Take that, Sir, which is due to you," giving the young man a hearty shake, and carrying him off with violence to some distance; "there," he said, "Mr. Fillygrove, I am sorry you oblige me to use you with contempt. Forbear, before ladies, the airs and language of a duellist; if, when we separate, you incline to that mode of satisfaction, I am quite ready to indulge you."

Mr. Fillygrove was rather inclined to be sick. Miss Sumelin had given a little shriek, and looked, and was indeed affrighted. Miss Wavel had infinitely more rage than terror.

"If I were a man," said she, "I would die before I would be treated in this manner."

"Good God!" said Mr. Fillygrove, "what would you have? Don't you see my dear Miss Sumelin is dying with fear; but don't be apprehensive, my dear creature; I would not distress you for the world; I will not call Mr. Hermsprong out; I won't, indeed, my dear."

"Miss Sumelin," said Mr. Hermsprong, "I am weary of these follies. With this gentleman and this lady I can have no concern: They do not entitle themselves to my esteem. If you will permit me to be your friend, I shall think it an honour. At least, give me the opportunity of half an hour's conversation with yourself. If after that you chuse to persist in your undertaking, with all good wishes for your future felicity, I must submit."

"Sir," said Miss Harriet, "I will attend you."

While Hermsprong was leading her back to the hotel, Miss Wavel began her abuse of Fillygrove; which she extended so far, that the young man's patience gave way; he retorted her abuse, and swore that he would go back to England without troubling himself any more about her.

"You — you fool," says she, "you have not sense to find your way back, — you know you have not. Have not I been obliged to direct every thing? and where will you have money to pay your passage?"

"I'll sell my watch," replied Fillygrove; "it's a gold one of my grandmother's," and he put his hand to his fob. "Zounds," says he, "it's gone. Where the devil can it be? I am certain I had it when I first met Hermsprong. Oh dear! sure I could not have lost it upon Miss Sumelin's bed, when, when, you know, Miss Wavel, we stayed a little after her."

Miss Wavel was frighted at this intelligence: "But come," says she, "we must seek for it. It's a very foolish thing, Mr. Fillygrove, for you and I to quarrel, so tenderly as we have been connected. And sure, if I did not love you, as dear Solomon says, beyond the love of women, I could never consent to give you up, for your own good, to a rival."[1]

Mr. Fillygrove confessed her goodness, and they returned to seek the watch.

In the interim a German girl, a lower maid servant came into the room where Mr. Hermsprong was reasoning the matter with Miss Sumelin, with this very watch in her hand; and asked the lady, in her own language, if it was hers?

"Lord bless me," says Miss Sumelin, "what does the girl say?"

"She enquires if that watch is yours," Mr. Hermsprong replied.

"No," Miss Sumelin said, "it was not; but (looking at it) it is Mr. Fillygrove's; I know it by the chain. Pray, ask where she found it?"

Upon madam's bed, was the answer.

"Upon your bed, Miss Sumelin," said Mr. Hermsprong.

"Oh dear," the young lady exclaimed, "what a vile story! what do you deserve, you lying hussey!"

The girl could not answer, for she did not understand; she perceived the young lady angry, but had no notion of the cause.

"Mr. Hermsprong," said the lady, "I hope you give no credit to this audacious creature."

"I will believe precisely what you would have me, Miss Sumelin," Mr. Hermsprong answered. And yet, notwithstanding his complaisant powers of belief, he did, at this instant suspect an intimacy which Miss Sumelin had not formed.

At this moment Fillygrove and Miss Wavel passed by the window, having sought the watch in vain. Miss Sumelin ran to call them in.

---

1 The love of David and Jonathan was "passing the love of women" (2 Samuel 1:26). Miss Wavel is apparently misattributing this sentiment to the lovers in the famously erotic *Song of Solomon*.

"Here," says she, "here is your watch, Mr. Fillygrove; and the girl says she found it upon my bed."

"That's impossible, Miss," said Fillygrove; "impossible;" and he began to abuse the poor girl in rough English, snatching the watch out of her hand.

"Is this the way," Mr. Hermsprong asked, "in which you reward the girl for her honesty?"

"Damn her honesty! what does she lie for? But, perhaps, you have bribed her to it," says poor Fillygrove.

"You will have the goodness to correct that expression," says Mr. Hermsprong, coolly, "otherwise, (seizing him by the collar) I shall take the liberty to cane you, Mr. Fillygrove, till you feel your error pretty sensibly."

"Well, I will, I will," said Fillygrove; "or what the devil would you have?"

"Very well, Sir. Now to the watch. Miss Sumelin, is it your pleasure to proceed in the enquiry, or permit it silently to drop?"

"Sir, I insist on enquiring. I can't bear such an odious supposition."

"This is your watch, Mr. Fillygrove?" asked Hermsprong.

"Yes, it is."

"Where did you lose it?"

"Zounds! that's what I want to know."

"This girl says she found it on Miss Sumelin's bed. Perhaps she mistakes one room for another. Will you, ladies, permit her to shew you."

"Yes, Sir," said Miss Sumelin, "and you shall go with us; for I will have my innocence cleared."

Mr. Hermsprong giving the maid directions, they all followed up stairs; and the girl, laying her hand on the bed in which the two English ladies had slept, "I found it," says she, "just here." Mr. Hermsprong interpreted.

"Oh dear," says Miss Wavel, "now I remember, I dare say it's all very true. You know, Mr. Fillygrove, that you came here this morning, to tell us of your meeting with this gentleman, and how he promised to be your friend. As to his friendship, one sees well enough what that is. And you know you asked Miss Sumelin to walk down into the garden; and when she was gone, you may remember how you threw yourself down upon the bed, and kissed the pillow on which she had lain; and how dearly you loved every thing that she had touched. To be sure then your watch fell out of your pocket."

"Yes, I remember all the whole circumstance now exactly," said Fillygrove.

"Very well," said Hermsprong; "you are satisfied, Miss Sumelin?"

"Are you satisfied, Mr. Hermsprong?" she asked.

"Perfectly," answered the gentleman. "To have been an eye-witness would scarce have convinced me more." Then giving the maid half a guinea, he dismissed her; and, addressing himself to Miss Wavel, he said, "You seem, madam, to have doubted the sincerity of my friendship for Mr. Fillygrove; you will doubt it no longer, when I advise him — to marry *you*. Miss Sumelin, shall I attend you to renew our conversation?"

This young lady followed without a word, astonished herself, and leaving Fillygrove and Miss Wavel in a state of stupefaction, which seemed to have deprived them even of the power of abuse.

The creeping, fawning explanation of Miss Wavel, with the awkward acquiescence of Fillygrove, had turned what was suspicion of Miss Sumelin, in the mind of Mr. Hermsprong, into a certainty of his mistake; and, by the consideration of all the circumstances, he was convinced Miss Sumelin was a victim of treachery. Nor was it difficult to convince Miss Sumelin also, who now recollected a multitude of little matters, which were, in her present disposition of mind, proofs; although till this instant, not any of them had scarce created a suspicion; such unmerciful work do the passions of man and woman kind, make with their judgments.

But the question of returning back to Falmouth, always brought Miss Sumelin into a fit of something anciently called in England, the pouts. A lady falls into this fit usually, when reason, propriety, decorum, are against a thing which she has a great inclination to do; when she is unable to say any thing in its favour, yet cannot get it out of her head, or heart, as the case may be. At length, much urged, this sentiment fell from her lovely lips, "That it was well known she left Falmouth to — to — to change her condition; and not to do it, — what should she be but an object of ridicule to every body."

Mr. Hermsprong began to grow weary, and consequently grave. A deviation from rectitude, he said, seldom produced any thing but a choice of evils; and he asked which would be the greatest, to marry Mr. Fillygrove, after what had passed, or not to do it?

She did not know, she said; then casting her eyes upon the ground, with an air so modest and timid, she added, to be sure, after what had passed, there might be persons she should prefer.

What Miss Sumelin meant, I dare not know. It is a little enig-ma, and I leave the solution to ladies. Mr. Hermsprong was trying to solve it, perhaps, for he was silent, when Miss Sumelin, raising her timid eye, and finding in Mr. Hermsprong's unanimated face, nothing that pleased her, she resumed her pouts, and remained silent to all the gentleman was pleased to say.

Quite wearied out, Mr. Hermsprong asked her if a walk, to see the town, would be agreeable.

"She could not be supposed to be much amused," she said, "in her situation."

"I see," Mr. Hermsprong said, "my services are disagreeable to you; so I beg leave to wish you happiness and a good morning."

Miss Sumelin had now some hours to herself. Angry at Mr. Hermsprong, she felt herself kindly disposed to the other delin-quents; one at least; for what signifies what he did before he was married; she durst say he would have been true and constant to her afterwards. Besides, she should never have known it, but for that impertinent Hermsprong.

But the culprit was not to be found, to reap the benefit of her forgiveness. Instead of him, she found Miss Wavel in the room they had slept in, all in tears. On the approach of Miss Sumelin, the tears fell in showers; and she had, besides, all the symptoms of going into hysterics. When she could speak, she told her tale: She did not deny her love for Mr. Fillygrove, nor its consequences; but she made it out so clear, that Miss Sumelin had the greatest of obligations to her, that of giving up a beloved youth, because he loved, and was beloved by another person, that Miss Sumelin became almost per-suaded she had acted upon the purest principles of friendship. A reconciliation took place; but where was Fillygrove? alas! an hour before Miss Wavel and he had resumed their quarrel; he had left her, threatening not to return. Poor dear young man! she feared his rashness; for he said something about the sea.

The dear young man, in the mean time, had met with Mr. Hermsprong upon the pier; and much to the surprise of the latter, accosted him with a diffident and humble air, begging permission to say a few words. He then informed Mr. Hermsprong, that he had been at two shops, in order to sell his watch; and not being able to make himself understood, had come hither to pick up an honest English sailor to be his interpreter, but had not been able to find one.

"Is it to compleat your intended enterprize with Miss Sumelin, that you desire to raise money by the watch?" Mr. Hermsprong asked.

"Oh, no, Sir; I have done with that; I want only to get back to England; and to pay Miss Wavel's passage; for I dare say you will have the goodness to take care of Miss Sumelin."

"Well, Sir, here comes the captain of the English packet, with whom I have agreed for Miss Sumelin's passage and my own. I will also agree with him for Miss Wavel's and your's; and I will pay him, as also your expences in Ostend. When we arrive at Dover, I will make you a present of ten guineas, to enable you to convey Miss Wavel back to Falmouth, if she chooses; but this upon condition, that you drop all clandestine intercourse with Miss Sumelin; nor attempt to speak to her before her arrival at Falmouth. I have no doubt but a prudent behaviour may still procure you Miss Sumelin, with the consent of her father; and when I see your frivolous vanity changed into the pride of good sense and rectitude, I will ask her for you."

Mr. Fillygrove promised every thing, and was directed to another inn, there to procure an apartment for Miss Wavel, and wait till he could be informed in what ship they were to go.

In the mean time the ladies were bewailing their mutual misfortunes, till they found themselves hungry. The hour of dinner was past. No one took notice of them. At length a billet arrived from Fillygrove to Miss Wavel.

"I wait for you to dine at the Pelican. Pray accompany the messenger. I have a great deal to say. Respectful love and duty to Miss Sumelin, but I must not see her."

At the same time a message came from Mr. Hermsprong to Miss Sumelin, requesting her company to dinner. No mention of Miss Wavel. These were extraordinary circumstances; but had there been no other reason with the ladies for compliance, curiosity would have been sufficient; and Miss Sumelin had hers compleatly satisfied after dinner, by Mr. Hermsprong, who informed her, with his true frankness of character, what he had done with respect to Fillygrove, and what he intended respecting herself. "And I leave it to your choice, madam," says he, "to permit me the honour of being your escort, or Miss Wavel. In the latter case, I shall not have the pleasure to see you again till your arrival at Falmouth; but I will take care your necessary expences shall be supplied."

Miss Sumelin pouted, as usual; and Mr. Hermsprong found her a companion so little agreeable to his taste, that he began to think it would be more for his ease to endure Miss Wavel. A similar revolution of sentiment had happened to Miss Sumelin: So, when Mr. Hermsprong told her that he should have the pleasure of giving up his opinion to hers, she answered, she had resolved to conform to his. A contest ensued; but as the lady had stumbled on the flattering supposition, that in a *tête-à-tête* of two days and nights, she might display all her charms; and Mr. Hermsprong having no sentiment which operated the contrary way with equal force, he gave it up, and quickly resigned himself to the dispensations of Providence.

To reward him, the lady drew forth her whole stock of airs and graces. She sighed; she languished; she had even moments of unutterable softness. "She is the daughter of my friend," he was obliged to say very often, and he said it with shortened breath; "shall I rescue her from disgrace, to plunge her into dishonour?" Conqueror, at length he delivered her safe into her father's protection, and made her his enemy for life.

CHAPTER XVII

MRS. MERRICK's death, an event which happened sooner than was expected, was scarcely more afflictive to Miss Campinet than inconvenient to Lord Grondale. It brought him into a terrible dilemma respecting Mrs. Stone, the person of merit I mentioned in my sixth chapter.

I know not what other consideration, except her merit and misfortunes, could have induced his lordship to have placed her at the head of his table, as well as of his household; but this post of honour she had now enjoyed for several years. If Miss Campinet resided at the Hall, all the laws of decorum required that Mrs. Stone should resign; but it is not, I believe, much to the taste of the female sex, to give up precedence. Lord Grondale explained the dilemma to Mrs. Stone, by way of asking her advice; not without hopes, that, struck by the necessity of the case, she would, of her own accord, make the offer of resignation. Instead of this, she offered to his lordship's consideration a plan of a very different kind;[1] an expedient,

---

1 That is, she asks him to marry her and threatens to leave him if he does not. It was not unusual for wealthy eighteenth-century men who kept a mistress to agree in advance to pay the woman a lump sum when the relationship ended, in addition to providing an annual income while the affair lasted and making provisions (cash or otherwise) for any children that might be born.

she said, which would reconcile all things; which his lordship had given her many reasons to believe he would one day have recourse to; and for which, to speak her opinion, no time was as proper as the present. Lord Grondale, not taking time for consideration replied to this with more hauteur than gallantry. The lady was offended, and said, since his lordship did not like the expedient she had proposed, he knew the alternative.

Now this alternative was almost as little to his lordship's taste, as Mrs. Stone's principal expedient: It required the payment of a very respectable sum of money, not less than 50001. which his lordship, from motives of pure benevolence, and charmed by her condescension, articled to pay, whenever choice or accident altered their respective situations relative to each other.

Lord Grondale's politeness and gallantry, returned upon him all at once.

"No, Mrs. Stone," he said, and he took her hand; "no, I find it absolutely impossible to part with you. Things must remain as they are."

So, since Mrs. Stone would not, Miss Campinet *must* submit; and Lord Grondale had the goodness to prepare her for the necessity, by the usual argument of great people — *sic volo.*[1]

CHAPTER XVIII

PEOPLE, young or old, excluded from society, are apt to contract oddities, particularly as was the case of Miss Campinet, the oddity of reflection. I do not mean, that ladies who live in the world do not think; they do very much; but their study is chiefly ornamental architecture; with what variety of graceful draperies to adorn the loveliest fabric of nature; with what stucco to increase its external brilliance. Miss Campinet having less occasion for this first philosophy of ladies, her studies were confined to inferior objects; to the operations of the human mind; the right or wrong of human actions.

---

1 I wish it to be so; Tave and Faulkner suggest an allusion here to Benjamin Flower's *French Constitution* (1792), in which the phrase "sic volo sic jubeo" (I wish it to be so; I command it to be so) is used to sum up the arbitrary practices of the French monarchs.

It did not appear to Miss Campinet that there was much of wisdom or virtue in Lord Grondale's general conduct regarding Mrs. Stone; but she had determined that it ill became a daughter to judge a father; and that filial obedience was almost the first of virtues.

Upon the strength of this singular conclusion, she sat down quietly to table with the person of merit, without assuming the privilege of young ladies, to pout, or purse up her pretty lips, or indulge herself in any of those tokens of contempt and dissatisfaction which nature or custom has provided for such cases.

But this was all. Her duty required she should treat Mrs. Stone with the exterior marks of civility; but not that she should associate with her; for besides this lady's suspicious situation, with respect to Lord Grondale, she was not polished; was little studious of intellectual entertainment, though by no means deficient in understanding; and rather an adept in the cunning which self-interest will usually dictate — even to ministers of state, when they quit — and when do they not quit? — the strait paths of rectitude, for those of crooked policy. Miss Campinet, therefore, rose from table with her father, and retired to her sitting apartment; there to read a little, to work a little, to weep a little, to think a little upon Lippen Crag, her providential delivery, and her proud deliverer.

CHAPTER XIX

IN the night of the ——, a storm, such as had not been remembered, rushed down Grondale vale, from north to south. It was accompanied by excessive rain, thunder, and lightning. The latter had damaged the spire of the steeple, and had set fire to a cottage, which was burned to the ground. The other cottages were mostly unroofed, and the straw carried to incredible distances.

The Reverend Doctor Blick, having been disturbed in the night, lay an hour longer than usual. When he had breakfasted, he thought it his duty to go about the village, and give spiritual aid, if any person wanted it. At the first cottage, he found Miss Campinet; who said, "I did not doubt but I should meet you, Sir, on the unhappy business of this morning. You find great devastation. The storm was terrible."

"Not being myself well," the Doctor answered, "I am only just come into the village."

"Here is a gentleman has been amongst the cottagers, ever since the dawn of day. All the labourers are at work to repair their respective damages. He promises their usual pay to all, and a gratuity over to those he finds most industrious. In the mean time, the butcher is stripped of his meat, and the baker of his bread, for the use of the women and children. His name is Hermsprong. Perhaps you know him."

"Yes," replied the Doctor. "Yes, I do know something of him. I wish I could say, something good. But, Madam, he is a proud haughty young man, who thinks too well of himself to pay a proper respect to his betters. Over and above this, Madam, he is an infidel; and you know, without faith, our best works are splendid sins."[1]

"So this profusion of benevolence is with you, Doctor, only a splendid sin?"

"Nothing more, Miss Campinet. A pure stream cannot flow from a corrupt fountain."

"You prefer faith, then, to charity."

"Certainly, Miss Campinet, to every thing: So, I hope, do you?"

"I hope I believe as I ought; but I own, Doctor, I feel a biass in favour of such splendid sins."

The conversation was stopped by the hasty approach of Mr. Hermsprong, who, with a respectful bow, said, "I hope I see Miss Campinet well?"

She answered with a courtesy.

"Never," he continued, "could I see her more lovely than when warm with the healthful glow of humanity."

"This is poetry, Sir," said the lady; "I must take care how I take it for praise; and Doctor Blick has been informing me, that benevolent propensities, without faith, are only splendid sins."

---

1 The phrase "splendid sin" occurs in poems by the Methodist leader John Wesley (1703-91) as well as in sermons by Wesley and George Whitefield (1714-70), another important early Methodist preacher. In his Sermon 58 ("The Method of Grace"), for example, Whitefield proclaims that without faith, "our best duties are as so many splendid sins." (See J.C. Ryle, *Select Sermons of George Whitefield*, London: Banner of Truth Trust, 1958). Doctor Blick is therefore — probably unknowingly — associating himself with the controversial Methodist reformers here, demonstrating yet again the elasticity of his orthodox principles. Miss Campinetet's rebuttal may be influenced by St. Paul's famous celebration of charity, which ends "[a]nd now abideth faith, hope and charity, these three; but the greatest of these *is* charity" (1 Corinthians 13:13).

"Surely," Mr. Hermsprong replied, "under any system, kindness to our suffering fellow creatures cannot be sin. But faith is the Doctor's vocation. It is his to speak comfort to the soul; and at yonder cottage, (pointing to a distant one) is a proper object of his care; a poor woman in agonies for her little one, who perished, I know not how, in the confusion of the night. To me belongs the inferior care of administering to the wants of the body."

"In this," said Miss Campinet, "I hope I may be permitted to share."

"Lovely Miss Campinet! your propensities are all amiable. The poor bless you. May they always bless you. But that I would not subject you to scenes of distress, there is an object —" said Mr. Hermsprong.

"Dear Mr. Hermsprong! don't think of my distress;" and Miss Campinet coloured rosy red as she spoke. Whether it was a glow of the heart, arising from the thought of being able to do good, or a simple blush at the "dear Mr. Hermsprong," I cannot exactly say. It was a lapse, no doubt; occasioned, perhaps, by a sudden warmth of sentiment. Mr. Hermsprong, however, did not appear to notice it in the least; but said, "The object I speak of, is a young woman, the school mistress of the village, thrown by this night's horror into premature labour."

"I know her," said Miss Campinet; "she is very respectable; but wants, I fear, aid superior to mine."

"A gentleman of the faculty[1] is sent for," Mr. Hermsprong answered; "but I fear the rashness of those about her: It is better to keep her a little longer in pain, than expose her to danger."

"I understand you, Sir," said the lady, "and will endeavour to be of use."

"Permit me to conduct you, madam. Doctor, good-morrow."

The Doctor returned a nod, and a look which had not in it much of courtesy; for he felt himself offended by the careless air of superiority assumed by Hermsprong. Nor could he but remember the Golden Ball, and the dignified manner of his bidding adieu there. Altogether, there was something in this young man which rendered it quite as eligible to the Doctor, to avoid as to seek a rencontre with him. He scorned, however, to be directed by the puppy, even to a work of salvation; so, instead of seeking the cottage of despair, he turned another way, asked a few questions,

---

1 That is, a doctor.

received mortifying answers, for they were in praise of Herm-sprong, and then took his way to the Hall.

CHAPTER XX

LET us now attend Miss Campinet to the house of parturition. It was a long walk. I am not certain whether Mr. Hermsprong did not put the poor woman to more pain than nature did for the sake of it; for when they arrived, the danger was over. But, upon the road, the lady's servant keeping a respectful distance, they had some little conversation. The lady began it with saying, she was sorry she could not acknowledge her obligation to him a better way than by words, and that she must be obliged to chance or misfortune, even for that opportunity.

"For the latter, Miss Campinet, it is I who ought to feel the sorrow," Mr. Hermsprong answered; "and indeed fortune, or whatever god or goddess has the disposal of this part of my fate, does not treat me well. When I consider who it was I had the happiness to save, — when I see her all beauty and grace, — when I hear her all intelli-gence, and hear of her all angel; I rise in my own estimation — I find myself higher than the Cæsars, and the other slaughterers, — nay, so high, that I almost think myself intitled to the reward I asked."

"To that slender reward, if you chuse to call it so, a much small-er degree of merit would have entitled you; but I am sorry you have learned to flatter."

"To flatter! nay, at most it is only truth a little heightened. In praise of beauty one becomes poetical. Are young ladies pleased to be praised with cold and exact precision?"

"It would be better perhaps they were."

"Possibly so; but since that is not their taste, what can poor young men do?"

"I am sorry our sex should lay yours under the necessity of esti-mating female merit by a false scale."[1]

---

1   Compare Mary Wollstonecraft's complaint that women "condescend to receive a degree of attention and respect from strangers, different from that reciprocation of civility which the dictates of humanity and the politeness of civilization authorise between man and man" and that, as a result, "they are treated like queens only to be deluded by hollow respect, till they are led to resign, or not assume, their natural prerogatives" (*Vindication of the Rights of Woman* OUP 1994, 125).

"Nay, Miss Campinet; men, unless they are in love, appreciate the merits of ladies very well. The error lies in custom, which seems to sanctify a little extravagance of expression in the cause of the fair."

"I could have wished your extravagance in that particular, Mr. Hermsprong, had been less."

"I am scarce sensible of any, Miss Campinet."

"I am."

"It is not proper Miss Campinet should think of herself as I do of her."

"Is not that, Sir, a confession that you do not think justly?"

"I must take the liberty to tell Miss Campinet, she has no right to dispute my taste."

"One may, at least, call in question the existence of the qualities you ascribe to the object of it."

"No, madam, they exist to me; and whilst they do so, can you wonder that I should wish to increase my happiness by your society, and hope for your esteem?"

"My esteem, Sir, you must always command; and I should injure myself to reject your society, did it depend upon myself. But Lord Grondale —"

"Thinks me deficient in respect to him?"

"I believe so, Sir."

"He thinks truly. Whether the frankness I have learned in my youth, be, in highly polished countries, a virtue or vice, I know not. Miss Campinet will pardon me, if the plain and simple truth to which I have been habituated, comes from me too soon and too unguarded."

"Every thing may be pardoned in favour of truth."

"Lord Grondale dislikes my manners, and I his. Humility to a proud man, is a price I cannot pay, even for life."

The sentiment, and the mode of utterance, made Miss Campinet turn to look at her companion. She had before thought him possessed of the finest face she ever beheld; it seemed improved now by the animation which lightened from his eyes. But young ladies are not permitted to look long or intently upon young men; so resuming her position, she said, "Do you know any country in the world, Mr. Hermsprong, where this price is not paid?"

"Amongst the Aborigines of America, Miss Campinet. Then, (added Mr. Hermsprong, with a smile,) I was born a savage."

Miss Campinet felt the strangest sort of feel; she never could tell what it was like.

"You astonish me, Sir," said she; "but there is mystery; you are not of savage parents?"

"No; of unfortunate Europeans; I might have been born in France."

"England, I presume, has had the greatest share in your education?"

"No, Miss Campinet; till a few weeks since, I never saw England; the language, equally with French, and that of an Indian tribe, I have spoken from infancy."

"But — your manners!"

"Cannot, I fear, be to the taste of English ladies. I have indeed been learning to dance and make a bow in France. It is six years since I have been endeavouring to acquire European arts. Of my progress I cannot boast. I cannot learn to offer incense at the shrines of wealth and power; nor any shrines but of probity and virtue. I cannot learn to surrender my opinion from complaisance, or from any principle of adulation. Nor can I learn to suppress the sentiments of a free-born mind, from any fear, religious or political. Such uncourtly obduracy has my savage education produced."

"I must own, Mr. Hermsprong, you interest me. You make me desirous of deserving your esteem and friendship. But, situated as I am — You know, Sir, I do not command in my father's house."

"Perhaps it is the only place where you do not, or might not, if you please."

"Did you," Miss Campinet asked with a smile; "did you learn this of the Aborigines of America? It tastes of France."

"One learns something every where."

"Is not flattery a diminution of that integrity of which you just now gave so pleasing a specimen?"

"I am told it is of the first necessity to ladies; as to please them, one goes out of one's way sometimes."

"If so, let them have it; but let it not be administered by the Hermsprongs of the age."

"I desire to please; especially the Miss Campinets, who are not too abundant. But how to please, I fear I have still to learn."

"I entreat you, go not to the school of flattery for it."

"So entreated, I will not, even for Miss Campinet."

They had now arrived at the door of the cottage, and finding the accoucheur come, and every thing in a fair way, nothing was left for Miss Campinet to do. Supposing Lord Grondale might expect her at breakfast, she took the road to the Hall, from whence this house was not far distant. But her conversation began to grow irregular; she seemed embarrassed. In reality she was afraid of her father's displeasure, if seen with Mr. Hermsprong; yet how could she hint her fears, or how be unpolite to a gentleman, she had more and more reason to esteem. Luckily he saw her embarrassment, and guessed its cause. He stopped; and taking her hand with the most respectful air possible, he said, "Miss Campinet will permit me, what indeed she cannot prevent, to interest myself in her happiness and peace. Fortune, I hope, will again and again give me the pleasure of this morning, without its calamity." He bowed, touched her glove with his lips, and was out of sight in an instant.

CHAPTER XXI

THE Reverend Doctor Blick found his lordship hobbling along the terrace, aided by his two sticks, and rather in a fretful mood. The butler had been informing him of the ravages of the night, and, which unavoidably followed, of Mr. Hermsprong's activity in repairing them. The person of merit also had mentioned to his lordship, that Miss Campinet had gone early out upon her charitable functions; and had added, that no doubt, in her progress she would meet Mr. Hermsprong; and that two such benevolent people could not meet upon so charitable a business, without being highly delighted with each other.

Lord Grondale, though sufficiently attentive to such matters, did not just now regard the profound humility of Doctor Blick's salutation; but asked him abruptly, if he had seen that strange impertinent fellow, that Hermsprong?

The Doctor answered, "Yes, my lord, I have just left him."

"What, where, when? I suppose you are grown intimate," said Lord Grondale.

"How can your lordship do me the injustice to suppose it?" said the Doctor. "I — I coalesce with a man who has failed in respect to your lordship? No, my lord. But going amongst my parishioners this morning, to endeavour to alleviate their miseries, I met the young man —"

"Sporting his ostentatious charity —"

"Just, my lord; the epithet is perfectly adapted."

"Saw you Miss Campinet?"

"Yes, my lord."

"And she, Sir, — what did she do?"

"Hermsprong told her of a poor woman in labour, and they went together."

"Together! the benevolence of that is admirable. Together! Rank and property have lost half their value, at least, in this liberal age. I believe, Doctor, you and I may live to see the unfortunate hour when they will have lost the whole. Such fellows! damn him!" said his lordship, with energy.

In the flow of holy effervescence, the Reverend Doctor Blick had almost said amen, to Lord Grondale's prayer; but it came across him, that to say Amen was an inferior office; so he chose rather to content himself with expressing his astonishment that any man, much more such a man, should presume to offend his lordship.

"But," continued the good Doctor, "it is a licentious age: Pride and insolence are the characteristics of young men now."

"I think, Doctor, I shall find a way to lower both."

"I hope you will, my lord."

"I never in my life so much disliked a man."

"He is shockingly disagreeable, my lord, indeed."

"They say he has travelled."

"So he says himself, my lord; but he owns it was on foot."

"A very convincing proof, in my opinion, of the strength of his purse."

"Undoubtedly, my lord; very convincing."

"Yet they talk of his generosity. Old women, I suppose, for pennyworths of snuff and tobacco; and they say, God bless his sweet pretty face; as he swells with vanity almost to bursting."

"Certainly," said the Doctor, laughing, or endeavouring to laugh. "For true humour your lordship has no equal."

"I suppose he has exerted himself to-day, in order to eclipse the lord of the parish."

"I dare say your lordship is right. I saw at once his charity, did not flow from Christian benevolence."

"For my part, I have no opinion of these charitable ebullitions."

"Your lordship is perfectly happy in your terms. Yes, ebullitions, — bubbles."

"Indiscriminate giving is not my taste: I chuse to consider my objects."

"If all charities had your lordship for a director, they would be bestowed more to the praise and glory of God, than I fear they now are."

"Does any body know where this young fool comes from?"

"No, my lord."

"A French refugee, perhaps."[1]

"Perhaps so, my lord."

"But he speaks English too well."

"That is a just observation, my lord."

"Probably he has spent his fortune, and comes to hide his shame where he is unknown."

"Exceeding probable, my lord."

"It is still more probable he never had a fortune to spend, and is now on the hunt for one."

"I confess, my lord, this is the higher probability."

"My daughter would be a pretty catch. A lucky hit, Doctor, that of catching the chair horse."

"Vastly lucky, my lord."

"Not that horses are apt to leap down crags; but to timid minds, terror magnifies possibilities into certainties."

"You look quite into human nature, my lord."

"Miss Campinet, like other sweet young ladies, has, no doubt, a tender and grateful heart; and what reward can be too great for an action so terribly heroic?"

"Your lordship is so humourous."

There are men — classes of men, I believe, to whom no human attainment is so useful and profitable as assentation. It is for the benefit of young beginners in this respectable art, that I have recorded this dialogue. Dr. Blick was an adept. He cannot but be a bishop.

CHAPTER XXII

THE terrace on which Lord Grondale was now exercising Dr. Blick and himself, had a spacious prospect. Lord Grondale, at the instant of concluding his last sentence, happened to cast his eyes on the spot where Mr. Hermsprong was taking leave of his heroic daughter, at the conclusion of the 20th chapter.

"There, Blick, there!" cried his lordship; "damn it, there!" For anger will not be always obedient to polished manners; and lords,

---

1   Refugees from the French Revolution began arriving in England in the early 1790s, often meeting with suspicion and distrust; for an example of a contemporary work treating this topic, see Charlotte Smith's poem *The Emigrants* (1793).

nay parsons, will swear on sufficient provocation. As Miss Campinet approached the garden gate, Lord Grondale, full of rage, flew to meet her with all the velocity of a man crippled by gout. It happened that Mr. Glen was at this instant passing by, from Sithin, where he had slept the night before; and where he had informed himself concerning a young woman, who had once waited on Miss Campinet, and with whom she was deservedly a favourite. This young lady asked Mr. Glen of her; his answer was, that she seemed every day to grow worse.

"Alas!" said Miss Campinet, "I fear then there is little room to hope."

"Indeed, Miss Campinet," answered Glen, in a tone of sorrow, — "indeed I have no hope."

At this critical moment, Lord Grondale, inflamed with rage, burst through the gate.

"What impertinent language is this," said he, furiously; "how dare you, Sir, speak to my daughter in such terms?"

"I do not comprehend your lordship," was Mr. Glen's reply.

"Miss Campinet," said her father, "walk in, and wait my permission to go out again."

"What have I done to deserve this, Sir?" asked his fair daughter.

"Every thing I should wish you not to do. Five minutes since you were coquetting with that impertinent puppy, that Hermsprong, who comes from you know not where; and now you were permitting this worthy gentleman to talk to you of his hopes. A man who ought to think himself honoured by such permission to your woman."

"Indeed, my lord," said his fair daughter, weeping as she went in; "indeed you are in an error."

"That now is woman," said his lordship; "I must not believe my eyes;" then directing a stern look at Glen, "nor I suppose my ears."

"For Miss Campinet's sake, my lord, I will, if you chuse it, explain the simple words which have shook your lordship so horribly," replied Mr. Glen.

"I ask no explanation," his lordship exclaimed; "I will receive none. I disgrace myself, by condescending to talk with you at all."

"I am happy in your contempt, my lord," replied Glen.

"There, Doctor," said his lordship, "there!"

"I am shocked, my lord," said the complaisant Doctor; "Mr. Glen, have you lost your senses? Do you know the respect, I should say reverence, due from such as you to such exalted characters as Lord Grondale?"

"I think I do," Mr. Glen replied; "and to such exalted characters as Dr. Blick; and I pay exactly what I believe I owe."

"Such audacity, my lord, I never saw before; and hope I never shall again," said the Doctor.

"Just as often," Glen replied, "as you presume to treat me thus."

"Presume," said the Doctor, waddling two or three steps towards him.

"Presume," replied Glen, meeting him with firmness.

"Come in, Doctor," said Lord Grondale; "let us leave the reptile;" and the garden door was slapt to with a force which shook the wall.

CHAPTER XXIII

THE house in which Mrs. Merrick had lived, and of which she had a lease for life, was to be sold. It was the property of a Mr. Jones, who had, when young, occupied it, and the little estate around it, had married, and with an income of 400l. a-year, had lived respected, without running in debt. Unfortunately, the death of a cousin introduced him into the possession of as many thousands per annum. He began to live, and in a few years found it convenient to sell. Bloomgrove, for so this house was called, was ordered to the hammer; it having been previously offered to Lord Grondale, at a price his lordship refused to give; not because he thought it much too dear; but because, being told that it would, upon his refusal, be sold by auction, he thought no body would dare to bid against him, and he should get it cheap. And, indeed, so persuaded was the country around, that Lord Grondale, to whom it was the more desirable, as it was surrounded by his own estate, would be the purchaser at any price, that on the day of sale not many people of property attended, and those were soon silenced by the stern looks of Mr. Roger Calvart, his lordship's agent, all but one.

About this time Lord Grondale had no company, and had given the reverend Dr. Blick a general invitation to dinner, which, had received almost as general an acceptance.

On the day of the auction, half an hour before dinner, arrived Mr. Roger Calvart, to whom his lordship gave audience in his library. This over, they entered the dining room. Mr. Calvart warm with bustle and business, Lord Grondale with vexation. An awful silence prevailed during dinner, interrupted only by his lordship's and the Doctor's frequent call for wine.

The servants having withdrawn, the Doctor recollected the auction, and addressing Calvart, hoped he might with his lordship joy of the purchase.

Many an unpaternal, I might say, malignant glance, had his lordship during dinner, cast upon Miss Campinet, who began to tremble, though she knew not why.

The Doctor's question was answered by Calvart only with a shake of the head; but it opened his lordship's mouth, already predisposed to eloquence by wine.

"No," said Lord Grondale, looking at his daughter, "it is Miss Campinet you must congratulate; it is her hero who is the fortunate purchaser."

"My hero, my lord!" said the blushing Miss Campinet.

The parson was eating a nectarine; it fell from his hand; and his paralytic jaws denoted his profound astonishment.

"These premises," said his lordship, "which I have been laying out for so many years, which are so convenient to my estate, and in all respects so desirable a purchase, has this young coxcomb persisted in buying, when every body else had politely given up the contest. Not content with this insolence, he must add contempt to it; for when Mr. Calvart sent a friend to him, to say his opponent was bidding for Lord Grondale, and that his lordship would consider it as an obligation, if he would desist, he turned from him with a cursed sneer, and instantly bid 20l. more, though the rules of bidding only required 10l. But if I forgive the affront! And how the devil the fellow intends to pay for it, I cannot conceive; unless indeed he can find credit upon the strength of his favor with Miss Campinet."

"I shall be much obliged to your lordship," said his fair daughter, with some degree of spirit, "when you do Mr. Hermsprong the honour to make him the subject of your conversation, to be less personal to me, till I have really given you occasion."

"I cannot," his lordship replied, "consider the occasion as wanting. Witness that day, for ever memorable in the annals of Grondale, when the joint benevolence of this hero and heroine flowed a pure torrent, through the streets of this metropolis. Witness the apprehensive spirit of the lady, when any one presumes to question the gentleman's merit. Witness this purchase, which, without a view to your beauteous self, and these domains, is so ridiculous, that absurdity's own self would never have stumbled upon it."

"It is my duty, Sir, to bear all you chuse to inflict," said Miss Campinet, now in tears, and rising to withdraw.

"She sat like patience on a monument,"[1] cried his lordship, as she passed the door.

Mr. Roger Calvart hung his head; the parson forgot to applaud; and Mrs. Stone, by no means a malignant woman, an enemy to Miss Campinet rather from situation than malevolence, rose and retired, saying, as she went out, "Fie, fie, my lord!"

"Hay!" says his lordship, "what, I have been too hard upon Missie today, have I? Come, push the bottle, gentlemen; I am in the humour to be merry. This rascal has diverted me; if I live I will drive the country of him."

This was a sentiment law and divinity could both applaud; and they began in earnest to concert ways and means; but the rapid movements of the bottle prevented any thing being cogitated, worthy such genius, conjoined to such good will.

CHAPTER XXIV

A MONTH now passed away at Grondale Hall with tolerable peace. Mr. Hermsprong was mostly absent from the village; Miss Campinet scarce heard the mention of his name, except when Lord Grondale chose to make him the object of his ingenious satire. If simple tranquility be all that young ladies ever desire, she had almost all she desired. We must however, own it was but a sleepy felicity, till the arrival of Miss Fluart gave it a degree of animation.

Lord Grondale, who, when out of humour one morning, had been indulging his daughter with his usual effects, was crossing the hall into his study, (I had better call it his calculation room) when he was met by Mrs. Stone, with an eye rather fiery, and a check a little inflamed.

"My lord," she said, "did you invite young ladies here to insult me? if you did, I must tell your lordship that —"

But she was prevented from imparting to his lordship this piece of information, by the entry of Miss Fluart, followed by Miss Campinet.

"My lord, your most obedient. I hope I see you well."

---

1 *Twelfth Night* II.iv.115. The line describes a woman pining away from unacknowledged love.

"Much obliged to you, Miss Fluart," his lordship answered rather gravely; "pretty well."

"I have flown twenty miles this morning, to see Caroline here, and she receives me with tears. Either I am an unwelcome guest, or your lordship must have been scolding her."

"Miss Fluart, I can reprove, and Caroline can deserve it, but I cannot condescend to scold."

"So then, you have been naughty, Caroline. My lord, you must appoint me her governess. In one month, I dare say, I shall make her almost as wise and prudent as myself."

"Probably," answered his lordship, half deigning to smile; "would it be one of your lessons to affront people?"

"Oh dear! who can I have affronted?"

"A person of merit, I assure you, though she condescends to take upon herself the office of regulating my family."

"Goodness, what a mistake I have made! She was so kind as to welcome me just as a Lady Grondale would have done; so, though had not heard of it, I concluded your lordship had taken a wife; accordingly I paid my respects. It surprised me, to be sure, to see her bounce off as if she was affronted; but, my dear lord, you must make it up for me; and in return, I will take this naughty girl to her dressing-room, and correct her; so, my lord, good morning."

Now, it must be owned Miss Fluart did fib a little; for she knew Mrs. Stone very well; but the whim of mortifying the poor woman came into her head; who indeed forgot propriety in her officious welcome; and whom Miss Fluart could not forgive for taking her friend's place at Lord Grondale's table.

VOLUME II

CHAPTER I

OF the conversation that passed between our fair friends, at this their first interview, little has come to my knowledge. Towards the close of it, Miss Campinet said, "You see, my dear Maria, the state of things with us, and the causes of my father's displeasure. All I have to do, is to submit, and comfort myself with the reflection, that I have not incurred it by any indecorums, or any contumacy of my own."

"Yes," Miss Fluart answered, "there is great consolation in being whipped for having been good. But let us leave unnatural fathers, and talk of natural things. You allow that this Mr. Hermsprong is very handsome?"

"I did not say so, Maria. I am no judge of the very handsome in men."

"Have you any disorder in your eyes, my dear?"

"No; I have seen him too little, notwithstanding, to determine so important a point."

"They say of us, that we decide this at a single glance."

"I have had more cause to think of his bravery than his beauty; and I have thought of his benevolence more than of either. One might almost call him the guardian angel of the poor."

"Yes, of poor young women, who are going to take imprudent leaps, either into matrimony, or down crags. For the rest, his charities are whims, I suppose, or vanities, as most charities are."

"One would imagine, Maria, you were a pupil of Mandeville."[1]

"I have not the honour to know the gentleman; but one looks and compares, and so one draws conclusions."

"Not very candidly, I think."

"That is as God pleases, child; one draws them how one can."

"Well, my dear Maria, howsoever you may draw our conclusions here, let me entreat you to spare your wit in my father's presence; and do not needlessly irritate Mrs. Stone."

---

1 Bernard Mandeville (1670-1733) was notorious for his cynical views of society and of human nature. He argued, among other things, that charity can arise from selfish motives, writing in his "Essay on Charity and Charity Schools" (added in 1733 to *The Fable of the Bees* [1714]) that "Pride and Vanity have built more Hospitals than all the Virtues together" (Penguin 1989, 269).

"Surely, Caroline, you think I have no discretion; I, who love so well peace and plumb pudding."

When summoned to dinner, the ladies found in the dining apartment Lord Grondale and the Rev. Dr. Blick. His lordship appeared in good humour, and said, "Sit down, ladies — sit down, Doctor, Mrs. Stone will be here presently."

Miss Campinet took her accustomed place, the gentlemen theirs.

"Oh," says Miss Fluart, "it is I then who am to do the honours of the table; upon my word, this is a new etiquette."[1]

Then taking Mrs. Stone's chair, she called upon the Doctor, with great gravity, for grace. But in the Doctor's sensorium there must have been some little confusion; for instead of, "Lord bless and preserve," he began with, "Lord have mercy upon us." Lord Grondale frowned at his daughter, as if suspecting this a contrivance betwixt them; Miss Campinet, much hurried, said, "My dear, you have mistook; that is Mrs. Stone's chair."

"Oh dear!" cried this volatile lady, "I wish Mrs. Stone was either Lady Grondale or not; one shall be always making mistakes."

Miss Campinet blushed at this specimen of her friend's discretion; Lord Grondale looked ugly; the Doctor did not know how to look. A little Mrs. Stone relieved this embarrassment, by now taking her place. The Doctor mumbled something that passed for grace. Pythagoras might have presided at dinner, so little was there a want of silence.[2]

The whole of things not being to the taste of the young ladies, they withdrew as soon as possible. Lord Grondale followed them to

---

1 It was the place of the hostess to "do the honours of the table"; that is, to ensure that all the guests were properly served and to signal the departure of the ladies at the end of the meal. In formal eighteenth-century society, the hostess would be the wife of the host, or, if he were widowed or unmarried, a daughter or other female relative. In placing his mistress — or, indeed, anybody except a wife — over an adult daughter living with him, Lord Grondale is committing a shocking breech of etiquette, as Miss Fluart emphasizes.

2 The Greek philosopher Pythagoras (born c.582 B.C.) imposed strict rules of austerity on his disciples and founded an order which imposed five years of silence on initiates.

the door with his eye, and then said, "Don't you think, Doctor, the world vastly improved since you and I were boys?"

Had the Doctor only heard this question, he would have answered, "Undoubtedly, my lord." But he saw it too, and his reply was a "No" — of no small tone and emphasis.

"A fine thing, this commerce, Doctor; it doubles production, and enlarges all sorts of qualities but good ones. I can remember when young ladies were something more civil, and something less impertinent than now. I can remember when they paid visits only when invited by the master of the house; and when they would have thought it indecent to have affronted even their inferiors. Now their superiors cannot escape; for in point of family, Mrs. Stone is Miss Fluart's superior. This girl is a child of commerce, and thinks, to be young, to be a hoyden, and to have a fortune, excuses every thing. What is it to her, who I chuse to do the honours of my table at my own house? But I suppose there may have gone abroad a rumour, that Mrs. Stone and I, disregarding ceremony, have chosen to live together as man and wife. And whence such rumour? Why, because I acknowledge Mrs. Stone's merit, and treat her with the attention she deserves. Even were it so, Doctor —"

"Oh, my lord!" exclaimed Mrs. Stone, "I beg the supposition may not be made."

"For argument's sake only," his lordship answered. "What more should we do than imitate the patriarchs? Doctor, can that be sin?"

"No," answered the obliging Doctor; "no, my lord; on the contrary, I maintain, that it is to the leaving their simple manners, that the present degenerate races of mankind owe so much of vice and misery."

"Very true, Doctor. And what, pray, is con — con — I believe we must borrow a word from the Latin; for when the vulgar use a word, they always contaminate the idea. I ask, then, what is con-suetudinage[1] but marriage without forms? And what are forms?

---

1 This is a term that Lord Grondale has apparently coined from the word "consuetude," which refers to customary practice, especially customs treated as unwritten law (OED). The word for which he is groping and chooses to avoid is presumably "concubinage."

Rules — rather than laws — of civil policy, which it may be sometimes expedient to comply withal, and sometimes not."[1]

"Howsoever," said Mrs. Stone, "this sort of marriage may be convenient and agreeable to men, to women it is good for little but to subject them to insult and contempt."

"Trifles," his lordship replied, "beneath a sensible woman's notice."

"Very sensible women, my lord, may not chuse to lose their reputation."

"Amongst silly people," said his lordship, "a reputation lost is often a reputation got."

"Yes, my lord, amongst those who are degraded themselves."

"There are situations of this sort, Mrs. Stone," said his lordship, with a little air of pride, "which do not merit the name of degradation."

"I know of none, my lord."

"It was not always, madam, you viewed things in this light."

"This is another blessing of the situation your lordship is pleased to praise. If simple women complain, they are ordered to look back upon their folly, even by those to whom they have made the greatest of all sacrifices."

"Upon my honour, ladies are not wanting to themselves when they estimate the value of their favours."

"I do not see," said Mrs. Stone, looking at the Doctor, "how they can be rated too high, if, as the clergy tell us, we risque heaven by them."

"The cant of methodists," said his lordship. "The church of England has more liberal notions, — has she not, Doctor?"

In his appeals to Dr. Blick, Lord Grondale was seldom disappointed; nor had he now reason to complain; except of prolixity;

---

1   Conservative novelists of the time frequently attacked the radicals by attributing such lax ideas of marriage to those under the influence of new "French" ideas; the idea that sensible women should not be deterred from unconventional behaviour by fears of social condemnation is also one which is repeatedly associated with radical thought. Mary Hays, for example, in her *Emma Courtney* (1796), has the heroine insist that she could maintain her virtue and honour, even if she loses her reputation, while living in a monogamous relationship with a lover who, for whatever reason, could not marry her. By putting these ideas in the mouth of Lord Grondale, the embodiment of church-and-king orthodoxy, Bage is audaciously turning the conservatives' rhetorical weapons against them.

for the learned divine, having at great length, explained how marriage and consuetudinage existed together in patriarchal times, proved that what was right then could not be wrong now; and that it was scarce possible a lord should be wrong at any time.

With the Doctor's conclusions, Lord Grondale was better satisfied than Mrs. Stone, who did not see in them any towards advancing her to the dignity of Lady Grondale.

CHAPTER II

WHEN the fair friends had reached their apartment, Miss Campinet began a tender expostulation with Miss Fluart, entreating her not to indulge her vivacity on improper occasions.

"In pity to me, my dear," she concluded, "you should restrain your lively genius. Lord Grondale is my father; he may have his failings, but is it fit for a daughter to see them? In short, my dear Maria, he is my father; I say every thing in that."

Miss Fluart, with composed gravity, answered, "Yes, my dear — that — that sanctifies him."

"How can you, Maria, so pervert my meaning? I refer to the duty I owe; a duty which forbids my giving him offence."

"Very true, child," Miss Fluart replied, with continued gravity. "Yes, about this high transcendent duty — yes, it is all true. Pray, my dear, did you ever hear, or see in the dictionary, the word reciprocity? I assure you, the politicians make great rout about it."[1]

---

1 The idea that there should be reciprocity between governors and the governed attracted the radical political writers of the day. Thomas Paine, for example, opens the second part of *The Rights of Man* (1792) by proclaiming that "The mutual dependence and reciprocal interest which man has upon man, and all the parts of a civilized community upon each other, creates that great chain of connection which holds it together"; earlier, he had argued about the "reciprocity" between duties and rights: "What ever is my right as a man, is also the right of another; and it becomes my duty to guarantee, as well as to possess" (*Common Sense, Rights of Man, and Other Political Writings*, OUP, 1995, 214, 165). In extending this political argument to domestic life, Bage is following Mary Wollstonecraft, who argued strongly that women should not be expected to submit to the arbitrary wills of their husbands, any more than citizens should submit to arbitrary rule by despots.

"My dear Miss Fluart, I cannot bargain with my father."

"I dare say not, Caroline; unless the bargain is all on his side. Mrs. Stone, too — a very reverend person, — almost like a mother; it is possible she may have failings; but it is not necessary to see them."

"For me, it is not, Maria. She has good qualities."

"Oh, yes, quite useful to Lord Grondale; a sort of necessary person; who keeps naughty people of fashion from disturbing his lordship's domain; and so preserves the dear daughter of her adoption from the vices of a dissipated age, and the contagion of bad example. And of good, too — some people would say; and would ask whether this was a proper situation for Miss Campinet, the daughter and heiress of Lord Grondale; the favourite of nature as well as fortune; whom women pity, and men want to adore; debarred from society, and the common pleasures of life, by pure paternal affection. Oh Caroline!"

Miss Fluart's vivacity here yielded to her tenderness. She shed tears, and with tears Miss Campinet answered.

"If crying would do," said Miss Fluart, recovering her usual tone, "what wonders might we not be able to effect. But it is spirit we want."

"I own I have it not."

"It is the more necessary, then, you should be under the protection of one who has. I shall take you under mine. I find myself qualified to be school mistress, to father lords, who have only learned to love themselves."

"I must advertize you, my dear, that my father is rather irritable."

"You need not, Caroline; I know this."

"When angry, Maria, he may not be perfectly polite."

"Will he beat me, Caroline?"

"No, — not that, I hope: But he has a way of talking sometimes not quite agreeable to all sorts of people."

"Yes, — and so have I. We shall agree prodigiously."

"I imagine it may come into his mind to say, 'Miss Fluart, I am accustomed to be treated with proper respect every where; in my own house I think it indispensable. If you cannot prevail upon yourself to comply with this state of things, I shall be happy to see you at Grondale Hall, when you have overcome this little difficulty.'"

"To which," said Miss Fluart, "I answer, 'My dear Lord Grondale, surely when I endeavour to correct any little errors you may fall into from a small acerbity of temper, I pay your lordship the most proper respect imaginable. But if your lordship happens, from weakness of understanding, to think otherwise, I am willing to oblige you, provided I may take my pupil with me. She has not quite fallen into your lordship's error of judgment; she does not yet think herself absolutely infallible; though I must own she is rather too much like her father. But you know, my lord, I have undertaken to make her wise, docile, and prudent, like myself.'"

"Very well," Miss Campinet answered; "this must succeed with Lord Grondale. That error of judgment, and weakness of understanding, are the most conciliating expressions imaginable."

"If my tongue does now and then make a little wound, I can heal it with my eyes. Then I can stroke him, and say, 'Pray, pray.' And for a last emergency, kiss him: This, I know, is irresistible."

"You know, Maria?"

"Yes, with elderly gentlemen; you do not imagine I would venture upon so desperate an expedient with a young one?"

"No, Maria, I do not."

"No indeed; and moreover, I must tell you a secret; but you must not reveal it; nor whisper it even to the reeds."[1]

"Bless me! is it of such importance? I die to know it."

"No, don't die; I will sooner trust you. Attend: Young men are my aversion."

"Aversion?"

"Yes, indeed; and judge if I have not cause: They have absolutely made me sick of flattery; once the most palatable of all food. I fear I never shall endure it again."

"I dare say you will, my dear, with a little wholesome abstinence. Of what species may be the culprits, who have reduced you to so sad a state?"

"Soldiers in red coats, and sailors in blue. If you are for love and leanness, I recommend one of the former. If you chuse intervals

---

1　King Midas was supposedly punished by being given ass's ears when he chose Pan as the winner in a piping contest with Apollo. He concealed this deformity from everybody except his barber (or, in some versions his wife), who was sworn to secrecy. Unable to keep utter silence, the barber whispered the story to a hole in the ground, from which reeds grew which repeated it every time the wind blew through them (or, in some versions, the reeds were made into pipes which proclaimed the secret whenever they were played).

betwixt your love fits, one of the latter. There are creatures too, called bucks. Did you ever see a buck, Caroline? Not the tame creature of the park or the forest, but the wild buck of London or Paris. An animal which bounds over all fences. Breakfasts in London; dines at Newmarket; devotes six days and nights to the fields of sport, of hazard, and champagne; and having done all that he has to do, that is, lost his money, returns to town, to the arms of his fair Rosabella; dozes away forty-eight hours between love and compunction; awakes; damns all impertinent recollections; sends for an Israelite; signs, and is again a buck. It is a terrible siege I have sustained from one of these. There was treachery in the garrison, caused by a present cockade and a distant coronet.[1] I have held out, notwithstanding and at length escaped to take refuge with you."

"You are welcome, my dear," Miss Campinet replied, "and I hope safe. This animal, I suppose, is not bred in these parts; for I have never seen one; and indeed I dislike the description so much, that I hope I never shall."

"If you could get into a convent, Caroline, or if you never move from these silent precincts, it is just possible. The creatures are at present in a state of vast multiplication; every noble and genteel family begets one or more. But begging your delicacy's pardon, they have their attractions."

When young ladies chuse to philosophize upon attraction, they are unusually eloquent; and their ideas flow with a velocity with which few pens are able to keep pace. Mine flags, and admonishes me to end the chapter.

CHAPTER III

"GRANT," said Glen, "that we have been in a progressive state of improvement for some centuries; and that the aborigines of America have not."

"I allow your progressive state," Mr. Hermsprong answered; "and if you will have it, that all is improvement, be it so. You have built cities, no doubt, and filled them full of improvement, if magnificence be improvement; and of poverty also, if poverty be improve-

---

1   That is, a soldier with prospects of inheriting a peerage.

ment. But our question, my friend, is happiness, comparative happiness, and until you can trace its dependence upon wealth, it will be in vain for you to boast your riches."

"It appears to me," said the Reverend Mr. Woodcock, "that we have all the requisites for happiness which the untaught races of mankind have, with the addition of all that can be extracted from art and science."

"This," said Glen, "appears to me an uncontrovertible argument."

"And perhaps is so," Mr. Hermsprong replied; "but of this addition your common people cannot avail themselves. Generally speaking, if unoppressed by labour or poverty, have you observed in this rank, a deficiency of those pleasurable sensations, which we agree, constitute happiness?"

"No," said Glen; "no," said the parson, "I think not."

"It should seem," Mr. Hermsprong said, "that nature in her more simple modes, is unable to furnish a rich European with a due portion of pleasurable sensations. He is obliged to have recourse to masses of inert matter, which he causes to be converted into a million of forms, far the greatest part solely to feed that incurable craving known by the name of variety. All the arts are employed to amuse him, and expel the *tedium vita*, acquired by the stimulus of pleasure being used till it will stimulate no more; and all the arts are insufficient. Of this disease, with which you are here so terribly afflicted, the native Americans know nothing. When war and hunting no more require their exertions, they can rest in peace. After satisfying the more immediate wants of nature, they dance, they play; — weary of this, they bask in the sun, and sing. If enjoyment of existence be happiness, they seem to possess it; not indeed so high raised as yours sometimes, but more continued, and more uninterrupted."

"In this comparison, Sir," said Mr. Woodcock, "you seem to have forgot our greatest pleasures, those drawn from intellect."

"They also have exertion of intellect," Mr. Hermsprong replied. "Their two grand occupations require much of it, in their way; and who, think you, make their songs? They have indeed a different mode of using their understandings, and a less variety of subjects; but our point is happiness. I know not that they derive less from intellect than you."

"Do they read?" Mr. Glen asked.

"They do not," replied Hermsprong.

"You do," said Glen. "Would you give up the pleasure you derive from this, for any pleasure these people have?"

"No," Mr. Hermsprong answered, "I would not. Reading is, as it were, a part of my existence. But, when with those people, my hours of reading were theirs of evening sport. My pleasure was perhaps more exquisite; theirs more lively. They ended with a salutary weariness, which disposed them to sound repose; I, with head-ach perhaps, and with a yawning lassitude that disposed me to sleep, indeed, and also to dream. But in reality, is reading all pleasure? or is it pleasure to all? Are there not amongst you, who read because they have nothing else to do? to pass, without absolute inaction, those hours which must be endured, before the wonted hours of pleasure arrive? Or, is reading all profit? Is knowledge the sure result? Your contradictious disputations, eternal as it should seem, in politics, in religion, nay even in philosophy, are they not calculated rather to confound than enlighten the understanding? Your infinite variety, does it not tend to render you superficial? And was it not justly said by your late great moralist, every man now has a mouthful of learning, but nobody a bellyful?[1] In variety of knowledge, the aborigines of America are much your inferiors. What they do know, perhaps they know better. But we are wandering from our original question, from happiness, to the *cui bono*."[2]

"And is there," said Glen, "no pleasure without a drawback, which you can allow us to enjoy in a superior manner? Not love, for example?"

"Of this," said Mr. Hermsprong, smiling, "I am little qualified to speak. I left America before I could well fall in love according to nature; and have not yet learned all the refinements which constitute its value in Europe. All I have observed is, that you are not satisfied with it in the simple way in which our American Indians possess it. With you the imagination must be raised to an extraordinary height; I might almost say, set on fire. And this you perform by dress, by concealments, and by sentiment, like sugar, treble refined. But l repeat, this is a subject on which I cannot speak."

---

1 The "late great moralist" is Samuel Johnson (1709-88). He had outraged a generation of Scots with his comparison of their education to "bread in a besieged town: every man gets a little, but no man gets a full meal" (James Boswell, *Life of Johnson*, 1791. OUP 1982, 627).

2 To whose profit, or (more loosely) who benefits. The phrase originates in orations by Cicero (106-43 B.C.), in which he insists on the importance of motive in legal cases.

"So well, perhaps, as Mr. Glen," said Mr. Woodcock; "who has indeed sustained some of its rudest shocks."

This sally of the parson's rendering Mr. Hermsprong curious, Glen was under the necessity of giving a summary of his life, much in the manner he has previously given it to his readers; who will remember the share a Mrs. Garnet of Lime had in it; her misfortunes and subsequent distress. Mr. Hermsprong, on whom the relation of the misery of others had a saddening power, became more particular in his enquiries respecting this venerable lady; but when he learned that she was the aunt, the neglected aunt of Lord Grondale, his eyes flashed fire: He became at once thoughtful and silent; and being now near the village, they separated for that day.

CHAPTER IV

ON the next morning Hermsprong came to Mr. Glen's apartments, and found him writing to Mrs. Garnet, in answer to a letter lately received from her, written not in the whining manner of a mind sunk and debased by calamity; but with a dignified sorrow which seemed to think complaint beneath it.

"But," said Hermsprong, when he had read this letter, "for the honour of human nature, I hope Lord Grondale knows not of this."

"It is," replied Glen, "a rule in that noble house, never to suffer the mention in it of a name which has been supposed to degrade it. Most willingly his lordship would not have known; but Mrs. Garnet herself wrote him an account of her situation, when she had recovered from the violence of her first grief. This letter not being honoured with the least notice, the good lady, whose mind, softened by sorrow, turned with a fond wish of reconciliation to her only relatives, for she had heard with pleasure of the growing goodness of Miss Campinet, requested me to endeavour, by personal application, to know the real disposition of Lord Grondale's mind respecting herself. Though, (continued Glen) I did not love, — I did not fear his lordship; and I went immediately to execute my commission. I found him just alighting from his chariot at his magnificent portico. Not to hurt my cause, I accosted him with all the exterior marks of respect; and with that appearance of humility which is required in this, and I believe most other countries, from little persons to great ones. I began my tale; his lordship began to frown; but I had settled it with myself before, that the frowns of a lord one does not love, are not so killing as the frowns of a lady one does; so I proceeded with increasing intrepidity. His lordship's patience, however, soon gave way; and he interrupted me with this question: "Your name is Glen, I think?"

"It is, my lord."

"Grooby's bastard of Patten-place?"

"That is not my fault, my lord."

"Tell your employer she has rendered herself still more despicable by her agent; and learn another time to speak to Lord Grondale with your hat off."

Hermsprong's eyes seemed to flame. — "Did you not kick the fellow?" said he.

"Good!" replied Glen; "you are not yet quite acquainted with our manners. We English plebeians are not supposed to be deficient in freedom, but we don't kick lords. We have tolerably awful ideas of rank."

"By heavens!" said Hermsprong, "the son of a king would not have escaped it from me, after such an insult."

"Yes," said Glen, "but you say you are a savage. To say the truth, I almost forgot my politeness at that critical moment. I said, 'Before you became a lord, it would have been well to have learnt the manners of a gentleman.'

"His lordship deigned not a reply, but walked into his saloon, with a look that ought to have annihilated so insignificant an atom as myself.

"This heinous affront, of talking to his lordship," continued Glen, "with my hat on, was given because it rained, and because his lordship stood sheltered by the portico, I at the bottom of the steps, sheltered only by a keen north east wind. Yes," continued Glen, "I did put on my hat unbidden; and there, as far as regards his lordship, I have kept it ever since."

How far these young gentlemen proceeded in their animadversions on Lord Grondale, is immaterial to the public. It is only necessary to remark that Mr. Hermsprong soon left Mr. Glen's apartments, saying, he had an engagement at many miles' distance.

CHAPTER V

SOME weeks had passed at Grondale-place, with a decent quantity of order and tranquility. Mrs. Stone sat unmolested in her chair of honour; and Lord Grondale, if he felt now and then the sting of Miss Fluart's tongue, was recompensed by the delightful feeling which the touch of youth and beauty is supposed to impart to elderly gentlemen. For this young lady had the prettiest kittenish moods imaginable; in which she would sometimes take possession of his lordship's lap; or draw him on to a small game of romps; or say agreeable things respecting his person; the more grateful, as his lordship, in this particular, had almost begun not to flatter himself.

Whether Miss Fluart had or had not conceived any roguish design against the peace and dignity of Lord Grondale, my readers must decide from subsequent events. What is certain, is, that perceiving herself increase in favour, she enlarged her flattery and familiarity, till it was evident Lord Grondale took so much pleasure in her society, that he would sometimes step out of the path of greatness to seek it. But we are at a time when the grubs, hatching in his lordship's *pia mater* had scarce begun to crawl; it will be time enough to delineate them when they are well formed maggots.[1]

It was the fourth Sunday after Miss Fluart had been a guest at Grondale, that his lordship declared his intention of going to church; for he went there, I never knew why, very often, for a man of his rank. Mrs. Stone did not go to church; not for want of piety; but because she could not sit with ease in any seat but Lady Grondale's; and his lordship had not yet invited her thither in a way which she could perfectly approve.

As going to church is a family act, Lord Grondale gave a place in his state coach to the young ladies. As they entered the church yard one way, they were met, almost at the church door, by a group of three, which did not seem to give Lord Grondale much pleasure. It consisted of an elderly lady, rather infirm, hanging upon Mr. Hermsprong's arm, and followed by Mr. Glen.

Some small confusion Lord Grondale could not avoid betraying; he averted his face, however, and hastened to his seat, without a proper attention to the politeness due to Miss Fluart at least. The other trio passed into the seat, now Mr. Hermsprong's, in consequence of his purchase.

---

1 A maggot is a foolish idea; the *pia mater* is the innermost membrane lining the brain.

The Reverend Doctor Blick, I know not by what sort of inspiration, this day out did himself. It was the 14th of July, an anniversary of the riots at Birmingham;[1] where a quantity of pious makers of buttons, inspired by our holy mother, had pulled down the dissenting meeting houses, together with the dwelling houses of the most distinguished of that unpopular sect. The Reverend Dr. Blick did not say this was exactly right; he only said, that liberty had grown into licentiousness, and almost into rebellion. Indeed nothing could be more true; for to take the liberty to burn my house, for drinking my neighbour's health (the imputed crime) would be rather rebellious with regard to the laws, and licentious with regard to me.

"If ever the church can be in danger, it is so now," said the good Doctor. "Now, when the atheistical lawgivers of a neighbouring country, have laid their sacrilegious hands upon the sacred property of the church; now, when the whole body of dissenters here have dared to imagine the same thing. These people, to manifest their gratitude for the indulgent, too indulgent toleration shewn them, have been filling the nation with inflammatory complaints against a constitution, the best the world ever saw, or will ever see; against a government, the wisest, mildest, freest from corruption, that the purest page of history has ever yet exhibited. Besides this political daring, one of their divines, if any thing divine could be predicated of so abhorred a sect, has absolutely denied the most important tenet of our holy religion, the trinity in unity; has endeavoured to take from us the comfortable doctrines of atonement and grace; and indirectly, the immortality of our precious souls; for unless they are immaterial, how can they be immortal?[2]

---

1 The so-called "Church and King" riots in Birmingham in July 1791 were attacks on the property of local men who sympathized with the French Revolution, sparked by a dinner given to celebrate the fall of the Bastille. Bage was deeply shaken and angered by these riots, as he indicates in his letters to his friend and business partner William Hutton, whose country house was burnt down by the rioters. See the introduction for further discussion of this topic.

2 Presumably a reference to Joseph Priestley (1733-1804), the main target of the riots, and a Unitarian leader. Among other things, Unitarians believe that God exists only in one person and that Jesus was an inspired human prophet, who could not therefore redeem humanity by his suffering — hence the reference to the denial of the Trinity and of

But," said the Doctor, rising in energy, "what can be expected from men who countenance the abominable doctrines of the rights of man? Rights contradicted by nature, which has given us an ascending series of inequality, corporeal and mental; and plainly pointed out the way to those wise political distinctions created by birth and rank. To this failure of respect to the dignitaries of the nation, and let me add, to the dignitaries of the church, is to be ascribed the alarming evils which threaten the overthrow of all religion, all government, all that is just and equitable upon earth."

This discourse must have been agreeable to Lord Grondale, if he had the satisfaction to hear it. But, besides, that great men do not usually attend to sermons, his lordship's cogitations were probably on other subjects, for he hurried from his seat with peculiar precipitancy; not staying, as usual, to receive the bows of his humble tenants; and was in the coach some minutes before the ladies, who had some courtesies to perform, were able to join him.

CHAPTER VI

IT was a week after their last parting, before Mr. Glen again saw Mr. Hermsprong, who called again to say adieu, and inform his friend, that a certain necessity obliged him to be in London in three days; and that he had to request of him to go to his house, and to entertain there a stranger who arrived last night; and whom he must be so unpolite as to leave.

"But you may be at London," Mr. Glen replied, "in two days, or almost in one."

Atonement. The French had disestablished the Catholic church early in the Revolution, something which would unnerve Blick, who profits enormously from state provision for the Anglican church in England, a practice which was criticized by radicals, including Bage (see the debate printed in the review of *Man as he Is*, in Appendix B.1). The toleration of dissenters to which Blick refers was, at least in theory, very limited indeed, as nobody in England and Ireland who was not a communicant in the Anglican church could attend a university, sit in Parliament, hold certain civic or professional offices, or worship without having their place of worship licensed by the Anglican hierarchy. In practice, however, "occasional conformity" — that is, taking communion at least once a year — could enable a Protestant dissenter to participate in civic life.

"On foot?" said Hermsprong.

"Surely, Mr. Hermsprong, you cannot think of walking?"

"Oh, man of prejudice, why? in what other way can I travel with equal pleasure?"

"Pleasure! pleasure in England is not attached to the idea of walking. Your walks we perform in chaises."

"I pity you for it. For myself, I chuse not to buy infirmity so dear."

"Yes, the mode is dear I allow; but what is that to you, who value money so little?"

"My friend, who has told you that?"

"Your generosities."

"Pshaw! in my journey hitherto through life, I have only taken a taste for different gratifications; which, how should I be able to indulge, if I spent all my money in accommodating myself? For not squandering my money too, I have another reason, which I feel at my heart. I must be independent as far as social man can be independent. In other words, I must be free from the necessity of doing little things, or saying little words to any man. But enough of this," added Hermsprong; "I must bid you farewell for a week; and entreat you will spend that week principally, or wholly at my house. Respecting my friend I need say nothing: You will like each other. Farewell."

Occupied with an increasing respect for this, as it appeared to him, extraordinary man, Mr. Glen took the road to his house. He overtook, on the road, a young woman, a native of the village, with a small bundle under her arm.

"How far are you going, Sally?" he asked.

"Oh, Mr. Glen," she answered, "I am going to live at Mr. Hermsprong's."

"In what capacity, Sally?"

"As chambermaid."

"I hope it will prove a good place to you, Sally."

"Thank you, Mr. Glen; I dare say you do; for you have a kindly heart. And for that matter there is not many people of finerer [sic] characters than my master that is going to be, if one may believe what poor bodies say. Howsoever, I must needs tell you that I was a bit afraid, because he is a young gentleman, and not married; for servants have nothing but their characters; and if that goes all goes. So he sends for me last night, and so I went; but I could hardly look up at him for thinking about this. So, just for all the world as if he could see in a body's thoughts, he said, 'young woman, it is not so much into my service you will enter, as into that of a lady, who is so good as to consent to reside with me for the present.' 'Then, Sir, says I, be you married?' and my face was all in a glow. He smiled, and said, 'I am not; but you will not like the lady the worse for that.' Then he asked me my wages; and I thought I would ask enough, because, you knows, Mr. Glen, one may bate. However he did not make one word; but took me into the parlour to as fine an old lady as ever I saw in all my days, that had come an hour before, in a post-chaise, as I understood afterwards. And my master said to her, 'I ought not, madam, to intrude business upon you so early, but here is a young woman of good character, who, I hope, will suit you as your more immediate servant.' Now my mistress looked as if she wanted to speak, and could not. So he walked out; and then she told me I was to be chambermaid; and now I am going to my place."

The hall door opened before Mr. Glen could knock; and in an instant he found himself in the presence of Sally's venerable mistress.

"Good heavens!" he exclaimed, "and is it Mrs. Garnet I am so happy to see? oh! I comprehend it all. My excellent young friend!"

"Excellent indeed!" the good lady exclaimed, the grateful tear falling down her cheeks. For some time it was the congratulating eye alone that spoke. When Mr. Glen expressed a desire to know how this agreeable event was brought about, "Oh!" says Mrs. Garnet, "I will tell you all.

"On Wednesday morning, as I was poisoning my breakfast by bitter remembrances, a note was delivered me to the following purpose: That a stranger was charged with compliments from Mr. Glen, and begged permission to wait upon me. You may be certain what would be the answer. He came; we talked of you; and he said many things in your praise which could not but be grateful to me. 'But,' said he, 'my friend requested me particularly to observe, if there were any traces in your expressive countenance, which might seem to denote declining health; and I fear I do see something.' I answered, that age would have its appropriate signature. 'I have not,' Mr. Hermsprong said, 'any peculiar skill in the science of physiognomy, but with eyes to see, something may generally be seen. In your very intelligent face, madam, I see something more than the effects of time, I see anxiety.'

"It was the tender and respectful air which accompanied these words, more than the words themselves, which reached my heart. I could not answer. He took my withered hand, and touching it with his lips, said, 'I fear, madam, this must appear an impertinent freedom in a stranger, but be assured, I have no impertinence at my heart. Two things, Mr. Glen has taught me to respect in you, your virtues and your sorrows; but who can see sorrow, and not wish, as far as possible to alleviate it?'

"'You appear to have humanity, Sir,' I answered, 'and I doubt not that I have your good wishes.'

"'Over and above the inevitable stroke of destiny, madam,' Mr. Hermsprong said, 'I learn from my friend, that fortune has been unkind to you.'

"'Yes, Sir; poverty has struck me, now I am old and helpless; but age brings me this comfort, I have less time to endure it.'

"'May it be permitted me, madam, to turn the injustice of fortune to my own benefit?'

"'I beg, Sir, you will be explicit.'

"'Most willingly, madam; only once more let me entreat your pardon for my presumption.'

"'I know not that you have yet committed the offence.'

"'I fear I shall too soon. I am a young American, without father or mother; but with a fortune that sets me above the necessity of employment. Left early to my own bias, I contracted a passion for travelling; and I have indulged it to satiety. I desire to settle, to be stationary, at least for a time. The wild and romantic scenes of Cornwall, with its natural curiosities, have pleased me, and engaged my attention. Grondale and its environs have particular beauties. I have taken a house there; and I should give dignity to myself, madam, if I could prevail upon you to honour that house with your residence. It is the house in which the amiable Miss Campinet has so many years resided.'

"So extraordinary a proposal from a stranger struck me with a certain degree of astonishment, which must have been visible to Mr. Hermsprong, for he continued thus:

"'I perceive, madam, my request is going to meet the fate, such presumption deserves. Stranger as I am, I durst not have made the proposal, but that within a few hundred yards of this house, you have a friend who has all the respect and reverence for you which you yourself can wish, in whom you have entire confidence; and is it not probable also that Miss Campinet may wish to pay you the duty she owes, and increase your happiness and her own?'

"'Indeed, Sir, you hold out flattering allurements; but, Mr. Hermsprong, permit me to ask what good you propose to yourself in this?'

"'To myself, madam, a great and most essential good. Sensible of the weakness of youth, I seek in you a corrective friend; and if I am so happy to deserve it, a mother.'

"Mr. Hermsprong said this with eyes so animated, and a countenance so expressive and intelligent, — I think I never saw a face at once so handsome and so manly, — I was upon the point of conceding to his request, without more consideration, when Lord Grondale came across me, and with him a tribe of reflections, never conducive to my health or peace.

"'I fear the terms I am upon with Lord Grondale,' I answered, 'will prove an insuperable bar.'

"'I cannot,' Mr. Hermsprong said, 'think him of the least importance. What, madam, after his proud and injurious treatment? What is Lord Grondale to you? His benevolence has never been exerted on your behalf; and were it now offered, I hope you have too much pride to accept it.'

"'And is there not,' I replied, 'a pride which might be supposed to say, Can the aunt of Lord Grondale accept the benevolence of an entire stranger?'

"'Why, my dear madam,' says Mr. Hermsprong, gaily, 'if you are subject to fits of family pride, I know not with what weapons I can encounter so formidable a foe. But have the goodness to consider whether it is a pride of reason.'

"'No, Sir, — I allow it. It is a pride of feeling.'

"'Then, pray, madam, oblige me so far as to try to conquer it, or expect in the evening to have it wrenched from you by force of arms.'

"With these enigmatic words, and an air of great respect, he withdrew.

"His absence was a few hours, and I used them in considering his proposal. For the affirmative, were Mr. Hermsprong's open and manly behaviour, Miss Campinet, you, and my poverty; for the negative, my pride. Unable to conquer this obstinate feeling I was still fluctuating when he returned. He spent the evening with me, — a confidential evening. He opened his heart, and a most amiable and generous one it is. All his communications I cannot disclose; but he sought and obtained my entire confidence, nor could I longer resist his wishes."

CHAPTER VII

IN a week Mr. Hermsprong returned. His salutation of Mrs. Garnet was equally respectful and affectionate. Again and again he thanked her for the honour she did him, and for the pleasure she gave him by her kind condescension.

Of the subjects of conversation the evening produced, one was Miss Campinet. Mrs. Garnet had never seen this young lady. She had heard her spoken of, indeed, much to her praise. Mr. Glen was profuse in her applause, and exciting in Mrs. Garnet the tenderest wishes. To love, and to be loved by a relation so amiable, so benignant, she said, was all that was now wanting to compleat her felicity. But the tender interest they had in each other was torn asunder by pride and prejudice;[1] and this pride and this prejudice, she feared, had been infused into the tender mind of Miss Campinet.

On the Saturday evening, Mrs. Garnet mentioned her perplexity about going to church. She seldom failed, she said; she thought it her duty; but circumstanced as she was, she knew not how to resolve on going. She looked up to Mr. Hermsprong for his opinion.

"If, dear madam, you think it a duty, I know of no consideration which ought to exempt you from the performance of it. Surely it is not you who ought to be embarrassed. Let Lord Grondale blush, — if he can blush," said, emphatically, Mr. Hermsprong.

"I am really very weak," said Mrs. Garnet.

"Yes, madam, and for that weakness, or any weakness arising from fear, you must permit me to invert the order of things, and become your preceptor, as in all things else you must be mine. To you, what is Lord Grondale? Can you fear a man whom you have acquired a right to pardon? A man whose mind is mean — so mean as to incite him to commit acts of injustice, of inhumanity! can he be feared? He, whose life has scarce been marked by one act of energy? Who owes the little consequence he possesses to his title and his money? How feeble must be the resentments of a man humiliated by his vices? Oppose him with the manly spirit of conscious rectitude, you will find him a child; a sulky, pouting one indeed; but still a child. If you want conviction, I dare engage to give it you, for I know myself marked out for the object of his mean and secret persecution."

---

1 This phrase was used in a number of books before Jane Austen's day, so even though Austen owned a copy of *Hermsprong* (see Tave 1, Butler 85-86), it is not likely, as Tave emphasizes, to be the source of Austen's title. Frances Burney's *Cecilia* (1782), which features the phrase several times in the final chapter, is a possible source for both Austen and Bage.

"You astonish me, Sir," said Mrs. Garnet, and Glen could have said the same, "by the boldness of your language."

"It was imposed on me as a duty by my father," Mr. Hermsprong answered, "to speak, when I did speak, with the spirit of conscious truth; and to act, when I did act, with the spirit of conscious justice. I have obeyed my father; and hope I have been rewarded, as he promised me I should, by a proper portion of firmness and intrepidity. If this, as I suspect, has the appearance of boasting, I answer, that to the weak and enervating humility of thinking, or pretending to think, worse of myself than I deserve, I am, and desire to be, a stranger. That I am not the first of men, I know. I know also that I am not the last. I see not the difficulty of man's becoming a judge, tolerably just, of the temper of his mind, as well as of the temperature of his body; and learning the lesson, conceived so hard to be learned, of thinking himself, what he is. I have energies, and I feel them; as a man, I have rights, and will support them; and in acting according to principles I believe to be just, I have not yet learned to fear."[1]

I wish the world, that is the original thinkers in it, would meet together in some barn, it need not be very large, and determine what is to be thought of such pretensions. Is this the stuff of which the pride of our people of rank and fashion is made? That it is pride of some sort, I have no doubt; for I, Gregory Glen, the son of nobody, felt myself raised, exalted by it. I almost began to think myself a man. But it is a word of bad augury. Kings like it not; parsons preach it down; and justices of the peace send out their warrants to apprehend it. Let us leave it to its fate; and only observing, that in consequence of Mr. Hermsprong's spirited support, Mrs. Garnet assumed courage enough to go to church, accompanied by the two gentlemen; and this was the trio which infused, as parson Evans would say, a trempling of mind into Lord Grondale, and almost suffused his cheek.[2]

---

1 Energies of the mind, which would enable their possessor to overcome conventional, restrictive codes of behaviour, was a favourite topic for radical debate; the concept is derived most immediately from William Godwin's *Political Justice*. The idea of the rights of man would then, as now, immediately be associated with Thomas Paine, although Mary Wollstonecraft had also written a pamphlet by that name.

2 Shakespeare's Parson Evans in *The Merry Wives of Windsor* cries "Pless my soul, how full of cholers I am, and trempling of mind!" (III.i.8). Substituting "p" for "b" was one of the standard techniques for representing a speaker with a Welsh accent.

CHAPTER VIII

THE dinner of this adverse sabbath passed over rather unpleasantly at Grondale hall. His lordship was grave and silent. At such a time, how could Doctor Blick talk? Miss Fluart was busy in repenting a little indiscretion towards Mrs. Stone, and Mrs. Stone in concealing her mortification. And Miss Campinet was engaged in the study of her father's countenance, where she saw a certain indefinable something she never saw before.

When the evening came, the young ladies, as usual, chose a walk. A favourite one was Lippen Crag. I know not what made it so to Miss Fluart; but with Miss Campinet, no doubt, it was piety. With due gratitude to providence, and to the agent it had been pleased to employ on so gracious an occasion, she delighted to view her danger, and tremble at her escape. Even Mr. Hermsprong, whose walks were leagues; whose meditations the whole phenomena of nature; even he has been known more than once to stride a few miles out of his way, to look at this terrible crag, to think better of himself for having been this agent of providence, and to sigh that Caroline Campinet should be the daughter of Lord Grondale.

To this classic spot, — not classic yet, — it must wait till this adventure has become the subject of an epic superior to the Iliad, — came the young ladies about seven in the evening; and amongst the objects viewed from the summit, was the same group of three they had in the morning met in the church yard. Though the walk was to her rather a long one, Mrs. Garnet ventured upon it, from a desire to see the scene of her grandniece's danger.

A small tinge of the rose, on the cheek of Miss Campinet, gave the intelligence of something to Miss Fluart.

"My dear," said Miss Campinet, "I think we had better return."

"Yes," said Miss Fluart, "but not by the way we came. For if I am right, the other way comes your hero, and probably his mother; though I thought he had none. You know, my dear, I have not seen him this month; and, to tell you the truth, I long for it very much. What pity it is, he should be a savage, and not love lords."

Miss Campinet, though not without a little real or seeming reluctance, yielded to the inclinations of her friend. The parties met. The gentlemen made their obeisances. The young ladies returned their courtesies, but with something like a reserve on the part of Miss Campinet, and passed on.

They had proceeded an hundred yards, perhaps, and Miss Flu-art was beginning to give vent to a small matter of ill humour at this stupid formality, when a step was heard behind and a voice that said, "And is pride too the attribute of Miss Campinet?"

She turned about. It was Mr. Hermsprong who had spoken thus, and there was something a little like indignation in his face.

"Why," said Miss Campinet; "why, Sir, am I accused of pride?"

"Know you that lady?"

"No, Mr. Hermsprong, indeed I do not."

"Her name is Garnet now, once Maria Campinet, the sister of your grandfather, the late Sir William Campinet. Can she be total-ly unknown to you?"

"I have heard my late aunt mention a Mrs. Garnet, who was said to have disgraced her family by marriage."

"Oh pride! pride! Was she never the subject of Lord Grondale's discourse?"

"Never that I know of. I believe it is a rule of our house, never to speak of any branch of it who have offended."

"Not to-day did Lord Grondale speak of her?"

"No, Sir: My father was not quite as usual to-day, but I know not the cause."

"She is the cause; that venerable lady; the sister of his father. That pride should be a giant, and humanity a dwarf!"

"Is my father the cause of this apostrophe?"

"Yes, good heavens! yes. But pardon me, Miss Campinet, to you such things should not be said. Your gentle nature knows not bar-barity. You are too just and too good for pride of this odious stamp. I have distressed you. I entreat your pardon. My indignation was just, but ought not to have been disclosed to you."

Mr. Hermsprong now gave Miss Campinet a summary of Mrs. Garnet's history. It was with some pathos he drew a picture of her distresses; and concluded with the hopes and wishes Mrs. Garnet had so fondly and tenderly expressed.

The recital drew many a sigh from Miss Campinet.

"Indeed," said she, — "indeed Mr. Hermsprong, I wish to pay my duty to my venerable relation, — to pay it this instant; but, sit-uated as I am, is it proper?"

"Why not, Miss Campinet?"

"Mr. Hermsprong, your benevolent virtues excite my admira-tion. As a brother, I could consult and confide in you. But you hate or despise my father. This is too visible. It grieves me. Yet I must express my wonder at so fixed an aversion. My father may be proud; but is it so uncommon to be proud? Or is it uncommon for a person to be angry at another who defeats a favourite purpose? This unhappy prejudice prevents me from considering you as the proper person to give me the advice I want. I long to pay my duty to my respectable aunt, —— but my father! Need I say more?"

"You are ever amiable, Miss Campinet, even in your errors."

"Errors! can filial obedience ever be error?"

"I have been taught, and taught by a father, to attend to the truth of things only, and to reject all prejudices that lead to injustice. An illegal act you must not do, even by the command of a father; and ought you to do a wrong one?"

"But surely it may be wrong to do a right thing, when prohibited by a father."

"What, if that right thing be a duty also, and the prohibition pride, prejudice, or caprice?"

"And ought a child to erect herself into a judge of her father's motives?"

"Adieu, Miss Campinet. I must join the respectable Mrs. Garnet, to whose calamities I now fear you will add one deeper than most of those she has already suffered."

"Stop, Mr. Hermsprong, I beg you stop. Whatever be the consequence, I entreat you to introduce me to my revered aunt. Whatever be the consequence, I will obey the impulse of my heart. Do you condemn me, Miss Fluart?"

"No, indeed."

"Miss Fluart," said Hermsprong, "I ask a thousand pardons; I have sinned dreadfully against politeness."

"I was indeed afraid I should not have had the honour of Mr. Hermsprong's notice," said Miss Fluart.

"Pardon me, madam; my mind was full; and full indeed it must have been, when it shut my eyes to the charming Miss Fluart."

"When your compliments do come however, they come in a full stream."

"No, Miss Fluart, I am but a learner of this art, and awkward as learners usually are. But see, Miss Campinet; Mrs. Garnet has stopped. Permit me to introduce you to each other."

Mr. Hermsprong broke the first cold forms of ceremony; Mrs. Garnet looked, rather than spoke her satisfaction, and embraced her dear relation with ardour. Miss Campinet entreated indulgence for errors; and hoped she might be able to atone for past neglect, by future attention. A little while they walked together; and then parted, much delighted with the rencontre.

CHAPTER IX

THIS pleasure, to Miss Campinet, was at her return, damped by the still gloomy appearance of Lord Grondale. Mrs. Stone was indisposed, and Doctor Blick gone home; so his lordship and the young ladies sat down to supper in solemn silence. When the table was disserved, Miss Campinet ventured to say, "I fear you are not well, papa." His lordship's answer was not in his kindest manner. It was a question rather sternly asked; "Who were those people you were walking with on the moor?"

"The lady was Mrs. Garnet," Miss Campinet replied; "the gentlemen, Mr. Hermsprong and Mr. Glen."

"It is very remarkable, Caroline," said his lordship, "that if there be people in the world I more particularly dislike, you are sure to select them for your acquaintance and favourites."

"Indeed, papa, they are not selected; they are my acquaintance by accident. Mr. Glen indeed was known to my late aunt; and was very obliging in procuring me books and music. Mrs. Garnet I never saw, nor scarce heard of, before to-day. To Mr. Hermsprong I owe my life. I ought to be grateful; but your lordship not approving, I dare only be civil. If we meet, it is merely by accident."

"Accident," his lordship answered, "is a most useful person, and the greatest pimp in the creation. Accident, I suppose, carried you back to these people, after you had passed them."

"No, Sir. I did not know Mrs. Garnet till Mr. Hermsprong followed to reproach me for not taking notice of her. It was then I first learned our consanguinity, her merit, and her distress. I thought it my duty to pay her my respects. I hope I have your approbation, papa, and your permission to repeat them. Mrs. Garnet is at present Mr. Hermsprong's guest."

"Very good," said his lordship; "how admirable is the artless simplicity of young ladies! If you are grateful, Caroline, you will raise an altar to accident. Accident carried you to the brink of Lippen Crag, and placed your hero there. Accident has made him leave off a life like that of the wandering Jew.[1] Accident has enforced him to buy a house, and settle in this charming neighbourhood.

---

1   According to medieval legend, a man who mocked Christ on the road to Calvary and so was condemned to wander the earth until Judgment Day.

Accident, no doubt, introduced him to my fool of an aunt; and accident caused him to bring her here. So accident has opened you a road into Hermsprong's house; and made that which the world would call a breach of decorum, seem a duty."

"How cruel this is," said Miss Campinet, bursting into tears.

"My dear," said Miss Fluart, "his lordship means nothing by all this, but to shew his ingenuity."

"I mean all I say, and more," Lord Grondale replied.

"Then," said Miss Fluart, "it is the compleatest triumph of pride and prejudice[1] over poor common sense, that has ever fallen under my notice."

"Now," returned Lord Grondale, "for a specimen of your ingenuity."

"But I cannot really believe that it does appear to your lordship, that Mr. Hermsprong sought Mrs. Garnet with a view to give Caroline an opportunity to come to his house."

"Such may be my suspicions, I presume," Lord Grondale answered, "without any impeachment of my understanding."

"I allow it to be very cunning, and very characteristic," Miss Fluart replied; "I only deny its truth."

"I can very readily suppose, Miss Fluart, that you know the truth better than myself; but I cannot so easily suppose you will impart it to me."

"Why not, my lord?"

"Oh! it is absurd in me to imagine that so immaculate a lady as Miss Campinet should have secrets she would not chuse a father should know; or that she should have a friend who would not chuse to betray her."

"So kind a father must claim unlimited confidence. But Caroline is bashful; so I will tell your lordship a plain tale, that will convince you of its truth, if your lordship does not find it inconvenient and disagreeable to be convinced."

To this Lord Grondale made no reply.

"Mrs. Garnet," continued Miss Fluart, "has been known to Mr. Glen many years. He is rather a compassionate man, and always lamented, though he could little relieve her distress. In talking over the memoirs of the house of Grondale with Mr. Hermsprong, Mrs. Garnet came to be spoken of; and this stranger, a compassionate

---

1 See note 1, page 170.

man also, took it into his head, that the aunt of Lord Grondale ought not to want bread; and having now a house of his own, he went to her, and prevailed upon her, I know not by what arguments, to accept this house as her asylum."

"The arguments," said his lordship, "may be guessed at."

"They may, my lord; but they may be guessed at wrong, if in benevolence, your lordship will see nothing but cunning, and in integrity, nothing but self."

"It is not absolutely necessary, Miss Fluart," said his lordship, with much dignity, "that things should appear in the same light to you as to me. I presume I have seen more of the world than you have. With me, the simple credulity of youth is past. Men are benevolent for many purposes; some not very laudable. And in your opinion, is it extremely absurd to suppose that a young fellow, whom nobody knows, who has no connexions, or keeps them secret, should be an adventurer and desirous of making the most of his good fortune?"

"And why, my lord, is suspicion, with her ifs and ands, so forward, and candour so backward? What better criterion is there to judge of men as well as trees, than by your fruits ye shall know them."[1]

"Judge as you please, Miss Fluart, and give me leave to do the same. Only, when you chuse to favour me with your ideas, have the goodness to spare your inuendoes; and do not suppose my conduct to Mrs. Garnet is without cause."

"Oh dear! my lord, I never supposed any such thing; every body knows there are two causes."

"May I enquire what they are?"

"Oh, — but it is not polite to call every thing by its proper name. Besides, your lordship may be angry."

"Politeness to Lord Grondale does not seem to make a part of Miss Fluart's necessities. His anger indeed might be rather disagreeable; but it cannot be excited by the opinions of a mob."

"This is a most convenient way of thinking for the great; in whose favour mob does not now form many of its notions. On other accounts, as well as Mrs. Garnet's, it accuses Lord Grondale of pride and avarice."

His lordship nodded.

---

1 Matthew 7:20.

"As to avarice," continued Miss Fluart, "it is a substantial cause; I have nothing to say against it; nor indeed against pride much; what would rank be good for without it? But as the sons of nobility honour the daughters of plebeians, when they happen to be rich; I do not see why the daughters of nobility may not honour the sons of plebeians, for like causes."

"I believe, Miss Fluart, it is better to avoid discussing opinions of this sort. What I expect from my daughter is obedience; and I dare say I shall have it, — if Miss Fluart pleases."

"What, my lord! implicit obedience and unconditional submission."

"Even so, Miss Fluart."

"That never sits well upon men's stomachs, and hardly upon women's; though I must own they are properly brought up for it, — some of them."

"I think not, if you mean Miss Campinet. But we shall see. The first mark of obedience I exact from her is, never, on any pretence, to enter Hermsprong's doors."

"May I not be allowed, Sir," said the timid Caroline, "somewhere to pay my duty to my aunt."

"No; I forbid it; she has no claim upon your duty. That woman is renounced; and the renunciation is a family act."

"This is very hard indeed," said Miss Campinet, the tears pouring into her fair eyes. "I hope I have your lordship's permission to retire."

"I find no difficulty in indulging you in that request," said his lordship; and the mortified Caroline hastily withdrew.

After a few minutes' silence, during which the rose and the lily had contended for empire in Miss Fluart's pretty face; she said, with a smiling archness, "Pray, my lord, how long do you intend to live?"

"As long as possible," returned his lordship.

"That is really very cruel now. If it was not for that terrible resolution," continued Miss Fluart, going to him, and stroking his face with playful wantonness, "I don't know but I should offer myself for this girl's stepmother; for I love authority and a coach and six; and though your lordship's commands are so perfectly reasonable, yet that headstrong girl will think it hard to obey them."

"Greater hardships," Lord Grondale said, "may possibly be the consequence of disobedience."

"Certainly, my lord; for I shall withdraw the light of my motherly countenance from her, and make her stand in a corner, till she cries, — pray, pray."

"This is a subject, Miss Fluart, that might, without much impropriety, be treated with less levity; and as I am not disposed to trifle, I must beg leave to wish you a good night, with this concluding observation: If Miss Campinet assumes the liberty of disposing of herself, without, or contrary to, my approbation, I shall assume the liberty of disposing as I please of the affection and property of Lord Grondale."

The conscious sense of dignity which swelled his lordship's features, on the conception and delivery of this sublime and beautiful sentiment,[1] cannot be described, nor I presume, felt by plebeian souls; and surely none but plebeian souls will condescend to read these humble memoirs. Miss Fluart seemed about to reply; but Lord Grondale waved his hand by way of prohibition; rang for his valet; wished Miss Fluart an awful goodnight, and retired.

CHAPTER X

MISS FLUART went to her friend's apartment, whom she found still in tears. "This crying must be a sweet pretty amusement, Caroline," said she; "you are so fond of it. Could not you teach me the art, my dear?"

"I hope, Maria," Miss Campinet answered, "your tears will flow for others; never for yourself."

"Then you do not find them pleasurable?"

"Comparatively so, Maria; for they relieve pain."

"And this pain too is a sort of favourite very often, if one may judge by the ready admission he finds into gentle bosoms."

"The secret of keeping him out would indeed be invaluable."

"I have it, my dear. It is a discovery of my own; and is nothing more than a profound reflection how troublesome and useless a gentleman he is."

"Alas! he enters before the reflection."

"In that cafe we must turn him out; and if one sort of consideration will not effect it, a wise person, like myself, will try an hundred others. Pray, my dear, have you ever made an estimate of the quantity of your father's affection?"

---

1 A phrase recalling the title of Edmund Burke's first published work, *On the Sublime and the Beautiful* (1757).

"An estimate! Sure, Maria, it is inestimable."

"Yes, my dear, when in full growth. But Lord Grondale's don't seem to be in that state of dimension."

"This is a subject, Maria, that lies very near my heart."

"I understand the reproof, my dear. But that heart I want to take a naked peep into; to see if it is composed of true feminine matter; if it prefer girandoles[1] and the heart-ach, to a simple candle and content."

"I see the extent of your question, my dear Maria. But suppose I could determine to buy peace with the loss of fortune, would not that peace be as much wounded by my own breach of filial obligation, as by my father's unkindness? If then, (continued Miss Campinet, with a faint smile,) the heart-ach must be born, one may as well have the girandoles along with it."

"Why, this now, Caroline, is ingenious; and I dare say ingenuous; it is so like the rest of the daughters of Eve; and yet it leaves me still in doubt, whether this meek and humble duty has its foundation in love, money, or one or other of the ten commandments."

"You are very whimsical, Maria."

"And you, Caroline, instructive. I had got into the foolish way of thinking that women did not love tyrants, whether husbands or fathers."

"It is a sight of every day, Maria, that women, wives at least, continue to love the tyrants, when the tyranny has become almost insupportable."[2]

"Depend upon it, it is nothing but a habit of fondness the silly things have acquired, and not had time to get rid of."

"But, Maria, a tyrant is a very harsh term; too harsh, I hope, to be properly applied to Lord Grondale."

"Oh quite; for what has he done, but govern with absolute sway, as great men ought; and turn his daughter out of doors, to make room for persons of merit."

"And Mrs. Stone has merit, Maria; let us do her justice; and if my father chooses to treat her more as a friend, than a servant, what right have I to complain?"

---

1 Elaborate, decorative candle holders.
2 An observation made by eighteenth-century feminist writers; for example, compare Mary Astell: "women are for the most part wise enough to love their chains and to discern how very becomingly they fit" (*Some Reflections upon Marriage,* 1700).

"Oh, no! — he might have married her, and begat you a few loving brothers."

"Certainly he might; and had he given me a respectable mother, so far from considering it as an injury, I should have rejoiced at the event."

"Well, Caroline, since you are so fond of respectable step-mothers, I will try to accommodate you. I have some thoughts of taking that dignity upon myself; and am glad to find you in such dutiful inclinations."

"And have you consulted Lord Grondale, mama?"

"Yes, his eyes; and eyes will sometimes betray the secrets of elderly gentlemen, as well as of young maidens. So God bless you, my dear child; be a good girl; and go quietly to sleep."

CHAPTER XI

ALL tyranny, that excepted which young ladies exercise over their lovers, Miss Fluart held in tolerable detestation; that of Lord Grondale over Miss Campinet was not the less odious to her, because it assumed variety of shapes. When his lordship was under the gentle influence of pure genuine ill humour, it was the stern frown of authority, that bears not the shadow of disobedience or contradiction. When the dining table had procured him a cessation of this overflow of bile, and disposed him to hilarity, it was the most bitter irony, that his lordship, and for this he did not want talents, could invent. There was, however, a middle humour, in which he permitted Miss Campinet to enjoy a certain degree of tranquility; and this desirable portion of harmony, Miss Fluart was desirous to produce in Lord Grondale as often as possible. Her powers of blandishment were not small, and she broke through her own disgust, to exert them for the service of her friend. In the beginning of her little romps with his lordship, she had to contend with a certain hauteur which seemed to say, why should I thus condescend? It was however soon apparent to this young lady, that but for this sense of degradation, her sportive play would not be in the least disagreeable.

In a little time, this dignified sensation appeared to have given way; Lord Grondale seemed growing into fondness; and Miss Fluart was taken with an irresistible inclination to subdue his lordship wholly. She flattered herself it was for the sole purpose of being enabled essentially to serve her friend; and if this was the leading motive, who will blame her, if a desire to plague his lordship, or if a little gratification of vanity were assistant causes. Nothing, however, was farther from her intention, than to become the wife of Lord Grondale; and it was therefore a necessary consequence, that nothing on her part should be said or done, that could legally, or in *foro conscientiæ*,[1] be construed to bind her to such an event.

On the part of Lord Grondale, it was a war of pride with the senses. On some small occasions, he said to himself, "This little gipsey has certainly an inclination to become Lady Grondale"; and when she had said to him one day, — how amiable you would be, my dear lord, if you could always preserve this good humour and vivacity, he became assured of it. Love, like other chronic passions, — I had like to have said diseases, — has its fits of progression and retrocedence, its hot and cold fits. Lord Grondale experienced this. Soon after, he said, "She has 20,000l." and this associated with the lady's other prettinesses; and finally became the grand auxiliary of love.

Now these were the respective states of mind of the lord and lady, on the morning of that unholy sabbath, when the spectre of Mrs. Garnet appeared in the church-yard. His lordship forgot he was under the necessity of being always in good humour; Miss Fluart forgot it was her business to keep him so; the affair of the evening increased his lordship's irritability; this revived Miss Fluart's satirical vivacity; and the melancholy consequence was, the expulsion of love and badinage from the respective breasts of the gentleman and lady; and when they would have been restored, but for an accident, is more than I can say.

At the extremity of the pleasure ground, bordering on the moor, Lord Grondale, soon after his accession to the estate, had built a sort of pleasure house, an octagon, on an artificial mount. It had obtained the name of the pavilion. In his earlier years, his lordship made of it a sort of temple of fame, and adorned it with the portraits of his own best hunters and racers, and of those who had obtained the greatest renown on the arduous plains of Ascot and Newmarket. This taste declining, these portraits had given place to paintings of another species, capital, no doubt, his lordship having been considered as a connoisseur.

This pavilion Lord Grondale made a kind of sanctum, it was open only to himself, a few of his more particular friends on their

---

1 That is, in conscience, though not strictly in law.

annual visit, and once a week perhaps, usually on Sunday evening, to the person of merit. So it happened to be on the eve of that sabbath, so mortifying to Lord Grondale. From thence it was they saw the movements of the parties, as described in our 8th chapter of this volume; which "tortured his lordship almost to madness,"[1] and subjected Mrs. Stone to his stern rebuke, for the mere endeavour to reason him into placidity.

It was several evenings after this, when Lord Grondale had begun to long for a few of Miss Fluart's sugared sweets, and Miss Fluart to wish he would, that this young lady was strolling the pleasure grounds alone; Miss Campinet having determined that evening to write to Mrs. Garnet; a thing she had attempted every day since her father's prohibition, but in which she had not yet succeeded to her mind. A few yards from the pavilion, turning a walk, Miss Fluart almost ran against Lord Grondale. The good peer said, with a tone of good nature, "Have I the pleasure to see Miss Fluart here, and alone?"

"Caroline is indolent," Miss Fluart answered; "she chose the zephyrs of her own apartment, rather than the zephyrs of your lordship's groves. Oh dear, (she continued) now I think of it, I have long had a desire to take a peep into your lordship's pavilion, where you have never yet invited me."

"I invite you now, then," said Lord Grondale, hobbling up the steps, and unlocking the door.

"I hear," says she, ascending, "it is a little palace of paintings."

The first object which struck her view, was herself, her beauteous self, many times multiplied. This was fascinating no doubt, but she got rid of it as soon as she could, and threw her eye on a lovely piece, representing Jachimo taking notes of the mole cinque spotted on the beauteous bosom of Imogen.[2] The next was Atalanta, straining to recover the ground she had lost by the golden apples; her bosom bare, her zone unloosed, her garments

---

1 Compare *Othello* II.i.291-92, when Iago gloats over the idea of tormenting Othello "by practicing upon his peace and quiet / Even to madness."

2 *Cymbeline* II.ii.iv. In the scene in question, the evil Jachimo spies on the lovely and virtuous Imogen while she is sleeping; he later describes the mole he has seen on her breast to her husband in order to convince him that she has been unfaithful.

streaming with the wind.[1] From the four following pieces, the pavilion might, not improperly, have been denominated the Temple of Venus. The first gave the goddess rising from the sea. The second, asleep; a copy of Titian. The third, accompanied with Juno and Minerva, appealing to Paris. The fourth, in Vulcan's net with Mars.[2]

However capital these might be, they were such as ladies are not accustomed to admire in the presence of gentlemen. There was, however, a superb sofa; on which a lady might sit down with all possible propriety. Miss Fluart did sit down; but the prospect from thence rather increased than diminished a little matter of confusion, which she felt on the view of the company she seemed to have got into.

She was rising to leave the pavilion, when his lordship, in the most gallant manner possible, claimed a fine, due he said, by the custom of the manor, from every lady who honoured that sofa by sitting upon it. His lordship meant simply a kiss, which I believe he would have taken respectfully enough, had Miss Fluart been passive; but, I know not why, the lady seemed to feel an alarm, for which probably she had no reason; and was intent only upon running away, whilst his lordship was intent only upon seizing his forfeit. A fine muslin apron was ill-treated upon this occasion; a handkerchief was ruffled, and some beautiful hair had strayed from its confinement, and wantoned upon its owner's polished neck. She got away, however, from this palace of painting, and its dangerous sofa.

"Upon my word, my dear Miss Fluart," said his lordship, getting down after her as fast as he was able, "you are quite a prude today.

---

1 In Greek mythology, Atalanta promised to marry any man who could outrun her in a footrace; if she won, her opponent would be put to death. She eventually lost to a young man who tossed golden apples in her path to distract her while she was running.

2 Four scenes from classical tales of Venus, all of them popular subjects for artists. The most famous painting of the birth of Venus is by Sandro Botticelli (1455-1510); it now hangs in the Uffizi Gallery in Florence. Titian (c.1488-1576) probably completed a sleeping Venus by the older painter Georgione (1477-1510) which is now owned by the Dresden art gallery. It is impossible to know if Bage had any specific images in mind for the other scenes. There are many paintings of the judgment of Paris, and while Venus trapped in bed with Mars by Vulcan's net was a less popular subject, there are numerous works showing Venus and Mars as lovers.

I thought you superior to the nonsense of your sex, the making such a rout about a kiss."

"A kiss! Lord bless me," said Miss Fluart, "I thought from the company your lordship had brought me into, and the mode of your attack, you had wanted to undress me."

Lord Grondale burst into an immoderate laugh, and declared it was the drollest idea in the world. Miss Fluart laughed too, and stopped to hear his lordship's exculpation; which she accepted without much difficulty, having a favour to ask, that could scarce be granted, except in his lordship's very best humour.

Whether a kiss refused is more a promoter of love, than a kiss granted, or whether there is any thing inflammatory in pulling a young lady's cloaths to pieces, it is certain Lord Grondale now found himself very seriously in love.

After they had walked together a little time, his lordship said, "My dear Miss Fluart, you are the most charming, the most irresistible girl in the universe. In pity to myself, I must avoid you, unless — unless I could learn to behold you with less affection, or inspire you with more."

"Oh dear!" returned Miss Fluart; "why, your lordship's love fit is come on again. I thought it had been gone for good. But I hope, as it has got a trick of coming and going, it will not incommode your lordship much."

"Miss Fluart," said the peer, gravely, "I could wish to be serious on a serious occasion. Can you, — a few minutes ?"

"Oh yes, certainly, upon a serious occasion. But I thought love had been a lighthearted airy thing, all joy and sport. If it is so solemn I shall not at all like it."

"Should you, Miss Fluart, if I should offer to lay my rank, my title, my person, and fortune at your feet — should you think it worth a serious consideration?"

"Why, my lord, these are very serious things, no doubt; one should like to tread upon some of them. But, indeed, my lord, you would lose too much, if I should accept your rash offer. How can your lordship expect greater felicity than with a person of Mrs. Stone's merit? In whom, you have one of the best of wives, without a wife's odious prerogative."

"You suppose, then, I have improper connexions with this lady?"

"I did not say any thing about improper connexions, my lord; they may be very proper, for any thing I know — for your lordship."

"That Mrs. Stone is any thing more to me than my housekeeper, who has any right to suppose?"

"Only that in the ordinary course of things, housekeepers do not preside at great tables; so one presumes there may be an extra measure of kindness."

"Mrs. Stone is a person of family under misfortunes."

"I adore your lordship's generosity and condescension; more especially as one of her misfortunes is loss of character in your lordship's service."

"I presume Miss Fluart is in this mistaken."

"Nothing more possible. It may be quite the contrary. She may have gained character for ought I know. But whether Mrs. Stone's be loss or gain, yours, my lord, will be certain loss by the change. Oh, but perhaps your lordship does not mean to change. Perhaps you intend this lady shall preserve the presidency."

"My dear Miss Fluart, how could such a notion enter your head?"

"By the eye, my lord. One looks at Miss Campinet. One reasons upon past events. One makes conjectures of the future."

"I look upon my daughter as a guest only. She will probably marry. Mrs. Stone is an excellent manager. I did not think it prudent to offend her, and disarrange my household."

"And I really think it would be better for your lordship to continue prudent. I am not qualified to represent Mrs. Stone."

"Thou art the oddest girl."

"Yes, I know it, and advise your lordship accordingly. A staid grave man like you, and a peer of the realm, to think of a giddy flirt like me. Consider, my lord, if you should repent, and I dare say you will, a wife is not so easy to get rid of."

"Oh, — I will run all risques."

"Then I shall take whole years of courtship; and after that you will have to fight half a hundred duels; for I have a little army of lovers, and a cross guardian who frights them away."

"Miss Fluart cannot want admirers; but may I presume to ask, is there one more favoured than the rest?"

"No, not one; unless they take it in their heads, as your lordship may do, that looking at them, and hearing them talk, is favour."

"And your heart, my dear Miss Fluart, is quite free?"

"Oh quite! and likely enough so to continue; for to tell you a secret, my lord, a fop is my aversion; and there are so few men, young men now, who are not fops."

"That is a most admirable sentiment; and manifests great solidity of mind. You must be Lady Grondale."

"I don't feel the necessity of it, my lord."

"But I do."

"It requires vast consideration; more than my poor brain will ever be able to bear. So take notice, my lord; and don't say hereafter, that I have encouraged your lordship in so silly a pursuit. Besides, what would Mrs. Stone say?"

"Be persuaded, my dear Miss Fluart; Mrs. Stone is nothing to me."

"No, — I cannot give your lordship credit for so much ingratitude. But let us talk no more of it till this day twelvemonth. Once a year is quite enough. And now, my lord, when do you expect your annual visitors?"

"Very soon; a month perhaps."

"It will be about the time my guardian requires my return; and as your visitors are all unaccompanied by ladies, I presume it would be your lordship's wish, Miss Campinet should be absent. Will you give her leave to accompany me to Falmouth during that time."

"Hermsprong will follow her there, perhaps."

"My lord, I do not pretend to take upon me to answer for things over which I have no controul. This I can assure your lordship, I have no cause to suppose he will; or that he would be well received by Caroline if he did."

"You will return with her?"

"If your lordship invites me."

"Be assured of that; and I shall commit Caroline to your care with perfect confidence; assured you will not permit her to stain the honour of a noble house, of which, I hope, you will soon be the greatest ornament."

"My lord, if you indulge in such suppositions, have the goodness to ascribe your disappointment, when it comes, to its true cause, the ardour of your imagination."

They were now at the hall door. His lordship took the way to his library, to indulge the ardour of his imagination. Miss Fluart to her friend's dressing-room; and shewing her habiliments to Miss Campinet, "See," said she, "your gallant father."

"Yes, I do see," answered Miss Campinet, gravely.

"Oh," said Miss Fluart, "and so do I, — an advertisement that you have imported a new cargo of wisdom. But don't unpack till my next folly. This I cannot repent of, since its consequence is so delightful. I have obtained your father's leave that you shall go with me to Falmouth, during the time his riots are to last."

"Indeed it is a most pleasing consequence to me. I did not dare to indulge myself in the hope it could ever be obtained."

"Acknowledge my powers of persuasion."

"Most willingly; though I must own, (looking at her little dis-arrangement), they appear to have been oddly exerted."

"Yes, I have been with your father in his pavilion."

"It is a favour, I believe, granted to very few."

"To none, my dear, but persons of merit. And indeed it ought to be confined to the deserving few, it is so charming. At one's entrance one is struck with a view of the most pleasing object in the world — one's own dear self, reflected from eight mirrors. Then there is such a variety of carving, and gilding, and painting. And the pictures, Caroline; as a connoisseur you must have admired them; but I, who have no pretensions, could hardly, for pity's sake, look upon such poor naked objects. My dear, for all they were god-desses, very few of them had any cloaths to their backs. So I sat down upon a sofa, and such a sofa, Caroline, it is certainly alive. Then comes my lord, and seizes me as a stray upon his premises. So I got up and ran away — not, as you see, without some little disarrangement. After all, it was only a kiss his lordship wanted, by way of fine; and I am sure he should have had a dozen, if he had bargained for them, as the price of your going to Falmouth."

"Thank you, my dear; but I don't advise you to be lavish of this sort of coin; lest you should diminish its value."

"Never fear."

CHAPTER XII

AT length Miss Campinet had finished her letter to Mrs. Garnet; not one with which she could be perfectly satisfied, but after many trials, as much so as any thing she could produce.

To MRS. GARNET.
Most revered madam,
The pleasure I promised myself from paying my duty to the only relation of my own sex, so respectable for her virtues and her misfortunes, so long unknown, and seeming to be sent me by the kind hand of Providence, was infinite; so is my disappointment. My father forbids my attentions, and never could he have more severe-ly taxed my obedience. Whether I owe implicit submission to a command I cannot help thinking as unjust as cruel, I am in doubt. Condescend, dear madam, to instruct, to guide me. If you say, Come, — although I should not chuse openly, and as it were in

defiance, against his direct commands, yet I would endeavour to find some more concealed mode of indulgence. To Mr. Hermsprong's house, indeed, I must not come, after the harsh things my father has said to me on the subject, and the injustice he has done me by ill-founded suspicions.

"Whatsoever may have been the prejudices which have produced a prohibition, to me so painful, I know them not. If I am acquainted with my own heart, it feels for you only the sincerest esteem and affection; and that I may one day be permitted to shew them, is the prayer of,

Dear madam,

Your most dutiful and affectionate,

CAROLINE CAMPINET

P.S. Since the above, I learn from Miss Fluart, that my father permits me to accompany her back to Falmouth, and stay there a month or two.

This letter cost Mrs. Garnet many tears. She answered thus:

My dear niece,

My disappointment also, is infinite. Much of my dependence, for the comfort of my declining years, I had placed in you; and much, the idea of being known and beloved by you, aided Mr. Hermsprong's persuasion to remove to my native place. Cruel Lord Grondale! but to you, my dear, I will not complain; nor can I encourage you to act openly or secretly, against your father's commands. I should only open a new source of calamity to myself, by involving you.

No, my dear, at present let things remain as they are; I will comfort myself with the knowledge, that you would treat me kindly, if you might.

From the hint you give me respecting Mr. Hermsprong, I comprehend what would probably be Lord Grondale's inference, were you to come here. Lord Grondale, indeed, mistakes when he supposes Mr. Hermsprong capable of any clandestine proceedings whatever. He is the warmest idolater of truth, the most determined enemy of duplicity I have ever known. Whenever my dearest niece changes her condition, the best possible wish for her is, that her choice may fall on such a man. To know, is to love him. That you may have an agreeable journey, prays

Your affectionate aunt,

M. GARNET

"To know, is to love him. Alas! then," said Miss Campinet, with a sigh, "I wish my father knew him, or I did not."

CHAPTER XIII

ALL men who chuse to govern by force or fraud, find suspicion a pretty constant attendant upon their machinations. Knaves are necessary for spies upon honest men; rogues, for spies upon knaves. As Lord Grondale travelled generally, like most great men, upon the high road of *je le veux — Telle est mon plaisir*[1] — it was expedient for him to know, if there were people about him, who durst assist his daughter in disobeying the orders he had honoured her with respecting Mrs. Garnet; for he took care these orders should be no secret. He well knew also by what little arts he could gain intelligence. In less than two hours after Miss Campinet's footman had brought the answer from Mrs. Garnet, it was known to Lord Grondale that he had been there, though nor exactly for what purpose.

This footman his lordship ordered into his presence, and said to him, with a brow of awful menace, "You have been at Hermsprong's this morning?"

"Ye — ye — yes," says the man, hesitatingly.

"What was your business?"

"To — to — carry a letter, my lord."

"To whom?"

"To Mrs. Garnet, my lord."

"From whom?"

At this question, it flashed into the mind of the man, that something was in agitation against the peace of his mistress; so he answered, "From Miss Fluart, my lord."

His lordship rang the bell.

"Let Miss Campinet know I desire to speak to her in the library."

She came.

---

1 I wish it; such is my pleasure. This phrase, associated with the arbitrary Bourbon monarchs, again links Grondale with *ancien régime* tyranny.

"Here," says his lordship, — "here is your footman tells me he has taken a letter from you to Hermsprong's this morning."

"No, my lord," says the man, "I did not say so; I said from Miss Fluart."

"And why did you say so, James?" said Miss Campinet; "I am sorry any motive should make you deviate from the truth. Yes, Sir, James took a letter from me to Mrs. Garnet."

"And brought you an answer?"

"Yes, Sir."

"I desire to see that answer."

"I hope you will not desire it, papa."

"Oh, then I guess the contents. Very agreeable it must be, to find myself the butt of the slander of an aunt who has disgraced her family, and of a daughter who probably will disgrace it very soon."

"Here is the letter, Sir: It is indeed a breach of confidence; but my aunt will pardon it, when she knows what a cruel inference it was intended to obviate."

Lord Grondale read the letter, and this was his comment, which he did not chuse to restrain, though Miss Campinet's servant was still in the room, waiting his lordship's commands.

"Yes — yes — cruel — cruel on both sides. On one, I endeavour to prevent an old woman from being a pander to her grand-niece; on the other, a young fool from running head long to drown herself in a sea of folly. But of this, Miss Campinet, and of your disobedience to my positive commands, another time. At present I have business."

Miss Campinet, I know not whether most terrified or disgusted, withdrew.

"Now Sir," said his lordship, "for you. I pay you your wages, not to tell me lies, but to obey my orders."

"I had no orders," replied James, rather sullenly.

"When I think it necessary to give general orders, I expect my whole family to observe them."

"My lord, I did not know I was your servant; I lived with Mrs. Merrick six years; when she died Miss Campinet retained me."

"Is it so, Sir? I shall take the liberty to discharge you notwithstanding. Make your bill, and carry it to Brown."

"I shall carry it to my mistress, my lord; I have nothing to do with Brown."

"Out of my sight, you insolent puppy."

"I never desire to come into it, to see the best young lady in the world, used worse than a negro."

James went immediately to Miss Campinet, who, smiling through her tears, thanked him for his good will, but reproved him for telling stories; and having made him a handsome present, said, when Lord Grondale's passion was over, she hoped she might obtain permission for him to return.

James answered, he should prefer her service to every other, if she was her own mistress; but he had rather work day-labour than live in a house where he must see his mistress ill used; "and curse me," added James, "if I will, whilst I have life and limb."

"My dear," said Miss Fluart, when James was gone, "while I have life and limb I will never be your mother-in-law;[1] and yet you do want some such body to take care of you."

"Indeed I am little able to take care of myself."

"Now, Caroline, keep the Vth commandment, and honour your father, — if you can. No doubt, it is a very pretty duty, when it is possible to be performed. Where it is not, children must do as well as they can. Dissimulation, I hope is not one of the seven deadly sins; for it is monstrous convenient on certain occasions."

"If it ever is a necessity, Maria, sure it is the most disagreeable one that can be imposed upon an ingenuous mind, and yet you, my dear, have taken it voluntarily upon you."

"No, indeed. It is a necessity imposed by friendship."

"My heart thanks you, Maria; but my judgment is against you."

"I am content with your heart, my dear."

"When Lord Grondale discovers the deceit, as soon he must, shall I be the better treated for it?"

"I think, my dear, I can make his lordship dance the dance of expectation a couple of years at least; and whilst I am mother expectant, I hope I may be able to dispose of my daughter in an honourable manner."

So saying, this mother expectant withdrew in a most matronly manner to her own dressing-room.

---

1 Stepmother.

CHAPTER XIV

IT was on the following morning Lord Grondale received a letter, whose contents were these:

My Lord,

A certain James Smith, hearing I wanted a servant, has offered himself, and might suit me, could I depend upon his veracity. Of this, I have certain reasons to doubt, and imagine your lordship can have no objection to satisfy me respecting this essential part of moral character.

Obedient to the forms of politeness, I am

Your lordship's obedient servant,

CHARLES HERMSPRONG

Mr. Hermsprong received this answer:

Sir,

I am ordered by Lord Grondale, my master, to let you know that he does not understand what right you can possibly have, to trouble him with your concerns; or why you should expect he would condescend to answer impertinence.

Your servant to command,

SAMUEL GRANT

P.S. Having obeyed my lord's orders, I hope you will not take it ill, for how could I do otherwise? But as to James Smith, he's as honest a fellow as ever broke bread; and as to his being a liar, I don't think he ever told a lie in his life, to do any body any harm; as for a joke I can't say.

On the next day Lord Grondale had the following.

Is it necessary to Lord Grondale that I should never know any thing personal of him, but his pride? Or hear, but of his meanness? If James Smith, as I learn from all but your lordship, he may, can be depended upon for veracity, for what virtues may we depend upon Lord Grondale? For justice? when he can discharge an honest servant for simple obedience to his duty. For kindness? when he can prohibit his angelic daughter from all correspondence with his own venerable aunt, than whom, a more respectable lady the house of Grondale never produced. Is a vindictive spirit so necessarily a constitutional ingredient of noble blood, that twenty-five years, many of them years of suffering, cannot dispose a noble mind to forgiveness? Or, is the marrying a man of honour and probity so deadly a sin, that no time, no misfortune can obliterate it? If Mrs. Garnet, not knowing its value, threw away any part of the pride she might be supposed to inherit, did she diminish any of your lordship's stock? But of what quality is that pride, which bends to mean suspicions, and still meaner actions? Could Lord Grondale demand to see Mrs. Garnet's letter to his daughter? Could he read it? And after reading it, could he stigmatize his venerable and virtuous aunt with the horrid appellation of pander to her niece? I have not the egregious folly to suppose that what I have written, will give your lordship any sentiments, but of indignation. You will be astonished at the presumption of an obscure person, daring thus to address a man of your rank and fortune. I claim, however, and shall always claim, the right to hear and see; the right to contemplate human actions; and the right to despise those I should blush to commit. Alas! the man who is destined to become your lordship's biographer, must find his motive in money; and matter of elogium in his invention. But even invention should have some foundation in truth; and there are some traits of your lordship, perhaps in the more early part of your life, which would puzzle a Jesuit to justify, or a poet to turn to praise.

CHARLES HERMSPRONG

This letter was delivered to Lord Grondale, soon after dinner, before the desert, the wine, or the ladies had left the table. His lordship was even in good humour, for he thought he had repelled Hermsprong's impertinence with proper dignity, and never did he contemplate himself with more complacency, than when he believed he had kept this dignity in high preservation.

Unless physiologists would do us the favour to explain what motions, solid or fluid, are going on within our microcosms,[1] when from a state of placidity we grow in an instant raving mad, I know not why we novel writers should be at the trouble of noting the outward marks with precision, such as redness of face, or lividity, with swearing, or gnashing of teeth. It is sufficient to say, that Lord Grondale, on reading this fatal epistle, lost at once his

---

1 "Jocularly used for 'body'" (OED).

patience, his paternity, and his politeness. He threw it at Miss Campinet, saying, "It is to you, Miss; to you, I am obliged for this insult; but, assure yourself, you shall repent it to the last hour of your life."

Mrs. Stone, alarmed at this sudden rage, rose and left the room; Miss Campinet took the letter, trembling, and read, or seemed to read; for indeed she was too much agitated to understand more of it, than that James Smith, probably, had reported the conversation in Lord Grondale's library, and that this was a letter of reproach.

His lordship in the meantime amused himself with pacing the room with angry steps, (strides they should have been, had the gout so pleased) and exclaiming, "The insolence of the scoundrel! to dare to insult a peer of the realm, a man of my rank and consequence! But I will rid the country of him if it costs me 5000l."

"I am sorry, papa," said Miss Campinet, when his lordship appeared to have recovered his powers of attention, "I am sorry, but I hope you do not impute to me things of which I have no knowledge."

"How do I know that? How could that insolent fellow know what passed betwixt you and I, but by your communication?"

"I had the mortification to receive your lordship's cruel reproof before James Smith."

"Are you sure you did not give him a hint how agreeable his tale would be at that damned house?"

"Is it possible my father can suppose it?"

"Easily. Duty and propriety are soon lost, when girls get love in their heads."

"I should be miserable under your displeasure, Sir, had I not the comfort of knowing it is unjust."

"A pretty sentimental flight that; and might have had something in it fifty years since. Daughters now, don't grow miserable for such slight causes as a father's displeasure."

"I beg leave, my lord, to retire."

When Miss Campinet had left the room, Miss Fluart said, "I must own, my lord, I thought you rather more of a philosopher."

"Who can philosophize under such damned provocation?"

"Why, not Lord Grondale; the more is the pity. And of what colour may this mighty provocation be?"

"Read that cursed letter."

"Why, I must own," said Miss Fluart, after reading, "it seems to be written with great force of contempt."

"It is beyond endurance."

"But after all, is there much wisdom in suffering one's tranquillity to lie at the mercy of every man who can call names?"

Lord Grondale answered this by a new execration of Mr. Hermsprong.

Miss Fluart continued. "Your lordship has surmised that this young man might presume to raise his aspiring hopes as high as Miss Campinet. This letter must convince you that he can have no such pretensions; for no man, not absolutely an idiot, could take so preposterous a method of courtship."

"My dear Miss Fluart," said his lordship, "you are my better angel; you tranquillize, you charm me. What are a thousand daughters compared with so sweet a friend?"

When Lord Grondale's fond fits came on, he had a way of making love with his hands; not very disagreeable perhaps to young ladies from young gentlemen; but very much so from old ones.

To divert this manual operation, Miss Fluart said, "I perceive, my lord, that Caroline puts you very oft, as Shakespeare says, into impatient thoughts; not, I believe from any fault of hers, but because your lordship's imagination has gone astray, and has fancied the things that are not.[1] Would it not conduce to your lordship's peace, therefore, to permit us to make our journey to Falmouth immediately?"

"If I could hope, my dear Miss Fluart, that a wish to return was included in the wish to go, I should be happy."

"There are three things I should like to give your lordship, — faith, hope, and charity; but I despair of two of them; and where they are not, I think hope should not be."[2]

"Oh! give me that," said his gallant lordship, "and I will take every thing with it you wish to give."

"Oh, but, my lord, matrimony follows hope; does it not?"

"I answer from your own Shakespeare, — 'tis a consummation devoutly to be wished.[3]

---

1   Shakespeare's Desdemona fears that she will "put my father in impatient thoughts / By being in his eye" (I.iii.239-40). Compare also *Julius Caesar* V.iii.67-69: "O hateful error, melancholy's child! / Why dost thou show, to the apt thoughts of men / The things that are not?"

2   Compare 1 Corinthians 13.13

3   *Hamlet* III.i.63-64.

"But that was death, not matrimony. Indeed they are both horrid things. I verily believe I shall never be able to endure the thoughts of either."

"You are a dear capricious girl," said his lordship; "I feel I can have no will but your's."

CHAPTER XV

ALL ladies know, — for all ladies read novels — how extremely dangerous the roads of England are for female travellers, who happen to be young and handsome. The banditti who infest these roads, are of the higher order of mortal men; such as seldom arrive at the gallows, whatsoever may be the pains they take to do it; lords, knights, and gentle squires. It is their cruel practice to seize, and carry away, *vi et armis*,[1] that is, in chaises drawn by flying horses, that distinguished part of the fair sex, called heroines; and confine them in very elegant prisons, where they sometimes cut off their heads; though more generally, the sweet creatures are, as in days of yore, under the protection of some magician, by whose potent aid they escape without much injury. Surely I did not consider these things, when I turned my two lovely girls into this wide world of danger, with no other guide but their own discretion; a quality indeed inherent in, and inseparable from, the dear sex; but deprived of a little of its original elasticity, by having passed through the hands of that great grandmother of us all, the too credulous Eve.

For this time, however, they escaped all danger; and were set down at the house of Mr. Sumelin, who received them with so little ceremony, that one might conclude he was really pleased to see them. But Mr. Sumelin's deficiency was amply supplied by his lady and eldest daughter, whose pleasure and happiness were so profuse, that the same wicked concluder might say, all the cordiality lay in the expression; and indeed there was so much of it, that Miss Charlotte Sumelin was under the necessity of speaking her welcome by the eye; an eye moistened by the tear of pure pleasure. Friendship, they say, is of two sorts, that which is to be felt, and that which is to be said. Both here, at the service of our fair travellers; and whilst

---

1 By force of arms.

they make their choice, and form their arrangements at Falmouth, let us leave them, to attend our principal personage, Lord Grondale, now unhappily tormented by two almost incompatible passions, love and revenge.

The business imposed upon his lordship by each of these was highly disagreeable. Mrs. Stone had been, and indeed still was, of great personal utility to his lordship, and it was a matter of infinite difficulty to inform her, that her services would in a short time be no longer required. It would, or should be, quite as difficult to put in execution against Mr. Hermsprong, laws which he had never broke. For against the laws of England, or any laws but of pride and arrogance, he had not offended; but, such is the constitution of great and noble minds, an affront is more unpardonable than a crime.

"Mrs. Stone," said his lordship, one day when he had gathered together a sufficient quantity of courage to begin the meditated battle, "I could have forgiven that scoundrel, Hermsprong, a thousand affronts, better than that cursed one of purchasing Bloomgrove. It has been long intended by me, as a sweet and honourable retreat for you, my dear Mrs. Stone, when (for the world is full of incidents) any thing should happen which might make it expedient for us to separate; for there I might hope still to be benefited by your wisdom and prudence."

Now certainly this was as civil and polite a speech as could well be found to begin a quarrel with; and yet there was in it something not quite agreeable to the lady. She had long desired to be Lady Grondale. It was a trifle on which she had set her heart; it was a reward she thought due to her merit and services; and she had contemplated the probability of it, arising from his lordship's increasing infirmities, till it had almost become certainty. It was not therefore without some degree of alarm, she had observed his lordship's behaviour, for she could not avoid seeing some tender looks at least, to Miss Fluart; it was preposterous indeed to think it could have any consequences; yet she did not like it. All the civility, therefore, of his lordship's speech, could not atone for the idea of separation which it inculcated, and which threw her into a momentary astonishment, not without some mixture of resentment. Recovering a little from this, she replied, "She wished she could compliment his lordship upon his sincerity, as well as his politeness."

"How is that, madam."

"Deeds, my lord, are a better proof of sincerity than words. Had my wisdom and prudence been of value to your lordship, you would have taken the obvious means to make them your own for life."

"Means may be obvious, madam, that may not be proper."

"Your lordship must do as you please, and I as I can. If you are not satisfied with my care and attention —"

"Very much so, Mrs. Stone; but to tell you the truth, I am disposed to marry. My daughter has offended me; she has got that Hermsprong in her head. To disinherit her requires some troublesome legal operations. A shorter and pleasanter way would be to give her a brother. I cannot expect this of you, Mrs. Stone."

"A son of your own, my lord?" said the lady, with an arch grin.

"Why not, madam? I know of no physical impossibility."

"Nor I of any physical probability. But your lordship may have a son for all that, if you marry prudently. May I be permitted to ask if your lordship has fixed upon the lady?"

"Miss Fluart."

"Miss Fluart!" echoed Mrs. Stone. But the air and tone with which she said them is not for my pen to describe.

"Miss Fluart!" she repeated after a pause.

"What is there incongruous in this?" his lordship asked.

"Oh nothing, nothing! the congruity will be prodigious. Ages so near; tempers so alike; the lady so willing to make the most of her charms. O yes! you will have a son."

"When you are in the humour to make black white, and a devil of an angel, madam, I know no person with finer powers; but at present I beg you will not put them to the proof."

"I must, however, take the liberty to tell your lordship that this affair is as dishonourable with respect to me, as it is ridiculous with regard to yourself; and take my word for it, my lord, the repentance will be bitter."

With this prophecy Mrs. Stone flew out of the apartment.

CHAPTER XVI

OVID de amore[1] informs us, and I inform my fair readers, that lovers may be divided scientifically into three classes; the naturals, the non-naturals, and the mixt. The first are those who think only

---

1 Ovid's first work, *Amores*, was a collection of love lyrics, but he does not
   divide lovers into three classes in this quasi-scientific manner, which
   seems to owe as much to Linnaeus as to classical poetry.

of the persons of their mistresses, the second of their purses, the last of both; but of such a variety of proportions, with adjuncts and conjuncts; the genera, the orders, the species run into one another so unlike any other earthly beings, that I fear it will take me years to arrange and describe them, so as the British fair may reap the full harvest of my labours.

Had my system been now compleat, of what advantage might it not have been to my two lovely girls at Falmouth; whose arrival caused as great a conflux of beaux as a race ball. Never were libations to Cornish divinities more full and frequent. Man, we know, is a plant, and is thought by many, something more. It is because the theologians and philosophers have not agreed about this something more, that botanists have never been able to compleat their classifications; so Miss Campinet, for want of science, shrunk, like the sensitive plant,[1] from the touch, and as much as possible from the looks of all her votaries, and wearied them out by a silent but steady reserve.

All but Sir Philip Chestrum, a gentleman of sufficient consequence to induce us to say something of his lineage and something of himself.

His father was a citizen of London, where, till the decline of life he lived unmarried, intent only upon acquiring fortune. Yet he was a reasonable man; he said to himself "I will stop at a quarter million; and then I will enjoy myself." This laudable resolution he kept; and purchasing an estate in Cornwall, retired to it for enjoyment. He became sheriff, and afterwards was created a baronet, for some of those services for which baronets and greater than baronets are now created. Notwithstanding all this, he grew weary of rural tranquillity, and was obliged to marry, to prevent excess of ease. In this he succeeded well; for he married Miss Raioule, a maiden lady, not much more than forty; of a very ancient family, with small fortune, but great dignity of thought, and energy of speech. This lady bore Sir Philip one child only, a son; but unaccustomed to the business, some part of it seemed imperfectly per-

---

1   Any of several types of plant with leaves that fold in on themselves when touched. Bage is referring to the Linnaean system of plant classification throughout this passage; developed by the Swedish botanist Carl Linnaeus (1707-78), it helped provide a more scientific basis for botanical observations.

formed; for the child was feeble, small, and half animated. He grew, indeed, to the height of five English feet, but not equally. His legs bore too large a proportion to his body. In short, he might resemble that important personage, who, Sir John Falstaff said, looked like a man made after supper of a cheese paring.[1]

Sir Philip died five years after the birth of his heir, leaving him to fight his way against death and the faculty;[2] and his lady to fight hers against enemies almost as hostile; against the corruptions of uncontrouled affluence; and against a host of lovers, all of the class of the non-naturals. So far neither had yielded; the lady was supposed to have obtained a solid victory; for she had past her twelfth lustrum; for poor Sir Philip, he was doomed to war eternal.

In this young gentleman's case, there was no occasion to consider the arguments for public and private education; his constitution and his mother, both determined for the latter; but the office of preceptor was almost a sinecure, for dear Sir Philip was too weak for study and never stood in the least need of correction. When, therefore, he arrived at the age of freedom, he found himself possessed of great wealth, without the least inclination to spend it; of unbounded pride, without the necessary judgment to correct it; of literature, not quite none; and of the smallest possible quantity of human kindness. With gentlemen he had no commerce; was well received by mothers and aunts; but by daughters and nieces with the glance of scorn, or the ill concealed titter of contempt.

CHAPTER XVII

MISS CAMPINET was the first young lady he had seen, on whom, unawed by the fear of ridicule, he durst bestow his affections. Sweetness of temper, attention to please, unwillingness to mortify, were habits of this young lady's mind; and she could not suddenly break them, even for Sir Philip. Several times he had looked at her with all the love his eyes were capable of expressing, and once or twice had ventured on broken hints to express his admiration. As often he had led her to her carriage, and once was her partner at an assembly, without giving herself airs of derision. To such fascinating sweet-

---

1   *2 Henry IV*, III.ii.250-51.
2   That is, the medical faculty; doctors.

nesses Sir Philip had been little accustomed; the divinity of Grondale stole his heart, like a thief in the night;[1] and by her gentle demeanour at length emboldened him to speak.

It was on a tea visit to Mrs. Sumelin. Miss Campinet had declined the card table; and Sir Philip having cut out, placed himself by her. He did not immediately speak, because it came into his head, that now was the time to say something; something that should express his affection; and also impress Miss Campinet with a high idea of himself. The young lady, attentive to her knotting, gave him what time he pleased. At length he opened with, "I think, Miss, you are the most agreeable young lady I ever saw in my life."

"I thank you for your good opinion, Sir Philip," said Miss Campinet, without taking her eyes from her work.

"Many young ladies," the baronet continued, "use me with ill manners. I cannot tell why; for if I am not so handsome as some are, there is nothing about me that's frightful; and they ought to consider my birth and family. But most of the young ladies hereabout are such scornful giggling creatures; and I can't tell for what neither. I should blush to make a Lady Chestrum of any of them. My family, Miss Campinet, is very great and noble by my mother's side. She was a Raioule, a great name in English history. I have some thoughts of changing my name to it, by act of parliament; for Chestrum is but an odd sort of name. Beside, my father was in trade once, and his title a new one; so people looking more at his side than my mother's, I don't get so much respect on account of my family as is my due. Should not you like Raioule better than Chestrum, Miss Campinet?"

"It is softer," the lady replied; "it has more vowels in it."

"I knew you would like it best, for you have the finest taste. Pray, Miss Campinet, how far do you count?"

"Twenty," answered Miss Campinet, after a pause of a few moments, till she conceived the meaning of the question.

"Twenty! twenty descents you mean from the first stock. But to what king's reign? Lady Chestrum goes up by her father to Richard the First."[2]

---

1 Compare 1 Thessalonians 5:2 and 2 Peter 3:10.
2 Richard the First of England, also called Richard the Lionhearted, reigned from 1189-99. "The first stock" to which Sir Philip refers would be the first member of the family to establish a name or a fortune for himself and the number of "descents" would be the number of holders of the family lands or titles.

"I fancy," said Miss Campinet, "my father goes up to Noah, if not to Adam."

"Now, that's turning it into a joke, and its no joke I assure you. People of family, now there are so many levellers about, ought to be more careful than ever. Lady Chestrum says, that now a days it is the only thing one can value oneself upon; for as to money, that is every body's that can get it."

"So I think is title."

"But it is not every scrub that can get it."

"Not quite."

"To be sure, it is a monstrous shame to see new families spring up so like mushrooms."

"They will be old in time."

"But then, how did they get their honours? Not in fields of battle, like the Raioules."

"Don't you think it as honourable to get money as to kill men?"

"No, — not in an honourable way; in war and battle. If it is, why do histories talk about Cæsar and Alexander, and them?"[1]

"For no good reason, indeed, that I know of."

"But it is a poor pride that's founded upon money."

"I scarcely know a pride that is not poor. Is it not Solomon who says, pride was not made for man?"[2]

"For who then?"

---

1   Several radical writers attacked the celebration of ancient lineages and of military leaders in history. Thomas Paine, for example, mocked claims of Norman descent (such as Sir Philip is making here) in *Common Sense* (1776): "A French bastard landing with an armed banditti, and establishing himself king of England against the consent of the natives, is in plain terms a very paltry rascally original — It certainly hath no divinity in it" (OUP 1995, 16). In *Caleb Williams*, William Godwin features a scene in which Caleb challenges the haughty Falkland, who is obsessed with reputation and personal glory, to explain why Alexander is called "the Great" when he caused so much death and destruction.

2   Although the Book of Proverbs, most of which is attributed to Solomon, includes many injunctions against pride (see, for example Proverbs 16:5: "Every one *that is* proud in heart *is* an abomination to the *LORD*"), this quotation in fact comes from Ecclesiasticus (10:18), one of the books of the Apocrypha. The author of that book names himself as Jesus, son of Sirach (50:27). Peacocks, of course, are proverbial for their pride.

"Peacocks, probably."

"But will women let them have it?"

This was so good a conceit, that it took Sir Philip two minutes to laugh at it. Miss Campinet then resumed.

"I can readily allow, Sir Philip, that women are as proud as men; but I think men disgrace themselves by being proud of the same silly things. Men may be poets, philosophers, artists; every thing that adorns or improves society. Man may be liberal, benevolent; his pride, if he must have pride, should be founded on merit; and that merit should be his own."

"As if any thing could be more a man's own than what his father leaves him. As to your philosophy, and all that, a gentleman may either have it, or not have it; it makes no difference. He is neither more nor less a gentleman. Whether I read Greek and Latin or not, I am the same man, am I not? and born of the same father and mother?"

"The latter, Sir Philip, no doubt; and will be as well received at the herald's office."

"Yes, and at court too, Miss Campinet; I have been amongst the courtiers, I assure you; but they never asked after my learning; but whether I was church and king; and if I had any boroughs?[1] And why not? Every man to his trade. I should have been amongst them before now, for my talents lie that way; but Lady Chestrum thinks I have not strength to bear the fatigues of government."

"That is great pity indeed."

"Yes, is it not? But you are the most kindly hearted young lady that ever I saw. I could not help loving you, if I would. Now I'll tell you a secret. Lady Chestrum and I don't always hit it; she has such odd fancies. Would you believe it? she is every now and then for hearing me my catechism. I take physic to please her twice a week; and if I have not stools enough, I must have another dose. I eat just what she would have me; I dress just as she would have me; and yet she scolds. I assure you I am forced to keep cordials in my closet, to raise my spirits; and they will hardly do sometimes. I sleep very ill; and if I wake in the night, and find myself all alone, I feel so uncomfortable. Now, pray tell me, Miss Campinet, don't you think I had better marry?"

"It is not my business to think for Sir Philip Chestrum."

---

1 See note 1, page 72.

"I awake," continued the baronet, "sometimes all in a sweat for fear; and say my prayers till my teeth chatter in my head. Now, if I found a sweet pretty young lady, such an one as I know who, by my side, it would be quite another thing, don't you think it would, Miss Campinet?"

Miss Campinet was considering whether she should laugh or be angry. Sir Philip went on.

"To be sure, a man of my family and fortune might marry when he pleased, and pick the world through almost. But there's very few, very few indeed, Miss Campinet, that would suit me. I assure you, I have a refined taste. She who wins my heart must have beauty and elegance. I should like a good fortune too, for wives now a days bring expences. Lady Chestrum insists upon family. Now, pray, Miss Campinet, do you know ever a young lady who would suit me?"

"You seem to have a full sense of your own merits, Sir Philip; and as you rate them, I really do not know any woman who can deserve you."

"Now I do know one. Shall I shew you her picture?"

"I have no great curiosity, Sir Philip."

"Oh — but I promise you, you will like her; see now if you don't." And the gallant Sir Philip held a pocket mirror to her eyes. "I need not tell her name, need I, Miss Campinet?"

Miss Campinet was on the point of answering with uncommon asperity, when a bustle at one of the card tables prevented her. Sir Philip was called upon to play.

"I shall play so well now," said he: "you cannot think, Miss Campinet, how happy you have made me."

In this Sir Philip was perfectly right; Miss Campinet could not think what she had said or done to make him happy; but formed the instant resolution, — could Miss Campinet have so little benevolence? — not to be so lavish of her power in future, if she could find out in what it consisted.

CHAPTER XVIII

ONE morning, at breakfast, Mr. Sumelin had the misfortune to scald his fingers, simply for the common cause of such accidents, doing one thing, and thinking of another. Mrs. Sumelin, as is usual in these small domestic cases, began to scold.

"If I had broke the cup, madam," Mr. Sumelin answered, "it would have been a crime inexpiable, but by a new set. This is, I suppose, a regular tax upon husbands; I submit to it; but I really cannot submit to the not being allowed to scald my own fingers."

"It was so thoughtless, Mr. Sumelin," said his lady.

"Was it not rather too much thought?" asked Miss Fluart.

"It's all one," Mrs. Sumelin answered.

"To the tea cup," said the husband, "or to things which want understanding."

"I suppose that means that I want understanding," said the lady.

"There is very extraordinary news from Constantinople, my dear," said the banker; "fifty of the grand Signior's[1] wives were brought to bed in one night."

"Fifty! Mr. Sumelin," said the astonished lady.

"Fifty," replied the banker.

"Wives, papa?" asked Miss Sumelin.

"No — not precisely what we should call wives in England; but something very like them. You must know, the Grand Signior buys his ladies; and for the honour of your sex, I must tell you, that some of them have cost him 1000l. English money; whilst a man who sells for 100l. must be extraordinary. I suppose his highness's female stock may be rated at 100,000l. so you see, my dear (to Mrs. Sumelin) it is not the number which is the wonder, but the all of one night. His sublime greatness had a small fit of astonishment about it, and sent for the head of the Kislar Aga, to make it more comprehensible. This is the chief of the black monsters, appointed to preserve the chastity of the Seraglio; whose head, however, for they had brought it without its body, could give the sultan no possible information. His sublimity assembled an extraordinary divan; and this divan, judging only by their own experience, were upon the point of giving an opinion very unfavourable to the poor women, when the mufti rose, and made an oration of twenty-five minutes, in that silent country, one of the longest ever known. The purport of it, was to shew, that the power of the prophet of God was not limited to so small exertions. If God pleased, all the women in the world might be brought to bed in one night; and perhaps the prophet might intend to reward the piety of our most august monarch, king of the kings of the earth, by this display of his unbounded liberality. What do you think of it, my dear?"

---

1 The grand Signior was a title of the Ottoman emperor; a "divan" was the privy council formed to advise the sultan on matters of state; a mufti is a religious leader.

"To be sure, Mr. Sumelin, if it be true, its rather odd."

"One meets with odd things every day. A most extraordinary odd gentleman has been with me this morning; Mr. Hermsprong; he requested I would pay his compliments to Miss Campinet, and Miss Fluart, and ask permission to pay his respects; though he could not, he said, presume for that favour on any claim of his own."

"Oh dear!" said Miss Campinet.

"But he imagined Miss Campinet would be pleased to hear of the health of Mrs. Garnet."

"Indeed I shall," Miss Campinet answered.

"It is very true," said Miss Fluart, "that the gentleman never danced with Miss Campinet at a ball, nor has any other of the usual claims to her acquaintance; saving one's life, indeed, may be something; but then it was an unavoidable accident; he could not help it; and so it is well paid by a little private gratitude. But, pray, Sir, why do you give Mr. Hermsprong the character of odd and extraordinary?"

"Simply, because one does not every day see such an one. Is it not extraordinary, that a gentleman should think of nothing, when he speaks, but truth? and are not his sentiments almost as singular as just? Then he is engaged in the oddest business."

"Is that a secret business?" Miss Fluart asked.

"Many a gentleman would be ashamed of it," the banker answered. "It is the condescending to notice poor objects in distress, and taking the trouble to relieve them. As I am his banker, I have the honour to know several of these objects."

"Sir," said Miss Fluart, "I had before lost half my heart; if I hear more, the whole is in danger."

"Yea, Maria," said Mr. Sumelin; "but these objects are all females."

"Indeed!" said Miss Fluart; "that circumstance may alter the nature of the benevolence. What sort of females, Sir?"

"Sailors' wives — not very tempting, I must own, — one excepted, whom I once saw; a foreigner, young, beautiful, and unfortunate. But her history you must learn from him. I am unacquainted with it."

"And when," Miss Fluart asked, "will this unpresuming gentleman presume to wait upon us?"

"He asked when you would be most at leisure? I answered, at dinner."

"But," says he, "I so seldom dine."

"Dine!" says I, "zounds! you eat I suppose."

"Copiously," he answered; "but betwixt eating and dining there is such a difference."

"What difference?" I asked.

"An English dinner," he answered, "is so melancholy."

"Melancholy! really" said I, "I never before heard the word so applied."

"If to dine," he answered, "were only to eat, twenty minutes would be ample. You sit usually a couple of hours; and you talk, and call it conversation. You make learned remarks on winds and weather; on roads; on dearness of provisions; and your essays on cookery are amazingly edifying. Not much less so are your histories of your catarrhs and tooth-achs. Not content with this mass of amusement, you continue your beneficence to that unfortunate viscus, the stomach, under the name of dessert, till it almost faints under the obligation. No matter; spur it on with wine. It is said, that physicians have much increased in your country; one great reason may be, because you dine."

"Then I must not presume," said I, "to ask you to dinner?"

"Yes," he answered, "you may. I have some reason to suspect the human intellect at your table in higher preservation. At least, I can feast my eyes."

"So at three today you may expect him."

CHAPTER XIX

AT three, then, Mr. Hermsprong entered the dining apartment. His figure was interesting. Not quite made indeed after the model of the Apollo, in the Belvidere, but full as pleasing perhaps except to persons steeped in virtu.[1] But he had faults; one for which it would be difficult to procure pardon in the court of politeness. It

---

1 The Apollo Belvedere, a statue now in the Vatican museums, is a Roman copy of a lost Greek original. It was seen, in the eighteenth century, as a model of masculine beauty and, more generally, as a work exemplifying the glories of classical art. The term "virtu" was used to describe a refined taste, usually shaped by classical or Italian culture; by the end of the century, it was often employed mockingly, as it is here, to imply self-conscious or foolishly pretentious refinement.

was a sort of secret contempt for politeness itself; or rather for its forms; forms so numerous and trifling, that they destroyed its essence. It was quite disagreeable to Mrs. Sumelin and Miss Harriet, to see them, that is to say, the bows, the smiles, and the graces, hurried over to-day, in order to address himself more particularly to Miss Campinet, for whom he had brought a letter from Mrs. Garnet.

During dinner, Mrs. Sumelin asked a question or two, which put Mr. Sumelin in mind of a certain malady with which his lady was afflicted, that of desiring to know other people's concerns. He was afraid lest the inquisition itself, or the mode of it, might not be to the taste of his guest; and therefore very bluntly and honestly asked Mr. Hermsprong's pardon before hand, for any offence which might be committed, by asking impertinent questions.

"Impertinence cannot be intended," Mr. Hermsprong replied; "conversation, to be agreeable, must have a certain degree of freedom. Grant me the liberty of not replying to questions I chuse not to answer; and ask what you please."

"Pray, Sir," said Mrs. Sumelin, "do you design to settle in England?"

"That, madam, depends on certain circumstances," Mr. Hermsprong replied.

"Pray, may one be so free as to ask the nature of those circumstances?"

"Certainly, madam; and it is one of those questions I take the liberty of not answering."

"Perhaps," said Miss Sumelin, "the gentleman comes a courting, and does not know yet if he shall succeed."

"I like the perhapses of young ladies, they are so pretty and interesting. But no, madam; I did not come to England to court; perhaps I have found the disposition since my arrival."

There was a small tinge of red on Mr. Hermsprong's cheeks, as he said this. He had thrown a wandering and rapid glance amongst the other young ladies, who could never precisely determine at whom it was directed.

"You call yourself American?" said Mr. Sumelin.

"By birth; but of European parents."

"Which country, Sir, had the honour of your education?"

"That honour, Sir, is due to savage America. I left it only four years since. Since when I have seen many countries."

"And which do you like best?"

"All have something to like, and something to dislike."

"Is there no one to which you would give a general preference?"

"If you are a true Englishman, you will be angry that I do not, without hesitation, answer England. But I have not yet known it sufficiently. Hitherto, I have only travelled; and I have observed, that one lives well every where, if one has money, and ill, if one has not. Every where, with money, one gets friends. Every where they give us good dinners, as you do to-day. Every where one may fall in love; and every where be happy, if one knows how."

"Have you in any country seen happiness more diffused than in England?"

"If by happiness you mean money, I think not."

"Money produces the conveniencies of life, and its comforts; these produce happiness."

"It produces also the pride, the vanity, the parade of life; and these, if I mistake not, produce in their consequences, a tolerable quantity of the anxieties; and anxiety is not happiness."

"To depreciate money, is to depreciate commerce, its mother; this the English will not bear."

"I know it well; but I suppose there may be too much even of good things."

"We say, the more commerce, the more property."

"This is changing the idea. Individual happiness was the question; not national prosperity. Your debts and other blessings flowing from the best of all possible governments,[1] impose upon you the necessity of being the first workshop of the world. You labour incessantly for happiness. If you find it, it is well. But savages, like me, have no idea of the happiness of incessant labour."

"Of such savages as you I have no knowledge; those I do know, have not seemed too abundant in felicity."

"It is from the habits of civilized life, as you call it, that you have derived this opinion. They have notwithstanding no inconsiderable portion of positive happiness; and a still greater of what may be called negative; they want the far greater part of your moral causes of misery."

"And one physical — food."

"There are improvident characters among them; and the number is not diminished by your rum bottles; but they have in gener-

---

1 Another allusion to *Candide*'s "best of all possible worlds"; see note 1, page 73.

al enough, though not what you would call plenty. No — what they most fail in, is intellectual pleasure. To enlarge their felicity, I ask not your gaudy habiliments, to puff them up with the silliest of all the vanities; I ask not your glittering equipages, to give them at once pride and debility. Keep your palaces and pomp. Keep your splendid abundance, and its diseases. Give them simple plenty, strength, and health. Give them to multiply the objects of their reflection; and to extend the powers of their mind. That, to me, would seem the happiest state of society in which all its members had the power, so to alternate the employments of the mind and body, that the operations of each might be enjoyment. So would the rich man's curse be avoided, that of not knowing what to do with himself; and the poor man's also, that of knowing it but too well."

"And where is this state of society to be found?"

"Alas! no where, — not even in America."

"Not *even* in America! As you lay the emphasis, you seem to think America approaches nearest your state of society."

"I do. Yet still at an immense distance from the ultimatum."

"Perhaps it is impracticable?"

"I fear it is. Manners must change much; and governments more. The first is possible; for manners are addicted to change. The latter is hopeless. Governments do not change; at least for the better."

"There are who say, that of America is excellent. There are who say it is superiour to ours."

"That you cannot believe."

"Not easily."

"You are a good Englishman. But I believe, indeed, their government would not do for you."

"Why so, if it is good."

"A simple government, without money to buy men, is little adapted to a people who will do nothing till they are bought."

"You suppose, then, we have no patriotism."

"Which of your patriots would prefer a civic crown, to a bank note, or a purse of guineas?"

"You are severe upon us."

"No, — it is simple observation. I call you no names; I lay no crimes to your charge. I impute to you nothing worse than the having followed the usual course of things. You are rich; and addicted to pleasure, to luxury. It is a consequence that has always followed wealth; and a consequence of this addiction is political carelessness; the immediate precursor of political corruption. But, Mr. Sumelin, I understand it is not the custom here to talk upon politics before ladies. I am told it is a breach of politeness."

"Is it not your opinion, also, Sir," Miss Fluart asked, "that the subject is improper for our sex?"

"I think no subject improper for ladies, which ladies are qualified to discuss; nor any subject they would not be qualified to discuss, if their fathers first, and then themselves, so pleased."

"You do not then," said Miss Fluart, "approve our mode of education?"

"Not quite."

"Faith, nor I neither," said Sumelin. "Women have too much liberty."

"I, on the contrary, think they have too little."

"Too little," exclaimed the banker. "English women too little liberty!"

"Well, then," Hermsprong replied, "they have too much."

"Yes," Sumelin answered, "that is indubitable to me. But, you, — is it the love of paradox which makes you maintain contrary propositions?"

"Perhaps," Mr. Hermsprong returned, "we may be reconciled, if, as I suspect, you mean that English young ladies of a certain age and rank have too much liberty of person. This I am ready to grant you, *pro gratia*;[1] if you will have the goodness to allow they have too little liberty of mind."

"To so courteous an antagonist," said Sumelin, "I would allow all I could; but this — this is really too much. And, pray, Sir, when they carry their pretty persons to routs and Ranelaghs, balls and masquerades, do they not carry their minds with them?"[2]

"Yes," Mr. Hermsprong answered, — "such as they have; minds imprisoned, — which, instead of ranging the worlds of physics and

---

1 Freely. The idea that fashionable amusements were turning women into frivolous pleasure-seekers was one that most reformers, whether evangelicals such as Hannah More or radicals such as Mary Wollstonecraft, could agree upon.

2 Routs were fashionable parties and Ranelagh was a place of entertainment in Chelsea, containing pleasure gardens and a large rotunda; it was a site for concerts, masquerades, and other amusements.

metaphysics, are confined to the ideas of these routs and Ranelaghs, with their adjuncts of cards, dress, and scan — I beg pardon — I mean criticism."

"And are women such things?" asked Miss Campinet.

"Some women are such things, Miss Campinet," answered Hermsprong. "Some are what they ought to be."

"There are very few of this latter description though," said Miss Fluart archly. "Did you ever see two?"

"Not two at a time, perhaps — out of this company."

"I declare," said Miss Fluart, "I will have nothing to do with your insidious exceptions."

"Be not angry with me, my dear Miss Fluart; be women what they may, — I am destined to be an adorer. Be angry at Mr. Sumelin here, the indiscriminating Mr. Sumelin. Be angry at Mrs. Wolstonecraft, who has lately abused the dear sex, through two octavo volumes. Who affirms that the mode of their education turns the energies of their minds on trifles."[1]

"Energies!" says Sumelin, with a certain tone.

"Energies," firmly repeated Hermsprong. "Who has presumed to say," he continued, "that the homage men pay to youth and beauty is insidious; that women for the sake of this evanescent, this pitiful dominion, permit themselves to be persuaded, that their highest glory is to submit to this inferiority of character, and become the mere plaything of man. Can this be so?"

"Now, the devil take me," said Sumelin, "if I know what either you or this Mrs. Wolstonecraft would be at. But this I know, that the influence of women is too great; that it has increased; is increasing; and ought to be diminished."[2]

"Well, then," Mr. Hermsprong answered, "let it be diminished on the side of —charms; and let its future increase be on the side of mind."

---

1   *A Vindication of the Rights of Woman* (1792) was published in one volume, which Wollstonecraft intended to follow with a second, but she never had an opportunity to write it. Her notes for the unwritten volume have been published in her collected works, edited by Janet Todd and Marilyn Butler (7 volumes, 1989).

2   An allusion to what was then a famous Parliamentary motion about the power of the Crown, made by John Dunning (1731-83) on 6 April 1780; see Namier and Brook, eds., *The History of Parliament: The House of Commons*. 3 vols. London, 1964, 2:368.

"To what purpose?" the banker asked, "To invade the province of men? Weaker bodies, you will allow, nature has given them, if not weaker minds."

"Whatsoever may be the designs of nature, respecting the sex, be her designs fulfilled. If she gave this bodily weakness, should education be brought in to increase it? But it is for mind I most contend; and if 'a firm mind in a firm body,[1] be supposed the best prayer of man to the gods, why not of women? Would they be worse mothers for it? or more helpless widows?"[2]

"No," said Sumelin; "but they would be less charming figures."

"Whilst they think of their charming figures, as much as you suppose them to do, Mrs. Wolstonecraft must write in vain."

"And when," the banker asked, "will they think less of them?"

"When," answered Hermsprong, "they are better taught."

"And when will that be?" again asked Sumelin.

"I know not," his opponent returned. "The change, if change there can be, must begin with men. Lovers must mix a little more wisdom with their adorations. Parents, in their modes of education, must make less distinction of sex."

"Mr. Hermsprong," said Sumelin, "this is pretty, and sentimental, but it cometh not of knowledge. There are two things co-existent with women, and co-eternal; admiration of fineries and of themselves. Eve, the hour of her birth, saw herself in the lake, and found herself more fair, more amiably fair, than her dear Adam; and her dear daughters will do the same, as long as clear water and looking-glasses exist."[3]

"With all imaginable deference to Milton's authority and yours, Mr. Sumelin, I must be of opinion, that women would leave the lesser vanities, and learn lessons of wisdom, if men would teach them; and in particular, this, that more permanent and more

---

1   More usually "a sound mind in a sound body"; Juvenal, *Satire X*, 356.

2   Compare Wollstonecraft, who, in *A Vindication of the Rights of Woman*, criticizes men for thinking that women should be "guarded from care, and all the rough toils that dignify the mind" and argues that better education will make "more observant daughters, more affectionate sisters, more faithful wives, more reasonable mothers — in a word, better citizens" (OUP 1994, 230-31).

3   In *Paradise Lost*, Eve becomes enthralled by her own beauty when, after she first awakens, she sees her reflection in a pool.

cordial happiness might be produced to both the sexes, if the aims of woman were rather to obtain the esteem of men, than that passionate, but transient affection, usually called love."

"Transient!" exclaimed Miss Fluart; "then inconstancy, I suppose, is one of the virtues of man."

"No, Miss Fluart, nor of woman; but is it very common for husbands to preserve the ardor of lovers?"

"No, indeed!" said Mrs. Sumelin.

"Nor can it be, madam, how much soever the ladies may wish and expect it. I suppose it is one of nature's positive laws, that even diamond rings worn a while, cease to raise that glow in a lady's bosom, which first possession excited."

"I think," said Mrs. Sumelin, "it is not very polite to compare a lady to a diamond ring."

"Would a rose, dear madam, be more to your taste? but the most fragrant odour of that, you know, is on the first application."

"You might compare us to better things, I think," Mrs. Sumelin said, "than either roses or diamonds."

"To angels? Unfortunately I know nothing of angels; and I make it a rule, not to talk of what I am wholly ignorant."

This produced a toss from Mrs. Sumelin, a general smile, but no answer; till Miss Campinet, fearing the subject might be dropped, said, "You seem to wish a considerable change in women, Sir; what would you have them be?"

"Very much like Miss Campinet; sensible, just, beneficent."

"Would not you have them like me too?" Miss Fluart asked. "Am not I also a model of perfection?"

"I do not know perfection."

"Not even in Miss Campinet?"

"Not even in Miss Campinet."

"It is but few hours since I was told, I had not a fault."

"And did you believe it?"

"No doubt."

"I have been often told, that in very, very civilized countries no man could hold up the mirror of truth to a lady's face, without ill manners. I came to try."

"And have you succeeded?"

"Have I been guilty of ill manners?"

"Why no — not violently. Still less can you be accused of politeness."

"Alas! I am distracted betwixt truth and politeness. What would I not give they were one and indivisible."

"It would be a great change indeed," said Mr. Sumelin. "But do you think women would be gainers by it?"

"I know not what ladies call gain. They would be beings of reason."

"And dare you," says Miss Fluart, "dare you look a lady in the face, and tell her she is not a being of reason?"

"When I look Miss Fluart in the face, I do not think of reason."

"Of what then?"

"Of beauty and good humour?"

"This will not do. I shall not be so bribed. It is the cause of my sex. Say again, if you dare, that women are not beings of reason."

"Did I say so?"

"Yes, by implication."

"I see my error. My rash and daring tongue is corrected by my eyes. Your pardon."

"So good a cause," cried Sumelin, "so cowardly given up."

"I suspect the cause is not good. We are, like unhallowed satyrists, involving in one promiscuous censure all the fair daughters of men. Let us be more just, Mr. Sumelin, they are our equals in understanding, our superiors in virtue. They have foibles where men have faults, and faults where men have crimes. In the gaiety of conversation it may be allowed, at least it will be assumed, to put the whole for a part, perhaps a small part; but it would be wise in man, when he makes the error of woman his contemplation, not to forget his own."

In saying this, Mr. Hermsprong rose to go.

"I suppose," said Miss Fluart, "this is what you call the amende honorable, and that it will absolve you of all your sins. But I move, to punish you, by confinement to our society, the rest of the day."

"What unheard-of cruelty! but your motion is not seconded."

"I second it," said the younger Miss Sumelin.

"Motion is always followed by debate, you know. Grant me one hour to fulfil a promise, and I will return, to endure the sentence of my judges."

"Is your promise to a lady?" Miss Fluart asked.

"It is."

"In such a case, who can refuse?"

When Mr. Hermsprong was gone, and after two minutes' silence, Mrs. Sumelin said, "I declare now I do not like this young man at all."

"Nor I," said the eldest daughter.

"That I can easily believe," said the father; "it has a cause; but your cause of dislike, Mrs. Sumelin, I can but guess at."

"He has not the least bit of politeness," said Mrs. Sumelin.

"A little, my dear, you might allow him; I own he does not appear to have sufficient for every lady's necessity."

"His notions are quite shocking," said Mrs. Sumelin; "don't you think so, Miss Campinet?"

"I thought his ideas singular, madam," this young lady answered, "but not shocking."

"But they are vastly foolish," said Miss Sumelin; "how absurd it was to talk of women doing men's work?"

"One may excuse the absurdity, supposing it to be one," said Miss Campinet, "for the sake of the compliment. Few men will allow us capacities for their employments."

"It is no compliment in my mind," said Miss Sumelin, and so will ladies think the remainder of this century, let Mrs. Wolstonecraft say what she will.

CHAPTER XX

MR. HERMSPRONG did not return in an hour; it was more than two; and Miss Campinet and Miss Fluart were just gone their usual evening's walk. He joined them, but had no longer the face of gay hilarity with which he had left Mr. Sumelin's. He seemed more than pensive. An air of soft melancholy rendered him more interesting to Miss Campinet, who thought he had lately wept; and that he could scarce now suppress the starting tear. She could not help asking, and with more apparent interest than this question is usually asked with, "Are you not well, Sir?"

"Not ill, Miss Campinet, unless the mind has diseases."

Miss Campinet could not pursue the inquiry. She found she could not trust her voice. Miss Fluart, however, who had no taste for the silent pensive walk, said, "Perhaps you have found the lady ill, Sir?"

No answer.

"Perhaps inattentive to your complaints?"

"I have not made her any, madam."

"Or you may not have been properly attentive to her, and she may have been upon the tender reproach?"

"I hope I shall give no lady cause for reproach."

"When a gentleman pays a visit to a lady in a gay humour, and returns in a sad one, one guesses there must be a cause."

"And that cause — love?"

"A very possible conjecture; especially if the lady is unmarried."

"Yes," said Hermsprong, with a sigh, "she is unmarried; indeed unmarried; the widow of an hour."

"Oh dear!" said Miss Campinet. Then after a pause she asked, "Is her misery aggravated by other circumstances? Can I assist her? Is she in want?"

"Of kindness; not of bread."

"Is there any secret in her story?"

"None. She is of a genteel family in France; of the small noblesse; and was designed for a nunnery. A Monsieur Marcour, late an officer in the navy, and who had a small independent fortune, taught her to dislike her destiny. To have him, it was necessary to run away with him, and she did so.[1] Reconciliation with the lady's family was a vain attempt. Indeed it would have added little to their happiness; and to their fortune, its value would have been negative.

"Mr. Marcour conducted his lady to St. Maloes, where they lived in much felicity. War being declared against England, he accepted the command of a ship of the line, which not being yet ready, he went on a cruise, as captain of a privateer. His first days were fortunate. He sent in to St. Maloes two prizes of value; but about the 8th day was himself taken, and carried into Falmouth. In the engagement he received a wound, the cure of which was not advanced by ill fortune and a prison.

"Three days since Mrs. Marcour arrived, spent with fatigue and grief; for she had been obliged to pass first into Holland,[2] and forced to sell her gold watch; and other valuable trinkets, before she could prosecute her journey.

"I happened to have made a little acquaintance with poor Marcour, and was with him when his lady arrived. I cannot describe their meeting — I cannot — words cannot describe it. I am little addicted to the melting mood. At most human complaints I laugh; for most of them are created and fed by our follies. But this — this is of war, — and it is not, I find, prudent to call war a folly. There

---

1 Escaping convents, a common motif in gothic fiction, was a plot device that seemed to fascinate Bage and his contemporaries; compare Hermsprong's later story of his own parents.

2 Following England's declaration of war on France in 1793, there was no direct transportation or communication between the two countries.

have been philosophers, and even divines, such as they are, who have said, that wars were means of providence, to prevent the too great multiplication of mankind.[1] If providence has decreed it, submission is our duty; but it requires indeed a revelation to convince us, that omnipotence can find no expedient more adapted to its benevolence, than this terrible scourge of the human race. Till this revelation arrives, I wish — but it is folly to wish."

"But poor Mrs. Marcour," said Miss Campinet.

"How, Miss Campinet, is agony to be described? How, a mixed mass of tenderness and horror? On the part of the lady, swoonings and embraces; of the gentleman, fortitude, struggling against affection and despondence. By degrees these violent emotions subsided; nor indeed could they have been much longer supported but at the expence of life. It was then my business to administer comfort in my way, and to entreat Mrs. Marcour to permit me to procure for her better accommodation than could be had in such a place. With a look, half expressive of thanks, half of reproach, she asked if it was possible, in her situation, to feel accommodation? To enjoy comforts of which Mr. Marcour was deprived? For refreshment, however, I did prevail; and then left them to enjoy the extreme of misery, in comfort."

"This," said Miss Fluart, "is the oddest mixture of phrase."

"I give it you, dear madam, to alter and amend. It was the first arrangement of words to express my conceptions, which offered themselves, and I seldom take the trouble to wait for a second."

"You visited your friends next day, I am sure," said Miss Campinet.

"The certainty, madam, does me honour, Yes, I did; and found wretchedness —not less perhaps — but less turbulent. The surgeon, having dressed his patient, whispered me, there were some appearances of gangrene. I called in Doctor Brown, to prevent its progress, which I believed, was happily effected. This morning I was assured Mr. Marcour was out of danger. It gave me spirits, and

---

1   This idea, today most commonly associated with the Anglican clergyman Thomas Malthus (1766-1834), who shocked and angered radicals and optimists when he published his *Essay on the Principles of Population* in 1798, has antecedents earlier in the century. Faulkner, following Tave, gives William Derham's *Physico-Theology* (1714) and John Bruckner's *Philosophical Survey of the Animal Creation* (1768) as possible sources.

Mrs. Marcour felicity. Indulging hope, I left you to call in upon them, and went, as usual, into the room without ceremony. The silence surprised me. They were lain down both together upon his miserable bed. Thinking them asleep, I was going to retire, but catching a glance of Mr. Marcour's face, there was something in it which did not look like sleep. In short, my dear ladies, he was dead, and Mrs. Marcour in a fainting fit by his side. How long she had lain thus insensible to her own existence, I know not, nor do I yet know the circumstances of Mr. Marcour's death, nor even its cause. For the relief of the lady I ran immediately to Doctor Brown. We procured lodgings, and conveyed her to them still insensible; since then, she has recovered and relapsed several times. She has a nurse, and the doctor is still in attendance. I promised to relieve him. In this situation, if I do not appear to take pleasure even in your company, ladies, I am sure you will pardon me, and you will have the goodness to excuse my request to you, to shorten your walk. Mrs. Marcour knows no one but myself. I wish to be present at her recovery."

"I insist upon it, Mr. Hermsprong," Miss Campinet said, "we do not detain you an instant; and, pray, tell me, can I be of service in any way?"

"Not to-night, Miss Campinet," Mr. Hermsprong answered.

"Promise," said she, "to inform me when I can; and impose what duty you please upon me."

Mr. Hermsprong took her hand, and putting it respectfully to his lips, bowed, and vanished without a word.

Either in the story itself, or in Mr. Hermsprong's manner of telling it, there was something that repressed the gaiety even of Miss Fluart, and the ladies walked home in silence.

CHAPTER XXI

ON the next morning Miss Campinet rose earlier than usual, and when she came down to the breakfast parlour found Mr. Hermsprong there. He came to give her intelligence respecting Mrs. Marcour; for she appeared to have taken an interest in that lady,—an interest, which, as Mrs. Marcour was unknown, could arise from humanity alone; and compassion for the unfortunate, accompanied with benevolence, was precisely what, in Mr. Hermsprong's opinion, raised the female character to the highest degree of perfection.

"I am sorry to acquaint you, Miss Campinet," he said, "that there is not yet room for the exercise of your gentle humanity. Mrs. Marcour's fever and delirium, for this is the present state of her disorder, are very high; and the physician scarce ventures to give hope."

"I am sorry, indeed," Miss Campinet answered with the quivering lip and moistened eye; "has she children?"

"Three."

"This is unfortunate; otherwise I know not but death may be a more desirable event to her, than life."

"So it appears to me, Miss Campinet; but as this is a circumstance in which we are not allowed to be guided by opinion, I have contrived to send information to St. Maloes, and hope, notwithstanding communication is stopped with France, I may still be able to get her conveyed thither in case of her recovery."

"One can scarce conceive a more distressing situation. I envy you, Sir, this monopoly of doing good; can you not oblige me, by permitting me to share with you in serving Mrs. Marcour."

"Not at present, Miss Campinet; but if you can extend your charity to other objects, here I stand, ready to receive any portion of it."

"My charity is only for those who want," said Miss Campinet, smiling.

"I want," answered the gentleman.

Miss Campinet shook her head.

"You are incredulous, Miss Campinet; but to a man so little accustomed to it, dejection of spirits is a disorder, and relief from it, a want; you do, however, relieve me, whether you intend it or not. To see you, to look upon you, is to me a certain degree of happiness."

In the lovely cheeks of Miss Campinet arose the blush of apprehension.

"Nay, Miss Campinet," he said, "do not, I beseech you, be angry. At least do not let me have the mortification of believing pride to be the cause of that anger."

"Have I deserved this, Mr. Hermsprong?"

"Have you not been angry, Miss Campinet?"

"No — what could possibly make you imagine it?"

"Fear. I have seen sometimes a reserve — a forbidding reserve — I know not how to interpret."

"Not how to interpret right. Reflect a moment. You know my father's prejudice respecting you, Mr. Hermsprong. On his side, I have feared anger; on yours, the imputation of ingratitude. As one or other of these opposite sentiments prevailed, I do not deny that my behaviour has not at times been inconsistent."

"Amiable candour! No, — I never accused you of ingratitude. Your just and generous bosom is not a fit residence for such a guest. You are all excellence."

"Upon my word!" says Miss Fluart, just entering, "it must be owned, that if Mr. Hermsprong cannot flatter, he can say very agreeable things, now and then; only that his powers seem rather limited as to their objects."

"Shall I exert them, and tell Miss Fluart she is every thing that is charming?"

"Do," replied Miss Fluart, "if the effort will not be absolutely insupportable."

"It is impossible to express how I desire to please; but whilst I am saying agreeable things to one lady, I am saying disagreeable things to another — if another hears."

"Wretch!" said Miss Fluart.

"My dear Miss Fluart, you should pity, not abuse me. Born and bred a savage, I was not early initiated in the noble art and science of flattery. I am learning as fast as I can, and then —"

"And then you will have the goodness to say civil things to other poor girls; at present it is Miss Campinet alone —"

"Whom I cannot flatter."

"For how can excellence be flattered?"

"I own it is a large, and may therefore be a suspected expression of my respect and esteem for Miss Campinet."

"Yes, — respect and esteem — love cannot be one of the brotherhood; for he is the greatest of flatterers."

"And of fools — if we view him in the old romance; and in the new; he seldom obtains much of my reverence."

"You are a most sublime and incomprehensible person. Can any thing please you that mortal men and women do?"

"Yes, something; but allow for my defective education, and honour me with your instructions. My dear Miss Fluart, what is love?"

"Pshaw! a fiddlestick."

"A good comparison; so love produces harmony or discord according as it is handled. Or what do you think of a top? which can stand no longer than whilst it has the vertigo."

"Pray, good Sir," said Miss Fluart, with a reverent courtesy, "may I take the liberty of inquiring your age?"

"Five and twenty, mistress, come Childermas-day."[1]

"Very early, Sir, to have imbibed so perfect a contempt of love."

"I, Miss Fluart, — I, the ardent votary of love, — despise it! What worse have I said of it, than that it is not immortal; and that when it dies, and leaves not behind it its best offspring, esteem and affection, no married pair have cause to erect a mausoleum to its memory."

"Betwixt love and affection, Sir," said Miss Campinet, "you appear to make a nice distinction."

"A distinction without a difference," answered Miss Fluart.

"I am not to cater for other minds; as far as I know my own sensations, I feel there is real difference."

"Your own sensations! I wish I could see them," said Miss Fluart. "I fancy I should see some out-of-the-way things."

"Yes," Mr. Hermsprong answered, — "for example, love; love for your fair self bursting into flame the moment you were pleased to sprinkle it with a few drops of Cupid's oil."

"And what for Miss Campinet? Affection?"

"If affection conveys an idea of something as soft as love, and durable as life."

"And, pray, Sir, is this your first declaration?"

"I have seldom seen Miss Campinet; when I have, I must have made this declaration, though not in words."

"And when made in words, ought it not to have been whispered in the lady's ear?"

"Why should love and truth be whispered?"

"That all people may not hear. Lord Grondale, for example."

"And why should he not hear?"

"Because, it is probable he would say something not quite pleasant."

"What would he say?"

"Shall I say for him?"

"If you please."

"Young man," says the lady, with a little imitation of the dignity and tone of Lord Grondale, — "young man, it is a thing that appears to me a little extraordinary, that you should make pretensions to my daughter."

---

1 December 28; it was the day marking the slaughter of the Innocents by Herod.

"What is there extraordinary in it, my lord? Every man's daughter may be pretended to."

"Your presumption seems to have made you forget her rank and fortune."

"It is true; I have thought only of herself."

"Do you know, Sir, there is not a nobleman in England who ought to disdain her alliance."

"Miss Campinet, my lord, cannot be seen and disdained."

"And you, Sir, presume to aspire."

"I presume to love her, my lord; the presumption of aspiring is really a phrase not within my comprehension."

"What, Sir! you suppose yourself her equal?"

"The poor word, my lord, has been so used and abused; has been made to mean so many things it did not mean, that I do not chuse to have any thing to do with it."

"Do you pretend to be a man of family?"

"As good as your's, my lord; and yet it never gave me a moment's exultation."

"And your fortune, Sir?"

"Above your lordship's; for it is equal to my wishes, and superior to my want."

"Sir, I must inform you, that your answers are vague and unsatisfactory; before I condescend to give you my daughter, I must have a more particular account of your family, Sir; of its alliances, Sir; and of your rent roll."

"Upon my word, my lord; here is a great deal of difficulty in this country, to bring two people together, who are unfortunate enough to have property. For my part, I have thought little of what your lordship thinks so much. I have thought only that I was man, and she, woman, — lovely indeed, but still woman. Nature has created a general affinity between these two species of beings; incident has made it particular betwixt Miss Campinet and me. In such situations, people usual marry; so I consent to marry."

"You consent to marry! really the tone is high."

"But that I love the gentle Desdemona, I would not my unhoused free condition, put into circumscription and confine for the sea's wealth."[1]

"Oh, pray keep your unhoused free condition; I promise you, you shall have no daughter of mine."

---

1 *Othello* I.ii.25–28.

"I promise myself I shall."

Miss Campinet could no longer restrain her inclination to laugh, which having indulged a few seconds she said, "But is this peremptory *Shall* of yours, with Miss Campinet's consent or without?"

"Certainly with," replied Hermsprong.

"Oh," says she, still laughing, "I was ignorant of that circumstance."

"I have faith and hope," the gentleman answered, "you will not long remain so."

"Till that point is cleared up," said Miss Fluart, "we had better defer what his lordship has further to say."

The coming in of the rest of the family put an end to the conversation.

CHAPTER XXII

I must now carry my readers back to Grondale, to the consequences of the quarrel between the noble peer and Mrs. Stone. That lady's spirited reply, though not very grateful to his pride, or the present state of his feelings, furnished him with an opportunity of resentment exactly adapted to his wishes. Accordingly he resented with great dignity and prudent perseverance; nor could the lady obtain admission to his presence by any submission she thought proper to make. In a few days, therefore, she left the Hall, in that sort of agreeable humour, which women, and men too, I believe, experience, when they happen to be suddenly and rudely checked in the career of interest, of pride, or vanity. This affair so happily terminated, gave his lordship a renovation of spirits. He wrote Miss Fluart the news of this happy event and was so courteous as to say, that he should leave the choice of the future housekeeper to herself.

He was now more at leisure to consider his other equally important concern, how best to rid the country of that poison to his pride, that Hermsprong. Dr. Blick had been some weeks on duty at Winchester, so that unfortunately his lordship was deprived of the very properest person possible to give advice on this occasion, for he would have given it *con amore*, and quite to his lordship's taste. Lord Grondale therefore was obliged to be content with what might be suggested by his own wisdom, and that of his attorney, Mr. Corrow, of whom I made honourable mention in a former chapter.

Mr. Corrow had a prodigious respect for Lord Grondale, and for money; and would have done for one, or both of them, any thing or every thing that the law, in any of its latitudes, would have enabled him to do. To press down to the earth, and under it, a poor man, is easy; it is the work of every day; but to make a man, with money in his purse, guilty of crimes he never committed, requires a superior fund of knowledge of the more tortuous parts of law, and superior intrepidity. Mr. Corrow did not care to promise too much, in a case which might possibly run counter to his prognostic; nor did he chuse to deprive his lordship of hope, because law without hope, he knew, was apt to come to an untimely end. He talked therefore about it and about it, till his lordship found himself well wearied, if not well informed; so he dismissed Mr. Corrow, with a promise of peculiar reward, if, by his exertions, he should rid the country of a man so odious.

From this great object, however, his lordship's thoughts were diverted for a time, by the receipt of the following letter.

Though personally unknown to your lordship, I request the honour of your lordship's particular attention. It is possible the name of Sir Philip Chestrum may be unknown to your lordship, but I presume your lordship cannot be ignorant of the illustrious name of Raioule. The family of Chestrum is indeed new, the late Sir Peter being the creator of his own fortune; but the Raioules were the splendid supporters of the dignity of the nobility of England, from Richard Cœur de Lion to George the First; when the Earldom lapsed, through defect of male issue, and the large family estates having been divided amongst five coheiresses, have gone into other families, so that the illustrious name of Raioule is sunk and lost. I, a descendant of this noble family, was married by my parents to the late Sir Peter Chestrum, and bore him a son and heir, the present Sir Philip Chestrum, who joins great elegance of person and manners to high birth on the part of his mother, and high fortune on the part of his father; for his estate is 15000l. a year. This young man has been captivated by Miss Campinet, your lordship's daughter; and from the flattering manner in which that charming young lady has been pleased to receive his addresses has the highest hopes of success. This induces me to apply for your lordship's approbation, on the receipt of which Sir Philip will wait upon your lordship to confer upon settlements, and other matters requisite to precede so important an event. Expecting your lordship's answer, I have the honour to be

Your lordship's most obedient servant,

HENRIETTA CHESTRUM

P.S. Should your lordship better like the illustrious names of Raioule or Campinet, I shall have no objection to Sir Philip's resigning that of Chestrum, and taking, by act of parliament, that which you approve.

There was something in this letter, which a plain man of common sense and excitable lungs might have laughed at; but to the noble sentiments of the noble lord to whom it was addressed, it was perfectly congenial. I understand that in this island of Great Britain, at the time I am now writing, birth is the first virtue, and money the second; some indeed may dispute the precedence; but all will allow that one or both are *sine qua nons*, without which virtue is not. Lord Grondale had both, and both were flattered by Lady Chestrum's letter. His lordship's reply therefore was the most polite and gracious possible; and it expressed a sort of desire, that the business should be begun and ended with as little loss of time as might be agreeable and convenient to her ladyship. It was Miss Campinet who suggested this; Miss Campinet, who would, his lordship imagined, be rather a superfluity at Grondale, when he was at the top pinnacle of felicity, by the possession of the charming Miss Fluart.

To the charming Miss Fluart he wrote also, and in a very lover-like strain; for he said, he counted the days and the hours, till the time he might expect the return of his fair conquerante. This time, in pity to his sufferings, he hoped she would abridge; and do Miss Campinet the honour to return with her as soon as possible; because Lady Chestrum had made proposals which his lordship very much approved; and had therefore required Miss Campinet's return, to receive Sir Philip's addresses. "For," added his lordship, "it appertains to my honour and dignity, to marry my daughter properly and speedily, that she may not throw herself away upon that low fellow, that Hermsprong; whose impertinencies toward me still continue, or rather increase. For what, my dear Miss Fluart, do you think he has lately done? set up a carriage; and under pretence of calling it Mrs. Garnet's, has presumed to put upon it a part of the arms of the house of Campinet."

His lordship's last letter, on this important occasion, was to his daughter; whom he reproached with having received Sir Philip's addresses without his permission; which failure, in point of duty, notwithstanding, he might be brought to overlook, in consideration of her happiness. Lastly, he fixed the time for her return.

Before we relate the effect of these letters. Let us see what further had passed betwixt the enamoured baronet and his fair enslaver.

CHAPTER XXIII

SIR PHILIP's declaration we have seen in a former chapter; after the discovery of which to his mamma, her address to Lord Grondale, and his lordship's answer, it did not occur to Sir Philip, that any thing more was necessary on his part, than now and then to attend his sweet mistress, and to look kind and gracious.

At first, this was performed with the baronet's usual abilities; but the increasing intimacy betwixt the lady and Mr. Hermsprong, gave a shock to the kind heart of Sir Philip, and in the place of gracious *doux yeux*, produced looks of sullen gloom and fits of resentment.

This increase of intimacy was occasioned by the unfortunate Mrs. Marcour, who, when she recovered her recollection, was kindly visited by Miss Campinet and her friend; and more than once, when Miss Fluart was less disposed to compassion, by Miss Campinet without her; on which occasions she was accompanied by Mr. Hermsprong only. This alarming circumstance was whispered to Sir Philip, by the generous Miss Sumelin, who, since her disappointment at Ostend, had sometimes permitted a little malignity to enter her gentle bosom; and which was peculiarly excitable by Mr. Hermsprong and Miss Campinet. Sir Philip, indeed, did not presume to complain, or indeed to speak at all to his mistress, more than common good manners demanded; he was satisfied to view the fair form, which so soon would be all his own; and was by no means so solicitous to entertain his mistress alone, either on the subject of love, or his new discovered cause of complaint, as she was to avoid the giving him such opportunity; not because she had the least conjecture of what was transacting, but because she did not like the concluding sentence of their last *tête-à-tête*.

So were things when Miss Campinet received her father's letter. It was astonishing; not that she should be the subject of Lord Grondale's reproaches on any occasion, or no occasion at all; but that she should receive Sir Philip Chestrum's addresses so kindly, when she had not the least suspicion of having received any addresses at all.

It was morning when the letters were delivered, and the ladies were just going, under the escort of Mr. Hermsprong, to call upon Mrs. Marcour. They broke the seals without ceremony; and it must have been very amusing to Mr. Hermsprong, to see laughter bursting from the coral lips of Miss Fluart and indignation flashing from the blue eyes of Miss Campinet. As neither of them, however, chose to make Mr. Hermsprong acquainted with the cause of these different emotions, they were obliged to suppress them for the present, and proceed to the business of the morning.

Mrs. Marcour was now in lodgings a mile from the town, for the benefit of country air. On their return from this visit they were overtaken by Sir Philip Chestrum's carriage, which stopped opposite to them, and from it alighted with unusual alacrity, Sir Philip himself, and in his hand the letter from Lord Grondale to Lady Chestrum.

"Now, Miss Campinet," said the gallant baronet, "I hope I have got something to please you; I hope you won't be so shy; and as you will fancy my company as well as that gentleman's."

"Never —" said Miss Campinet, with emphasis.

The baronet stared and wondered.

"Is it to you, Sir Philip," said this young lady, with indignant scorn, "is it to you I am obliged for the information given me by my father, that I have received your addresses?"

"But you seem to be angry, Miss," said Sir Philip; "if I did, where was the harm?"

"The harm lies in the falsehood," the lady answered.

"But where lies the falsehood?" Sir Philip asked.

"Do you persist in it, Sir? When, Sir, or where, did I either accept, or you offer me any addresses?"

"Dear Miss, don't you remember? It was last Monday was a fortnight. Stay, it was Tuesday; for grey Bess tumbled down and broke her knee as we went home, and next day we had the farrier; and that was Wednesday; you may see the scabs;" and Sir Philip pointed to grey Bess's knee.

This proof did not appear so satisfactory to Miss Campinet as Sir Philip probably expected; for she said with increasing scorn, "Answer my question, Sir."

Sir Philip stammered, — Miss Fluart laughed, — Mr. Hermsprong smiled; and Sir Philip, growing angry, said, "As to you,

Miss Fluart, ladies may say any thing; but as to this gentleman, it is neither mannerly nor respectful for him to laugh at nothing."

"If a man laughs at nothing," Hermsprong answered, "what is there to be angry at?"

"But," said the baronet, "I know you laughed at me."

"Then certainly, Sir, you do not suppose I laughed at nothing."

"I wonder what you can find to laugh at about me?"

"Vulgar people, unaccustomed to elegance, might laugh at the profusion of ornament, which decorates your person; and indeed Sir Philip Chestrum is always super-abundantly genteel."

"What signifies that to you, Sir? As if I did not pay for every thing I wear; and as if I wore any thing out of fashion. But this is only a put off. I desire you to tell me the truth."

"You are a most pertinacious enquirer after truth, Sir Philip," said Hermsprong, smiling. "Suppose I should have laughed at the idea of your having mistaken Lord Grondale for Miss Campinet, and in consequence, of paying your first addresses not quite in the right place."

"I say, Sir," said the baronet, and stopped, unable to articulate for anger and trepidation.

"At your leisure, Sir Philip," said Hermsprong; "if you are not prepared to say now, take time."

"Sir," said the baronet, in a rage, "you are —"

"Do not call names, if you can help it, Sir Philip; it subjects gentlemen sometimes to inconveniences."

"I never saw such an odd kind of man in my life," said the baronet; "you are enough to provoke a standing tree."

"Better provoke a forest than such a man as Sir Philip Chestrum," said Hermsprong. "Ladies, shall I entreat the favour of you to be walking on. I have an apology to make Sir Philip."

The ladies went on.

"I shan't chuse to stay behind," said Sir Philip.

"What, not to hear my apology?" replied Hermsprong.

"That's talking more like a gentleman," said the baronet, "but the main point is to refrain keeping company with Miss Campinet."

"A hard article, Sir."

"But it must be; for I am to marry her, and then it belongs to me to tell her who she is to keep company with."

"Husbands have great prerogatives I see. But till you are her husband, I should imagine she ought to be left to her own choice."

"But I think otherwise; for evil communications corrupt good manners."[1]

"What evil do you suppose I should communicate to her, Sir Philip?"

"No body knows any thing about you here; so you might tell her any thing; and she might take a liking to you."

"I am not afraid of that."

"But may be I may."

"What are your fears to me, Sir Philip?"

"There — now you are off again. This is not talking like a gentleman."

"To talk like a gentleman is to tell Sir Philip Chestrum that I will obey his commands."

"Why not? I am a baronet, am I not?"

"So they say. And your commands are that I should not come into the presence of Miss Campinet?"

"Yes, — its what you ought not to do."

"And what is the consequence, if I should have the presumption to disobey?"

Sir Philip, not approving this question, I suppose, did not answer.

"Perhaps you will call me into the field of honour."

"It may be I may," said Sir Philip, assuming dignity.

"It will be great honour to me to meet Sir Philip Chestrum there; and since I am afraid I cannot dispose myself to obey his orders respecting Miss Campinet, the sooner the better."

"But," said the baronet, with a little trepidation, "I shall not do you no such honour; as I don't know whether you are a gentleman. John, draw up." For there was a sawed and painted railing, which divided the carriage from the foot road.

"Good morrow, Sir Philip; shall I carry your compliments to Miss Campinet?"

"No, — I shall send them by no such person; for I dare say you are no better than you should be."

"That I dare say too," replied Hermsprong.

"Perhaps an Irish fortune hunter; or some such take in gentleman," said Sir Philip, making up to the stile.

---

1 1 Corinthians 15:33.

"One moment, Sir Philip, if you please. You have fallen into a little error of language which I am desirous to correct you for; and since you do not chuse to consider me as a gentleman, you will not complain that my correction is not perfectly polite. Do you chuse to be thrown over the rails, or whipt with nettles?"

"I chuse neither," said Sir Philip; "John, Thomas, — murder!"

Hermsprong did not throw Sir Philip, he only lifted him gently over the rails, and set him down softly on the other side; at the same time said, "if I hear any more of these liberties of language, respecting Miss Campinet or myself, I shall correct them in a manner far less agreeable to you." But the footman had now leaped the railing, and was coming to his master's assistance.

"Friend," said Hermsprong, "I have no quarrel with you — keep yourself out of harm's way." The man, seeing his master safe, and probably not liking the rencontre, took quietly Mr. Hermsprong's advice.

Hermsprong was in an instant with the ladies, who had seen the transaction; though they had not heard the dialogue. He found Miss Fluart laughing; Miss Campinet in terror.

"You have terrified me exceedingly," said this latter lady; "Mr. Hermsprong, do you consider consequences?"

"In these pleasant sallies of humour," Hermsprong replied, "one seldom does consider consequences. Does Miss Campinet suppose some terrible ones are to arise, from Sir Philip's resentment? Will he swear the peace against me?"

"He will bring his action of assault and battery," said Miss Fluart.

"Then, my dear Miss Fluart, you will be my evidence, I did not beat him."

"Of Sir Philip," said Miss Campinet, "I do not think; his ideas of revenge will probably be, like all his ideas, mean and inconsequential. But is there no other person of whom Mr. Hermsprong might reasonably be afraid?"

"None," replied the gentleman.

"May not all this go misrepresented and aggravated to Lord Grondale?"

"Of what consequence is that to me?" asked Hermsprong.

"Mr. Hermsprong," said Miss Campinet, with a degree of solemnity, "you have been lately endeavouring to persuade me you entertain an affection for me."

"And in this persuasion, my dear Miss Campinet, I hope I have succeeded."

"How can I think you desire it, Sir, when upon no occasion, you take the trouble to conceal your contempt of my father?"

"I think not of your father; it is you, not him, I love; from you I expect my happiness, not him."

"In this country," said Miss Fluart, "fathers, of rank and fortune especially, have great powers over their children."

"They have indeed, if they have the power to direct or control their affections," said Hermsprong.

"Perhaps," Miss Fluart replied, "they do not reach that point quite; but pray is not love a much more lively and lovely gentleman when he has golden wings?"

"I have not the honour to know love with golden wings."

"Let us descend, — Lord Grondale has great efficient powers in his strong box; such as love, airy as he is, may need."

"I cannot condescend to mix the idea of strong boxes, with felicity and Caroline Campinet."

"You are a sublime mortal; but do you know a lady called Prudence?"

"I hope I do."

"And will she allow Miss Campinet to give up a splendid fortune for love and Mr. Hermsprong?"

"If that is a necessary consequence, I hope she will."

"On the part of Miss Campinet, I presume this requires a tolerable portion of humility."

"Not more, I hope, than Miss Campinet possesses."

"To ladies who have been brought up in affluence and splendor, they are said to become necessaries of life."

"Affluence may be Miss Campinet's, as high, if she pleases, as she herself can wish; but if grandeur, in its usual glittering forms, be to her a necessary of life, I fear it is not mine to supply it. Millions of revenue would not make me exchange the comforts of life for its parade. I have seen splendor in all its fantastic forms, till I sicken at the idea. Give me, heaven! any life, but the life of grandeur."

"Friend," said Miss Fluart, "with these sentiments you ought to look no higher for a wife than a barber's daughter."

"I have one better hope," answered the gentleman.

"And that one," said Miss Fluart.

"Caroline Campinet," replied Hermsprong.

"Have I," Miss Campinet asked, "ever given such hope."

"I know not," he replied, "whether you have given, or whether I have stolen it from you. That I have it is certain, and it is certain also, no power but that of Miss Campinet can take it from me."

"Mr. Hermsprong," said this young lady, with a more serious air than usual, "that I esteem you much, I own; but if you imagine that I can, in your favour, disregard my duties —"

"I ask no sacrifice of duty," Mr. Hermsprong answered, "nor any sacrifice, except of prejudice. In return, Miss Campinet will not require of me the sacrifice of my integrity to pride; or meaner still, to money."

The entrance into the town prevented further conversation.

CHAPTER XXIV

IT was now become necessary for the ladies to communicate to each other their respective letters from Lord Grondale. Miss Fluart was kindly angry for her friend; Miss Campinet was kindly sorry for hers; whose affair with her father she thought was becoming awfully serious. On expressing this apprehension, Miss Campinet received an answer quite characteristic from her fair friend.

"To serious girls, like you," said Miss Fluart, "this affair might be vastly embarrassing; to mad creatures, like myself, it is nothing. All things, as Sir Philip says, are to be put up with from young ladies, especially if they are wild and handsome. As oft as his lordship indulged himself in making love to me, I took care to inform him, that I did believe I never could bring my mind to marry him. I shall write, to renew his memory on this head; and to give him the pleasing intelligence that this mind continues as foolish and obstinate as ever. Think not of me, my dear, but of yourself. It is probable Lord Grondale may indulge himself in a little persecution, as you will call it; though to me it would be pastime. Had I a father who took it in his head to marry me to a man I disliked, were he as stern as old Cato,[1] I should say, 'Venerable Sir, it is I who am to be married, not you; it is I, who am to bear his follies and his humours by day and by night, not you; it is altogether my own affair, and ought to be regulated by my own feelings. I allow you have a right to advise, and I give you leave to advise, provided you

---

1   Cato the Elder (234–149 B.C.) was famous for his strict and austere morality, seen even at the time as being a throwback to an earlier, more severe version of Roman Republicanism.

do it quietly. But I tell you beforehand, I will not take it, if it be to throw myself away upon that odious Sir Chestrum; or not to throw myself away upon that Hermsprong.'"

"Stop, dear whimsical girl, stop; and tell me if you think I am likely to throw myself away upon this last named gentleman?"

"Why, you know, my dear, the man says he will have you. I do think he is an obstinate person; and how you will be able to resist the man, and his obstinacy too, I do not know."

"You think me favourably disposed to him."

"Yes, rather."

"And you think that disposition strong enough to make me risque Lord Grondale's displeasure, and its consequences?"

"Yes, — all but one."

"Pray, favour me with your opinion of Mr. Hermsprong."

"He is moderately tall."

"Pshaw!"

"Tolerably handsome."

"I care not."

"Rather genteel too, if he would dress more en coxcomb."

"Can you praise him no better?"

"I have given him all the attributes which carry our daughters of blood and ton so fast into Scotland;[1] what would the girl have?"

"I had rather hear of the attributes of his mind; his good sense, his knowledge; his cool collected fortitude; his intrepidity; his contempt of meanness; his sentiments so noble, so exalted, so soaring above the reach of common minds."

"Very good, my dear. Yes, you will be able, by prayer and fasting, to risque all consequences. I wish, however, we knew something of his birth, parentage, and education; or are you willing to take him, as they advertize for stolen goods, and no questions asked?"

"I am not so far advanced, Maria. That I esteem him, I own; so much, perhaps, that it would be difficult for me to make another choice; but between esteeming and taking, there is some difference. I wish for happiness, and shall not chuse to risque it by imprudence."

---

1 Scotland, unlike England, permitted the marriage of minors without parents' permission, so Gretna Green, on the Scottish-English border, became synonymous with runaway marriages.

"Especially the imprudence of losing a duchess's revenue?"

"If by this I lost only the freaks of greatness, I think I could be comforted."

"You are an apt scholar, my dear; and take your philosophy very fast; if you can get enough of it to overcome female vanity, you will have done a wonderful thing; something like a miracle I believe."

"Does it appear so difficult to conquer that vanity which is to be gratified only by things one does not want?"

"Not want? Change the expression, my dear; vanity creates almost as great wants as hunger, and much more teazing."

"If I can contrive to want the vanity, I can make shift, perhaps, without the gratification."

"Yes — if love can expel vanity — one need not complain of its weakness."

"I will talk no more to such a perverter of meanings; let us mind our business."

CHAPTER XXV

THIS business was writing to Lord Grondale; a most arduous task to Miss Campinet. She desired to write dutifully; but there was a certain degree of indignation which rather weakened the expression. She wished to assure Lord Grondale, she never had encouraged Sir Philip; and this was easy; but she also desired to say explicitly and dutifully, that she never would; and she found this an insurmountable difficulty. The English language did not supply words to express what she meant, without conveying at the same time, a sort of intention to have a will of her own; an offence she feared her father would be little inclined to pardon. She confined herself therefore to informing his lordship that she detested Sir Philip Chestrum, and always must detest him, for endeavouring to impose upon her father with a direct falsehood.

Miss Fluart, far from being embarrassed, with her accustomed playfulness wrote as follows:

My Lord,
Your lordship's favour of the 14th would have been more agreeable to me, if it had not been quite so loving; and written upon the supposition that your lordship and I had absolutely agreed to intermarry with one another, as they say at Doctor's

Commons;[1] whereas, your lordship will be so good to remember, the agreement was only conditional; that is, if I could bring myself into a proper and wife-like affection for your lordship; which condition being not done and performed, the obligation to marry, as your lordship knows, becomes null and void. To be sure I endeavour to conquer this little difficulty, and if I am so fortunate as to succeed, I will send an express to your lordship with the agreeable intelligence.

I really do not know what to say respecting Mr. Hermsprong's putting any part of your lordship's arms on Mrs. Garnet's carriage. If he has sinned against the sacred laws of heraldry, your lordship does not want the inclination to punish him. What but silly things can be expected from a young man, who throws away his money upon gauds for old women?

Your lordship requires Miss Campinet to return, in order to receive the addresses of Sir Philip Chestrum. I would recommend to your lordship to receive these addresses yourself; for if they are offered to Caroline in person, they must inspire her with invincible disgust; and this is not the state of mind in which so just and tender a father as your lordship would wish a daughter should marry. Indeed, my lord, there should be a little affection, if it be no more than sufficient to prevent a nausea, which possibly might affect an elegant young woman upon the pawings of a bear or a monkey. You know, my lord, this is what I am waiting for; and when it comes I am ready. But indeed, and indeed, I must wait till it does come; and so ought all sober minded young women, like

Your lordship's most obedient servant,

MARIA FLUART

CHAPTER XXVI

THESE letters being sent to the post, Miss Fluart sat down to dress, — Miss Campinet, to think. Twenty minutes had scarce passed in these operations, when Miss Fluart broke in upon her friend's reverie with this abrupt question. "Pray, my dear, what did

---

1 The London courts where, among other things, one could apply for marriage licences.

Mr. Hermsprong mean by saying that Miss Campinet might, if she pleased, have affluence as large as woman's wish."

"Indeed," replied her fair friend, "I do not know. Perhaps we misunderstood the expression. Perhaps it might be a flight of sentiment, meaning nothing more than that if Miss Campinet would not wish for wealth, she might have as much as she desired."

"You are quite ingenious in your explication," said Miss Fluart; "but it is not quite satisfactory, child. May I not take the liberty to ask him?"

"By no means," answered her fair friend. "It would appear as if I were really looking forward to a connexion with Mr. Hermsprong; and I would not have him suppose I am employed about any such consideration."

"Ah, my dear! but how if he supposes such a wicked thing, without your permission?"

"Then, if he is disappointed, he will not have a just cause of accusation against me."

"No — it will be all against his stars; and perhaps, Caroline, you may be rather angry at yours. However, if your delicacy has declared war against your curiosity, mine have not quarrelled, and I shall certainly set him to talk of his forefathers, this day, upon our walk to Mrs. Marcour's."

Miss Campinet was going to be urgent with Miss Fluart, not to hazard such a step, when, instead of the gentleman, they received from him the following note.

Mr. Hermsprong's compliments to Miss Campinet and Miss Fluart, — a little necessity detains him from them and happiness, possibly for the whole day, — if so, to-morrow he hopes will not treat him as to-day will have done.

The ladies had now another turn given to their curiosity; what could be the necessity? Was it another of his benevolencies? What could be the object? They wished for dinner; they wished for Mr. Sumelin; who probably might know his engagement. But neither did he come; and the sun set upon their curiosity; and the moon gave them not the light they wanted.

Mr. Sumelin, the next morning at breakfast, seemed disposed to be grave, sententious, and laconic. He expected questions, and he had them.

Mrs. Sumelin, in a querulous tone, said, "You came home monstrous late, Mr. Sumelin."

"Yes — monstrous late, Mrs. Sumelin."

"I suppose you spent your evening, as usual, at the tavern."

"As usual, at the tavern."

"I think you'll live there after a while."

"Any thing to oblige you, my dear."

"I wonder what it is that makes taverns more agreeable to gentlemen than their own houses?"

"Love of independence, madam."

"Pray," Miss Fluart asked, "had you Mr. Hermsprong?"

"No."

"You did not see him yesterday?"

"Yes, I did."

"Pray, where?"

"At Justice Saxby's."

Miss Campinet gave a little start.

"On justice business, may one ask?" said Miss Fluart.

"On justice business; Hermsprong the delinquent."

Another start.

"What had he done?" Miss Fluart asked.

"Maliciously, contumaciously, *vi et armis*,[1] he had thrown over rails into the high road, no less a man than a baronet of this realm, — no less a man than Sir Philip Chestrum; and put him in fear of his life."

"Oh dear!" said Miss Sumelin, "was ever any thing so shocking?"

"I always said he was a headstrong young man," said Mrs. Sumelin. "And so I suppose they have sent him to jail; and to be sure he deserves it."

Mr. Sumelin did not reply to this. Miss Campinet's seat seemed uneasy. She set down her cup.

"What is your opinion of him, Harriet?" Mr. Sumelin asked.

"Sir, I always thought him a very proud man."

"And you, Charlotte?"

"I have seen so little of him," said this good-natured girl, "that I have only had time to remark his good qualities."

"Well, Miss Fluart?"

"He must have some bad qualities, Sir, for he is a man; but really I have not yet made a catalogue."

---

1 See note 1, page 197.

"Shall I have the honour of your opinion, Miss Campinet?"

"Whatsoever may be his faults, Sir, I think his virtues predominate."

"It is evident that Mrs. Sumelin and Harriet are the best judges; for he is bound over to his good behaviour; and I am his surety for peaceable demeanour. But here he comes; and I leave him to your correction. Sir, you have friends here, who are so good as to own that you have faults. One thinks you have a hot head; another that you have pride in it. Others have not yet dissected you. Carry your cup as even as you can here, Sir; for if these swear the peace against you, ten to one they will require other bonds than mine for their protection."

"Keep me, Sir, in happy ignorance," said Hermsprong, "to whom, in this charming society, I have the misfortune to be disagreeable."

"Be ignorant, if you can," said Sumelin, as he retired. But indeed the happy lot of ignorance was denied him, merely because he did not take the precaution to shut his eyes.

"I hope," said Hermsprong, "you are not disposed to punish Mrs. Marcour for my faults; nor me so heavily as not to permit my attendance."

"I think, Caroline," said Miss Fluart, rising to put on her cloak, "I think that punishment would be too grievous even for this sinful offender."

Miss Campinet seemed to think so also, for she rose to prepare for departure. Poor Charlotte looked as if she wished it too; but Mrs. Sumelin said, she could not possibly spare her this morning.

VOLUME III

CHAPTER I

THEY were no sooner in the fields, than the ladies required of Hermsprong a full account of the movements of the renowned knight, Sir Philip Chestrum; which he gave in such a manner, that the fair ones could with difficulty confine themselves to that placid and dignified smile, which that great schoolmaster of grace, the late Earl of Chesterfield, prescribed in lieu of laughter, to all the sons and daughters of men, who happened to be gentlefolks born.[1]

The morning was fine; Hermsprong proposed an extension of their walk, and to call on Mrs. Marcour on their return. Miss Campinet assented; Miss Fluart owned she was too much of the fine lady to relish long walks; but, says she; "there is a condition —"

"In my power?" asked Hermsprong.

"Yes," Miss Fluart replied; "It is, that you will talk of yourself; you are an odd, out of the way mortal; but I suppose you had a father and mother notwithstanding; and I want to know whether they were as odd as yourself."

"Relators of their own memoirs have seldom a right to unlimited credit, but I shall obey your injunctions with all the regard to truth I can. That I shall be without spot or blemish, you may reasonably expect; but I perhaps may have the candour to own, that my father, mother, and et ceteras had their faults. You will conclude, from my name, that I am of Germany.[2] My grandfather was a man of rank and affluence. My father the second of three sons. His younger brother and himself, at the respective ages of twenty and twenty one, were rivals in love; and this brother, by a series of treachery, and with a cunning one finds it difficult to believe could be the inhabitant of so young a breast, brought my father, almost in the same moment, under the heavy displeasure of my grandfather, and the still more insupportable misfortune of killing, as he

---

1 Philip Dormer Stanhope, 4th Earl of Chesterfield (1694-1773), wrote in his famous letters of advice to his son (first published 1774) that "Loud laughter is the mirth of the mob, who are only pleased with silly things; for true wit or good sense never excited a laugh, since the creation of the world. A man of parts and fashion is therefore only seen to smile, but never heard to laugh" (ed. David Roberts, OUP 1992, 107).

2 Hermsprong's disingenuity here is inconsistent with strict Godwinian principles, a point emphasized when he later claims that he misled Miss Campinet from motives of delicacy — a sentiment more appropriate to a world of romance than to one built around ideas of political justice.

then believed, his dearest friend in a duel. He was obliged to fly; and his elder brother being then on his tour, he joined him in France. His reception was cool and disgusting; my father found it impossible to bear. Sick, and almost in absolute penury, he went to Bagnieres; wrote thence to my grandfather; and entreated pardon and subsistence. The latter was granted. There was a servant in the family, not much older than himself, for whom my father had conceived an attachment, and who had drooped and neglected business ever since his absence. This man my grandfather pitched upon to carry some immediate relief to his unfortunate son, together with his last commands. These were never more to set foot in his native country, which he had so disgraced; to change his name; and never on any account to claim an alliance with his family. On these conditions, he gave him leave to draw on his banker for 6000l. My father, hurt almost to death by such injustice and such cruelty; abhorring the treachery of one brother, and disgusted with the polite nonchalance of the other, willingly returned the messenger with the required acceptance.

"But the man had also conditions to make. He told my father, he never intended to return. His intention in coming was to offer his service to himself, and if he was not accepted, to try his fortune in America, where he had a brother. 'And, Sir,' says the man, 'in whatever place, or whatever station of life you chuse to settle in, you must have a servant; and one that will serve you for less wages, and with more fidelity you will never find. For, Sir, if I may presume to say it, I love you; I know you have been basely betrayed; and I know one of the agents in the plots which were laid to entrap you. I will go back, if you will permit me to return; otherwise not; for I have ill treatment to complain of as well as you, though not so atrocious.'

"This offer my father accepted with pleasure. His servant, Claus, performed his journey with celerity, and came back to Bagnieres, enabled to disclose to his master the whole system of treachery by which he had been undone. This I cannot relate, nor think of without rage and horror. It is a black perfidious tale; much I wish never to have known it; much to be able to blot it from my memory. Its closing scene was the ruin of the young lady, by this brother, who had supplanted my father in her affections.

"There was at Bagnieres for health, a young French lady, Mademoiselle Ruprè, the daughter of a rich weaver at Nantes. My father and she had formed an acquaintance, and it was at the time when Claus returned ripening apace into love. On my father's side, perhaps resentment aided the passion; for he believed the lady he had loved in his own country a party in the perfidy of his brother.

"Having recovered her health, Miss Ruprè returned to Nantes, partly accompanied, partly followed by my father. Mr. Jean Ruprè, my maternal grandfather, was extravagantly fond of his only child, and also extravagantly fond of his money. By permission of Miss Ruprè, my father waited upon him; obtained an audience; told his love; but at the same time told his disgrace, and consequently the state of his fortune. Mr. Ruprè perceived in an instant, he was not a proper match for his daughter; and informed him of this perception with rather less politeness than a courtier would have used upon the occasion.

"This grieved Miss Ruprè, and she undertook one day to reason with her father, and know his objections. He had but one — money; for what was 6000l. compared with her expectations? Miss Ruprè said, that money did not make happiness; for she had read much, and this sentiment is to be found in a prodigious number of books. Authors in general, know money does not make their happiness; and thence conclude rather too hastily, it could not make that of other people. Now it did make Mr. Ruprè's; who fell into a passion at his daughter's quotations, and abused the poor rogues who chuse to live by writing nonsense, rather than by honest industry.

"A month had passed away in these reasonings and rebukes, when Mr. Ruprè, a man of business, and accustomed to decision, proposed to his daughter three gentlemen, all men of substance and industry, for her choice of one. Not one being to her taste, she rejected all. Mr. Jean Ruprè was scarce ever before in so great a passion. He was a pious catholic; yet he swore — yes he swore — one of these, or a nunnery should be her portion.

"Opposition, especially parental, is the true blow bellows of love; the metaphor is coarse, but I am told it is true. Miss Ruprè said to her father, with great respect, 'since it must be so, Sir, I chuse the nunnery as the lesser evil.'

"Mr. Ruprè had drank a good deal of Burgundy in the course of these pleadings, by way of calming his passions. It had assisted him in his arguments, and had made him understand that daughters had no rights but the rights of obedience. He laid this down to her as an incontrovertible proposition. She answered with a smile, she had never before heard of those rights. So, a few days after, her ignorance was rewarded by a convent.

CHAPTER II

"LOST to his country, to fortune, and to love, my father had almost sunk into despondence. There was at Nantes a young man, of German extraction, a Mr. Germersheim, whose father was settled as a merchant in Philadelphia, and who had sent this son upon a mercatorial[1] tour to Europe. This tour he had now compleated, and was at this time loading his father's vessel, in which he was to return home. It had happened to this Mr. Germersheim also to fall in love, and very fortunately with the most intimate friend of Miss Ruprè. But this lady was one of six daughters, and her father had neither the wealth of Mr. Jean Ruprè, nor Mr. Ruprè's passion for it. Every thing had been agreed upon, and nothing but the sanction of old Germersheim, every day expected, prevented the immediate union.

"An acquaintance had commenced between my father and this young man, which a knowledge of each other, had matured into a cordial esteem. They had no secrets; and Germersheim revived my father's hopes, by offering him America for a country; his power with Miss Lissot, to endeavour to prevail upon her friend to make herself happy; and his assistance in the new world to any establishment he should fix upon.

"Most willingly, if nunneries were in the same estimation as they have been, would I give for the benefit of the fair, not only the ingenious contrivance by which Miss Ruprè was liberated, but all others which have ever come to my knowledge, or entered my imagination. For most willingly, any way, every way, would I counteract the diabolical policy that has dictated such cruel abstractions.[2] But, thank heaven, and common sense, nunneries are no more, or no more in estimation, at least, in France; so that I have only occasion to say, Miss Ruprè arrived safe at Philadelphia, accompanied by Mrs. Germersheim, and on the day of her landing, became the wife of my father.

"When rapture had a little subsided —"

"That is," said Miss Fluart, "when love began to die —"

---

1   Mercantile.
2   This reflection on the French abolition of convents is typical of radical writing of the era; see, for example, Helen Maria Williams' comments on the subject in her *Letters from France* (1790). The law allowing monks and nuns to leave their convents if they desired was passed on 13 February 1790.

"And something better," continued Hermsprong, "had succeeded in its place, it became necessary to think of the future. My mother had written to her father, imploring forgiveness, I suppose, but not expressing much of penitence; he did condescend to answer, that as her husband had forfeited his life by the laws of France, he could not return thither. That her life was not forfeited, because she had not professed; but, no doubt she would prefer a husband to a father, and love to duty. For his part, he never was a man that liked to pay for that which he had not; and as he had not now a daughter, he did not chuse to pay for one. Indeed he had supposed that heaven had been speedy in its vengeance; for he had heard that the Concordia, the vessel she was believed to have sailed in, was lost off Cape Finisterre, and all perished. Now it was true that the Concordia was lost, and that they had intended to take the voyage in her; but had changed their purpose; and hired the Arethuse; principally because Germersheim's vessel, being heavy laden, could not accommodate the ladies, so well as was desired. This very circumstance too, of sailing in the Concordia, my father had written to a young gentleman of his own country, his friend, he believed; but from whom he never heard more.

"Mr. Jean Ruprè concluded, by informing his daughter, that it would be useless to trouble him with any more letters, — as she had brewed she must bake; as she had made her bed, so she must lie in it; and for his part, he would try if an obedient wife would not console him for the loss of a disobedient daughter.

"My father, at the same time, received a short latin letter, in a distorted hand, anonymous, dated Paris, to inform him, he was not safe in Philadelphia; nor in any American port. That Monsieur had the patronage of the convent; that the court had entered into his resentment, or rather that of the abbess; and that dark designs were forming against him.[1]

"This friendly letter, my father always supposed, came from a gentleman, a secretary in one of the public offices; with whom he had become intimate at Bagnieres.

"It was now time for removal, for action, for decision. Unfortunately it happens, that almost in every country, a gentleman suddenly reduced to penury, is the most helpless of human beings, and

---

1 "Monsieur," used alone as a title, would usually refer to the brother of the French king, although Louis XV (king in the 1760s, when this story is presumably set) had no siblings.

my father has often confessed how strongly he felt this impotence. Once he had thought of giving public lectures in philosophy, for which, as far as knowledge was requisite, he was well qualified; or taking the superintendence of an academy; being a good master of several living languages, and eminently so of English. But these schemes, and similar to these, could not now be thought of; and were not indeed promising from another cause; the quarrels then arising between America and her mother country.[1]

"Mr. Germersheim the younger, cultivated the fur trade. At this time, he had with him, the son of a Nawdoessie chief,[2] employed on a trading embassy. He had sufficient English to be understood; and my father, fond of seeing man in a less civilized state, was delighted to converse with him. It occurred to my father, that by this man's means, he might find an asylum, gratify his ardent desire to know man, assist his friend's business, and employ himself to advantage. He proposed it to Germersheim, who himself had thought of the scheme, but motives of delicacy had prevented his mentioning it. It was soon agreed upon. Stores were sent to Michillimakinac, to await my father's call. He himself set out with the Nawdoessie, for winter was coming on; and my mother, then pregnant, was prevailed on to stay at Philadelphia till the ensuing spring.

"It appears to me," said Hermsprong, "that the story I am telling you is very tedious, and totally uninteresting." The ladies, with more politeness than veracity perhaps, assured him to the contrary. "I cannot, (says he) make it entertaining; I must make it short.

"My father was well received. The head man of the village, whose name was Lontac, and who had acquired the appellation of the Great Beaver, received him into his tent. There was a commerce of civility, but none of language. To remedy this, my father

---

1 This passage suggests that Hermsprong's father arrived in America in the mid-1760s, during the unrest caused by the Stamp Act, a date which fits reasonably well with the information that Hermsprong is in his mid-twenties at the time of the main action, which is apparently more or less contemporary with the date of publication.

2 The Nawdoessie lived west of the area that is now Michigan; Fort Michillimackinac was the main trading post linking the eastern and western Great Lakes region. Bage's main source of information here was probably Jonathan Carver, who travelled in that area roughly at the time that we can assume the fictional Hermsprong family were moving there. See the introduction for further discussion.

availed himself of the son's assistance, and during the winter months, learned enough of their language, to be able to communicate all the ideas he believed would be necessary for their mutual accommodation.

"Early in spring my father sent for stores, and having distributed presents of rum and tobacco, there was a meeting of head men, from all the Nawdoessie villages, whom the Great Beaver addressed thus: 'Six moons ago, a man from the American people came hither, brought by my son, to strengthen peace betwixt us. He has learned our language. He loves our customs. He will reside with us a vast number of moons; perhaps till the great spirit calls him away. He has a wife and people. We must build him a wigwam; large, that it may be unto us a storehouse of all the good things we want from the European people. He will be our friend. When we go to war, he will aid us with his counsel. When we return from hunting he will buy our skins. So we shall have powder and guns, cloth to warm us in winter, and rum to cheer us.'

"The Great Beaver's speech was well received. The wigwam was built; large and commodious. The stores were deposited. My mother and myself, for I had made my appearance in this best of worlds, arrived safe, with our European servants, our books, our music, our instruments of drawing, and every thing that could be supposed to alleviate the solitude my mother had pictured to herself.

"This afflicting solitude, however, did not arrive. The people were civil and attentive; Lontac's family obliging; and there was novelty in the scene. My father even found it difficult to procure leisure for the studies and amusements he most liked. When he could, he read, wrote, drew the rude scenes around him; and kept up a correspondence of philosophy as well as business with Mr. Germersheim.

"My mother was a very good woman; not without her prejudices indeed, but a good woman, and a zealous catholic. She loved my father; she saw him in a place of safety and happy. She was happy herself, except when she thought of France, her father, and the convent. The last disturbed her most. She feared she had committed a crime; she had no confessor, and could not absolve herself. She confessed indeed to my father who consoled her always, and would have given her absolution, had she been pleased to accept it. At length it came into her mind, that greater sins than hers might be expiated, by a conversion to christianity of a few Nawdoessie females. How did she know, but she might be the agent appointed by God, for producing this salutary change in a whole people?

"Lodiquashow, the wife of Lontac, the best of squaws, the most obedient of wives, had never presumed to sit down in the presence of the Great Beaver, till she had brought him six children. With her my mother determined to begin the great work, and applied herself to learn the language with an assiduity which surprised my father. Perhaps she began her pious labour before she had attained sufficient powers of explanation; for although Lodiquashow heard my mother with the most patient attention, nor once offended by interruption, contradiction, or remark — all the assent my mother was ever able to attain, was, the Great Spirit and Lontac only know.

"Unable to produce any effect upon the stupid Lodiquashow, or the two daughters, who still remained ungiven away in marriage, she determined to try her powers on Lontac himself. Sixty moons, however, passed away before she durst venture; partly owing to a fear she had not yet acquired the full force of the Nawdoessie tongue; and partly to a sort of awe of this venerable chief, who was himself an orator, and who was much beloved, respected, and obeyed.

"At length my mother asked an audience and obtained it. It appeared indeed to Lontac to be an inversion of order, that the Great Beaver should lend his ear to a woman for instruction; but there is in these people a politeness derived from education, as well as ours, which qualifies them for patient hearers, to a degree I have never observed in more polished nations.

"What most of all astonished my mother, was, that though Lontac, after a few lectures, seemed himself to put her on speaking, and to be amused, if not instructed, she could seldom obtain an answer, and when she did, it was only to thank her for the pains the took on his account. It is true, he did not always understand; when he understood, he did not always approve; but it is only for a native American to arrive at so high a degree of politeness, as to testify disapprobation, only by a respectful silence.

"Wondering that any human creature should be deaf to persuasion, and blind to the sublime truths she had now so oft explained, she began at times to be angry, and ladies are seldom angry without a little gentle abuse. Entreated, almost commanded, to answer, Lontac spoke with all possible gravity, and the greatest respect, as follows:[1]

---

1 As Faulkner and Tave have pointed out, this story is derived from a similar anecdote related by Benjamin Franklin. See Appendix C.1.

"'One day's journey west of this place, there is, as you have heard, a large lake called the White Bear; because white bears were numerous on its banks, and disputed the sovereignty of the adjacent lands with man. About a thousand moons ago, when the war had lasted many generations of bears and men, the two powers agreed upon a truce, and met on a certain bank of the lake, in order to have a talk. When the orators on both sides —'

"'On both sides!' exclaimed my mother.

"Lontac proceeded. 'Were preparing to speak, a figure arose from the midst of the lake, of vast dimensions; viewed on one side, it seemed to be a bear; on the other, it seemed to be a man. The white bear part of this awful figure, waved its paw in the air, to command silence, then said, with a terrific voice —'

"'Was ever any thing so preposterous!' cried my mother. 'Sure it is impossible you should believe it.'

"'Why impossible?' answered Lontac, 'it is tradition handed down to us from our fathers. We believe, because they said it.'

"'Bears speak!' again exclaimed my mother.

"'A serpent,' answered Lontac, 'spake to the first woman; an ass spake to a prophet; you have said so, and therefore I believe it."

"'But,' said my mother, 'They were inspired.'

"'So was the half white bear. The Great Spirit inspires every thing.'

"'But this is so excessively absurd,' said my mother.

"'I have not called your wonders absurd,' Lontac replied; 'I thought it more decent to believe.'

"'What have I told you so preposterous?' asked my mother.

"'Many things far removed from the ordinary course of nature,' Lontac replied, 'I do not presume to call them preposterous. It is better to believe than contradict.'

"Such obstinacy of politeness provoked my mother, almost as much as contradiction could have done; she told my father what a stupid creature she had undertaken to instruct; and desired that he would endeavour to bring him to the light of truth. My father answered, 'My dear, they have had missionaries, whose holy lips have hitherto failed. Perhaps our mysteries are too refined for their gross understanding. Perhaps the time appointed by providence for their conversion is not yet come.'

"'I despise them,' said my mother, 'prodigiously.'

"'Do, my dear,' my father replied, 'as much as you can with civility, people who are always doing you services, and shewing their regard. I despised them myself, till I found them my equals in knowledge of many things of which I believed them ignorant; and my superiors in the virtues of friendship, hospitality, and integrity.'

"'I shall never be easy amongst them,' said my mother.

"'You will indeed, my dear,' answered my father, 'When you don't think of converting them.'

CHAPTER III

"IT is my intention," continued Hermsprong, "to give you a sketch only of my father and mother's story, for in their pacific retirement, there is little to gratify curiosity; nothing to excite your compassion; nothing to inspire terror. But I have deviated from my intention, perhaps improperly, merely because this conversation, amongst many others, I found amongst my father's papers after his decease; and imagined it might give you a taste of savage politeness."

"So far," Miss Campinet answered, "from wishing you to abbreviate such communications, I could listen with pleasure to more, I fear, than you with pleasure can give; for to you they are old; to me, not new only, but strange; and as pleasing as strange.[1] I admire the old Indian; the more perhaps, because I could not expect from such a man so much of sentiment, and so cool and firm a mode of expressing it. Whatsoever might be the error of his opinions, they flowed naturally from his education. But of yourself, Mr. Hermsprong, you have yet said nothing."

"Of myself, Miss Campinet, I have nothing to say, but that the active part of my life was spent like that of other young Indians, whose very sports are athletic; and calculated to render man robust, and inure him to labour and fatigue. Here I always found my superiors. I could not acquire the speed of many of my companions; my sense of smelling was less acute, — my sagacity inferior. I owe this probably to the sedentary portion of my life, spent with my father in learning languages, in mathematics, in I know not what. My father, always thinking of Europe, was desirous I should have a taste, at least, of the less useful, but more ornamental parts of knowledge. In consequence, I am superficial. I have a mouthful of many sciences, a meal of none.[2] In this I believe I resemble the

---

1   Compare Desdemona's reaction to Othello's tales: "She swore in faith
    'twas strange: 'twas passing strange, / 'Twas pitiful: 'twas wondrous pitiful"
    (I.iii.159-60).

2   Compare note 1, page 160.

generality of young Englishmen. It is fashion here — and surely a people more obedient to fashion never have existed — never can exist."

"Such was the life I led amongst the aborigines of America; I am fond of the remembrance of it. I never there knew sickness, I never there felt ennui, I even loved some of my copper-coloured companions —"

"And none of your companionesses?" asked Miss Fluart.

"Oh no, — I was too young. Love is there a simple lesson of nature. They never experience its pains; they never refine upon its pleasures. Yet the modesty of their young women is uncommon. They have delicacy also, and respecting men, a timidity of which here I have seen not many examples."

"And this timidity towards men," says Miss Fluart, "is what I suppose you would principally recommend to us."

"Not I indeed. My recommendation to the ladies would be, to acquire minds to reason, understandings to judge; for when they will take the trouble to reason a little, and judge for themselves, they do it so well, that propriety of action must follow of necessity, and then they are —"

"What, Sir?" asked Miss Fluart.

"Women, madam," Hermsprong replied; "Heavenly women; such as a man might take to his bosom with a possibility of an increase to his happiness."

"Indeed!" said Miss Fluart; "well, you are prodigious at a compliment; and under your tuition we must be amazing creatures. But pray, Sir, proceed."

"What more have I to tell my lovely hearers, but that I grew up in the grace of God, and in the keeping of many of the ten commandments. That I could almost run up a tree like a squirrel; almost catch an antelope; almost, like another Leander,[1] have swam over a sea to a mistress, had I had one. That at the end of ten years, my father found himself affluent to his own satisfaction; and meditated a return to Philadelphia. This was prevented by the war that gained England the loss of her colonies.[2] Two years after, I lost my

---

1 Leander, although famous for his swimming, drowned while swimming the Hellespont to be with his beloved Hero.

2 The dryly ironic phrasing here recalls some of Bage's other satiric writing about the pointlessness of the English cause in the American Revolution. See, for example, the dialogue from *Mount Henneth* quoted in the *Monthly Review* (Appendix B.1).

father by an inflammatory fever; an incalculable loss; for his instructions were my daily benefit; his fond affection, my daily happiness. Almost the affliction sunk my mother to the grave. She wrote to France. She asked again of her father forgiveness; but she asked nothing else. On the contrary, she informed him that she had wealth sufficient to enable her to spend the remainder of her life where and how she pleased. No other possible plea could so soon have disposed my grandfather to compassion. He forgave her now with all his heart. He even desired she would hasten to comfort his old age. For it must be owned, that, except money, he was poor in articles of comfort. His old friends, or rather companions, had deserted him for heaven; a loving widow, whom he took into his house, and to his bosom, after my mother's leaving him, but whom he would not marry, had been negligent in the household economy, had found means to divert some sums of money from their destination to the chest, and had even failed in the point of honour; for my grandfather had bargained, and, as he thought, paid dear enough, for her whole person.

"Before the expiration of a year, by the kind aid of Mr. Germersheim, we were safe in France. I was then sixteen; my grandfather thought I was too wild and rude. The ladies of our affinities were shocked to see me enter a room so ungracefully; so they sent me to learn to dance. My grandfather thought proper that I should be well skilled in book-keeping. Of the latter school, however, I did not like the confinement; of the former, the frivolity and grimace. I told my mother this, and desired her leave to run over France, in the way I had been over great part of America since my father's death; that is, on foot, attended only by a man to carry a few changes of linen et cetera —. Perhaps I should not have obtained her consent, had not a great decrease of plumpness and animal spirits, made her apprehensive I was beginning to suffer by so great a change of habits. In seven years, then, I had made excursions half over Europe;[1] in which time I lost first my grandfather, and little more than two years since, my mother. I have succeeded to the fortunes of both; and not liking the situation of things in France, I sold

---

1   Bage is inconsistent in his dates. In his first dialogue with Mr. Sumelin, Hermsprong says that he has been in Europe only five years; later he says four (see pp. 89, 209). That would mean, given the contemporary setting implied by other incidents in the novel, that he arrived in Revolutionary France as a young man, rather than, as here, arriving in pre-Revolutionary France as an adolescent.

all I was able, and have dispersed the money into different banks, principally in England, Italy, and America. Lastly, I have come over into England, to look at it; resolved, if I did not find it more suited to my taste than the rest of Europe, to return to America; buy 30,000 acres of land,[1] and amuse myself with peopling a desart."

"I hope, then," said Miss Fluart, "you have found England to your taste?"

"Yes, — I have found Miss Campinet in it."

"Eh, — well!" Miss Fluart exclaimed, "and so, then —"

"And so then, like all true lovers, I find I have but one want."

"You want Miss Campinet?"

"I do."

"Wise men, they say, when they want a thing, take the properest means to get it."

"I hope I do. I take the means of probity. Miss Campinet shall see me as I am."

"Your probity, Sir, is a little of the inflexible."

"Can probity be otherwise? what is it else, than doing what is right? Or what you think is right?"

"But the affair does not depend on Miss Campinet alone."

"In my opinion, it does. It is she alone whom I desire. She loves me too. I am bold enough to make the confession for her; because she dare not make it for herself."

Miss Fluart burst into laughter. Miss Campinet only smiled, and said, "Suppose it so, Mr. Hermsprong, of what consequence is it, since you will not take the trouble to conciliate my father?"

"That trouble, could I stoop to take it, after what is past, would be in vain. I am honoured with his inveterate hatred. I am marked for his persecution. Were it possible, he would hunt me down. At his malice I laugh. The wounds he would inflict are terrible. The wounds he can inflict are harmless."

"But," said Miss Campinet, with emphasis, "he is my father."

The reply was, "How do you know?"

Miss Campinet started. "Would you have me," says she, "impute infamy to my mother?"

"No, my too apprehensive Miss Campinet, no. But fathers

---

1 Again, there seems to be a minor inconsistency; near the end of the novel, Hermsprong refers to 60,000 acres of land already in his possession.

ought to be known by their cares, their affections. Tell me now, and let no prejudice arrest your judgment, are there obligations binding on one party only? obligations which are not reciprocal?"

"It is a question of too great range, Mr. Hermsprong; but suppose it so," said Miss Campinet, "does a breach on one side dissolve the obligation on the other?"

"I think so," replied Hermsprong.

"Let us try now," said Miss Fluart. "Here am I now, your wife, the most charming creature in the universe; in two years you begin to wonder what made you think so. You find another quite as much to your taste. You play the false. Am I at liberty to return the favour?"

"Yes, my most charming creature in the universe; yes, as far as respects myself. But in this case, you have contracted an obligation with society also. Society does not think itself so much injured by the lapse of the male. In short, you bear the children. To you, I need not point out the important deductions from this single circumstance."[1]

Nor, indeed, had it been necessary, would Mr. Hermsprong have had time; for they were now entering Falmouth. This long conversation had been interrupted at Mrs. Marcour's, and afterwards renewed. I thought it useless to mark the interruption.

CHAPTER IV

IT is time to think of Sir Philip Chestrum, a gentleman now, of too much consequence to us, to be neglected. From the field of action lately commemorated, the insulted baronet drove home, and poured his griefs into the gentle bosom of his mamma; which swelled, as all gentle bosoms do, when a naughty man gives them justifiable causes of anger. When this subsided, she had the goodness to consider what could be done for her darling, and her dignity. She was not so cruel as to harbour any of those principles of revenge with which persons of high honour call one another into

---

1 This was a conventional idea in eighteenth-century thought, expressed most bluntly and forcefully, perhaps, by Samuel Johnson: "Boswell. 'To be sure there is a great difference between the offence of infidelity in a man and that of his wife.' Johnson. 'The difference is boundless. The man imposes no bastards upon his wife'" (*Life*, OUP 1982, 1035).

the field. She found a better expedient, and more consonant to that moderation of mind, which Sir Philip felt on the occasion. It was first, to swear the peace against Hermsprong, which was done in due form; and then to proceed to Grondale Hall with his complaints, his pedigree, and his rent-roll.

Sir Philip found at Lord Grondale's, several gentlemen accustomed to pay his lordship an annual visit. The most conspicuous of these were a Mr. Lowram and Sir John Wing. Mr. Lowram was rather in years, grave generally and silent, and sometimes thoughtful. Sir John had not yet began to think. It was first necessary he should lose his money and mortgage his estates, that he might have something to think of. For he was young, not incumbered with too much understanding, and just entering into genteel life under the auspices of Mr. Lowram, a distant relation. The rest of the party, were three gentlemen, all elderly, who, with Mr. Lowram formed a groupe of the most easy manners; so much alike, there was scarce a perceptible difference of character. Perfectly genteel in their address, and voluble (Mr. Lowram excepted) without much meaning; all gamesters, but less gamesters than *bon vivants*, all victims of gout, save one, hitherto preserved by a true carbuncle face.[1] Not men of hunting, nor addicted to the sport, of the field, their earliest hour of rising was eleven. By one they had compleated their toilets, and met to breakfast, after which they sat down to whist, in the sociable small way; that is, what they call guinea points.[2] If I thought an explanation necessary to any one of my male or female readers, I would give it; but with this lamentable degree of ignorance, no person, in this enlightened country, above the degree of peasants, can be charged. At five, our uniform party

> Tried all hors d'oeuvres, all liqueres defined.
> With spirit drank, and greatly daring, dined.[3]

---

1   That is, he has a badly pimpled face. Gout was, at the time, associated with excessive indulgence in rich foods and alcohol.

2   A guinea was a pound and a shilling (there were twenty shillings in a pound). Wagering this sum on every point won or lost in a card game would normally be considered very high stakes gambling — note that Glen lives on an income of £80/year.

3   Alexander Pope, *The Dunciad* (1742), IV. 317-18. The lines are slightly misquoted; Bage substitutes "with spirit" for Pope's "judicious."

Leaving this pastime about nine, they indulged themselves with a few throws of the dice; resigning themselves with more liberality, and more directly to fortune, without presuming to interfere in her decisions by any efforts of the head. A light supper, and a little warm punch, concluded the evening, and carried them to repose, well satisfied with having spent the day in a gentlemanlike manner. Thus, not much indebted to wisdom, and not stinted with any thing that is now called folly, glided the even tenor of their lives;[1] guilty of no actions which deserve a record, but in the annals of oblivion, one excepted, which looked so much like wisdom, and being quite a curiosity in its kind, I hope I shall please my readers by the communication of.

Mr. Lowram was a younger brother, and designed for the church; but the death of his father, and the more sudden one of his brother, whilst he was yet at Oxford, threw him into the possession of several thousands a-year, and into genteel societies, very capable of instructing him how to spend it. He proved too a docile scholar, and being blessed with a steward who knew business, and did not very strongly invite him to the consideration of his own affairs, till half his estate was gone, the first ten years of genteel life was quite a whirlwind of joy. To think at all was then become a heavy task; and to think of œconomy, an insupportable one. He did however advance so far in reformation as to make several prudential resolutions; and nothing was wanting but the power of keeping them. A salutary sickness detained him in his apartment several weeks; he was seized with fits of prayer and penitence; and having made the most astonishing reflections, and anatomised man in general, and himself in particular, he formed, yes, and executed the following scheme of things.

Imprimis. To dismiss his steward and sell his estates.

Secundo. To divide the 30,000l. raised by these means into two equal parts.

Tertio. To sink one for an annuity; and depose the other with an eminent banking house, for a fund for gaming.

But the *quarto et ultimo* was the crown and perfection of provisionary wisdom. By a clause in the annuity agreement, he agreed to forfeit one half of it, if ever he drew out the last of the 15,000l.

---

1   An allusion to lines about the poor in Thomas Gray's "Elegy Written in a
    Country Churchyard" (1751): "Along the cool sequestered vale of life /
    They kept the noiseless tenor of their way" (75-76).

deposited for his gaming fund. And upon this fund, not applying a guinea of it to any purpose but its own, had he gamed for the last thirty years; and had the good fortune, at the time we are now arrived at, not to have sunk it above one third.

CHAPTER V

A LITTLE before Sir Philip Chestrum's arrival, Lord Grondale had received the letters from Miss Campinet and Miss Fluart, mentioned in a former chapter. Neither of these pleased him. In his daughter's, there was concealed rebellion in the garb of duty; in Miss Fluart's there was — he did knot know what. It was not easy for a man of sense not to have a glimpse of perception, that she might be laughing at him; but pride happily came to his aid, and stifled the odious idea in its birth.

Lord Grondale soon perceived the state of Sir Philip Chestrum's intellects; but his rent roll was sound; and that ought to be, and generally is, the care of every good father.

When the baronet had given his lordship a full account of his lands and monies, intermingled, as Lady Chestrum had ordered, with certain genealogies of the Raioules, he proceeded to complain of Miss Campinet, as having greatly altered her courteous demeanor towards him, ever since the arrival at Falmouth of one Hermsprong, come from foreign parts he believed, and as conceited as sin. "He came about a month ago," said Sir Philip, "and since then I never could get her by herself, to tell her more of my mind."

"Damnation!" half said, half thought his lordship. "And Miss Fluart?"

"Yes — Miss Fluart. They three are always together; and they fetch long walks in the country, with a pretence to see a sick woman that comes from France. And it was but last Monday, when I had got your lordship's letter to Lady Chestrum, I overtook them altogether; and because I told Miss Campinet she ought to give me more of her company and him less, he behaved so monstrous rudely, I was forced to swear the peace against him."

"Really!" said his lordship, half ashamed of his destined son-in-law; "I hope he did not offer to lay violent hands upon you?"

"Yes, he did; he flung me over a rail; it was a mercy he did not break my bones."

Here his lordship made a long and thoughtful pause. It is probable a little contempt for Sir Philip, mingled with the desire he had to be angry at Hermsprong. At length his lordship burst out in angry exclamations: "Such licentious behaviour — a baronet — probably soon to be a peer — assaulted *vi et armis*[1] — by a fellow whom no body knows — it is insufferable."

"Yes, — quite insufferable, my lord."

"If he was a gentleman, one would call him out."

"Yes, my lord, but who would dirty his fingers with a man that is not a gentleman?"

"We must consider how we can punish him."

On the next day Mr. Corrow was sent for; the business laid before him; and Lord Grondale suggested a hint, that Hermsprong might possibly mean a robbery. This was ingenious; and Mr. Corrow, desirous to serve so good a client to the utmost of his abilities, pondered upon it, examined the baronet's two servants, cogitated again, and at last declared to his lordship it was quite hopeless.

"But," said his lordship, "it might serve to throw him in prison."

"I fear," said the lawyer, "no justice would commit him."[2]

"If Doctor Blick was here," said his lordship; "and he will be here in a fortnight. He has been some time at his canonry."

"Yes, Doctor Blick is the very gentleman; he would not scruple to oblige your lordship," said Mr. Corrow.

"In the meantime," proceeded Lord Grondale, "attack the fellow immediately with an action of assault and battery. A jury will give large damages, when they consider the rank of the offended person. At any rate, my interest, joined to Lady Chestrum's, may make this county no longer a desirable residence for the fellow."

Of late Lord Grondale had been so agreeably engaged, his time had passed so pleasantly, that he had thought of Miss Fluart with less ardour; of Hermsprong with less violence; of his daughter not at all. Bitter remembrances were now renewed. The day, indeed, allowed him no time to indulge them; but they intruded upon his pillow without contributing to his repose. Miss Fluart! could it be possible, a simple girl, raw from the boarding school, should dare to

---

1 See note 1, page 197.
2 There was no regular police force in eighteenth-century England, and so the protocol for arrest and imprisonment was very different from modern practice. Justices of the Peace (see note 1, page 75) could not try serious charges, but they were responsible for deciding if those accused of such crimes should be brought to trial, and could, if necessary, hold them in jail until their cases were heard. Godwin attacks the injustices and potential abuses of this system in *Caleb Williams*.

conceive the idea of playing upon such a man as Lord Grondale? Certainly it was impossible. And yet to be thus familiar with Hermsprong! the man on earth he most abhorred! What was this but deceit — but treachery, aggravated by indignity? Women are devils.

Yes, I, Gregory Glen, the humble compiler of this authentic history founded on facts, — I, have more than once tried to be angry with some fair creature, who having smiled on me, smiled afterwards on another. I too, have called women, devils. Charming devils though, my heart forced me to confess. Even when I was most disposed to be angry, some delightful retrospect — some something or other, prevented my making any great progress in wrath. So, probably, was it now with Lord Grondale; for, alas! lords, in love, are men, meer men. Some something pleaded for the fair Miss Fluart, and opposed her utter condemnation. So his lordship's final resolve was, to recal his daughter instantly, and peremptorily. To invite, or rather to suppose it certain, that Miss Fluart would return with her; this, if she did, all might yet be well. If not — women were devils! he would force his daughter to marry Sir Philip, and never think of woman more.

CHAPTER VI

LORD GRONDALE would have delayed putting in practice the resolution he had formed, till his guests, whose visit was almost expired, had taken their leave. But it was still ten or twelve days to the Newmarket meeting, which called them away;[1] and what might not such a time produce? His lordship wrote therefore to Miss Campinet in the most positive terms, to Miss Fluart in the most polite, commanding the first, and requesting the last, to set out immediately for Grondale, but without assigning a cause, or mentioning Sir Philip Chestrum or Mr. Hermsprong. Some speculation, his lordship's letters must necessarily cause at Falmouth; Miss Campinet, however, disposed herself to instant obedience; and Miss Fluart, not bearing the thought of deserting her fair friend at so gloomy a crisis, his lordship had the pleasure of seeing her alight from the chaise with his daughter, a day sooner than his expectation.

---

1   Regular horse races, at Newmarket.

It was evening, and rather, for Lord Grondale, an unfortunate hour, for the orgies to Bacchus had just ended, and the society was engaged in making exchanges of property, not by bargain and sale, but by a summary appeal to chance. I am told that this affair seizes upon man, and binds him down in chains stronger even than those of love. Difficult as it is to believe this, I must own Lord Grondale's movements this night will not assist me to confute it. His lordship did step in to the ladies for a moment indeed, but it was only to say, that politeness rendered it indispensable to him not to leave his guests, and to request Miss Fluart to have the goodness to command in his house. To his daughter he did not condescend to speak.

In the morning his lordship sent a message to Miss Fluart, that he would do himself the pleasure to breakfast with her. He rose an hour earlier than usual, and had the satisfaction to find her alone in the breakfast room. Fortune had been kind to him the preceding evening; he was higher in his spirits than in a morning was usual to him; Miss Fluart appeared to be more lovely than ever; as fast as he could fly, he flew to embrace her; he forgot the letter she had written; her commerce with Hermsprong; every thing but herself

But there was a sort of repelling coldness in Miss Fluart, which would soon have brought him to a soberer sense of things, had not Miss Campinet entered; and before she could well pay her duty to Lord Grondale, and observe the man of gallantry changed into the stern father, was followed by Sir Philip Chestrum. That the baronet was in the house, Miss Campinet very well knew, and expected his morning visit; yet she almost started at seeing him. He bowed; her returning courtsey was scarce perceptible. He bade her good morning; if she answered, it was too low to be heard.

"I dare say now," said he, "You did not expect to see me here."

"Certainly, Sir," she answered, "I did not wish it."

"No," the baronet replied; "No, Miss; I know you had rather have seen Mr. Hermsprong."

"What is it to you, Sir," she answered, with strong contempt, "Who I had rather see?"

The baronet was confounded, and his lordship rather surprised; but the entrance of servants, with breakfast, put, at present, an end to recrimination.

When breakfast was ended, Sir Philip again ventured to address his mistress, but received a cold look, and an ungracious answer. Lord Grondale then thought proper to say to his daughter, "A little more deference to my friends, Miss Campinet would not misbecome you."

"If I see Sir Philip only as your friend, my lord, I ask his pardon."

"Of that hereafter, Miss Campinet; good manners from my daughter is due to every guest."

"As guest, my lord; if I had not suspected Sir Philip in a very different character, I should not have presumed —"

"I think, Miss Campinet," said his lordship, with an awful solemnity, "I think you know, from my own communication, that this gentleman comes in no character unapproved by me."

"I am sorry for it, my lord."

There was a something in his daughter this morning, which Lord Grondale had not before observed; a something which militated against one of his most firm opinions, that unconditional submission was the duty of a child, and especially of a daughter. He felt in his bosom the swell of parental, or more perhaps of lordly dignity; but a few moments' consideration shewed him it would be better to stifle it for the present, and learn from Miss Fluart what he had to expect, both from his daughter and herself.

He then said, "As it is possible, Miss Fluart, that Sir Philip may have something particular to say to Miss Campinet, I shall be happy if you will have the goodness to favour me half an hour in the library."

"I attend your lordship," answered Miss Fluart, rising; "learn of me, Caroline, to be gracious."

CHAPTER VII

LORD GRONDALE began the conversation, by expressing the degree of happiness he felt from Miss Fluart's condescension, in returning to Grondale; and hoped it was the prelude to more favourable intentions. At the same time, he must own himself alarmed at what he heard from Sir Philip Chestrum.

"Why, yes, my lord, if Sir Philip has any talent, it is that of being alarmed, and communicating his alarms to his friends. Don't you find him intolerable, my lord? How many times a day does he tell your lordship of his horrors? I fear he may have infected your lordship with hypochondriacism."

"Perhaps so; for he has told me, that Hermsprong has constantly attended my daughter, ever since she has been at Falmouth."

"Yes, I dare say; that is perfectly in Sir Philip's stile of information. When does he go? I knew your lordship would never be able to endure him."

"You evade my question, Miss Fluart. Has Hermsprong ever attended Miss Campinet at Falmouth?"

"Oh, yes! he has been in her company several times. There was no avoiding it, if one was ever so desirous; for my guardian is his banker; but I believe there was no desire to avoid him."

"You, Miss Fluart, knew he was my aversion."

"Yes, my lord; but I did not perceive that he inspired any one else with aversion. He is pretty generally liked. My guardian says he is the most manly character he ever knew. Quite a Phenix."[1]

"A Phenix?"

"Yes, such an one as one sees but once in a century."

"Miss Campinet too! I suppose she thinks him a Phenix?"

"I suppose so, my lord; but she is prudent of speech; she seldom says above half what she thinks."

"And what does she say?"

"Only that he is a young gentleman of extraordinary merit."

"And that is half what she thinks?"

"Somewhere thereabout; one cannot be very exact."

"Miss Fluart, may I depend upon you for candour and ingenuousness?"

"They are scarce things, my lord; but all I have are at your lordship's service."

"Are you most my daughter's friend, or mine?"

"Your daughter's assuredly. Your lordship asked me for love, not friendship."

"Surely they are inseparable."

"I cannot judge of that for want of experience."

"Is it, Miss Fluart, is it your intention, or is it not, to honour me with your hand?"

"Your lordship has so many inexplicable questions."

"Inexplicable! Miss Fluart."

"Yes, my lord. A woman's mind is not so easy to be known. Besides, your lordship ought to remember, that this affair depends upon a certain contingency."

"What contingency?"

---

1 Miss Fluart seems to have the story slightly wrong, although the phoenix (the more usual spelling) is used to signify something rare or uniquely valuable. It is a mythical bird, only one of which is alive at any one time. At the end of its lifespan (which varies in different versions of the story), it incinerates itself, and a new bird arises from the ashes.

"Upon my acquiring a proper affection for your lordship; and you know, my lord, love, like death, will come when it will come."

"It is possible, Miss Fluart, you mean to trifle with me."

"Not quite impossible, my lord. To this little inconvenience men generally subject themselves when they become lovers."

"I was in hopes, my fortune, rank, and title, might have claimed an exemption."

"Could not your lordship have established a better claim upon age and wisdom?"

"Philosophic ladies, like Miss Fluart, know how to appreciate and despise the foolish things of this world, such as rank, fortune, and title."

"Oh no — they are vastly alluring; I dote upon them. When did a woman despise brilliant trifles?"

"They, possibly, would be Miss Fluart's principal objects in an union with Lord Grondale?"

"To be sure, — one never hears of young women marrying for the venerable qualities of their lovers."

"The declaration is a little alarming. Since the lady knows so well why she marries, it would not be amiss, perhaps, if the gentleman should endeavour to develop his motives."

"Yes, but don't tell the lady."

"My dear Miss Fluart, you are at present too much en badinage.[1] I will postpone my suit to a more serious hour. Only have the goodness to give me some further information respecting Hermsprong and his designs."

"Why, he designs to have Miss Campinet."

"Indeed! this is clear and explicit. And she him?"

"No — she don't know her own mind. There is a little war, I believe, betwixt inclination and duty."

"Are you of opinion, Miss Fluart, that such a match would do honour to the house of Grondale?"

"It might bring a little happiness into it, my lord."

"Happiness! Miss Fluart."

"Yes, — to Miss Campinet, at least."

"And is it possible you can approve of her seeking her happiness by an alliance with an unknown person, a vagabond, for ought she can tell, and who she knows is my aversion?"

"But she does not know why he is your aversion, my lord; or

---

1 Joking or talking frivolously.

why you call him names; and young women like to have their fathers reasonable sometimes."

"Is it of any consequence to Miss Campinet to know, that if she marries Hermsprong, she loses all my fortune?"

"That will be vastly kind, my lord; and who must she marry to secure it?"

"Sir Philip Chestrum."

"Now, dear, my lord, do chuse a man a little lame or blind, or humpbacked, or bending under the weight of time or pleasure; let him be any thing but — Sir Philip."

"Is it that you believe Sir Philip an idiot?"

"Not quite. He can take care of his money and himself; and does not walk into a well with his eyes open. But you know he is silly, my lord; and that weakness of understanding is peculiarly disagreeable to Caroline."

"Miss Fluart," said his lordship, increasing the solemnity of his tone, "I fear Miss Campinet has not had in you so prudent a friend and monitor, as I had hoped."

"If, as I suppose, by prudence, your lordship means money, you are probably right; for as I have always thought it the greatest prudence in the world to make ones self happy, my advice has been mostly directed to that object; and certainly it has been honest advice, at least, for it has been to do what I would myself do in the same case."

"To marry Hermsprong?"

"The question has never come fairly under discussion, my lord. When it does, I shall assuredly decide in the affirmative, if the alternative be Sir Philip Chestrum."

"All that I can gather from this conversation, is, that I have nothing to hope from you, Miss Fluart, for myself, and every thing to fear for my daughter."

"As to hope, but that your lordship seems to have no great opinion of my talents for giving counsel, or I would advise you to give it up; for it depends, you know, upon your becoming amiable, and this does not seem your lordship's forte. For your fears — there may be some foundation, if you fear your daughter's happiness."

"Grant me patience! is there no happiness for her but with Hermsprong?"

"It is a conclusion to which she may soon arrive, if your lordship continues your very politic tyranny in favour of Sir Philip Chestrum."

"Politic tyranny! you are a lady, Miss Fluart. One scarce knows how to apprize a lady, when she takes liberties."

"Oh dear! these are nothing to what I should have taken, had I had the honour to be Lady Grondale. I should have been always blurting out some impertinent truth or other. Thank God, my lord, for your providential escape."

"Miss Fluart, you have disordered me; perhaps broken my heart. I am no longer able to support this cruel conversation."

"Then good morning, my lord; when you chuse to hear me my catechism over again, I am at your lordship's service."

CHAPTER VIII

LORD GRONDALE remained in his study, not broken hearted quite, but rather in a pitiable situation. It was difficult not to conclude that Miss Fluart and Miss Campinet were in concert; and if so, the consequence was obvious. Miss Fluart would prove a jilt, and Miss Campinet a rebel to paternal authority. Whilst his lordship was tormenting himself, Sir Philip Chestrum entered, half angry, half blubbering, to complain to Lord Grondale of the fresh cruelty of his daughter.

"She says she never will have me. I told her I had set my heart upon it, and it would kill me to be disappointed, she said it would kill her to do it, and if one must die, she had rather it was me than herself. How cruel this was, my lord. I told her that your lordship had promised. She said your lordship's promise was not binding upon her.[1] I said every thing in the world to move her, nay, I went down upon my knees to beg her mercy; and just then, Miss Fluart comes running in, laughing as if she would split her sides. And she said, she believed your lordship wanted me in the library; and advised me to come to you, and comfort you, for she believed you was dying as well as me; for you had told her that your heart was broke."

"And shall I bear this? Shall I submit to this?" said his lordship, rising in anger. "A man of my rank, my dignity, my consequence, to be treated thus, by a giggling girl, a chit? No, — Miss Fluart shall

---

1 The idea that one person's promise could not be binding on another was one of the central arguments used by Paine and others against the concept of inherited authority.

feel I am not to be thus insulted with impunity; and as for Miss Campinet, — she shall know what it is to have an angry father. It shall be better for her, never to have been born, than thus to have excited my indignation."

His lordship indulged himself in threats against his daughter, to the joy and comfort of Sir Philip, till he began to feel himself faint; and fearing he might suffer by the indulgence, he endeavoured to mitigate his own rage; and having concluded by affirming upon his honour, as a lord ought to do, that Sir Philip should have her; dead or alive should have her; he dismissed the baronet, and sat down to repose himself.

The demons of hatred and vengeance were however too busy in his right honourable bosom, to suffer his return to much composure; and under the influence of these delectable guests, he rang his bell, and sent an order to Miss Campinet to attend him.

She entered trembling. The furies which raged in his heart, his lordship endeavoured to conceal by a solemnity of deportment.

"Your name, I think," said he, "is Caroline Campinet?"

This question, so awfully put, did not tend to strengthen the young lady's nerves. She answered by a courtsey.

"You will have the goodness, Miss Campinet," said his lordship, "to endeavour to answer by words rather than signs."

"You terrify me, Sir," said the lady.

"You have courage enough to disobey and insult me by your actions, madam; it is pity you cannot, like your friend, support your amiable propensities by words. I wish to know, Miss Campinet, whether you suppose yourself my daughter."

"Certainly, my lord."

"Have you ever heard of any obligation, any duty attached to this relation?"

"Certainly, Sir."

"But this duty does not reach so high as obedience?"

"Pardon me, Sir, I think obedience its first duty."

"Under certain limits."

"I believe, Sir, all the virtues have their limits."

"And to be set by daughters."

"No, — Sir. By reason alone."

"The reason of daughters."

"My lord, I am unequal to this. To a father, I cannot answer what my simple judgment would suggest."

"I am very sorry, Miss Campinet; I have infinite loss in the disability. It would have edified me much to have heard the rights of daughters, and the duties of fathers, descanted upon by so fine an understanding."

"My lord, permit me to retire."

"Not yet, Miss Campinet; will you first have the goodness to inform me, if a marriage with Sir Philip Chestrum be highly disagreeable to you?"

"Yes, my lord, highly."

"Are your objections to the man, or to its being what I wish?"

"Certainly, Sir, — not the latter."

"Let us hear them; silly ones I know they must be; but let us hear."

"My first objection, Sir, is to his weakness."

"Oh, — not so strong as Hermsprong."

"My lord, — I beg permission to withdraw."

"You have most apprehensive fears, Miss Campinet; I suppose you wish to persuade me that you want a wise, a learned husband."

"My lord, I do *not* want a husband. If I were desirous to marry, I own I should wish to be united to a man of sense."

"And you think Sir Philip Chestrum not a man of sense?"

"Yes, Sir."

"Comparing him, no doubt, with that miracle of understanding, and every human excellence, Mr. Hermsprong."

"My lord!"

"What pretty astonishment! as if you did not know that I knew this odious — I beg pardon, Miss Campinet, — this paragon I mean, has been your constant attendant at Falmouth."

"Constant, Sir! I have seen him occasionally, I own. I know not how I could have avoided it with good manners. Mr. Sumelin is his most intimate acquaintance."

"Another most opportune incident; accident I believe you call it. You are excessively fortunate, Miss Campinet. And to be able to join good manners to all these accidents. Good manners will now assist you in rising above the pitiful obligations of life. Good manners and filial duty will be found incompatible qualities. Although you, Miss Campinet, well know the just reasons I have for abhorrence of this fellow, good manners has obliged you to throw yourself in his way, to make him of all your parties; and good manners will teach you how little respect ought to be paid to the commands of a father, when they oppose your inclinations."

"I should have no support, Sir, under the burden of this severity, if I were not conscious I did not deserve it."

"Very well, — let us examine what a young lady means when she talks about her consciousness. I command you to marry Sir Philip Chestrum. You refuse to obey. Why? Your inclinations are otherwise disposed. Is it not so? Is not my statement perfectly accurate?"

"Is it not right, my lord, that I, whom marriage is to make happy or miserable, should be allowed a judgment and a will?"

"Undoubtedly, madam, you are persuaded that your judgment is as mature and ripe for this purpose, as your person?"

"My lord, I am your daughter, and must submit to whatever treatment you please."

"You are my daughter — prove it by your obedience."

"In every other case, my lord. I can honour Sir Philip Chestrum with no sentiment but of contempt."

"I have condescended, Miss Campinet, in this argument rather too much. Let us now come to a decision. Obey me, you have a father. If otherwise, I have not a daughter."

"My lord, I humbly conceive I know my duty, and am disposed to fulfil it; but I hope it is no part of my duty to make myself miserable for life."

"You reason, Miss Campinet; I also reason. It is my duty to give you sustenance because I have the honour to be your father; but I know of no law which binds me to bestow immense fortune upon a daughter, as a reward for disobedience."

"It is Sir, and it ought to be your pleasure, which determines as to fortune, whether I shall have little or much. To your pleasure, in that respect, I chearfully submit; and humbly request you will permit me the choice of that condition which is for ever to constitute my happiness or misery."

"From what pretty playbook have you learned these fine words? From all for love, or the world well lost?[1] And you really, Miss Campinet, prefer poverty and Hermsprong, to affluence and Sir Philip Chestrum?"

"I speak not of Mr. Hermsprong, my lord; but I prefer any condition to that of being Sir Philip Chestrum's wife."

"That being the case, Miss Campinet, and since it has cost you no more trouble to decide, I suppose all connexion between you and me is at an end. No tragedy, Miss Campinet. You will, no

---

1   The title of a 1678 play by John Dryden (1631-1700) about Antony and Cleopatra.

doubt, consider yourself in future as a free independent person, mistress of the superb fortune left you by your foolish aunt. It will procure you food and raiment; and so philosophical a lady, and so much in love, what else can she want? Tears! Pray, Miss Campinet, are they shed for your errors or mine? But you will weep better in your own apartment, where I request the favour of you to remain a few days, till the departure of my guests, whose visit I do not chuse to make uncomfortable by your tragic airs. You will also please to observe, that whilst you chuse to reside in my house, I expect you not to deny Sir Philip Chestrum access to you, should he, after what has past, condescend to desire it, at all proper hours. So, Miss Campinet, wishing you all possible felicity, I remain, as in duty bound, your most obedient father."

Miss Campinet, pierced with grief, but grief mixed with resentment, made a silent courtsey, and withdrew.

CHAPTER IX

ALTHOUGH Lord Grondale had succeeded so well, in mortifying his daughter, his brilliant malignity had failed in giving full satisfaction to himself. In this instance he found the indulgence of malevolence, not the certain road to tranquillity. But sensible of the utility of a mind disengaged, in the business he was going to enter into with his guests, he strove for composure, and the more certainly to obtain it, had recourse to a practice he had often tried with success on fretful occasions, the calculation of the interest due for his money on bonds and in the funds; and this pleasing operation would have restored him to tolerable sanity of mind, but for a note from Miss Fluart, requesting the favour of a few minutes' audience. His lordship's feelings became again tumultuous. Towards Miss Fluart his sensations were rapidly passing into dislike; if we may use so gentle a term; and in his present temper he would most willingly have declined the conference; for it may have been observed by my readers, that though his vanity as well as spleen, was gratified by the success of this triumphant satire, when his gentle daughter was the subject; over Miss Fluart he could boast no such gratification; but often smarted under the playful lash of this laughing, good-humoured, unmalignant girl.

But second thoughts are best, say the people of grey hairs; and something suggested to Lord Grondale, that Miss Fluart might be a messenger of unconditional submission from his daughter; might even be her own embassadress and bring at once the olive branch and myrtle.[1] Besides, politeness would be hurt by a refusal to see the lady, so he graciously replied, that he was much at her service.

Miss Fluart entered the room, not as usual, with a hop, step, and jump, but slow and solemn, and saluted his lordship with a low, silent, and most respectful courtsey.

Lord Grondale thought well of this. It denoted penitence, at least humility; so he rose with dignity, handed the lady to a chair, and then inquired the nature of her commands.

"My lord," said Miss Fluart, "it is to entreat, not to command, that I once more presume to come into your lordship's presence."

Here is a great alteration in language and in tone, thought Lord Grondale; and much for the better; I must be courteous, and smooth the road to penitence. His lordship therefore answered in his gentlest manner, "Miss Fluart could not yesterday have asked of Lord Grondale, what it would not have been an honour and a pleasure to grant."

"I think, my lord," The young lady answered, with inflexible gravity, "it was Friar Bacon's head that said so wisely, time was, and time is past; and what sage Greek was it, who left upon record, that youth has admirable talents for laying up regrets for age."[2]

"It is true, Miss Fluart; all people advanced in years, offer lessons of experience to youth, and wise are the young persons who profit by them."

"My lord, there is no making young persons wise. Don't think of it. I feel it is quite impossible. For myself now, — my time for wisdom is not come; my time for prudence is past."

"Is the latter irretrievable? Have you any particular instance?"

"Yes, my lord; I might have had the honour to be Lady Grondale you know."

---

1 Symbols, respectively, of peace and love.
2 Roger Bacon, a medieval monk and alchemist, supposedly made a brazen head, which, after saying "Time is," then half an hour later, "Time was," and finally, after another half hour, "Time's past," shattered into fragments. The story appears in *Friar Bacon and Friar Bungay* (1594), a play by Robert Greene (1560-92), and a number of poets, including Pope and Byron, allude to it. The "sage Greek" has not been identified; as Faulkner points out, Miss Fluart's comment is a generic warning to youth of the sort that sounds vaguely as if it might be attributable to somebody famous.

"And may, most lovely of your charming sex," said his lordship, half in rapture, and seizing her lily hand, "say so —,"

"No, my lord, I cannot say — though it be very prudent, and so, yet even prudence may have drawbacks upon its enjoyments. Wives may die of husbands' cruelties, as well as daughters of fathers'."

The lily hand of Miss Fluart slipped out of Lord Grondale's; a faint glow embrowned his sallow cheek. He repeated, "Cruelties! well, madam, without canvassing at present the propriety of the term as it respects Miss Campinet, cruelty to Miss Fluart would have been impossibility."

"The impossibility, my lord, never presented itself to me. Perhaps, indeed, you would not have ordered me to marry a being whose personal consequence would not raise him to the dignity of a church-warden; but your lordship might have had propensities of some other sort, which might not have coincided with mine; and then, my lord, if one may judge by the fate of those independent beings who have the misfortune to differ from your lordship in opinion or practice, my comforts would not have been too great, or extremely durable."

"Your friendship for Miss Campinet imposes upon your understanding, Miss Fluart; I am one of those unhappy fathers necessitated to force a daughter to prudence; and you call it cruelty."

"And your lordship paternal affection. An odd sort of affection too, to throw a child upon certain misery, to avoid a possibility of it."

"Miss Fluart, to hear of my daughter's marrying that Hermsprong, deprives me of patience. I would sooner follow her to the grave."

"No doubt, my lord."

"I would, by heaven."

"You need not swear it."

"And to hear you an advocate for it, galls me to the quick."

"Nay, my lord, prudence, if I had it, or self, or something I don't know what, whispers me I should be quite in the wrong to be its advocate. For Mr. Hermsprong says he loves me second best; and I verily believe I should stand first, if Miss Campinet was not my rival."

"And is the gentleman then of such infinite value as to have rival queens contend for him?"[1]

---

1 *The Rival Queens* (1676) was a play by Nathaniel Lee (c.1653-92); the queens in question were Roxana and Statira, two consorts of Alexander the Great.

"He is a most charming man, to be sure."

"This to me! Miss Fluart."

"Oh dear! why, would your lordship lay an embargo upon truth?"

"The more I talk with Miss Fluart, the more I find her an enigma."

"And you don't love riddles, my lord?"

"No, — they are troublesome till found out; and when found out, nothing."

"That is really the best thing I ever heard your lordship say, and so applicable, that I will not presume longer to intrude nothing upon your lordship."

"One moment more, Miss Fluart. You have played with me too long. I suspect you never meant me for any thing more than a dupe. I therefore call upon you in the most serious and solemn manner to say, is your mind irrevocably made up, never to be Lady Grondale?"

"Oh dear, — yes, my lord; II'll swear it upon the bible, if you please."

"I flatter myself, this determination has been lately made. Will you have the goodness to tell me what has produced it."

"Observation, my lord. It has appeared to me, that you have no talents for making women happy. Your forte seems to lie the other way; and one naturally loves ones self so well that one can hardly bring ones self to encounter assured misery, — even for a friend."

"Assured misery! Miss Fluart —"

His lordship stopped, finding himself rather too angry, and fearing for his politeness. After a minute's pause, — "While such are your notions, madam, I believe it may be better to postpone, at present at least, any farther conversation on this head."

"I have the honour to be of the same opinion, my lord."

"Pray, Miss Fluart, what was your intention in seeking me here."

"Simply to entreat the loan of your lordship's chaise one stage towards Falmouth, for Miss Campinet and myself."

"Miss Campinet must have the goodness, a little longer to wait my pleasure where she is."

"Have you not disclaimed her, my lord? Ordered her to consider herself no longer as your daughter? She has just told me so, in agony."

"It is no uncommon thing for fathers to forgive."

"Did Lord Grondale ever forgive?"

"Miss Fluart, I am not at leisure any longer to sport with repartee; you have given me some subjects of consideration, Miss

Campinet others. I cannot, as I ought, attend to these, whilst my guests stay. This will be a few days only; and this time it will be proper for my daughter to remain in her apartment. Over Miss Fluart, I have no right. To remain or depart will be at her own option."

"As I have partaken of Caroline's guilt, I ought to share her punishment; and under so illustrious a jailor — You do not mean to reduce us to bread and straw, — and so, my lord, adieu till better times."

CHAPTER X

THREE happy and quiet days succeeded these tumultuous scenes, in which Miss Fluart almost persuaded Miss Campinet, that fathers may be wrong. On the fourth, a note was received from Lord Grondale, sharply reproving his daughter for ill manners to Sir Philip Chestrum, and contumacy to himself. Indeed, Miss Campinet, unable to conquer her disgust to Sir Philip, had replied to his messages of permission to wait upon her, that she was engaged. Along with this note of his lordship's came one from Sir Philip to his mistress, that he would wait upon her at twelve; and another to both the ladies from Sir John Wing, to say, that unless forbid, he would take the opportunity of Sir Philip's visit, to pay his respects.

Of Sir John Wing I have spoken in a former chapter. He was now become the intimate and well-deserving friend of Sir Philip Chestrum, who, since his residence at Grondale-Place, had borrowed between two and three thousand pounds of him, simply to avoid telling his mamma, that he had entered with spirit into the science of whist; had made great improvements; and for which he had paid, as other young men pay; learning being never so valuable as when dearly purchased. Sir John Wing then became the confidant of Sir Philip's blubbering affection; and having wondered at the caprice which led his lordship to exclude his daughter and her fair friend from the society of his guests; and resolved it into jealousy, for his lordship's future marriage with Miss Fluart had been whispered amongst them; he took it into his head that this jealousy had himself for the principal object; and was quite willing, on his part, to give it a real foundation.

The young ladies, one from obedience, the other from curiosity, having granted the requested permission, the pair of baronets presented themselves, and the first compliments being over, sat down with the usual embarrassment of those who find themselves under a necessity to talk when they have nothing to say.

It was Sir John Wing who first observed that the wind was easterly to-day; on which Sir Philip remarked, that was the reason then why he found himself he did not know how-ish. Sir John said it was a damn'd bad thing to have a constitution subject to squalls of weather. "I myself," he continued, "have one of the first racers in the kingdom; he will beat half Newmarket when the wind is down, and north westerly; and Lord Titchfield's Quetlovaca beat him at Epsom, only because there was a squall at South East."

"A horse of great sensibility, Sir," said Miss Fluart.

"Yes, madam, I'll be bold to say, that I have as sensible horses as any in the kingdom; and know as well what they are about; they never run on the wrong side of the post."

"As men do," said Miss Fluart.

"That is a joke, a very good joke, madam. Yes, they do get wrong side sometimes. You did, Sir Philip, last night."

"One always loses," said Sir Philip, "with that Mr. Lowram, and that squinting gentleman, that never seems to look at his cards. I had rather play cards with these ladies, if they would let us."

"So had I, I swear," said Sir John.

"On our next open card playing day, gentlemen," said Miss Fluart, "we will entreat the honour of your company."

"What is the reason, ladies, we have not the pleasure of your society below?"

Miss Fluart. "Enquire of Lord Grondale, Sir; he does us the honour of protecting us. Our obligations to men are infinite. Under the name of father, or brother, or guardian, or husband, they are always protecting us from liberty."

Sir Philip. "Did not I tell you, Sir John, that Miss Fluart talked one thing always, and meant another. I bet seven to five she don't think women have any obligations to men at all."

Miss Fluart. "How do you think, Sir Philip, I could possibly fall into such an error. Are not you always taking care of us? Don't you want to take care of Miss Campinet?"

Sir Philip. "Yes, — that I do."

Miss Fluart. "And to keep her from harm, shut her up in a cage, as Lord Grondale does now."

Sir Philip. "I'd keep her a coach, and she should go out when ever she pleased."

Miss Fluart. "Indeed! that would be a large allowance of liberty. How can she resist?"

Sir John. "Would a coach tempt you, Miss Fluart. If it will, you shall have two, and go out twice as often as you please."

Miss Fluart. "And shall I have the accomplished Sir John Wing into the bargain?"

Sir John. "Yes, madam; and damme if I think there are three women in the kingdom I would make the offer to."

Miss Fluart. "But they say you are married already, Sir John."

Sir John. "The devil they do. To who, pray?"

Miss Fluart. "To Miss Chance."

Sir John. "Curse me if I ever heard her name. Was it in the papers?"

Miss Fluart. "Yes, in the Morning Herald. 'On Wednesday night a young baronet, not a hundred miles from Bloomsbury, lost twenty rouleaus of guineas, at Brookes's,[1] and took his revenge upon Champagne.' Now, a man that is married to two such dearly beloved wives as the bottle and the dice, can never desire another."

Sir John. "Damme, madam, but you have given me a set down."

And indeed Sir John seemed to feel it, if one might judge by his consequent silence.

"And you, Sir Philip, they say," resumed Miss Fluart, "Are beginning to love a la-mode Sir John Wing."

"Miss Fluart," said Sir Philip, "you never talk to be understood. I don't love nothing in the world so well as Miss Campinet."

"Oh but you will, and better, if you indulge in the agreeable society of Lord Grondale's present guests."

"But I never shall, and it is very unjust for you to say so. But you was always setting Miss Campinet against me."

"Was I? then, to be sure, it must be because I wanted to have you myself. Did not you think so?"

"If I did, I did not think we could set our horses together."

"Then we might have two stables, you know."

"But that would not do. If we did not marry, to live lovingly together, we might as well not marry at all."

---

1 One of the most famous and fashionable of the London gentlemen's clubs in the late eighteenth century. Its members included such notorious gamblers as the politician Charles James Fox (1749-1806) and the Prince of Wales, later George IV (1762-1830). According to a 1796 dictionary, a "rouleau" could contain anywhere from twenty to fifty or more guineas (quoted OED).

"What should hinder us from living lovingly together?"

"One cannot always like where one would."

"Why?"

"Fancies won't always hit."

"And when fancies don't hit, you think it better not to marry?"

"Yes, — every body thinks so."

"Does Miss Campinet's fancy and your's hit?"

"I can fancy she, if she can fancy me."

"Well, I have told you that I could fancy you, if you could fancy me. But you can't, you know; and you say that's a good reason for not having me. Now what's a good reason for you, may be a good reason for Miss Campinet."

This, as Sir John phrased it, was a sort of set down for Sir Philip; but he recovered, by saying, that he never broke his word in his life; and he had given his word to Lord Grondale.

"Then I'll go," said Miss Fluart, "and lay my unhappy case before Lady Chestrum; and I'll give her my word that I will have you; and then you must, I suppose."

"What, whether I will or no?"

"Miss Campinet is to have you whether she will or no, because you have given your word to Lord Grondale, is she not?"

"I won't talk to you no longer, Miss Fluart, you turn and twine one so; and it all signifies nothing; for Lord Grondale says she shall have me; and I can't sleep o'nights for thinking of her."

"Oh then you want her for an opiate."

"I wonder why people can't mind their own business. They say you be going to marry Lord Grondale."

"I never will though, unless Miss Campinet will have you. I should like you every bit as well for a son-in-law as a husband. Miss Campinet, will you take Sir Philip Chestrum for better or worse? This is, I believe, the first time of asking."

"No," replied Miss Campinet.

"And why?" Miss Fluart asked.

"I cannot fancy him," gravely replied Miss Campinet.

"Nor he me," said Miss Fluart; "how sadly we three poor creatures be crost in love. What is to be done, Sir Philip, with this perverse girl?"

"It's all along of you, Miss Fluart, and that there Hermsprong," said Sir Philip.

"Hush, Sir Philip," said this lively lady, "walls have ears; don't talk of that there Hermsprong, he's such a boisterous wretch you know."

"Yes, — there's a rod in pickle[1] for him though, I can tell you that; he'll be glad to get off where he came from, I believe; and then I hope, Miss Campinet, you won't be so cruel shy."

"Sir Philip," said Miss Campinet, "I cannot trifle upon a serious subject. I owe you civility as the guest of my father, but I will never be your wife."

"Never, Miss Campinet?"

"Never."

"What, not for all Lord Grondale? May be you may change your mind, when you know how bad he has behaved to my lord; and what a rogue and rascal he is; and a French spy; and come to inveigle people to America."

"Whatsoever he may be," Miss Campinet answered, "it will not lessen the distance between you and me. On no consideration will I ever be your wife."

"Oh dear!" said Sir Philip, half sobbing, "what have I done? You have never given me no reason."

"I will give you reasons now," Miss Campinet replied; "your understanding is weak; your spirit mean; and your mind malignant."

"I'm sure," said Sir Philip, rising in a passion, — "I'm sure you use me worse than any dog."

"So she does," said Miss Fluart; "I am quite ashamed of her; go, and tell her daddy."

So ended this love scene.

CHAPTER XI

SIR PHILIP CHESTRUM, disconsolate, followed the hasty steps of Sir John to the stable, rather mortified at such cavalier treatment of a man of his consequence.

"I am for a ride this morning, Sir Philip," said the latter gentleman, "shall I have your company?"

Sir Philip assenting, they mounted, and rode a mile in deep meditation, one upon the cruelty of Miss Campinet, the other on the impertinence of Miss Fluart. At length Sir John broke the long

---

1   A punishment. The phrase comes from an old practice of storing the birch switches used to give whippings in brine in order to keep them flexible.

silence by saying, "Damme if I understand these Cornish diamonds, as they are called.[1] This lady of yours took the liberty of saying very shocking things to you, Sir Philip; and that Miss Fluart too, —'faith she has a tongue."

"Don't you think Miss Campinet quite pretty?" Sir Philip asked.

"Yes, they are both pretty, — but so damn'd proud."

"Miss Campinet is reckoned quite contrary," said Sir Philip, half crying, "what in the world shall I do?"

"Why, do as I intend to do," Sir John replied. "Keep out of the way of these high flown beauties. Give me a girl of easy virtue, to visit when I like, and leave when I like; not a proud high-born thing, who because I have been foolish enough to marry her, thinks it her prerogative to black ball me whenever I do a naughty thing."

"But I do love her so," said Sir Philip.

"What breed of spaniels art thou of, baronet? Thou lovest the more, the more thou art beat.[2] Now, damme, I make it a rule never to love any thing that does not love me."

"If I had ever such a mind to be off, I could not for Lord Grondale; for my mother and he have quite agreed about every thing."

"Your mother and he! Pray, baronet, how old are you?"

"I am turned six and twenty."

"And in leading strings.[3] And so thou wantest a wife to lead thee, instead of a mother. For shame, be a man."

"You don't know my mother; else you would not think it so easy, to get out of her claws."

"As if the world was not wide enough. Take my advice now. In four days I'm off for Newmarket. Then we have made a party to shoot growse. Then for London, my buck. That's the place to cure thee of thy milkiness. Keep me company next winter, and if I do not bring thee into Cornwall next summer, cured both of thy love

---

1 "Diamond" could be used as a slang term for a beautiful woman; a Cornish diamond is a type of shiny quartz found in Cornwall — considerably less valuable or desirable than real diamonds.

2 The idea that spaniels cravenly fawned on those that beat them was commonplace in eighteenth-century writing; compare Mary Wollstonecraft's barbed comment that "Gentleness, docility, and a spaniel-like affection are ... consistently recommended as the cardinal virtues of the [female] sex" (*Vindication of the Rights of Woman* OUP 1994, 100).

3 Literally, strings attached to the clothing of young children who were just learning to walk; figuratively, an indication of continued immaturity.

and obedience, tell me I know nothing. I'll shew thee girls as handsome as Venus, and as kind as handsome. I'll introduce thee to Earls and Dukes. Break thy chains, and be a man of fashion."

"But you know," said Sir Philip, "I am not so tall, and sightly, and well shaped as most gentlemen are."

"Baronet, I'll shew thee amongst the lords the ugliest fellows in the kingdom. What's personal beauty in a man? no body thinks about it."

"But I shall never get Miss Campinet out of my head."

"There's nothing like one girl to drive out another. Love the whole sex, my buck; that's the way. Apropos, what dost think I chose this rough stony road for?"

"Because you did not know it, I suppose."

"Wrong, baronet; it was because I did. Do you see that pretty little snug red house in the valley? It contains two sweet girls. A little skittish though. A week since, in one of my rides, I saw them clambering up that hill. Egad, I gave my horse to my servant, and began to clamber after them. Off they sprung another away, and in ten minutes were got, like rabbits, safe in their burrow."

"What then? You did not take them for loose women, did you?"

"No — damn'd virtuous; but women sometimes change their natures. Now I heard a sort of whisper at Grondale Hall, — by the bye, that father-in-law of yours, Chestrum, has some damn'd bad points about him. I heard I say that Lord Grondale threatened their father with a jail, for an old debt they say, and none of the most honourable; but that is nothing to us, my boy; it will make the girls the more come-at-able."

"But what excuse can you find for going in?" Sir Philip asked.

"To inquire the road," Sir John answered; "one easily loses one's road in this cursed country. And then for the chapter of accidents."

Sir John alighted as he said this, and hung his horse to a gate; Sir Philip followed his example, it must be owned not with much alacrity; and they proceeded towards the house. But the chapter of accidents had prepared a scene unfriendly to that sort of love, which had crept into Sir John's bosom, at least. The doors of the house were open; no servants seen; nothing heard except a shriek from a distant room. Fear of seeing disagreeable things, or being involved in disagreeable consequences, prompted Sir John to retire; and his still more timid friend declared his resolution to go back. In passing out, they were met by Mr. Hermsprong, accompanied by the man servant of the family, a man of a respectable appearance, who, on seeing the arrest of his master, had ran of his own accord to a neighbouring village, to advertize a friend of Mr. Wigley's, of this unhappy business. This friend was not at home; and the man, on his return, had met Mr. Hermsprong, whom he knew, and who, having observed his distraction, stopped him to inquire into the cause. He told all he knew; and all he knew was, that his master had been arrested at the suit of Lord Grondale. He described this master as one of the best and most inoffensive of men; he had lived with him almost twenty years; and in all that time his master had no connexion whatsoever with Lord Grondale. His mistress too was an excellent mistress, and her two daughters charming young ladies; and they loved one another so, he was sure it would break his mistress's heart.

The story was more pathetic than was necessary to induce Mr. Hermsprong to fly to the relief of this afflicted family; and the more, as he suspected from the name of Lord Grondale, whom love, omnipotent as he is, could not make him think on without scorn and dislike, that it was most probably some act of tyranny or mean revenge.

On meeting the two baronets, Hermsprong touched his hat, and complaisantly[1] said, "I am sure I see Sir Philip Chestrum here from a motive of benevolence; I presume the same of you, Sir, whom I have not the honour to know."

Sir Philip looked sullen, Sir John rather confused. Neither answered.

"Have you seen the unfortunate Mr. Wigley?" Hermsprong asked.

"I don't know Mr. Wigley," said Sir John.

"Nor I," said Sir Philip.

"The ladies, perhaps," said Hermsprong.

"I don't understand by what authority you question us," Sir John Wing replied.

"I wonder what obligation I have to you, that I should give you an account," said Sir Philip.

"You are right, gentlemen; I perceive I was wholly mistaken," Mr. Hermsprong answered, and passed on.

"Who is the fellow?" Sir John asked.

"What, don't you know him?" Sir Philip answered; "it's that Hermsprong, that Lord Grondale hates so."

---

1 Pleasantly or courteously: the term did not have the negative connotations of its modern homophone "complacent."

"And whom his daughter loves."

"I wonder what she can love him for."

"Perhaps for throwing you over the rails."

"You need not fling that in my dish. He took me unawares."

"You were even with him. That swearing the peace against him was a damn'd spirited thing; and wise as spirited; for the fellow is cursedly muscular. So let us get out of his way."

Sir John spoke as he thought; but in a tone and manner as if he did not intend Sir Philip should believe he thought so. It brought upon the latter, however, one of his long sulky fits; so that in their ride back to Grondale, Sir John could not draw from him more than a monosyllable.

CHAPTER XII

CONFUSED and indistinct sounds directed Mr Hermsprong to the usual sitting room of the family. The most conspicuous object was Mrs. Wigley sitting. She certainly was not dead, yet she scarce seemed to live; nor had she fallen into a swoon, for her eyes were open, and she appeared to see, though not to observe. Her face, once so pretty, had lost its colour; her arms hung languidly down; and in a coffin, she would have been taken for a beautiful corpse. Her eldest daughter was on her knees; her head supported by her mother's lap; but her arms thrown round her mother's waist; whilst from her bosom came the bursting sigh, frequent and deep. Not far thence was the younger daughter in hysterics, held by the two maid servants of the family, profuse in tears and loud in lamentation. A little dog, the favourite of this young lady, was at her feet. And now he stood up, looked moaningly at her; turned three or four times, and lay down; then rose again; gave a mournful whine; turned round as before, and again lay down. This circle of movements the poor animal continually repeated. The last of the distressed group was Mr. Wigley himself, leaning against a wall of the apartment; and surveying the scene around him with an aspect half expressing grief; and half astonishment, bordering on stupidity. Near the door were a bailiff and his attendant, with faces rather of sorrow for their success, than of exultation.

The first reflection which occurred to Hermsprong, you might almost call it an exclamation, was, "What a total imbecility is here!" Yet, all weakness as he thought it, compassion sprung into his eye. He went up to Mr. Wigley, and in the kindest tone, said, "You will pardon a stranger for his intrusion, Sir, when you know my motive is to serve you."

It was evident Mr. Wigley did not understand, for he did not answer, and his eye had only the vacant stare. He addressed himself to Mrs. Wigley, who continued unmoved; but her eldest daughter raised her eyes, and met his, beaming with benignity.

"Resume your tranquillity, Miss Wigley." So he addressed her. "Assure your mother this affair will be without consequence."

"Must not my father go to prison, Sir?" said the pretty apprehensive sufferer.

"Most certainly not," Mr. Hermsprong answered; "if, as I learn from your servant, the affair is simply debt."

"Oh! but I fear it is large," said the young lady.

"Think not of it, Miss Wigley; endeavour to comfort your mother."

"Who, Sir, shall I say, —"

"My name is Hermsprong, madam; I fear a stranger —"

"Hermsprong!" replied Miss Wigley.

"Hermsprong!" repeated the bailiff.

The female servants reiterated the word. Mr. Hermsprong himself was astonished. It was new to him that his was become a name which humane people had learned to pronounce with transport. It even roused Mr. Wigley from his seeming stupefaction.

"Are you indeed Mr. Hermsprong?" he asked.

"Such is my name, Mr. Wigley; and my desire is to serve you. Put me to the proof. All will be well. Assure Mrs. Wigley so."

Then going to the bailiff, he said, "I am afraid, Sir, I have not credit with you sufficient to induce you to permit your prisoner and myself a conversation of half an hour in a private room?"

"Sir," answered the bailiff, "the sheriff must pay the debt, if he now escapes, and I and my sureties must pay the sheriff. Yet if you will give me your word — you know what I mean, Sir —"

"I do know what you mean; and give you my word, no injury shall accrue to you from the permission. I beg your acceptance too."

The bailiff declined his offering hand.

"My friend," said Hermsprong, "It is an acknowledgment of your humanity, not a bribe to neglect your duty. Your heart is too gentle for your office."

The bailiff took his present with a bow, and sighed as he received it. Mrs. Wigley was now fast recovering; she was made to understand Mr. Wigley was not to go to prison; and at present this was full consolation.

Mr. Wigley's tale was a plain one, and had all the marks of truth; for nothing was glossed over, nothing palliated; he confessed his youthful errors, and lamented them. His patrimonial estate was about 700l. a year, and he came to it at the age of twenty-one. Mr. Henry Campinet (now Lord Grondale) was nearly of the same age, both lovers of field sports, and almost inseparable. Their intimacy looked like friendship. The connexion was closer still, when Mr. Campinet became Sir Henry. London and Newmarket became the principal seat of pleasure. Mr. Wigley stood it five years, and might have stood it six, but that a salutary fever brought him leisure for reflection. He ventured on an accurate inspection of his own affairs; and found, that the interest of his debts exceeded the revenue of his estate. Sir Henry Campinet had the goodness to take this estate, to pay these debts, and to grant him an annuity for life of 200l. per annum, secured on the estate itself. It had never been raised, and Sir Henry Campinet had reason to be well satisfied with his bargain. Soon after, Mr. Wigley married a lady of some, but not large fortune; which he caused to be settled on herself. She had beauty too, and Sir Henry found it out. I suppose he thought it a privilege of friendship to share this with his friend; but Mrs. Wigley was simple enough to be offended at the proposal; and as he grew more importunate, was under the necessity of making a confidant of Mr. Wigley. Perhaps it was owing to the prudence of Sir Henry that the affair ended only in cessation of friendship. But great men are said not easily to forgive those they have injured. Vengeance may sleep, or seem to sleep even for years. But it may wake; and a contested election, in which Mr. Wigley had been active against the candidate supported by Lord Grondale, did awake it on the part of this nobleman. The only means of gratification now in his lordship's power, were such as himself must have been ashamed to use. At least I hope so; for to affirm any thing upon so obscure a point is beyond my daring. It was now approaching towards twenty years, since, at the adjusting a gaming account between these dear friends, Mr. Wigley appeared indebted to Sir Henry about 300l. For this a bond was given; Sir Henry at the time saying he would never accept the payment till his friend was 5000l. in bank. Two years after, whilst they were still friends, Wigley offered to pay it. Sir Henry said it was cancelled; and received the thanks of his friend for this act of generosity. For this bond, with its legal interest, was Wigley now arrested.

When the gentlemen returned to the sitting room, they found the ladies had recovered some degree of tranquillity, the hysterics of the younger being over. After saying some things to them, not a little consolatory, he addressed the bailiff.

"My friend, this debt must not be paid, for it is not due. Mr. Wigley chuses to contest it. I leave him therefore under your friendly guard, till I return to offer the necessary bail."

I need not be particular as to the conclusion; a few hours were sufficient to put an end to this detestable business, — and forever.

CHAPTER XIII

IT may be now expedient to look in at Grondale-Hall. In the apartments of the ladies, there was plenty of repose, but in those of the gentlemen, there was action of so great vivacity, that it dissipated harmony, and dissolved friendship. Sir John Wing, during the ride home, had again endeavoured to incite Sir Philip to be a gentleman of the very first world; and became convinced that he was fit for nothing but the lap of his mother, or his mother's maid; and therefore it was best to make the most of him for the short time they had to stay. He communicated this notion to Mr. Lowram, and he to the rest, except Lord Grondale. They agreed that it was a prudential business, and that they would enter upon it that very day, having fixed on Mr. Lowram himself to occupy his lordship's attention in the fullest manner possible. These associates began by complaining at dinner, one that he was stupid; another of a violent head ach; a third of want of appetite; a fourth of an unaccountable dejection of spirits. All however agreed that wine was the universal panacea. All therefore drank *ad libitum*,[1] and with such success, that every malady gave way. After this they proceeded to the proper business of the evening. When their accounts were closed, Sir Philip Chestrum was declared to have lost 5000l. Altercation ensued. At length they agreed to retire, and postpone the elucidation of these mysteries till the hour of breakfast. The tone of Sir Philip's complaints in the morning would have subjected him both to the mirth and the insults of the associators, had not Lord Grondale, (who thought it ungentleman-like to plunder his intended son-in-law, and exclude himself from any share) taken up Sir Philip's cause. The quarrel became so serious, that Lord Grondale's

---

1   Freely. "Stupid," in the previous sentence, is not used in its usual modern sense but rather suggests a temporary state of dullness or stupor.

guests announced their immediate departure, and this bosom society was dissolved for ever. That I may not have occasion to mention it any more, I shall say now, that a month after Sir John Wing waited on Sir Philip, at his seat near Falmouth, to offer him the polite alternative of paying his debts, or meeting him in the field of honour. Lady Chestrum said it was not in the paltry field of modern honour, her noble ancestors gained their laurels. So Sir Philip paid like a man of honour.

CHAPTER XIV

IT cost Lord Grondale some hours to get rid of his vexation, so as to be of proper temper of mind to meet Miss Fluart and Miss Campinet at dinner, to whom he had sent a card of invitation, or rather of command, to come. In this necessary work of tranquillising himself, he was assisted by the good Doctor Blick, who had returned from a long absence on the higher duties of his ministry; and had proceeded immediately to the Hall, to pay his usual tribute of respect and admiration where they were so justly due.

On sitting down to dinner, a little embarrassment arose. The head of the table was vacant, and Miss Campinet, not chusing to take it, unless ordered by her father, sat down in her usual place.

"My dear," said Miss Fluart, "Is not that your seat?"

"I do not offer it to Miss Campinet," said his lordship, "till she understands her duties; but if you, Miss Fluart, will condescend to take it, ——"

"I cannot indeed, my lord," this young lady answered; "I have not the proper merit."

It should seem by the cloud on his lordship's brow, that this speech did not meet his approbation. And indeed considering the sacrifice his lordship had made to the fair speaker, it was not gracious. But when will young ladies learn to say nothing they ought not to say? A cynic would say, never; but I am not a cynic. It is scarce reasonable to expect it while they are young, beautiful, and goddesses; that time past, I do not see the absolute impossibility of it.

The time of dinner was not very lively, but might have been instructive; for Lord Grondale called forth the whole abilities of Sir Philip Chestrum; and all the Raioules, with their fields *d'or et d'argent*,[1]

---

1 Fields of gold and silver; heraldic terms.

their feats of chivalry, their intermarriages, with all that the gentlemen of the herald's office think of the first importance, came forth in due procession, and stood before the wondring eyes of Miss Campinet. To this were added, and here Sir Philip was peculiarly eloquent, all the dresses of all the Countesses at the grand court days. Sir Philip had never before been so brilliant. Almost he had forgot the misfortunes of the preceding evening, when the indiscreet Miss Fluart, taking the opportunity of a pause, said, "Oh dear! I did not think there had been such famous folk any where, except the Amadises of Gaul, and the Don Bellianusses of Greece.[1] Pray, Sir Philip, were none of the Raioules hanged?"

"Hanged, madam!" said Sir Philip, his lips quivering with rage, "hanged!"

His lordship was shocked also; so much that he burst into an involuntary laugh, which all his power was unable to restrain. When this little convulsion was checked, he said gravely, "Young ladies are privileged. We allow them, Sir Philip, to say what they please. The pretty things have seldom any meaning."

"I subscribe to the wit and truth of this, as I do of most of your lordship's general remarks," Miss Fluart replied, "But really I had some meaning in the question; for surely if the exploits of many of Sir Philip's noble ancestors, as related by himself, were to be now performed, even their being lords would scarce screen them from the gallows."

"They lived in times of violence," his lordship said; and what more he would have said, must be for ever unknown, for Mr. Corrow was announced; Mr. Corrow, from whom his lordship expended intelligence of the gratification of that little matter of revenge with which he had indulged himself against Mr. Wigley. But Mr. Corrow had been under the necessity of accepting bail; and his lordship found himself under fresh obligation to that bird of ill omen, Hermsprong.

It was some time before Lord Grondale's anger would permit his ears to open to the consolations of his lawyer; who at length

---

1 Amadis of Gaul was the eponymous hero of a Portuguese or Spanish romance, which, in its earliest written form, was published in 1508 by the Spanish writer Rodriguez de Montalvo; *Don Belianus de Grecia*, another Spanish chivalric romance, was written by Jeronimo Fernandez in 1547 and later considerably expanded. Like *Amadis of Gaul*, it was one of the books to be reprieved from the bonfire of foolish romances in *Don Quixote*.

informed him, that he had proof that Hermsprong had endeavoured to entice Wigley to America; which, though not directly penal, might, in the present temper of the times, be made something of.

"And," said the lawyer, "I have hints of other little circumstances. He has read the Rights of Man;[1] this I can almost prove; and also that he has lent it to one friend, if not more; which you know, my lord, is circulation, though to no great extent. I know also where he said, that the French constitution, though not perfect, had good things in it, and that ours was not so good, but it might be mended.[2] Now, you know, my lord, the bench of justices will not bear such things now; and if your lordship will exert your influence, I dare say they will make the country too hot to hold him." This complacent idea restored his lordship to tolerable temper; so that he returned to the dessert with Mr. Corrow; who by the way, he desired to make Hermsprong the subject of his discourse. The obliging attorney knew it was not panegyric his lordship wanted; so he turned his talents to obloquy; and Hermsprong became, under his skilful hands, a tolerable monster of deformity. Unfortunately, the ladies, for whose good it was intended, were taken all at once, with hardness of heart, and all manner of unbelief. Nay, it was said, but it was too incredible to be believed, that twice the lively Miss Fluart made the lawyer blush.

CHAPTER XV

WHEN Lord Grondale came down to his book room the next morning, he found, among others, the following letter.

1　It was not illegal to read *The Rights of Man*, however controversial it was, but Paine himself was convicted of treason in absentia (he had fled to France) after the publication of the book.

2　Again, there was nothing obviously illegal in these comments, although the treason trials of 1794, in which several pro-Revolutionary writers were tried on the charge of high treason, had made some of the more radical thinkers nervous. The argument was that, by raising the possibility of changing the English form of government, they were implicitly "imagining the king's death," one of the grounds of treason (on this subject, see John Barrell, *Imagining the King's Death*, Oxford, 2000). They were acquitted, in part because of a brilliantly argued pamphlet by William Godwin, but the anxiety caused by their prosecution still helped dampen later radical rhetoric.

To Lord Grondale

Unless your lordship can prevent it, by some honourable satisfaction, a shameful tale is going to be told, in itself incredible, had it been told of other actors. It is of a nobleman who could call a man his friend; live with him for years in the greatest intimacy; introduce him into the gay scenes of fashionable life; permit — perhaps meditate — his ruin; attempt the chastity of his wife; foiled in this, persecute him with little arts; at length, pour the full urn of vengeance on his head — for virtue; for to support the freedom of elections, is surely political virtue, in every creed but the creed of courtiers. For daring to support our boasted constitution, while your lordship was sapping it, this man, whom you had every way injured, you dared to send to prison; you dared to arrest him for a debt, obsolete by the laws of your country, and cancelled by your own word. It was my happy fortune to be passing near his house, soon after your lordship's honourable attorney had seized his prey. The distraction of this unhappy house I would endeavour to describe, did I not know the attempt to inspire your lordship with feelings of pity would be fruitless. And for what could you thus desolate a respectable family?

"Could you but have seen, my lord! I saw; and have prevented ruin, and expelled despair. I have added one more to the black catalogue of crimes, for which I have your lordship's execration, and for which you are meditating my destruction. Come on, my lord. I offer myself to your lordship, for an experiment of what wealth and power, aided by malignity and the spirit of the times, can do against innocence.

C. HERMSPRONG

If Mr. Hermsprong thought, that by writing this letter, he should convey any spark of remorse or compunction into the breast of Lord Grondale, he deceived himself; it only made his lordship mad. In a paroxysm of rage, he sent for Miss Campinet. Instead of the polite irony with which he used to torment her, he now abused her in the vulgar tongue with all the power of language; spoke, though not very intelligibly, of the new insult he had received; swore, yes swore, he would stab her with his own hand, — yes, with his own hand, — sooner than she should be Hermsprong's. Finally, he gave her his last, positive, and peremptory orders to prepare for immediate marriage with Sir Philip Chestrum. Three days he would give her, to return to duty and chearful obedience. On the fourth, it should be solemnized even by force; if she were still so foolish and obstinate to render force necessary.

"Yes, pretty Miss," continued his lordship, "And consummated by force also, if your body be as refractory as your stubborn soul."

Trembling at her father's fury, and shocked by his menaces, Miss Campinet dared not to utter a syllable in reply; but receiving her dismission, retired to pour her tears in the bosom of her friend.

His lordship's next step was to send for Mr. Corrow, who lifted up his eyes in pious astonishment, that a man so daring as Hermsprong should exist. "But," says he, "your lordship shall be rid of him by some means."

"By any means," his lordship answered.

"Apparently legal," said the lawyer.

"*Per fas et nefas*,"[1] returned his lordship.

"By G–d," says the honest attorney, "I will have him taken up as a French spy, if your lordship will support me."

"I will support you," his lordship replied; "I will; and perhaps this is really the case."

"By the bye, my lord, I believe he is no more a spy than I am. His reputation is actually rising in the county. People of some consideration begin to talk of him, and give him credit for many virtues."

"Damn his virtues," his lordship answered. "How, Corrow, can you talk so like a fool."

"Nay, my lord," said the skilful attorney, "it is not I, for I am not a man to be deceived by appearances. But opinion, I am sure I need not tell your lordship, opinion is very powerful."

"We must counteract it, Corrow. We must be active, enterprising. I would give the man a thousand pounds who should remove him from the kingdom, so that I might never see or hear of him more."

Mr. Corrow promised and departed.

Lord Grondale then adverted to his daughter, whose timid spirit he doubted not he could bend to his will, but for the interference of Miss Fluart. This young lady he now hated as much as he once thought he loved her; yet to turn her out of his house was so violent a breach of politeness, he could not resolve upon it. So much however did he fear her machinations, that he sent re-iterated

---

1 Justly or unjustly.

orders to Miss Campinet, not to leave her apartments; at the door of the gallery, which led to these apartments, including Miss Fluart's also, he placed a confidential servant, as a sort of porter; with orders to permit no egress to Miss Campinet; nor letters or messages to pass that door, even to Miss Fluart, but by his own order.

If the case of the young ladies was pitiable, that of Sir Philip Chestrum was not to be envied. Lord Grondale and he were tiresome companions to each other. Into the ladies' recess Sir Philip could not gain admission; he dared not take rides into the country for fear of Hermsprong, now more than ever terrible to him. He durst not go home without Miss Campinet; for that would be to own he had deceived Lady Chestrum, in his representation of this young lady's affection for him; nor did he know how to answer the honourable calls which he feared would be made upon his purse by Sir John Wing, without the knowledge of his mother. So he took the wise resolution to stand by Lord Grondale, and marry his daughter, whether she would or no; or, as we elegantly phrase it, in spite of her teeth.

CHAPTER XVI

SO great was Lord Grondale's indulgence, that, except from apprehension, the gentle Miss Campinet had peace two days. On the third, his lordship thought proper to summon her once more, and the first stern question was, as usual, had she disposed herself to obedience.

Miss Campinet threw herself at her father's feet, and as well as she could speak for tears and terror, requested from his hand the death he had threatened, rather than Sir Philip Chestrum. To his lordship, this was disobedience, aggravated, as he thought, by reproach. His gouty hand was lifted up to strike. It fell — with no great violence indeed — but sufficient, with her fear, to lay the lovely Miss Campinet prostrate on the carpet. There he spurned her with his foot; then commanded her to rise, to leave his presence, and to prepare for marriage on the next morning, or for everlasting imprisonment, or something still more terrible; and so terrible was now his lordship's countenance, that his affrighted daughter rose, and as fast as her trembling limbs would permit, ran back to her own apartment.

The agitated frame of his lordship was this day destined to endure another shock; for before he could compose himself to tolerable tranquillity, he received the following.

I now take the liberty to thank your lordship for those kind intentions of which I am informed by public whisper. The assault and battery action of poor Sir Philip Chestrum is not a master piece of invention; but the accusation of inveigling Wigley to America, the reading the Rights of Man: Above all, your lordship's circular letter is admirable; in particular, the inference that I must be a French spy, because your lordship does not know my birth and parentage. Yet it is probable that something still more ingenious, more spirited, must be thought of, or I may still breath the same air with your lordship; still be your lordship's monitor; and perhaps the historian — of your virtues.

But I have more to thank your lordship for, and still more cordially, the treatment of your daughter. I love Miss Campinet, and though she has not told me so, I believe our love is mutual. But duty to her father obstructs the confession, and its fruits. Do not, my lord, be so cruel to me as to be kind to Miss Campinet. Let me entreat you to proceed in the same paternal course; shew her you are her tyrant, not her father; and confirm her affections irrevocably mine. Yes, my lord, still imprison her; still insult her with opprobrious language as false as malignant. Still force her to marry the *brave* and *respectable* Sir Philip; still stab her with your own hand, my lord, and you rivet her affections to the man on earth you most detest. But confine her still more closely, my lord; let not a mouse enter your doors without your knowledge; redouble your vigilance, or she may still escape you.

Your lordship will suspect perhaps, that I have a source of intelligence within your house. I have, my lord; but lest your anger should fall on innocent servants, I tell your lordship candidly, Miss Fluart is the traitress.

CHARLES HERMSPRONG

But for the opportune appearance of the good Doctor Blick, I know not whether his lordship must not have sunk under this fresh attack upon his nervous system; but this gentleman had a balsam which never failed in its healing powers, when applied to Lord Grondale's wounded pride. On this great occasion, it was copiously used, and the wound healed apace.

"But is it not, my good Doctor Blick," said his lordship, "is it not perfectly strange and unaccountable, that this man, who, from the first hour I saw him, has endeavoured to affront and offend me, should pretend to love my daughter."

"If any thing could be strange in such a man," the Doctor replied, "this would be so; but his intolerable pride and headstrong vanity —"

"Does he not know," said his lordship, interrupting the doctor, "that she will be only the heiress of my sister, if I please; and that offending me, she will have seven thousand pounds to her fortune, instead of two or three hundred thousand? for I assure you, Doctor, if she does not marry to-morrow morning, for no longer will I suffer my patience to be abused, I will take legal measures for her disinheritance. I will leave my fortune to hospitals," continued his lordship, "or to Bedlam."

"Your lordship need not be reduced to that extremity," said the doctor; "there are worthy individuals still, though the age is corrupt; men who would use your lordship's bounty for the service of mankind — men who —"

"Are dressed in black," said his lordship, "and, merely to serve mankind, pant after mitres and lawn sleeves."[1]

"Your lordship is so humourous," said the doctor; "but I hope the church is not really fallen into so low estimation with your lordship, that —"

"Why no," his lordship replied, "it was never so high as to fall."

These and a few more sallies contributed much to restore his lordship to his wonted state of mind; and consulting the reverend doctor, what ought to be done with Miss Fluart, it was concluded that her presence would probably impede or prevent the ceremony of to-morrow. Were she away, it was not likely so gentle a spirit as Miss Campinet's would resist her duty. On which conclusion Lord Grondale wrote the following note.

Lord Grondale's compliments to Miss Fluart, has received from Hermsprong another most insulting letter, wherein insolence is carried as high as it can go; and in which he informs him that Miss Fluart has given him certain intelligence which ought not to have passed this house. Lord Grondale therefore thinks Miss Fluart an improper guest in it, and requests the favour that she will leave it as soon as convenient. It is known to Miss Fluart that Miss Campinet's marriage takes place to morrow morning; of which, as Miss Fluart has always been an opponent, it is presumed she will

---

1 A clergyman would wear black; a mitre and lawn (a fine linen) sleeves are part of a Bishop's regalia.

not be a pleased spectator; and as Lord Grondale considers Miss
Campinet's refractoriness as the sole work of Miss Fluart, and
hopes to see no more of it, it will be more agreeable to him, if her
removal can take place before the hour. A chaise as far as Bodmin
waits her orders.

This was the answer.

Miss Fluart's compliments to Lord Grondale; is sensible that
many things have passed in his lordship's house, which ought not
to have passed there; she confesses the intelligence; allows Lord
Grondale's right to chuse his guests; and intends to depart at ten in
the morning; but without troubling his lordship for a chaise. At
what hour of the morning her friend is to be sacrificed, she does
not know; but thinks the sacrifice will not be compleated, when
Lord Grondale sees his daughter so changed, that even Sir Philip
Chestrum will shrink from her offered hand.

The morning came, and with it, to the two friends, the sad
necessity of parting. At ten the chaise appeared. The tender leave
was taken in Miss Campinet's apartment; and tender it must have
been, for Miss Fluart, unable to look up, her handkerchief before
her eyes, and sobbing as if her heart would break, ran through the
hall, and threw herself into the chaise. Miss Fluart's maid followed,
without the least symptom of distress, erect, and smiling a courteous farewell to those servants who were in the passage. Lord Grondale, whose dressing room fronted the court, had taken the trouble to slip on his morning gown, in order to enjoy the happy
minute when his house would be rid of one who had inflicted on
him such a variety of torment. He saw her enter the chaise, he saw
her whirled away, and I hope, said a prayer of thanksgiving.

CHAPTER XVII

I HAVE not thought it necessary till now to acquaint my readers,
that when Miss Fluart had extinguished the flame she had lighted
up in the right honourable bosom of Lord Grondale, his lordship
felt an inclination to reinstate Mrs. Stone in all her former rights
and privileges. Indeed she had been a kind nurse to him; and oft,
since her departure, had he missed her cherishing care, in the little
daily complaints to which his debilitated body was now subject.

She too, did not find herself happy in the deprivation of the power and pre-eminence she had so long possessed. No sooner therefore was the overture made on the part of the lord, than it was graciously accepted on the part of the lady; and there succeeded, as usual, after differences of this nature, a great increase of confidence. She had returned several days before Miss Fluart's departure, but she wished, if possible, it might remain unknown to the ladies, because Miss Fluart had not treated her with due respect.

The ladies did know it however; and indeed every thing that passed in the house which they chose to hear; for so great is the difference betwixt kindness and tyranny, that where Lord Grondale had only servants, Miss Campinet had friends.

An hour after Miss Fluart's departure, Mr. Corrow having arrived with the parchments necessary to be signed previous to the ceremony, and Doctor Blick every moment expected, it was thought proper to send Mrs. Stone to Miss Campinet with a message from his lordship, requiring her presence. Mrs. Stone accordingly sent in a message to the young lady, requesting permission to wait upon her. Miss Campinet's maid returned for answer, that her lady had lain down, being unwell; but should be glad to see Mrs. Stone.

On her entrance, Miss Campinet apologized for her unpolite reception, saying, that in addition to her other complaints she had a severe tooth-ach, which had swelled her face, so that she could scarcely speak to be understood. Mrs. Stone was sorry, extremely sorry, and said, after delivering his lordship's message, that if she wished a delay to the ceremony, on account of her health, she would endeavour to persuade his lordship to indulge her; although both the lawyer and the clergyman were come.

Miss Campinet thanked Mrs. Stone for her kindness, but declined the postponing the ceremony. Suspense, she said, was a disagreeable state of mind; nor did she chuse any more to irritate Lord Grondale. She said she knew she should fright Sir Philip when he saw her face; but she owned that gave her little concern; requested Mrs. Stone to carry her duty to Lord Grondale, and say, she would attend the company in a few minutes, hoping for all the indulgence her pain and weakness demanded.

Mrs. Stone having delivered her message, Miss Campinet was waited for with solemn and expectatious silence; and in a few minutes after she entered; her face almost covered with her handkerchief. Lord Grondale pointed to a chair.

"I am sorry, Miss Campinet," his lordship began, "to see you indisposed on a day which ought to be a day of joy; but a return to duty will best restore you to a quiet mind; and this, to personal health. I presume I now see you disposed to obedience."

Miss Campinet bowed.

"You are scarcely dressed as I could wish you for the occasion," his lordship continued, "but after the ceremony this little error may be corrected."

Again Miss Campinet bowed.

"Mrs. Stone," said his lordship, "will have the goodness to officiate as bridesmaid; this is a necessary consequence, Miss Campinet, of certain things which have passed, and which may now be buried in oblivion. It is first necessary to sign the marriage settlements, in which you will see that my paternal care of you has not been diminished by — but of that no more. Sir Philip, approach and sign."

Sir Philip did so.

"Now, Sir Philip," said his lordship, "lead your bride to the table." And in an audible whisper, he added, "salute her as your own."

"O dear, how happy I am," said Sir Philip, as he approached the lady.

It was her duty to take the handkerchief away to receive the salute. She did this with the greatest possible courtesy, and discovered to the enamoured bridegroom, not the face of Miss Campinet, swelled with pain, but the individual countenance of Miss Maria Fluart, with an arch smile upon it, that did not at all denote the timidity of a trembling bride.

Poor Sir Philip, as if he had seen the face of Medusa,[1] flew back, and encountered a girandole, which fell to the floor, a girandole no more. Of the astonished spectators of this extraordinary metamorphosis, the reverend Doctor lifted up his eyes and hands toward heaven, in pious wonder; the lawyer stared — a vacant stare; Miss Campinet's maid burst into laughter; Mrs. Stone had the utmost difficulty to refrain; Sir Philip's features bore all the marks of fatuity; and fire began to flash from the terrific eyes of Lord Grondale.

All were dumb; Miss Fluart saw the necessity of some one beginning to speak; so she addressed Lord Grondale very courteously.

---

1 In Greek mythology, one of the three Gorgons. Anybody who saw her face would be turned to stone.

"My lord, you seem disordered; I hope I have not been the unfortunate cause — I, who desire to do every body good."

Lord Grondale answering only with looks of fury, this young lady addressed Mrs. Stone, who, she said, she was quite happy to see on so joyful an occasion, and whom she congratulated on being restored to her rank and dignity. Mrs. Stone not answering, she applied to Doctor Blick.

"Doctor," said she, "You came to marry somebody, I presume. Is it of any importance to you who? I offer myself to your benediction. Are you ready, Sir Philip?"

The baronet looked a little surly, and began to pick up the fragments of the girandole.

"Oh dear," says the lady, "I fear I shall not be married to-day, unless your lordship, or you, Doctor Blick, will take pity on me."

At length Lord Grondale found his speech. "It is possible, Miss Fluart, you may think this frolic innocent, but consequences may flow from it which you may not expect."

"I am quite easy about that, my lord; provided the consequences follow that I do expect."

"What are those?" his lordship asked.

"The happiness of your daughter, my lord."

"Is happiness to be purchased by disobedience?" asked Dr. Blick.

"Yes, Miss Campinet's," the lady answered.

"I suppose you know, young lady," said the Doctor, "that it is my duty, my office, to advise, admonish, reprove —"

"In all Christian humility," replied Miss Fluart; "when Doctor Blick can prevail upon himself to wear that garb, I believe I may promise to become his humble scholar."

"Have you no reverence, madam, for the sacerdotal character?"

"Much, Sir, for the character; little for the mere habit."

"This, madam, to me!"

"This, Sir, to you."

"Do I appear in your eyes to wear the habit only?"

"Very much so, Sir."

The Doctor's cholor rose; he felt a suffocating sensation somewhere; a sort of swell about the praecordia;[1] but he suffered in silence.

---

1 The part of the chest around the heart.

As nobody seemed inclined to speak, Miss Fluart rose from her chair, made a low courtesy to Lord Grondale, thanked him for all favours, made him adieu, and walked gently out of the apartment, followed by Miss Campinet's maid.

The Reverend Doctor Blick's zeal now burst its bounds.

"If these things are to be suffered, my lord, farewell to all religion and morality."

"What can one do," said his lordship, "with a giddy girl?"

"The law corrects women as well as men, my lord; otherwise there would be no living with them."

"The law!" said his lordship. "Corrow — what say you?"

"No doubt, my lord; the law doth coerce women; but whether this be a case to which the law will apply, I have not duly considered."

"Were it my case," said the mild Doctor, "this impertinent young woman should never leave this house till she had atoned for her evil doings; for depend upon it, my lord, it is more she than Miss Campinet, that has crossed your lordship's inclinations."

"But how could I be justified in detaining her?" said Lord Grondale.

"I own," says Corrow, "I do not at present see the mode of justification, but I think, a little consideration, might shew us one, by the aid of Doctor Blick, in his capacity of justice of the peace."

"But in the mean time," said Lord Grondale, "the girl will be gone."

"Then, my lord," said the Doctor, "I advise your lordship immediately to go and stop her. I will forfeit my head if we do not find a legal and justifiable cause."

"Very well," his lordship replied; "I will delay her for a few hours, at least, till you have well considered."

His lordship left the room, to execute this gracious purpose.

CHAPTER XVIII

ALONG with his lordship went Mrs. Stone, not by any means as approving the design of detaining her, which she did not wish, and which she thought futile and illegal. They found Miss Fluart and Miss Campinet's maid ready, and at the instant of departure. Lord Grondale seemed flurried. His beautiful yellow face had taken a deeper hue. He spoke, and gasped as he spoke, so that he was not very intelligible. Miss Fluart most politely reached him a chair, and said, "Don't hurry yourself, my lord; take time; and do me the favour to inform me what has occasioned me the honour of this visit."

"Miss Fluart," said his lordship, "You are —"

"I know I am, my lord; but not very well what."

"Where is Caroline Campinet?"

"I really cannot tell, my lord; I have not seen her since ten this morning."

"And do you think, Miss Fluart, that I am a proper person to be thus played upon?"

"Very proper, my lord."

"And can you, madam, after all that has past, — can you hope to escape me with impunity?"

"Why," says Miss Fluart, with a roguish smile, "what can your lordship do?"

"It is you who have encouraged Caroline in her disobedience."

"It is so, my lord."

"And you have the effrontery to confess it to my face?"

"My dear lord, that is not a polite word to a lady; that effrontery — it is almost calling me an impudent baggage. However, my lord, I do confess it; and am much inclined to boast of it too."

"Probably you contrived the elopement of this morning?"

"Yes, please your lordship, I contrived the elopement of this morning."

"Perhaps concerted it with Hermsprong."

"Not impossible."

"Where is she gone?"

"Cannot your lordship guess?"

"To Scotland?[1] Death, madam, you do not mean it. If such is her folly, the remainder of her days shall be bread and water. And her husband, if he dare to be her husband, shall have the most rigorous punishment the laws can inflict. He shall know what it is to steal an heiress."[2]

---

1 That is, he suspects her of eloping; see note 1, page 235.

2 Until the early nineteenth century, "stealing" an heiress was a crime that could be punished by execution. It was not a law that was often invoked, however; in the opinion of Sir Robert Chambers, in his *Lectures on the English Law* (1767-73), "That this crime is now so little known may be in some degree the consequence of this law, but is more probably the effect of general intercourse and a more open state of life which gives fewer opportunities for forcing inclination and more of gratifying it" (ed. Thomas M. Curley, 2 vols., U of Wisconsin P, 1986, 1: 408).

"An heiress! why, has not your lordship had the goodness to disinherit her?"

"No, madam, that was intention only, not fact. She is still an heiress. The crime is capital, and you are accessory before the fact."

"Oh dear! how you take a delight in terrifying poor innocent young women. But, pray, my lord, what is stealing?"

"A carrying off, and a consequent marriage."

"Yes; — but when a man and a woman go quietly into a post chaise together, it may puzzle the judge and the jury, to determine whether the He carries away the She; or the She the He."

"The law, madam, respecting the delicacy of the sex, always supposes the man the seducer, and treats him accordingly."

"The law is vastly obliging to Caroline; but to poor I, who was only a secondary, it is monstrous cruel. But, my dear lord, can you have the heart to hang me? Me, whom you loved so well?"

"Have you, madam, any possible claim to my favour or indulgence? You, who have injured me in the tenderest points."

"Now, do let us hear those points, my lord; I should like to know what I am to suffer for."

"You gave me all possible reason to believe you designed me your hand."

"Certainly, my lord, you took the reason, if there was any; I always told you, I believed I could never prevail upon myself, to give my consent; and you see I was right."

"You meant I should believe the contrary. You meant to deceive."

"Perfectly sensible I was not a fit wife for your lordship, how could I think upon imposing a deceiver upon the just and generous Lord Grondale, whose character for integrity stands so high?"

"Dare any man impeach it?"

"That would be what you call *scandalum magnatum*,[1] would it not, my lord? But people will talk, especially women."

"Yes, women are immaculate; they never deceive or betray."

"A little of both sometimes."

"It is not impossible but Miss Fluart may feel herself guilty."

"Not of betraying; for when had I your lordship's confidence? Did you intrust me with the paternal resolution of killing your daughter with your own hand, if she would not marry Sir Philip Chestrum; the most contemptible of men?"

---

1   See note 1, page 60.

"Nonsense! how could it impose upon you?"

"On me it did not. But it terrified Caroline quite out of her senses, so that ever since she has been obliged to me for a little understanding. I taught her, that under your lordship's paternal affection, she could not possibly fail of being miserable; under Mr. Hermsprong's conjugal one, it was not impossible she might be happy. I taught her, that your lordship, having violated all the duties incumbent on you as a father, she owed you nothing as a daughter. Then Hermsprong wrote very moving letters, and said very moving things —"

"Said! what! interviews too!"

"Don't interrupt me, my lord. In short, I endeavoured to convince her you was one of the most odious gentlemen in all these parts. After which, I had nothing to do but to contrive to get her out of your right honourable clutches; no difficult matter, but that I had so much to do to make her perform her part; for if left to herself, she would have preferred death by your honourable and paternal hand. Don't you think you have great obligations to me, my lord?"

"Yes, by heaven, madam, and I will repay you. Out of this house you shall not stir, till I deliver you up to due course of law."

"And, pray, my lord, by what authority do you pretend to confine me? Watson, you are my servant now. I order you to follow me. We are under the necessity of leaving this hospitable house by force. Stand off, my lord."

His lordship now began to bawl out for his servants. The butler ran, the cook, and two footmen.

"Stop this woman," said his lordship; "stop her, I charge you."

"Let me see who dare," said Miss Fluart, producing a pistol, and almost overturning his lordship as she passed.

"Seize them, I command you," said the enraged Lord Grondale.

No one obeyed; and the intrepid Miss Fluart walked on to the hall door, which she opened herself unimpeded even by the porter. At the door of the garden leading into the village, she was received by Hermsprong and Glen; for historical veracity obliges me to make known to my readers, that this was a concerted plan, and that these gentlemen were prepared to rescue Miss Fluart by force, had any insult been offered her, of which they were to have been apprized by the butler, a respectable man, who had seen with equal shame and disgust, the infamous treatment, for so he scrupled not to call it, to which his beloved young mistress had been subjected.

CHAPTER XIX

SOME of the numerous complaints which afflicted the august person of Lord Grondale were supposed to arise from vitiated bile, and which the emotions he had lately undergone were not at all calculated to sweeten. An increased yellowness denoted his lordship to have undergone some change from the tempests which had lately shook him. The men of medicine called it jaundice; but whatsoever it might do to the body, it did not in the least alter the fabric of his lordship's mind.

On the third day after her departure, Miss Campinet wrote the following letter.

My heart is humble; it is tender; and beats towards its only parent; but I know not in what words to address a father who believes he has cause to be offended. It is with sorrow and regret I learn, that my friend's vivacity has led you, Sir, into the error of supposing that I had totally thrown off the duty of a daughter, and had gone off to Scotland for the purpose of marriage. No, my lord; I am with my respectable and venerable aunt, Mrs. Garnet. In my unfortunate situation, to whom else could I so properly apply, for shelter from malevolence. Nor is Mr. Hermsprong an inhabitant of the same house; his own delicacy pointed out its impropriety.

I will not deny, Sir, the high esteem I have for this gentleman, whose general manners obtain the respect of every one. I cannot forget that he ventured his life to save mine, and saved it. I regret the proud inflexibility of his behaviour to your lordship, for which I cannot account. This excepted, he is, what your lordship must like, if he were better known; for a spirit of undeviating rectitude, which spurns at every thing mean and selfish; an unruffled sweetness of temper, and a soul of benevolence, must merit, and obtain, your lordship's approbation.

But whatsoever may be my sentiments respecting this gentleman, they shall not interfere with my duty, if my father will listen to the request of his unhappy daughter. I promise, Sir, not to marry without your approbation, if you will have the goodness not to insist on my marrying against my own.[1]

---

1 This was the arrangement that Clarissa Harlowe had vainly sought to make with her own father in Samuel Richardson's immensely influential novel (1747-48). By Bage's day, this would have generally been seen as exemplifying the proper attitude of a dutiful child.

It afflicts me, Sir, to hear you are less well than usual; my most earnest wish, is, to be permitted to pay you always those affectionate duties and attentions, which would be so pleasing to me to perform, could I be allowed to hope you would be pleased to receive them from your most dutiful daughter

CAROLINE CAMPINET

Whatsoever Lord Grondale might have thought of the more dutiful and affectionate part of Miss Campinet's letter, he was much too irritable to bear the praise of Hermsprong. He chose to answer as follows.

To Miss Campinet

I know not why I should take the trouble to answer your eloquent and pathetic epistle, Miss Campinet, but to shew you I see through your little arts. You love — but do not, like Antony, chuse to lose the world for love.[1] You would wait a year, or, as you may hope, a month or two, till you have raised the marble monument over my grave; have shed a few pious and thankful tears upon it; and then perhaps dance around it with the man, who, ever since the first unfortunate moment I knew him, has taken every occasion to insult and offend me. But it is quite enough, Miss Campinet, to give him your fond heart and pretty person. To add my estate to it, would be to overwhelm him with felicity. This must be my care.

Fathers in general are accustomed to expect submission from their children, and obedience. I have a daughter who knows the rights of women, who stipulates conditions with her father; who talks prettily about duties and attentions; who takes the trouble to become her father's preceptor; and points out for his imitation a pattern of rectitude and benevolence, in a young puppy, who may, for ought she knows, be of the dregs of mankind, a mere fortune hunter, with all the simulation and dissimulation belonging to that class of human beings. It will however soon, sooner than you wish, be seen, whether the law will be as indulgent to him as a love sick girl. For the rest, give yourself no trouble, Miss Campinet, about your filial duties. I have no daughter.

GRONDALE

---

1   Another allusion to Dryden's play *All for Love, or, The World Well Lost*; see note 1, page 270.

P.S. Mrs. Garnet is to shelter you from malevolence! Yes, —
as the procuress does her innocent virgins. Could she shelter you
from my power, do you think, did I believe you worthy of its exertion?

CHAPTER XX

THIS was indeed a cruel letter; Lord Grondale had surpassed himself. Miss Campinet would have sickened and died perhaps, had
not Miss Fluart laughed; had not Mrs. Garnet soothed; and had not
Mr. Hermsprong reasoned. Whether his reasoning was just or otherwise, I do not decide; but I believe it was efficacious.

"Will Miss Campinet have the goodness to inform me, if our
actions can have better guides than the rule of plain and simple
justice? The condition of your being, would have carried you
almost instinctively, to have resisted your father, had he made a
sudden attack upon your life and happiness; ought he less to be
resisted because the attack is pre-meditated? Because the fault is
greater on his side, ought your obedience to be greater also? I had
a father, whom I always obeyed; whom I always thought it my duty
to obey, because his commands seldom wounded my feelings, and
never insulted my understanding. I loved him. Could I have loved
a tyrant? In vain would the reasoners of this polished country say,
every thing is due to the authors of our existence. Merely for existence, I should have answered, I owe nothing. It is for rendering
that existence a blessing, my filial gratitude is due. If I am made
miserable, ought I to pay for happiness? Suppose me the child of
an ancient Grecian parent, who, not chusing to support me, had,
according to the existing laws of his country, exposed me to perish.[1] Suppose me preserved and educated by a stranger, whose
compassion would not permit me to perish. Is it to the author of
my existence, or of the happiness of that existence, to whom I am
in debt? For a moment, lovely Miss Campinet, lay aside your pre-
conceived notions of duty, and tell me in what part of Lord Grondale's conduct to you, can you recognize the care and tenderness
of a father?"

---

1 Spartan — and early Roman — law gave the father the right to abandon
   unwanted children to die of exposure.

Miss Campinet was at first angry to hear paternity thus treated. Then she wept. With her tears, her compunctions seemed to decrease; and in a few days, she dared to admit of consolation.

They reasoned too at Grondale-hall, I believe, in a different manner. It was not of justice they talked; it was of law. To drive Hermsprong out of the kingdom was of the first necessity to Lord Grondale. His second great object was to disinherit his daughter.

For this, Mr. Corrow was ordered to consult the attorney general, and to take the proper steps immediately. Not quite content with this, his lordship wanted to force Miss Campinet home again; for considering how few pleasures he now possessed, the pleasure of tormenting could not be parted with, without great reluctance. But this, Mrs. Stone opposed, for she had spirit, and was by no means destitute of humanity. After one of those conversations, in which his lordship discovered more malignity than Mrs. Stone could bear, she told him plainly, that she would neither be an instrument of his inhumanity, nor a witness. The day that forcibly brought back Miss Campinet, should be that of her own departure from Grondale for ever; so his lordship was forced to be content with the instrumentality of law. Not less was his unfortunate lordship embarrassed by Hermsprong. Neither the obsequious doctor Blick, nor the zealous Mr. Corrow, were so positive in their assurances as they had been, for they had begun to fear. It had happened, that notwithstanding those irregularities of Hermsprong's character, which unfitted him for the society of English gentlemen; notwithstanding he eat only to live, and had not yet found out the ravishing pleasures of the bottle, or those still more extatic of cards and dice; yet there was something so engaging in his manners, that where he came, he pleased. Men, who could not find in their hearts to imitate it, applauded his benevolence; and all admired his free and manly spirit, which had shewn itself in many instances, which a good biographer would have thought it his duty to record. I am not a good biographer; and shall conclude this eulogium by saying, that he began to be considered as a man of property, as well as respectability; and that Mr. Corrow thought it wise not to go rashly and blindly on. But these were morning fears; the evening consultations had more of spirit and of expectation; and in the last of these, it was concluded, that Hermsprong should be summoned by Doctor Blick and another justice, before the whole bench, at the next quarter sessions; that the most able counsel should be retained, and amply paid for his utmost exertion. That the whole force of their artillery should be brought down at once, to obtain a commitment to prison. Once there, they might easily find means to retain him, till he would be sick of his confinement, and consent to exchange it for another kingdom.

CHAPTER XXI

WHILE the sessions were approaching and his lordship, with his co-adjutors, preparing the threatened thunder, news arrived that the miners were in a state of riot; the motive, dearness of provisions.[1] The second day's report was, that their numbers increased; that they threatened violence; that the magistrates durst not act. The third day's intelligence was still more alarming. There must be French agents amongst them. The fourth, that they were coming to pull down all lords' houses, especially Lord Grondale's; for he was a miner; had gotten rich by the sweat of their brows, and for any good he had ever done, they had never heard of it. His lordship justly alarmed, gave orders for an immediate journey to London; when in the evening of that day, he had the agreeable intelligence that the mob had dispersed without doing much mischief, and had returned peaceably to their labours.

Amongst the other minutiæ of information, it was told his lordship that Hermsprong was amongst the rioters, and had even been seen to give some of them money. Doctor Blick and Mr. Carrow, who knew his lordship's taste, were of opinion that he could be there for no good; and that it almost confirmed the suspicion of his being a French spy. After an hour's ingenious reasoning, it became a certainty; and on it, above every thing else, they grounded their expectations of a commitment.

In the interim, before the day of appearance came, no pains were spared to procure every kind of sinister information respecting Hermsprong. The inquiry was unfortunate. Mouths in plenty were ready to open in his praise; not one to his discredit. This operated in a wonderful manner. Doctor Blick found out, that no

---

1   There was some unrest among Cornish miners in 1795 (presumably the year in which the novel is set), but there was also considerable general alarm about food shortages and the possibility of riots throughout the 1790s, fears which reached their climax around the time of the writing of *Hermsprong*, in the famine year of 1795.

man would give himself the trouble to please every body, without great and uncommon motives. In proportion as he was plausible, he must be the more dangerous. His talents were finely calculated for the office of a spy; and a spy he certainly was. "I assure your lordship," said the good Doctor, an hour after dinner — "I assure your lordship, it is very seldom, very seldom indeed, that I have been mistaken in my judgments of men."

CHAPTER XXII

LORD GRONDALE had resolved to honour the county court with his presence. There was an impropriety in it, no doubt, which his lordship could not entirely overlook; but once the culprit was undoubtedly a French spy, it became a man, zealous for the welfare of his country, to overlook little improprieties, in the pursuit of an object of so great importance, as that of ridding the kingdom of a traitor.

Lord Grondale entered the court, attended by a numerous suite, amongst whom were half the bench of justices. In passing along the hall, he had the mortification to see Hermsprong elegantly and rather richly drest, in conversation with Miss Fluart, and accompanied by many gentlemen of genteel appearance. In Mr. Hermsprong's face appeared no signs of dejection, shame, or fear. He seemed all spirit and animation. His party took their seats, when the court proceeded to business, and he presented himself in obedience to his summons.

Doctor Blick first spoke: — "This young man, whom I believe to be a very suspicious person, and know to be a very impertinent one, I have summoned before me at this place, and at this hour, on the charge of Mr. Corrow, here present. It was for rioting, and sufficiently warranted my committing him to prison; but that I chose, in order that it might be the more solemn and efficacious, that it should be rather the act of this court, than solely my own. I call upon Mr. Corrow to inform the court of his grounds for laying the information."

Mr. Corrow rose, and delivered himself thus: —[1] "At a time when the nation is so greatly, excessively, and alarmingly alarmed, agitated, and convulsed; when danger is so clearly and evidently to

---

1   This phrase and the previous paragraph were added in 1799, replacing the following sentence from the 1796 edition: "Previous to moving for Mr. Hermsprong's commitment, it was necessary to state to the court the reasons for such motion, and the advocate his lordship had chosen, addressed the bench in the following words:".

be feared, dreaded, and apprehended, from enemies both exterior and interior, it behoves the magistrates of the several counties to be wakeful and vigilant in detecting, discovering, and bringing to condign punishment, all traitors who are working and hatching their wicked and diabolical plans in secret.

"A very terrible, dreadful, and alarming riot has, as you well know, been set on foot in this county, and there are also many and manifold reasons to believe that it was raised, excited, and supported by secret emissaries from France. A person who calls himself Hermsprong, I suppose the same who now sits here in obedience to his summons, was seen many times amongst them, was heard to harangue them, and what is in this case a most suspicious and atrocious circumstance, and I dare say your worships will think as I do, was observed to give money; to give money, gentlemen; please to take particular notice of this.

"That this person is not well disposed towards this government, in church and state, appears in various multitudinous modes and manners.

"He has also counselled and advised sundry subjects of this his majesty's realm of England, to migrate to America, and hath promised pecuniary and recommendatory aid and assistance to enable them so to do.

"Although there may be other particulars of a public nature, tending to criminate this person, I do not think a larger and more copious catalogue is necessary to be exhibited to this worshipful bench, because the proof of all will lie before a court of superior jurisdiction. But there are matters of a private nature, which indeed are rather to be considered as civil injuries, but the mention of which may serve to strengthen and corroborate the general idea that ought to be formed of such a person. What I mean, is the whole tenor of his conduct to Lord Grondale, a nobleman of the first consequence, whose numerous virtues it is not in my power to praise as they deserve. To this noble lord, his personal conduct, deportment, and behaviour, has been in a high degree insulting, not only in contempt to the noble lord's own person, but in interfering whenever he could do the noble lord an injury, or even a spite. Of this nature was his bidding against his lordship's agent, though otherwise requested, for a house lately occupied by his lordship's sister; and which, lying as it were in the centre of his lordship's domains, ought, in reason and the nature of things, to become the noble lord's property. This purchase, however, I presume to think, we shall shortly set aside in the court of King's-bench, by proving the purchaser an alien. This insulting purchase, made, it should seem, out of a bravado to the noble lord, is farther aggravated, by introducing into the house a relation of the noble lord's, who had been rejected by the family for an indiscretion, which his lordship's honourable house could not pardon. This person, Mr. Hermsprong, a stranger to her, who heard of her only by chance, has brought just under his lordship's nose, as one may say; and chusing to set up a carriage, I do not presume to know upon what means, under the pretence of its being the property of the noble lord's rejected relation, has had the presumption to put upon it the family arms, an indignity I suppose no noble lord could put up with. But all these things are trifles to what I shall now mention, the highest of all civil injuries, the seduction of the noble lord's daughter —"

Hermsprong, whose countenance had hitherto exhibited no stronger emotion than a placid smile, now suddenly rose. The act of rising, and the fire that sparkled from his eye, stopped the pleader. "Seduction, Sir!" said Hermsprong. But recovering himself, and bowing to the bench, he said, "I ask pardon of the court," then casting an indignant glance at the advocate, sat down.

There was something in Hermsprong altogether, which inspired the attorney with a sensation resembling timidity; at least, he lost part of that effrontery, so useful, and so used, in his profession; and said, in a tone less exalted, "The gentleman's interruption did not give me leave to finish my period."

"No," said the Reverend Dr. Blick, "it did not. To interrupt a gentleman in the midst of his pleading, is a high contempt of this court, and ought to be punished by commitment."

Hermsprong looked full in the worthy magistrate's face. It was a look which seemed to say, can this be possible? and it ended with a smile of such superlative contempt, that the doctor felt his cholor rise to an invincible height.

"If magistrates," said he, "are to be thus treated, — on the very bench, — in the actual performance of their functions, — I know not who will sit here — certainly not I."

A murmuring noise ran round the court. The justices had a sort of whispering conference, and seemed rather disposed to espouse the cause of their offended brother, when Mr. Saxby, who sat in the chair, a gentleman of the greatest weight upon the bench, having been bred to the bar, and leaving it on his accession to one of the largest estates in the county, demanded silence.

"I blush," said he, "when I see this court attend to the passions of any of its members, or of its own. What may be the nature of the particular offence given to our reverend brother, I know not; it was contained in a look; and this court, I think, has not cognizance of looks. As to the offence against the court itself, it was the smallest possible. It was an instant, perhaps a laudable impulse, and instantly and genteelly atoned for. I request there may be no farther delay of our proper business."

Doctor Blick making no answer, but by a look of swoln malignity, the lawyer proceeded.

"It was my intention to explain to the gentleman, that by the word seduction, I meant, not of the person, but the affections; which I suppose the gentleman does not mean to deny."

"Is it," Hermsprong asked, "is it permitted me to deny?"

"Better," Mr. Saxby replied, "when this gentleman has said all he intends."

"I was just on the point of finishing," replied the attorney; "for as to the gentleman's rude assault and battery on the person of a most respectable baronet, now in court, (for Sir Philip was of Lord Grondale's suite) that will be heard before another tribunal. It rests with the bench to determine, whether the causes I have enumerated are sufficient for commitment."

"It is not," said Hermsprong, rising, "from confidence in my own abilities, that I presume to address the court myself, rather than by the aid of an advocate, but, totally ignorant of what I could be accused, it was not possible for me to give instructions. Indeed the learned gentleman's oration has shewn me, how formidable a structure may be raised on a very slender base of truth. Fiction of law, perhaps, may be the learned gentleman's general guide, as it is in the particular instance of my having rudely beat a respectable baronet now present, whom, however, I appeal to himself, I did not beat. It is true, the respectable baronet did not comport himself quite to my liking, so I took the liberty to remove him out of my way; but with so cautious a delicacy, that so far from dislocating a limb, I did not even discompose a curl. For this offence, however, I am not called to answer at this tribunal.

"Respecting Lord Grondale, there is against me variety of charges. First, disrespect to his person. To this I plead guilty, and freely confess I have no respect for his person. If this be a crime in the English jurisprudence, I must be content to suffer the penalty.

"I am accused of bidding against his lordship's agent for a house put up to sale by public auction. In this, I offended not against law, I presume, but courtesy. I own I was advertised against whom I was bidding. But if Lord Grondale's agent meant to intimidate me by the mention of so great a name, I was under the necessity of shewing I was not to be so intimidated. If it was designed as an exercise of my complaisance, I did not think it fair to require such complaisance at an auction. I wanted a fixed habitation; I liked the romantic scenes around, and I had other reasons why I wished for a residence in the vale of Grondale.

"But in this habitation, I am accused of placing a relation of the family, a person of indiscretion, so great, that the noble house of Grondale could not pardon her. This person was no other than the aunt of Lord Grondale, who, unkindly treated at home, gave her affections and her hand to a Mr. Garnet, a merchant, affluent then, and of integrity untainted; of a character indeed, which, if noble lords would stoop from their dignity to obtain, would do them more honour than all the insignia the herald's office can bestow. The property of a merchant however is insecure almost to a proverb. He suffered immense loss in the West-Indies. He went in person to reinstate it. In this he was but little successful. On his return he perished by a wreck of his vessel. Of his remaining fortune, so much was swallowed by legal contention, that when his debts were paid, so little remained to the widow, that she has since struggled with every want but the want of pride, which would not permit her to ask or accept charity. The noble lord, her nephew, was made acquainted with her situation, both by herself and others. To every application his lordship answered, he knew her not. It was indeed true — he knew her not. When I did, it became my first wish that she would permit me to consider her as a mother. I applied for this valuable privilege; I obtained it; and so dear to me is the distinction, I would not exchange it for his lordship's barony.

"But the climax of my offence against Lord Grondale is the seduction of his daughter. I know not whether the laws of England give its advocates the liberty, however they may stand in an opinion of popularity, of saying any thing, every thing with impunity; of loading the opponent client with every obloquy that sinks his character from man to monster; but if they do not, you, sir, (to the lawyer) must answer me this charge in another court. I have not her person, though I hope I may possess her affections; whether won by philtres, or by what other seductive means, it may become your province, Sir, to explain.

"These are my private crimes, or what the learned gentleman, I imagine calls civil injuries. My public crimes are, that I have advised and promised to aid sundry of his majesty's subjects to migrate to America.

"That I may be a French spy. And

"That I have been a rioter.

"All that can be proved against me without perjury, I will save the court time, by open acknowledgement.

"There is a Mr. Wigley, probably known to many gentlemen here, who has had thoughts of quitting this country for America. This gentleman has asked my advice. I have given him information only, for I do not chuse to give advice which may hereafter subject me to reproach. If the court demands, or Lord Grondale desires, a full explanation of Mr. Wigley's motives and my own, I am ready to give it.

"The next charge against me is, that I may be a spy! Is then the state of this kingdom so deplorable that Magistrates think it their duty to act upon a may-be? Or, suppose it so, are suspicions so raised, are alarms so high, that actions, which candour and justice might equally as well attribute to laudable intentions, shall be so interpreted by malignity, as to become the pretence for depriving an innocent man of his freedom?[1]

"That I went amongst the rioters is true; and it is true that to some I gave money. Why may it not be supposed that this was done to allay the riot, as well as to foment it? Was I seen committing any acts of violence? Was I heard uttering any seditious harangue? If I was guilty of any illegal act, surely the proof lies with the accuser. What is his evidence? If it appear to you, as to the candid Dr. Blick, whose pious hope it would be pity to disappoint, I ask not your mercy — I demand your justice."

"The evidence must be reserved for the day of trial," said Mr. Corrow.

"Enough should be given," the chairman answered, "to justify our committing the gentleman, at least, which is what you desire of us."

No answer being given, the junior justice of the bench, a young

---

1   This paragraph is a 1799 revision of a passage that, in the 1796 edition, reads: "The next charge against me is, that I may be a spy. So, gentlemen, may you, if you please; but the accuser seems to have forgot to say by what deeds I have manifested this spy-ship. If these sentiments offend you, I am here to answer for the offence. I ask not favour; I demand justice."

Mr. Hermsprong here ceased to speak, and the court remained a few minutes silent. A sort of astonishment seemed to have pervaded it, I know not whether produced by Hermsprong's arguments or his intrepidity. At length the chairman said, "You have taken no notice of the leading charge against you, that of being amongst, and of giving money to the rioters."

"That I went amongst them," Hermsprong answered, "is true; and that I gave money amongst them, is true. My accuser says these must have been with a bad intention. I deny that it was so."

The paragraph then continues with the sentence beginning "Was I seen ..." and concludes with the words "the proof lies with the accuser. I demand his evidence."

man who had just qualified, rose and said, "Since nobody else will give evidence, Mr. Hermsprong, I will. I went amongst the mob according to my duty, and twice I read the riot act in vain.[1] I saw this gentleman amongst them, but knew not his design. On the third day I heard him speak, and his seditious discourse ran in these terms. 'My friends, perhaps it may be true that your wages are not adequate to the furnishing you with all the superfluities of life which you may desire; but these are unhappy times, and require of you a greater degree of frugality and forbearance. My friends, we cannot all be rich; there is no possible *equality* of *property* which can last a *day*. If you were capable of desiring it, which I hope you are not, you must wade through such scenes of guilt and horror to obtain it, as you would tremble to think of. You must finish the horrid conflict by destroying each other. And why should you desire it? The rich have luxurious tastes and disease; if you have poverty, you have health. Add but content, and you have all that is worth having here.' A turbulent fellow interrupted him here with 'Damn you, who are you? What business have you here preaching amongst us? As if we did not know what's what as well as you.' Mr. Hermsprong answered with great mildness, 'My friend, it is to little purpose who I am. I ask of you only to attend to the reasonableness of what I say. Truth is worth our regard, by whomsoever it is spoke.'

"'Damn you,' replies the other, 'I believe you are one of King George's spies, and no better than your master.' Mr. Hermsprong, without reply, knocked him down. This astonished the crowd, and not a hand was raised against him. The man rose with his head a little bloody, and was slinking. Mr. Hermsprong called him back. 'My good friend,' said he, 'I am sorry to have hurt you. Any thing you had said relative to myself, I should not so have resented; but to revile your *King*, is to weaken the *concord* that ought to subsist betwixt him and all his *subjects*, and overthrow all civil order. I hope you will be sorry for your passion, as I shall then for mine. Pray, accept this half crown; I give it with all my heart.' The man took it, though awkwardly; and this gentleman continued to speak to the crowd, 'I wish, my friends,

---

1 "Where twelve or more persons are committing a riot, it is the duty, under the Riot Act (1 Geo.1 [i.e., 1714], st. 2, c. 5), of the mayor, sheriff, and certain other officers to make a proclamation in the King's name, commanding them to disperse; and every person who obstructs the making of the proclamation, or continues to riot for one hour afterwards, is guilty of felony" (P.G. Osborn, *A Concise Law Dictionary*, 2nd ed. London, 1937, 278).

I was able to supply all your wants, and give you all your reasonable desires. But I am a single individual; you are many. If, however, there are any amongst you who have large families, now wanting food, I have some silver, and to such I freely give it. You, Sir, (he now addressed a man of the best appearance amongst them) you, Sir, are a neighbour. Neighbours only can know one another's wants. To you I intrust this purse. There is honesty in your face. I am sure you will dispose of it among those who want, and want the most.' The man, flattered with the distinction, withdrew to a neighbouring ale-house; and bribing a few of the most forward, and giving ale to others, he prevailed on them to disperse. I was separated from Mr. Hermsprong soon after, but heard that he continued late amongst them. The next day, however, not a man was to be seen; all was peace and order. If, therefore, the charge of this gentleman's being a French spy, for we have nothing to do with his demeanour to Lord Grondale, rests, as I suspect, on this affair of the riot, or on similar grounds, we have not the least possible pretence for commitment."

The justices withdrew to the grand jury chamber, and soon returned; disappointment and dissatisfaction appearing on the face of Doctor Blick alone.

Mr. Saxby, addressing Hermsprong, said, "There does not appear any overt act, Sir, on your part, for which you ought to be committed to confinement. It is said, however, that you are a foreigner, and in this country have no property, relations, or connexions which bind you to it. In these suspicious times we think circumspection, with regard to strangers, necessary. You will not therefore wonder that we require some particulars of you."

Mr. Hermsprong bowed.

"Of what country are you?"

"I was born in America."

"You have resided some years in France?"

"Not properly resided. My mother was a French woman. I have been in France some part of every one of the last six years."

"Which do you consider as your country?"

"Not France, certainly. England, if I may be permitted to reside in it in peace, otherwise America."

"By the name, your father must have been of German origin."

"It should seem so."

"Sir, that is not explicit. Is it so? or is Hermsprong your real name?"

"Can it be of importance, by what name an unknown individual chuses to be distinguished?"

"Every man incurring suspicion, who cannot, or who will not, give an explicit account of himself, is exposed to the animadversion of the magistrates. It is important to know your real name, that we may be put in the proper track of inquiry. If you conceal it, or assume one not your own, you give, against yourself, a strong cause of suspicion."

"I know not why I should seem to elude your inquiries, rather than invite them. I acknowledge your right to demand, and I obey. Hermsprong, though he bore it many years, was not the family name of my father. An individual of great distinction, now present here, ought to blush at the necessity for the change, which was of his own creation. My father's real name was Campinet. He was the elder brother of Lord Grondale. Had he lived, his proper appellation here would have been Sir Charles Campinet. I am his only son."

It is impossible to express the astonishment and the murmurs which ran through the court at this explanation. All eyes were turned upon Lord Grondale, who seemed to endeavour to be firm and collected, but was in too much real confusion to impose much upon the spectators.

When Mr. Hermsprong could be heard, he said to the bench, "The proofs of what I have now asserted, you gentlemen, will not now expect me to give. They will very soon be called for in the proper court; where I shall apply to be put in possession of the family estates, now possessed by Lord Grondale. I do not accuse him of fraudulent possession, for he believes my father dead very many years ago. Could I have respected his character, it is probable my claim might have lain for ever dormant, for I have property fully equal to my desires. So it might have lain, had his lordship condescended to think of the happiness of his amiable daughter. Whomsoever she had chosen as the partner of her affection — had she chosen — her happiness should never have been molested by me. A fortunate incident, and Lord Grondale's peremptory determination to sacrifice her on the altar of avarice, perhaps of revenge, aided I hope by some affection, has induced the young lady to consent to trust this happiness to my keeping, and I will guard it well. This circumstance, added to his being the brother of my father, should seem to call upon me for all possible respect for Lord Grondale; and willingly should I pay it, if filial piety would permit. But I cannot remember a father's wrong, and venerate their author."

Tears sprang to the eyes of Hermsprong, as he spoke of his father; and as far as appearances could testify, he was honoured with the approbation of far the major part of the court. No reply being made by the counsel, the senior justice informed Sir Charles Campinet it was not the wish of the bench to give him any farther trouble. Lord Grondale, not without some trepidation, rose and said, he was sorry to see so much credit given to an impostor; he trusted it would be short, and that he should take ample revenge on the seducer of his daughter, and the calumniator of his honour. His lordship was suffered to leave the hall with much less ceremonious attendance than he had entered.

CHAPTER XXIII

MAY I ask the philosophers if we may ever hope again for the good old times of Zeno?[1] The art of reflecting ourselves out of feelings is, I fear, wholly lost. It may indeed be possible, that we may be good stoics still, when the misfortunes of our friends call upon us for firmness in adversity;[2] but in our own, our sensibility is quite as keen as any reasonable person ought to desire. I meddle not with that other sort of sensibility, so fashionable, and so pretty to talk about, because I begin to be of opinion, it was made only to be talked about; having watched it ever since it was born, and never having yet seen it rob a man of his appetite, or steal a rose from the fair cheek of beauty.[3]

In the course of our acquaintance with the illustrious Lord Grondale, we have seen pretty well the nature of his feelings. Being

---

1 Zeno (c.340-264 B.C.) was the founder of the Stoic school of philosophy.

2 Compare La Rochefoucauld (see note 4, page 120), maxim 19: "We always have enough strength to support the misfortunes of others."

3 By the time Bage was writing, sensibility — that is, great delicacy of feeling — had become a suspect concept, although it was extremely fashionable earlier in the century and was still an admired quality if the writer took care to differentiate "true" sensibility from mere fashionable affectation. Mockery of sensibility had, by the mid-90s, developed a definite political edge; Paine and Wollstonecraft, for example, attacked Burke for evoking readers' sensibility with lavish accounts of comparatively mild, individual suffering while ignoring mass misery and institutionalized injustice. Conservatives, meanwhile, used similar tactics against the radicals. For a good overview of the subject, including a discussion of the complex political implications of the term, see Janet Todd's *Sensibility: An Introduction* (London: Metheun, 1986).

centered so compleatly in his dear and only self, he has had no chance of obtaining much of our esteem, except when he happened to be under the influence of love and Miss Fluart. At all times also, his chief governors seem to have been pride and revenge. Perhaps, since the unfortunate day of the sessions, the first of the useful qualities had lost something of its accustomed force. He could not disguise to himself his apprehension of the possibility, nay probability, that Hermsprong might be the son of his brother; for he had contented himself with the report of this brother's shipwreck, without thinking it at all necessary to be too nice and scrupulous in the investigation of its truth. Even did he live, it would probably be in some obscure corner of the earth where he should never hear of him more. For he stipulated to renounce his country, and being the fool of honour, he will probably observe his stipulation. His family having cast him off, he may have sufficient spirit to despise that family, and think it no longer worth a place in his remembrance. So disposed, he may never hear of our elder brother's death; and why should I go to inform him of it, by an impolitic research after himself.

So reasoned his lordship; and as it was the established custom of the family, never to speak of those who were thought to have disgraced it, and as his lordship lived very much in the world, where people learn to forget what they do not wish to remember, it is no wonder this brother should have been buried in oblivion. I believe Miss Campinet had never heard of him, or heard of him simply as one who had lived and died.

On the other hand, it would occur to his lordship in his happier hours, that it was impossible he should have been permitted to possess his estates so long unmolested, had this brother been in existence. That this was probably some young adventurer, who had come to the knowledge of this family anecdote; and having infatuated his daughter, wanted to make use of it to intimidate himself. Doctor Blick said it must be so; Mr. Corrow said it must be so; and besides, the law had so much of glorious uncertainty, so much of useful procrastination, that at the worst, years might pass away, before his lordship could be dispossessed. But although the reverend Doctor and the man of law said so, it was one of those cases in which men usually allow themselves the liberty of saying what they do not believe; for neither of them believed Hermsprong an impostor; and as, since the day of the sessions, he had made the principal conversation of the county, and this conversation ran wholly in his favour, both these gentlemen thought it highly necessary to take some step of humility, in hopes of future favour. But of these devotees to self-interest, it is no longer necessary, and far from agreeable to me, to write. It is the great Lord Grondale must occupy me now,

> Whose breast, hope and fear alternate swayed;
> Like light and shade upon a waving field,
> Coursing each other, when the flying clouds
> Now hide, and now reveal the sun.[1]

But the paroxysms of fear had been so much stronger than those of hope, that his lordship's nervous system was grievously shattered by it; and debility seemed to be coming so rapidly on, that his lordship, with all his strength, could not wholly avoid some intrusive reflections of death, and something after death. So little however had his lordship thought of any world but this, that those of another gave him but little satisfaction; and the faculty were called upon to chase away at once the danger and the apprehension.

CHAPTER XXIV

IN this state of things, Mrs. Stone imagined a little consideration for herself might be useful. Farther than the sum formerly mentioned, she had nothing in the pecuniary way to expect of Lord Grondale. Consequently she had nothing agreeable to expect, unless his lordship would comply with her darling desire, and make her Lady Grondale. This idea, she insinuated to his lordship on every proper occasion; but he, proving incorrigibly deaf, she determined to try the effect of menace; and actually told his lordship, that without this compliment she would stay no longer at Grondale place; and what was the compliment now, just when he was going to lose the best part of his fortune. She wondered at herself for desiring it; it was a proof that her love for him was superior to every other consideration.

Had Mrs. Stone been politic, she would have forborn the least allusion to Hermsprong. It had the effect of exciting his lordship's anger, both against the proposition and the proposer. He said some

---

1   Slightly misquoted from *Alonzo* I.i.255-58, a 1773 play by the then-famous Scottish playwright John Home (1722-1808).

provoking things, such as ladies are not pleased to hear. She answered with sufficient asperity. Their reproaches became wonderfully keen and personal. She repeated her threats of going; he bade her go to the devil. She would not go any where, she said, where there was so great a probability of meeting his lordship, to whom she now bade adieu for ever. It was to Doctor Blick's she retired, in consequence of the doctor's having often said, how happy he should be to see her at his house, a few days, whenever her convenience would permit.

The day after this important event, his lordship received from his fair daughter the following letter.

Sir,

When I received your letter, decisively renouncing me as a daughter, I had many bitter tears to shed; but I own I had resentment also, which prevented me from troubling you with importunate supplications. To avoid being the wife of Sir Philip Chestrum, I took, though with infinite reluctance, a step, for which I feared your anger, but did not expect its endurance for ever. Farther than as it has offended you, Sir, I cannot repent of it. As the wife of Sir Philip, I think I could not live. Of two dreadful evils, I had to chuse the least, if I could know the least, and I concluded your displeasure for a time, a less evil than misery for life. I received your renunciation of me as a daughter. It was my duty to submit; and I should never more have presumed to consider myself as the daughter of Lord Grondale, but for the very extraordinary, and to me unintelligible events, which have recently taken place. That Mr. Hermsprong is the person he purports to be, I have no doubt. Although to me, he never gave the least hint of such a circumstance, to my aunt, as she says, he gave absolute proof; or certainly she would not have accepted his presents, or have presided in his house. I own that I esteem him, and think highly of his probity; but I cannot resolve to give my hand to the man who reduces my father to adversity: That adversity, be it what it may, I entreat I may be permitted to share. Permit me, Sir, to return to your house, and to my duty; and suffer me to convince you, by more than words, that I am truly your affectionate and dutiful daughter

CAROLINE CAMPINET

Lord Grondale received this letter after a bad night, in an hour of low spirits, and indeed of humility; for he had begun to repent of his quarrel with Mrs. Stone, and was considering whether he should not secure her attentions to him, at her own price. This letter determined him in the negative. His daughter promised fair. She wrote as if she loved him; at least, as if she desired to love him. It would separate her too from Hermsprong. This last consideration determined his lordship; and he wrote the following condescending and gracious epistle.

Miss Campinet,
I permit you to return.
GRONDALE

On the receipt of it, at Hermsprong's, Mrs. Garnet wept, and remonstrated; Miss Fluart cried and scolded. The inflexible Miss Campinet persevered, with a kind of determined despair; and in a few hours had paid her duty to his lordship, who had the goodness to forbear at present any virulent reproach, and to permit her to withdraw to her solitary apartment.

CHAPTER XXV

IT would have been the easiest thing in the world for Lord Grondale to have learned to love his daughter, had it not been necessary first to unlearn to hate her; for I know not by what word of milder signification I can describe his present disposition towards her. I must do him the justice to say, there were hours, or minutes rather, when he strove against it, when he saw, when he felt she was amiable, and almost allowed it. So his behaviour for the first ten days was a little capricious. He did not indulge indeed in passion, nor talk of putting her to death with his own hand; he contented himself with only stabbing her to the heart with ironic taunts, when he was tolerably high in spirits; and when low, with kindly attributing his death to her. Not that he believed himself in any immediate danger, but was desirous his daughter should. In this he succeeded. She thought she saw her father visibly decline; she feared some part of that decline might be owing to her own disobedience; and therefore she bore the infirmities of his temper with the most enduring patience.

So much sweetness, and so much perseverance, could not totally fail of their proper effects. She saw, or hoped she saw, herself gaining upon his affections; and the satisfaction this gave her, was a compensation for the sacrifice she had made, at least for a time, of all the tenderest friendship had to give. Uncertain of her fate with Hermsprong, she resolved not to think of him; and she resolved this perhaps a thousand times a day.

Hermsprong had left England along with a Mr. Germersheim, the son of his father's friend at Philadelphia. It was he, who, along with Mr. Sumelin, and two other gentlemen, accompanied Hermsprong in the county court, and it was he whom Sir Charles (I will call him Sir Charles when I remember) intended to call upon to speak concerning his father, had it been necessary. These two friends had ran over half England together, and Mr. Germersheim having to go into Germany, Sir Charles had gone to accompany him as far as Dresden; so that Miss Campinet had seen him only once after the county court day, and that, before she had heard of his consanguinity to herself. A little resentment she felt, and expressed to Miss Fluart, that Sir Charles did not think her worthy of his entire confidence; and it is not impossible that this resentment might assist in carrying her back to Grondale Hall; for we are not always accurately acquainted with all the little springs which move us to action.

CHAPTER XXVI

AT the request of Miss Campinet, Miss Fluart promised to stay with Mrs. Garnet till Sir Charles's return. This was at the end of three weeks; and, Mrs. Garnet not being able, Miss Fluart told him the disagreeable news of Miss Campinet's re-elopement; wondring sometimes how her fair friend could be so dutifully silly; and sometimes weeping, with Mrs. Garnet, for the consequences. Sir Charles heard all, without offering the least interruption. As far as the matter depended upon words, he was the perfect philosopher; but his fine face betrayed certain internal emotions, which proved him "no philosopher at heart."[1] He even found it expedient to walk in the garden, whence however he returned in a few minutes, and sitting down by Mrs. Garnet, he took her hand, and with the

---

1 The phrase "no philosopher at heart" is in quotation marks, but no source for it has been traced. Bage might perhaps be misrecalling a phrase from the first of Alexander Pope's *Moral Essays*, "Epistle to Sir Richard Temple" (1734) — "You hold him no philosopher at all" (8) — although in context the line refers to a scholar who knows the world only through books.

kindest tone, said, "So fall, my dear and revered mother, the expectations I had built upon to secure my own happiness, and increase yours."

"No, no, my dear son," Mrs. Garnet sobbed out, "not fallen — our hopes are not entirely fallen."

"I know not, my dear madam, whether I can accommodate myself to prejudices, even in my Caroline, which appear to me to pervert justice and leave reason unconsulted. My father taught me to think and to judge — for myself. — One sole absolute command he left me, engraved upon my memory by a thousand repetitions. 'Do always what is right. — In most human occurrences this right is at once seen and acknowledged. Where discrimination is necessary,' would my father say, 'discriminate with strength and with care. When you have judged, that is the right to you.'"

"But if Miss Campinet errs, it is from a weakness so amiable," said Mrs. Garnet.

"That Caroline would be amiable with a thousand weaknesses, I can allow; but not that weakness itself is amiable. But let us not enter into the argument; I fear to sink in your opinion. That I am strongly disappointed, I must confess; yet will I not play the fool or the madman. I will not pine and waste the fruitful morning of my youth in love-sick indolence. So far indeed I must indulge myself, as to leave England, and return to America. There I may forget. Here, I cannot but remember. There too, I know how to pass my days with some amusement to myself, and some good to my fellow men. My grief is, my dear madam, that I must leave you — you, who I love as a mother."

"No, never — never shall you leave me by my own consent," said Mrs. Garnet. "Wheresoever you settle, that shall be my country for my few remaining years; for you are all to me."

Mr. Hermsprong kissed her hand respectfully, and, the tear standing in his expressive eye, withdrew to his study.

Having reflected there a while, he decided upon a certain course of action, and began it with the following letter to Miss Campinet.

A few hours since, Caroline, I was happy; for I had confidence. Now — but I wish not to move your compassion, when I have failed to convince your understanding. Since you have decided to renounce affinities and connexions, which so lately it appeared to you virtuous to form, we must submit. There remains only to clear myself of certain things which you have already imputed to me, and of others which it is probable you will; for you *can* be unjust, Caroline; and injustice has no limits.

It appears that you are offended, because I did not impart to you in full confidence the affinity I revealed to our respectable aunt. You are offended then because I respected your delicacy. To you, the secret must have been highly embarrassing; and you would earlier have thought it your duty to have become unjust to me. Or suppose, what really happened, that after the accident which brought us to the notice of each other, I desired your affections; and wished to owe them to personal merit only, if I had any which might prove agreeable to you, not to the adventitious aids of fortune or affinity: Was there any thing in this, which ought to have drawn your resentment upon me?

I learn also, that you had imputed my past slights and offences of Lord Grondale, to pride or caprice; now you consider me as the decided enemy of your father, and determine to treat me as such. Yes, — I own myself the decided enemy of your father, for he was so of mine. Not the open and avowed, but the concealed and treacherous enemy. My enmity is virtue, or of virtuous origin; his began and ended in vice. And are you sure, Caroline, that it is virtue in you to take the side of improbity, because it is the improbity of your father? But no more of this. I find it impossible to press upon you with the full force of conclusion. Your motives I can grant to be amiable, though I cannot grant that they are just.

Once, I think at your request, I related to you, faithfully as far as it went, my father's story, my mother's, and my own; permitting you to conclude, from the name I bore, that I was of German origin. My real birth being known, it follows in the general opinion, that I must prosecute my claim, and strip Lord Grondale of the family estates. That I came to England with that intention, I own. When you became known to me, I determined it should never be pursued in a court of justice. Learning that Lord Grondale was preparing to deprive you of the inheritance, I resume my claim; ready to relinquish it at your request, provided it is allowed to descend to you, as it would have done, had my father never existed. It is an object to me, only as it relates to you. For you I reserve it; and to you I yield it. Perhaps I have some right to your gratitude for this; and *by this*, I seek no more. Not to such causes would I owe your affections. You did love me, Caroline; I thought you did; and that thought was an inexhaustible source of felicity. That source is gone; to find one equally efficacious, perhaps is impossible; but I owe it to myself to resist undeserving misery. I go to America, having lost the tie which bound me to England. At this you will not be surprised. But should you not, to hear that Mr. Glen and the worthy curate of Sithin were emigrants for my sake? Should you not be more than surprised, if you heard that our dear and respectable aunt, advanced as she is in years, should declare her resolution to go where I go, and live where I live? This goodness I will repay with the utmost solicitude. I shall have friendship, Caroline, and I shall want it. To Miss Fluart I lend my house and its precincts, that she may be near you. Cherish her friendship, it is above all estimation. When she marries, or no longer occupies Bloomgrove, it is yours. So would I have been, Caroline. But — no more of this womanly effusion. I am ashamed of my lingering pen. Caroline, adieu!

HERMSPRONG

CHAPTER XXVII

IT was not till the following day that this letter was sent, for Sir Charles was interrupted by the arrival of Mr. Woodcock and Mr. Glen. These gentlemen spent the evening, for Miss Campinet being gone, Sir Charles considered himself as at home. It was upon this young lady principally the conversation ran, of which I am desirous to give my readers a specimen, to shew still more the excentricities of Hermsprong.

Mr. Glen had said he was sorry Miss Campinet had left Mrs. Garnet; but he did not allow, as a necessary consequence, that the connexion between Sir Charles and she must be broken.

"So I have told Sir Charles," Miss Fluart said; "if he will wait with patience and submission, he may reasonably hope for a successful termination."

"Patience and submission, my dear Miss Fluart, are not the qualities of a savage," Sir Charles replied; "we allow not the language of tyranny, even from pretty mouths."

Miss Fluart. "Savages are wonderful beings. You have no objection to the language of slavery from pretty mouths."

Hermsprong. "I have not all the savage ill qualities. I learned to hate the language of slavery in all its forms, especially in the form of adulation. I consider a woman as equal to a man; but, let it not displease you, my dear Miss Fluart, I consider a man also as equal to a woman. When we marry, we give and we receive. Where is the necessity that man should take upon him this crouching mendicant spirit, this excess of humiliation?"

Miss Fluart. "The arrow that Cupid shot you with was of lead. Or perhaps your heart has twenty thick coverings. It is the creed of a true lover that his mistress cannot have a fault."

Hermsprong. "Unhappily, my father bred me up to think for myself; and this error of education does not permit me to receive creeds of any manufacture but my own. So I fear I cannot rise to the exalted eminence of a true lover. Yet I love Caroline, and though I do not approve her quite so well, I must love her long. How happy I should be, has been the darling subject of my imagination, sometime past. How happy I might have been, will be so, for some time to come."

Miss Fluart. "When a man chuses to extinguish the torch of love, he easily finds the water."

Hermsprong. "Was not the water Miss Campinet's? She rejected me, did she not?"

Miss Fluart. "Has she said so, Sir?"

Hermsprong. "She has done so, my dear Miss Fluart; she has left us."

Miss Fluart. "Only to return for a while to her father."

Hermsprong. "Did he solicit this return, Miss Fluart."

Miss Fluart. "No. It was suggested by her duty."

Hermsprong. "By what was her leaving him suggested."

Miss Fluart. "By fear; or perhaps by love."

Hermsprong. "If the latter motive, it operates no longer, my dear Miss Fluart, and I have proved the point of rejection."

Mr. Woodcock. "Perhaps, Sir Charles, when you become a father, you will allow more force to the motive of duty, than you now seem to do."

Hermsprong. "Yes, — I may become a monster like Lord Grondale; and expect duty where I have deserved execration. But I am not that monster yet. Yet I seem to discern the relations of things; and if I do, Lord Grondale has no right to the duty of a daughter from one whom he has never treated as a daughter."

Miss Fluart. "I have urged this so often to Caroline, that I must own I cannot, with any conscience support the contrary."

Hermsprong. "Here Miss Campinet found almost a mother in consanguinity, and quite a mother in affection. Here she found a friend, not idly called so, but one who has proved her friendship, and nobly proved it. Here she found a man who loved her, and whom she said she loved. She left us all, and broke the tender engagements she had expressly or tacitly entered into with us; and all for a word; for what, but a word, is a duty not owed; and certainly not produced by affection. Me, above all, she left; for after what had past, she could not well imagine, that having manifested the utmost contempt for Lord Grondale, I could stoop to wait his pleasure, and humbly solicit him for happiness. If she expected this, she knew me not. If she did not expect this, she has made her election, and it is decisive against me. I must now make mine. For the sake of my friends here present, and particularly, my dear mother, for yours, I would stay in England; but having been struck with a disease in it, I fear I shall need another climate to promote my cure. Nor indeed do I well know how I can make myself useful in England for want of something to do. Nor do I yet see how I shall be able to accommodate myself to the existing manners of the rich. I cannot eat for hours, nor love candles so well as the sun. I cannot, I fear, submit to be fettered and cramped throughout the whole circle of thought and action. You submit to authority with regard to the first, and to fashion with regard to the last. I cannot get rid of the stubborn notion, that to do what we think is right to do, is the only good principle of action. You seem to think the only good principle of action is to do as others do. You allow fashion to be often folly; and believe it right to be fools, when you have so great a sanction; — and by some ingenious use or abuse of words, you are always and eternally right. It is my misfortune I cannot be right on such easy terms. Servile compliance is crime, when it violates rectitude; and imbecility, at least, when it is prostituted to folly. When it has become habitual, what a thing it has made of man."

"My friend," said Miss Fluart, "you have indulged yourself in a pretty satirical vein; but will not you have the goodness to allow us some good qualities?"

"Many, madam; I am not now drawing your whole picture as a people. I am only placing before you some of the things I dislike. As to your panegyric, it is a subject so copious, I dare not venture upon it so late in the evening. You will indulge me with one complaint more, and then I will confess that England abounds in amiable individuals, and that I am charmed with your arts and sciences."

"Well, Sir, — your one more."

"It is your politics, madam; a subject on which the English people delight to dwell on which, no two people ever thought wholly alike; and on which you have brought yourselves to so charming a degree of rancour, that you can bear no deviations from your own opinions. Before you can set up an undisputed title to an amiable people, you must first learn to agree to differ. Your religion has been teaching you love and good will to men ever since you were born, and you have not yet got beyond the primmer of the science. This it is that deforms your societies; or, to preserve your tempers, and politeness, drives you to insipidity and cards."

"Are these things better in America?" Miss Fluart asked.

"I think they are. It is true, they dispute there very much, grow animated sometimes, and sometimes indulge in personal abuse. But this is evanescent. To your polite hatred for opinion, generally they are strangers. I imagine they owe this to their diversity of religions, which, accustoming them to see difference of opinion in a matter of the greatest importance, disposes them to tolerate it on all subjects, and even to believe it a condition of human nature. Their government too, embraces all sects, and persecutes none; and when there is no reward for persecution, and no merit attached to it, I suppose it possible for men to refrain from it."

The conversation stopped here. After the silence of a minute, Mrs. Garnet said, "My dear son, for so I must call you, I see your difficulties here, and your prejudice, for so perhaps it is, for the country in which you were born. I cannot wish you less than all possible happiness, — and yet to part —"

Tears prevented her proceeding. Hermsprong, taking her hand, and kissing it with equal respect and tenderness said, "Madam, we will not part."

"Why, then we will not," said the good old lady with animation. "Of what importance is it to me where I die, so I live, whilst I do live, with those I love."

"I meant, madam, to stay in England for your sake; but if, on farther consideration, we shall determine the contrary, your travelling shall be rendered so commodious, you shall scarce know you move. But I must own, madam, I have no friends in America so dear to me as these who are present; to part with them will be a suffering —"

"I mean not to suffer," said Glen. "I presume I may be warmed with an American sun, and be nourished by American food, as well as yourself; existence is a double blessing, when we live with those we love."

The reverend Mr. Woodcock heard all this. He wished to speak; his lips quivered; a tear gushed from his eye; his head hung down; he gave up his hopeless attempt at speech.

Hermsprong observed this and said, "I interpret for you, dear Woodcock; your inclinations are with us, but you imagine obstructions."

"I do indeed," answered the parson; "a man with a family — without fortune — without talents; at least, any that can be useful —"

"Stop, friend," said Hermsprong, smiling; "and do not abuse thyself. I have sixty thousand acres of uncleared land upon the Potowmac. It cost me little. I have imagined a society of friends within a two mile ring; and I have imagined a mode of making it happy. In this, it is possible I may not reach the point I desire; but with common prudence, we cannot fail of plenty, and in time of affluence.[1] Of this hereafter. But you, Miss Fluart, what temptation can I possibly offer you?"

"Yourself, to be sure," answered this laughter loving lady.

"I love you," Hermsprong replied, "with every sort of love but one; that one is at present, Caroline's exclusively. If I recover it —"

"Don't trouble yourself," said Miss Fluart; "for though I love you with every sort of love but one, I love Caroline better; and if she is not amongst your collection, you may grub wood by yourselves."

"For that sentiment I cannot love you less," Hermsprong answered, and then changed the conversation.

CHAPTER XXVIII

THE letter to Miss Campinet, given in a preceding chapter, startled this young lady. She endeavoured to reflect with more precision than she had hitherto done; she began to doubt whether the step she had lately taken, was as meritorious as she wished to have thought it. The friends she had left had been uniformly kind,

---

1 This assumption is usual in the many pamphlets promoting emigration to America. The most optimistic writers — such as Gilbert Imlay — promised far more; anti-emigrationists warned direly of starvation and misery. (See, for example, the satire of emigrants' Utopianism in George Walker's novel *The Vagabond* [1799]). When Brissot de Warville set out for America in 1788, he was instructed by a friend to investigate the possibility of buying land for a colony in which a small group of like-minded Frenchmen could settle and form a society "better calculated for peace and happiness, than any now existing, or that ever did exist" (Jacques Pierre Brissot de Warville, *New Travels in the United States of America*. London, 1792, 60). See the introduction for further discussion.

whilst the little tenderness she had experienced from Lord Grondale, seemed more the effect of declining strength and spirits, than of sorrow or affection. Wine had still the power of elevating his lordship, and still, when elevated, he was disposed to taunt his daughter with his accustomed malevolence.

This secession from her dearest friends, had it not also the appearance of resentment against Sir Charles Campinet? What had she to resent? Sir Charles thought her unjust; perhaps with reason. How much more cause to think her so would he have, if she gave him reason to suppose her capable of desiring to deprive himself and his posterity of their undoubted right. Could she repay such generosity with such ingratitude, she must indeed deserve his contempt. With such sentiments, could she permit him to leave England? Could she bear to see him no more? These reflections, the last perhaps not least, disordered her even to sickness. The paleness of her cheek was visible to Lord Grondale, when she next went to receive his commands. She excused it as well as she was able; but her father, always suspicious, pursued her with such peremptory inquiry, that she was compelled, as she had been once before, to give him the letter, to avoid his ironic taunts.

Lord Grondale read this letter; it was generous no doubt; but as it was intended to operate in favour of his daughter, to himself it was no obligation. But how to render it beneficial to himself? This question, his lordship considered, as well as he could now consider, two or three succeeding days; during which he remained totally silent upon it to his daughter, who having nothing to say on the part of her father, wrote herself to Sir Charles Campinet as follows.

Surely, Sir Charles, you bear too hard upon a mind opprest, and harassed by opposing conflicts. However wrong I may have been, I have at least the merit of having been governed by your own first principle of action; I have done what I thought to be right. I have sinned, if I have sinned, against my own affections; for I make no scruple to say, those affections were yours. If, for a moment, I gave way to new sensations, testified by any little expressions of resentment at not being sufficiently confided in, or suspecting a now more implacable enmity to my father, forgive me; such error was evanescent, my judgment would have corrected it, if my heart had not. Not so influenced, did I leave Bloomgrove. It was the picture of my father, always before my eyes, reduced from grandeur to comparative poverty, sick in body, and unhappy in mind, which drew me thence. You do me wrong indeed, if you think me superlatively happy here; or that I left Bloomgrove without regret; or that I less love and revere my respected aunt; or that my Maria is less dear to me; or that I do not think of you, Sir Charles, often-er than now perhaps I ought; for — so easily to suspect — so eas-ily to accept the idea of separation — but no more of this. You make nice distinctions; too nice perhaps for human happiness; and I may now seem to you to depart from maiden modesty, and court your lost affections, — better lost, than so redeemed.

For your generous intentions respecting myself, I thank you; and wish to avail myself of them just so far, as that my father may breath out the remains of his short existence, for short it must be, untroubled by litigation. This awful event past, no consideration on earth shall induce me to withhold from you a tittle of your right. No law for me, Sir Charles; every thing you claim shall be yours.

CAROLINE CAMPINET

I write my aunt and friend, to entreat their pardon of a conduct too embarrassed to be blameless even to them.

CHAPTER XXIX

FORGIVE my nice distinctions, Caroline; love, they say, is always making them. You will not hold from me a tittle of my right. And what method, my fair cousin, will you take to enforce my accep-tance? For the daughter of Lord Grondale, I would have claimed every thing; of her, nothing. No — nothing but herself will I ever claim. The rest is air. Her heart was mine, is mine and may it ever be the happy lot of her

CHARLES CAMPINET

Our aunt, and our fair friend are all in tears, but they are tears of joy. Your letters have a fascinating charm in them, Caroline. They move all hearts as you direct.

So wrote Sir Charles in answer; and I believe communicated to his fair mistress a pleasure equal to his own. More letters passed, which it is not to our purpose to transcribe; only to say, that they drew closer together the knot which love had formed. In the mean time, the illustrious Lord Grondale, when disposed to meditate, fixed his attention on the means of turning the love and romance of Hermsprong to his own advantage. It accorded indeed ill with his pride to seem to compromise with a man he had so often declared an impostor; but as he could not avoid, in his more timid hours, owning to himself, the higher probability of the young man's being really his nephew, he feared two consequences. One, lest the evidence should be such as to render him ridiculous for not better informing himself; or stamp him with odium, if he was believed to have been better informed. The other, lest he should be obliged to live with diminished splendour, or perhaps to hide himself in obscurity; for the idea of dying, with which he had wished to impress his daughter, had been a passing idea with his lordship, of little force, and less duration. These fears began by degrees to sap his pride, now unsupported by the kind and cherishing hand of Doctor Blick, who, since the day Mrs. Stone had become his guest, or that on which Sir Charles had declared himself in the county court, had seen little of his lordship. Even the assiduous Mr. Corrow had failed in the usual frequent expression of his respect. Each of these gentlemen, though unknown to the other, being engaged in considering the best mode of transferring their invaluable friendship, to the future possessor of the power of patronage.

Lord Grondale then, after some days' consideration, and the strong contention of his pride with his interest, thought proper to indulge his daughter with a conversation, the tenor of which may be collected from the following letter of hers to Sir Charles.

My father has been kinder to-day, and more explicit than usual. He has ordered me to say, that if you can, in a private manner, convince him, you are the son, the legitimate son of his elder brother; if you will let your claim rest, and permit him to possess the family estates for life; if you will apologize for your past conduct; and engage to treat him with proper respect in future; on these conditions, he grants you his daughter. It is probable some, or all of them, may be disagreeable. If so — reject them, I entreat you. I ask no sacrifice.

CAROLINE CAMPINET

Sir Charles to Miss Campinet.

It is not necessary, my Caroline, it is not proper, that my reply to Lord Grondale's requisitions should pass through you. Fortune certainly shall be no bar to my obtaining you. But my honour, Caroline, my principles, they must be in my own keeping. I must not forfeit them, — even for Caroline Campinet.

Her devoted
CHARLES

Sir Charles to Lord Grondale.

My Lord,

I have the honour of a letter from Miss Campinet, wherein she proposes, as from your lordship, three conditions, herself the reward of my compliance. I know not what, that is just and honourable, I would not do for such a reward.

I must first convince your lordship that I am what I pretend. That I have evidence which must carry conviction to the minds of as many impartial people as hear and consider it, I am certain; but I believe, under certain circumstances, the human mind has a power to resist even conviction. I can send your lordship, a Matthew Clewes, whom almost thirty years may have taken from your remembrance; but to which, certain circumstances must unavoidably restore him. He was then a servant in the family, a favourite of my father's, and confidentially employed by him in a love affair with a certain Miss Debank, a lady, whose name will probably afflict your lordship with recollections. This man you endeavoured to corrupt; you did corrupt; and made subservient to your treachery; sent over to France, to my father; this man, struck with remorse, confessed his guilt, was forgiven, and at his earnest request received by my father as his servant. This he continued to be till my father's death, and has since been mine. From this person your lordship may learn, if you please, every occurrence of note respecting my father.

Your second proposition is of a kind too uninteresting to me, to occasion the least opposition — but your third — that I shall apologize to you — shall treat you with future respect!

You are my uncle, Sir, the brother of my father; and had you had my father's virtues, how sincerely could I have transferred to you, the duty and respect I owed, and always most willingly paid to him. His story was not told me by himself; it was written in latin; and pursuant to my father's directions, given me by my mother; when I arrived at the age of twenty-five; accompanied by some letters of yours, which unhappily too well prove your intention to deceive. Such testimony corroborated in every point by Matthew Clewes, I could not doubt; and my personal conduct to you, Sir, has arisen, not from resentment of the pride with which I was treated on our first rencontre; but from a deep abhorrence of principles which could deceive and betray a brother.

Should I ever be so happy as to see you in that state of mind, which would have disposed you to ask forgiveness of a too justly offended brother, I will ask yours; and not pay you exterior marks only of respect, but those interior ones, which cannot become your due, but by contrition, and true respectability.

CHARLES CAMPINET

CHAPTER XXX

AT the name of Matthew Clewes, Lord Grondale was seized with a cold shivering, the beginning, I should hope, if physioligists will permit, of that contrition recommended by his proud and inflexible nephew. But when the marks of repentance are genuine, and likely to endure, none but divines know; and as Doctor Blick, at this critical period, was either indisposed, or not disposed to attend his lordship as usual, we are not able to determine the state of Lord Grondale's mind in this particular. All we know is, that his lordship did not request the attendance of Matthew Clewes, and that Mr. Corrow did. This gentleman said that Lord Grondale was very unwell, and could not at present see him, the said Matthew Clewes; that himself was deputed to take his deposition; and therefore he desired him to say the truth, the whole truth, and nothing but the truth.

But Matthew was himself an intelligent fellow; and had besides the benefit of his master's counsel in this business. So he said, "I do not suppose, Sir, you would advise an evidence for your client, to explain to the opposite party the nature of his evidence, before he came into court; but as my master does not intend to imitate the crooked policy of lawyers, I may acquaint you, that I was with my late master in France, and took the voyage with him in the same vessel to America; that I was a witness to his marriage with Miss Ruprè of Nantes; was in the house when she was brought to bed of my present master; conveyed her and him from Philadelphia to the country of the Nawdoessies; lived there with them the best part of twenty years; was present at the death of my old master; and have attended Sir Charles ever since; and will to the end of my life, if I may; because he is all that is good."

"And do you think, fellow," said Mr. Corrow, "that a bold evidence like this, will procure your master the estate of Lord Grondale?"

"I do not know," replied Matthew, "how great a battle truth and law may have when they meet, but I know, that if law wins the contest, so much the worse for the country that is plagued with it."

"And I do assure you," Mr. Corrow said, "that Lord Grondale must win. Possession, you know, is eleven of the twelve points of law, according to the old saying;[1] and I think I can answer for keeping his lordship in possession in spite of your evidence. But it seems to me that it would be more for your interest not to give evidence in a losing cause; both because it might be better to have Lord Grondale for a friend than an enemy; and because his lordship is a man of very great honour; and bountiful as the sun to those who oblige him; and," the lawyer continued, "as you have lived most of your life out of England, you may like some other country better than this; in which case, I am sure Lord Grondale would make it easy and comfortable to you."

Pretty long, and rather insinuating, was this harangue of Mr. Corrow's, — for he graced it with much smile, and much sweetness of expression.

Matthew answered it, all at once in the Lacedemonian[2] way, I believe. "Fair words, Mr. Corrow, butter no parsnips."

The lawyer was not much displeased with the reply; so he smiled again, and said, "true Mr. Clewes, you are right; come to me again on Friday, and we will see how the parsnips may be buttered in the best manner possible. So Matthew departed; and ran to tell his master the progress he had made in the suit of *law* versus *truth*.

CHAPTER XXXI

BUT had this interview taken place, it might have been death to the reputation of Mr. Corrow as a lawyer; for Matthew had contrivances in his head, the success of which would have shewn the attorney deficient in matter of sagacity, or what is vulgarly called cunning; a part of character so essentially necessary to some gentlemen of the long robe, that without it, parchment is of no value.

Poor Lord Grondale, that sun of bounty that was to be, had the use of his left side taken from him, by a paralytic stroke. His mouth was distorted, and the muscles subservient to speech were almost immoveable. His memory seemed much impaired; and his percep-

---

1 More usually, possession is nine tenths of the law.
2 Spartan; that is, in this case, direct and to the point. Matthew's response, which is proverbial, means that promises are not enough.

tion of the objects around him greatly diminished. By degrees he recovered a part of these faculties; but the utmost endeavours of his physicians, could not prevent his advancing fast into a state of lethargy. One day, about a week from his being first struck, he suddenly awoke, as from a disturbed slumber; and answered his weeping daughter's inquiry with a "Thank you my dear," a word, which from him she had never heard before. He spoke it too rather more distinctly, than since his stroke he had spoke any words. He looked at Miss Campinet several minutes, and then said, "kiss me Caroline." She did so, and burst into a tender suffusion of tears. Half an hour after this, he said, "I must die." Miss Campinet sobbed. "I have been a hard father," he said, then sunk to sleep. When he awoke again he was visibly altered, and of this he seemed sensible. He spoke now with more difficulty, and seemingly with much earnestness. "My aunt," he said, "and Charles — send —." Miss Campinet, though not certain she understood him, dispatched an immediate messenger, who fortunately finding Sir Charles at home, Mrs. Garnet and he were ready when his lordship next awoke, to attend his call, if he remembered them. That he did do so was conjectured by Miss Campinet and the attending physician, from anxious looks cast alternately at his daughter and the door; for he could not now speak. Mrs. Garnet entered; Lord Grondale put out towards her, the only hand which now obeyed his will. His look asked forgiveness; hers granted it. He cast his eyes on his nephew, to whom he now held out his hand. Sir Charles took it with respect. He pressed it gently; Lord Grondale, with what strength he had, returned the pressure. Sir Charles understood this as an expression of contrition, and he marked his sentiment of it by raising his uncle's hand to his lips. It seemed to animate his lordship; he beckoned Miss Campinet to approach; he took her hand and motioned it towards his nephew. Sir Charles caught it, and imprinted upon it a respectful kiss. His uncle's last look seemed to express a faint degree of pleasure. But not longer able to support the effort of keeping awake, his head sunk upon the pillow, oppressed with his last sleep. He awoke and died. So closed the last act of Lord Grondale.

CHAPTER XXXII

IF the careless writer of a novel, closes his book, without marrying or putting to death, or somehow disposing, not only of his principal personages, but of all who have acted a part in the drama above the degree of a candle-snuffer, he creates an unsatisfied want in the minds of his readers, especially his fair ones, and they hardly part friends. As every body knows I live but to love and oblige these charming critics, I will in this chapter endeavour to prevent so sad a catastrophe to myself, and give them all the satisfaction I can. Bound, I presume, to give the preference to holy things, I shall begin with Doctor Blick; to whom it no sooner appeared that Sir Charles Campinet was Sir Charles Campinet, and that he would have the estates and the boroughs, than he began to think Lord Grondale was not so great, so very great a man, as he had hitherto supposed him. He even began to see several faults; and when he looked upon Mrs. Stone, his guest, advanced a little into the vale of years indeed, but of a fine person still, and considered all her merit, and all the obligations by which his lordship was bound to her, he could scarce avoid accusing, him of folly, if not ingratitude. No sooner were the funeral obsequies performed, than he wrote Sir Charles a copious epistle, in a stile of pompous humiliation, imputing his own behaviour to ignorance of his birth and quality; and stating many reasons why he ought to be forgiven.

Sir Charles wrote:

I forgive you, Sir, but do not like you. You will discover frankness to be my vice, and it will incur your displeasure. I fear we shall not be cordial neighbours. If on this account your residence here would be more disagreeable to you, and you should prefer another situation, I engage for Mr. Woodcock that he shall do the whole duties of Grondale and Sithin without increase of salary.

The doctor, in his answer, lamented his hard fate, in not being allowed the liberty to try to make himself agreeable. Hoped Sir Charles would one day think better of him; till when he must submit to necessity. That he accepted the condition, and was Sir Charles's

Most faithful,

Most obedient,

Most devoted servant.

Sir Charles allowed Mrs. Stone's claim upon the effects of Lord Grondale, and ordered immediate payment; a circumstance so agreeable to the doctor, that he wooed the lady, and won the lady, to wed, not love. They settled at Winchester; and as they are little visited, have the more time to despise and plague each other, which they do with great sincerity.

Mr. Woodcock is in possession of the parsonage, of the friendship of Sir Charles, and of 300l. a-year; I need not point out from what beneficent hand. As he is one of the best men, I hope he is one of the happiest.

The venerable Mrs. Garnet removed to the hall, and took possession of the chair of ease; and long may she enjoy it. Miss Fluart, not yet willing "to buy herself a master,"[1] establishes a little household at Bloomgrove. Once a day she quarrels with Sir Charles about *le bon ton, et la belle usage*;[2] and the greatest vexation she has yet to complain of, is, that she cannot vex him. She calls him savage; abuses his antediluvian ideas; and then tells her friend, with half a sigh, she will have a savage like himself, or die a maid.

Mr. Sumelin and his lady are one flesh, so says the church,[3] but they are two spirits. Upon submission, and the request of Sir Charles, Mr. Sumelin received Fillygrove into his compting-house, with leave to marry his daughter, if he can. Miss Sumelin demurs and pouts, and bids him remember Miss Wavel. It is not that she cannot forgive, or has lost all her first affection; but Mrs. Sumelin, has half persuaded her that Sir Philip Chestrum is the most accomplished man for most of the purposes for which a wise young woman should marry, of all men living; and that she may catch him if she will take trouble to angle. The mild, the gentle Charlotte Sumelin is yet uncourted; has asked and obtained her father's consent to live with Miss Fluart at Bloomgrove. For the unhappy Mrs. Marcour, Sir Charles obtained the means to convey her safe to her children.

"And pray," say a thousand of my fair readers all at once, — "pray, Mr. Glen, can you think of closing your book without giving us compleat satisfaction respecting Sir Charles and Miss Campinet. Many things fall out between the cup and the lip. They might marry, or they might not. Are we at liberty to suppose which we please? For what END then did you write your book?"

---

1 Compare Pope, "Epistle to a Lady" (1735), in which he writes that Phoebus has given the lady in question "beauty, but deny'd the pelf / That buys your sex a tyrant o'er itself" (288-89).

2 High fashion and polite behaviour.

3 Ephesians 5:31: "For this cause shall a man leave his father and mother, and shall be joined unto his wife, and they two shall be one flesh." This passage is also used in the marriage service in the Anglican Book of Common Prayer.

Pardon me, dear ladies. I knew, or thought I knew, that there must be a total conformity of conclusion in your minds respecting this great event; and my hopes were, that you would have the goodness to marry them, when and where, and how you pleased. But since otherwise is your pleasure, I, as in duty bound, submit.

It was in the 5th month after the death of Lord Grondale that the happy Hermsprong, the name he still best loves, led his blooming Caroline to the altar, — dressed in a white polonese[1] — pshaw — dressed in love and innocence I mean, — for of any dress, but of the mind, I know, — yes, — I just know a polonese from a cabbage net.

The union, I believe, will prove unfortunate only to the gentlemen of the law; for Sir Charles having no body to go to law with but himself, is under the necessity of not going to law at all; which will be so obliging as to give him a full title to his property, by what the gentlemen of this science call a rèmitter.[2]

---

1   A type of dress, supposedly influenced by Polish styles; it consisted of a robe with a skirt designed to be pulled up and draped to reveal an underskirt of a matching or contrasting pattern. The word could also be applied to the material used to make such a dress.

2   "[W]here a man hath two titles to lands or tenements, *viz.*, one a more ancient title, and another a more latter title; and if he come to the land by a latter, yet the law will adjudge him in by force of the elder title, because the elder title is the more sure and more worthy title" (P.G. Osborn, *A Concise Law Dictionary*, 2nd ed. London, 1937, 268). That is, while Hermsprong has claims to the property both as the son of the true owner and as the husband of Grondale's sole heiress, he will inherit it under the older claim derived from his father.

Appendix A: Bage's Life

1. William Godwin, from a letter to Mary Wollstonecraft, 15 June, 1797. (In C. Kegan Paul, ed. *William Godwin: His Friends and Contemporaries.* 2 vols. New York: AMS Press, 1970. 1: 262-63.)

[Godwin and a friend, Montagu, have called on Erasmus Darwin, who is away, but they meet his wife.] We asked of her a letter to Mr. Bage; but she said that she could not do that with propriety, as she did not know whether she had ever seen him, though he was the Doctor's very particular friend.

Thus baffled in our object, we plucked up our courage, and determined to introduce ourselves to the author of 'Hermsprong.' We were able to cite our introduction to Dr. Darwin by the Wedgwoods and our intention of having procured a letter from the doctor. Accordingly, we proceeded from Derby to Burton upon Trent, 16 miles. This is a very handsome town, with a wide and long street, a beautiful river, and a bridge which Montagu said was the longest he ever saw in the world. Here we slept, and drank Burton ale at the spring, after a journey of 48 miles. The next morning, between six and seven, we set out for Tamworth, 15 miles. At Elford, 11 miles, we saw Mr. Bage's mills, and a house in which he lived for 40 years. His mills are for paper and flour. Here we enquired respecting him, and found that he had moved to Tamworth five years ago, upon the death of his younger son, by which event he found his life rendered solitary and melancholy. The people at the mill told us that he came three times a week, walking from Tamworth to the mill, four miles; that they expected him at eleven (it was now nine); and that, if we proceeded, we should meet him upon the road. They told us, as a guide, that he was a short man, with white hair, snuff-coloured clothes, and a walking-stick. He is 67 years old, exactly the same age as Dr. Darwin. Accordingly, about a mile and a half from Tamworth, we met the man of whom we were in quest, with a book in his hand. We introduced ourselves, and, after a little conversation, I got out of the chaise, and walked back with him to the mill. This six or seven miles was very fortunate, and contributed greatly to our acquaintance. I found him uncommonly cheerful and placid, simple in his manners, and youthful in all his carriage. His house at the mill was floored, every room below stairs, with brick, and like that of a common farmer in every respect. There was, however, the river at the bottom of the garden, skirted with a quickset hedge, and a broad green walk. He told me his history.

His father was a miller, as well as himself, and he was born at Derby. At twenty-two he removed to Elford. He had been acquainted forty years with Dr. Darwin. The other acquaintances of his youth, were Whitehurst, author of 'The Theory of the Earth,' and some other eminent man whose name I forget. He taught himself French and Latin, in both of which languages he is a considerable proficient. In his youth he was fond of poetry; but, having some motive for the study of mathematics, he devoted his three hours an afternoon (the portion of time he allotted for reading) to this subject for twelve years, and this employment destroyed the eagerness of his attachment to poetry. In the middle of life, he engaged in a joint undertaking with Dr. Darwin and another person respecting some iron-works. This failed, and he returned once more to his village and his mill. The result filled him with melancholy thoughts; and, to dissipate them, he formed the project of a novel, which he endeavoured to fill with gay and cheerful ideas. At first he had no purpose of publishing what he wrote. Since that time he had been accustomed to produce a novel every two years, and 'Hermsprong' is his sixth. He believes he should not have written novels, but for want of books to assist him in any other literary undertaking. Living at Tamworth, he still retains his house at the mill, as the means of independence. It is his own, and he considers it as his security against the caprice or despotism of a landlord, who might expel him from Tamworth. He has thought much, and like most of those persons I have met with who have conquered many prejudices and read little metaphysics, is a materialist. His favourite book on this point is the 'Système de la Nature.' We spent a most delightful day in his company. When we met him, I had taken no breakfast; and though we had set off from Burton that morning at six, and I spent the whole morning in riding and walking, I felt no inconvenience in waiting for food till our dinner time at two, I was so much interested with Mr. Bage's conversation.

2. From William Hutton, "Memoirs of Mr. Bage," *The Monthly Magazine*, vol. XIII (Jan. 1802), 478–79.

Sir,

I waited, and earnestly wished, to see in your Magazine some memoirs of the late worthy Mr. Robert Bage. But none appearing after so urgent a solicitation, I think myself bound to pay a tribute to a departed friend whom I dearly loved, who stood one of the first in my esteem, whom I have known perhaps longer than any man living, and with whom I have lived in the closest friendship fifty years.

This uncommon but excellent man was born Feb. 29, 1728, at Darley, a hamlet in the parish of St. Alkmond's, Derby, where his father worked a paper-mill. Though he lived to the age of 73, he could not celebrate more than 18 birthdays.

His mother died soon after his birth, when his father removed to Derby, but kept the mill. He quickly married a second wife, and, as I well ·

remember, he buried her in 1732. He soon procured another, buried her, and ventured upon a fourth, who survived him.

Robert was put to school, so that I did not perfectly know him till 1735, when he was seven years old. He had made at that age such a progress in letters, that he was the wonder of the neighbourhood; he was then in the Latin tongue. My father often held him up to me for imitation, I being much bigger and older. I was then but little acquainted with him, for he moved in a sphere more elevated than I. At this time he was completely master of the manual-exercise, and I saw him instructing some young men. He afterwards was trained to his father's business.

In about 1751 he married a young lady, who possessed four accomplishments which seldom meet in one woman, fortune, beauty, good sense, and prudence; I might add a fifth, necessary for the peace of a family, good nature. I have reason to think he found more happiness in domestic life than is usually experienced. Having embraced the marriage state, he entered upon a paper-mill at Elford, four miles from Tamworth, which he conducted to the time of his death.

Some men's capacity opens at a late day, and some wither soon after the meridian of life, but Robert Bage's opened and shut with his existence. His enlivening sun shone with vigour during a long period of years. His talents, humanity, honour, and generosity, appeared, through the whole of his life, conspicuous to all who knew him. I could bring numberless incidents to establish every trait of his character: but as this would lead me into too wide a field, I shall confine myself to one or two proofs to each assertion. The *powers of his mind* were amazingly strong; these, in the early part of his life have already been noted. During my acquaintance with him he learnt music, and the French and Italian languages, without a master. Being inclined, in 1760, to learn the abstruse branches of mathematics, he applied to Thomas Hanson, a celebrated teacher, and spent a night in Birmingham once a week for instruction. As I was intimate with both, I sometimes attended, and before the scholar had been a month, I could easily perceive, though no adept myself, he was able to teach his master, nay, even set him fast. Perhaps part of this victory might arise from the easy fluency with which Mr. Bage delivered himself, while the master of figures was better formed for thinking than speaking.

His humanity will appear from his treatment of his servants, and even his horses, who all loved him, and whom he kept to old age.

Trade, which is thought to corrupt the mind, made no such impression upon his. Though he laid no stress upon Revelation, his dealings were stamped with rectitude; he remarked to me, "Fraud is beneath a man." He had no other love for money than to use it, or he might have left a much larger property than he did. In Feb. 1756, he asked me to spend the evening with him. He proposed a connection (not a partnership) which I accepted, and which continued, with small variations, according to the mutations of time, till the day of his death. From that date, perhaps, I have paid him 500 l. a year, upon the average, and always with *pleasure*, which proves this simple point, *I was treated with honour*. During this long course of 45 years he never gave me one cause of complaint. His *honour*, and peaceable temper, will farther appear from a remark he made while we travelled in a chaise from Wolsey bridge to Tamworth, in October 1795 — he had then been in partnership with a person in another concern near 15 years — "that they never had one word of difference since they met."

His generous cast of mind will appear from two, among many, incidents. I accidentally remarked that, "I had seen a distant relation of his, who was out of employment." — "Give him, (says he) upon my account (though he did not know him) five shillings a week till he gets into work." When the rioters, in 1791, had cruelly destroyed my property to a large amount, and obliged me, with my family, to run away without a shilling, and none durst take us in, we drove, among other places, to the Castle at Tamworth. I asked the people of the inn if they knew me? "No." — "I have no money to pay my way, or property to pledge." Their looks fell. "I am known to Mr. Bage, of Elford, whom I will request to pay my bill." Their looks and my credit rose together. He cheerfully paid it, blamed me for not coming to his house, and I could never prevail upon him to accept a return.

With all these rich *talents* and rare endowments he was mild in the extreme; an enemy to no man, and, I believe, never had one himself.

His reason for becoming an author was singular, and such as would have driven another out of authorship. I shall state the cause, and deliver the result as given me by himself in the chaise above mentioned. About the year 1765 he was induced to enter into partnership with three gentlemen in a wholesale iron-manufactory. The pursuit continued about 14 years, then dissolved, when it appeared he had lost a sum, which I have now forgotten, perhaps 1500 l. Fearing the distress of mind would overcome him, he took up the pen to turn the stream of sorrow into that of amusement; a scheme worthy a philosopher.

Appendix B: Bage's Fiction

1. *Monthly Review* on Bage's early fiction

[These reviews are taken from a single journal in order to give an overview of Bage's developing reputation from a more or less consistent perspective. Although not by the same reviewer, they all reflect the moderately liberal, moderately progressive editorial attitudes of *The Monthly Review*. The excerpts, which are printed as they appear in the review, even where there are slight variations from the original novel, indicate the political and social interests that recur throughout Bage's fiction and that were clearly shared by the *Monthly*'s reviewers. The length of the reviews and the excerpts — at a time when the more typical novel received only a few (often dismissive) sentences — is itself an indication of Bage's favourable reception, and while the *Monthly* is somewhat more enthusiastic than some of the other reviews, its tone is fairly representative. Even the rather less admiring *Critical Review* opened its ambivalent discussion of *The Fair Syrian* by proclaiming that "The author of Mount Henneth and Barham Downs demands a little more attention than we usually pay to novellists [sic]. His abilities, his humour, wit, and pathos, are above the common kind" (vol. 63 [Feb. 1787], 109). Bage himself seems not to have taken criticism too seriously. Shortly after the publication of Man as he is, he told William Hutton "What character it will have I know not; but if thou hearest any thing said of it in Birm^m — if good let me know — if bad keep it to thyself. I can digest flattery but hate correction" (Letterbook, Birmingham City Archives 486802 IIR 29, 100).]

a. *Mount Henneth: Monthly Review* 66 (Feb. 1782), 129–31.

We should indeed be mortified, if the very sensible and ingenious Author of this Novel meant a satire on the *Monthly* Reviewers by the little Critique which he himself hath drawn up *on his own performance* [See Appendix B.2]. Was there ever a work like the present, that even in the fulness of their spite, they were so unjust or so foolish as to pronounce destitute of 'wit, humour, plot, character, or keeping?' Let him point it out — if he can.

In the mean time, we think we shall be much better employed — no, not in pointing out the various beauties of *Henneth Castle* — for that would employ too large a portion of our Review — but in recommending it, with the most sincere conviction of its superior merit, to the perusal of our Readers: for we do not remember that we have, for many years, had the satisfaction of reviewing a work of this kind, that abounds with more lively strokes of wit, or sallies of fancy; with more judicious reflections, or pleasing and interesting characters. Its sentiments are liberal and manly, the tendency of it is perfectly moral; for its whole design is to infuse into the heart, by the most engaging examples, the principles of honour and truth, social love, and general benevolence.

To abridge this Novel, or even to give a general outline of its characters, plot, or *denouement*, would exceed the limits of our Work: we shall therefore present our Readers with only the following little episode, as a specimen of the Author's sprightly manner of reasoning on a subject which graver politicians have not discussed with more solid argument, in long orations in the house, or in laboured productions from the press.

"Carthage had settled colonies in the Hesperides, which in time grew to be worth something. Carthage desired to tax these fortunate islands. The fortunate islands did not desire to be taxed.

"The marrow of their negociations may be comprised in the following short Dialogue:

"*Carth.* We are to desire you, gentlemen, to submit patiently and lovingly to a few taxes which our country will do itself the honour to lay upon yours, as times and occasions may offer.

"*Hesp.* We must beg the favour of you to permit us to tax ourselves, as the people of your good country are accustomed to do, whom we are fond of imitating, and of calling our friends and brethren upon all occasions.

"*C.* To tax yourselves will not answer *our* purpose; for how can you be judges of what we want?

"*H.* At least as well as you can be of what we are able to pay.

"*C.* But if you give us no more than you like, that will probably be too little.

"*H.* And if you take from us what you please, that will probably be too much.

"*C.* We have laid a heavy load on ourselves for your emolument. Gratitude ought to induce you to submit to our demands.

"*H.* Honestly, now, did you do this for *our* sake or *your own*? But be it for ours, we are making your people a large return, by working for them with all our might. The greatest part of the whole profit of our industry has been always yours. Permit it to continue so. Turn all our trade into your own harbours, as you are wont. Tax in your own country the commodities you make us buy; but let us be favoured with the privilege your people so justly boast of as their greatest safeguard; let us give and grant our own money.

"*C.* As to the benefit of your trade, it may be something to our people in general. But what is that to the necessities of government? We want a benefit flowing full and fast into the exchequer. We don't understand your round-about way of sending it through the body of the people.

"*H.* We believe it; otherwise you would certainly be content with receiving it as you do, in the best manner possible, for the good of the whole.

"*C.* What we *have already* we have no reason to demand. — More, gentlemen, more; — and by the strait forward road.

"*H.* We cannot consent to it.

"*C.* Then, by G-d, we will dragoon you till you do.

"*H.* Pray, gentlemen, consider. — Let us beg you to hear what we have to say. — Let us beg it for both our sakes, gentlemen.

"*C.* Implicit obedience — unconditional submission — and your money, are the things we want, and will have.

"*H.* Win them and wear them.

"—— And so Carthage sent out fleets and armies, and spent as much of her own money in five years, as she had expected to get of her colonies in one hundred!"

b. *Barham Downs: Monthly Review* 71 (Sept. 1784), 223-24.

Some of the characters exhibited in this novel are the most execrable and abandoned that can disgrace human nature; they are almost 'too bad for bad report:' but they are contrasted by others which are peculiarly amiable and excellent, and shine with more than common lustre. Harry Osmond and his Annabella possess the softer graces; and they are here sketched with a free and easy, if not a delicate pencil. But the Author's talent lies chiefly in striking and spirited touches, and such particularly as convey lively images of objects under a light and ludicrous form. He is seldom serious; and his pathetic is sometimes dashed with an odd mixture of ridicule and irony. His object seems to be, to put his Reader into a gay humour; and he generally succeeds in his attempt: for, amidst the display of the most atrocious characters, he hath the art of repressing indignation by pleasantry.

Harry Osmond, disappointed in love, through the caprice and avarice of a false and unprincipled woman, hath the superadded misfortune of failing in business. After settling his affairs with his creditors, in a manner greatly to his honour and their satisfaction, he changes his name, and retires on the wreck of his fortune, to a small and sequestered cottage in the country, near BARHAM DOWNS, the seat of Justice Whitaker; who had two daughters, the youngest of which he was desirous of marrying to Lord Winterbottom; who had ruined himself by gambling, debauchery, and extravagance. Osmond, under the assumed name of Davis, meets the Miss Whitakers in a grove, the accustomed scene of his retirement. His manner of address interested the young ladies in his favour; and by their means he is introduced to the old justice, and a very agreeable acquaintance commences; — but which, in a short time, is interrupted by the jealousy of Lord Winterbottom. Here the plot opens: and it is carried through various scenes and embarrassments, both in England and on the continent, till Osmond's constancy is rewarded by the hand of his Annabella.

The leading principle of this Author's novels is *good sense*, animated by a spirit of freedom and benevolence, and expressed in a style peculiarly pointed and sprightly. But we see nothing original in either his characters or plots, though there is a novelty in the *manner:* we suspect that it will be judged too deficient in nature; that the *smart strokes* and *hits* of humour and wit strike the reader too rapidly; above all, that the ingenious Writer too frequently discovers a pruriency of fancy, which leads him too near the borders of indelicacy; and he is, moreover, chargeable with a levity of sentiment, which hath a strong cast of irreligion and infidelity.

In a work of entertainment, designed for general reading, every thing which hath a tendency to infuse loose ideas into the mind, and to unsettle religious principles, should be carefully avoided by every one who hath the real interests of virtue and the welfare of society at heart. We are sorry that so ingenious a writer as the Author of Mount Henneth, and Barham Downs, and who is so capable of affording amusement, without condescending to stand indebted to the tricks of meaner novelists for the means of gratifying a vicious taste, — we are sorry that *such* a writer should ever lay himself open to censure, or give cause for a reflection, which we make with reluctance, and which nothing but a sense of the duty we owe to the Public could have drawn from us. We shall, however, rejoice that we have made it, if by this means he should be led, in future, to correct an error which shades the beauty of too many pages of his otherwise admired novels.

c. *The Fair Syrian: The Monthly Review* 76 (April 1787), 325-29.

It is unquestionably the business both of the dramatic writer and the novelist, "to hold as 'twere the mirror up to nature; to shew virtue her own feature, vice her own image, and the very age and body of the time his form and pressure." The man of genius, therefore, who writes with the view of affording amusement to his readers, will, when selecting materials for his work, make choice of such particular incidents and scenes in life as may be somewhat familiar to the people in general, but which are still of such a nature as to admit of amplification, and which will allow him to exercise his inventive faculty in a certain and limited degree; that is, in such a degree as that he do not "o'er-step the modesty of nature," or in all events, that probability do not receive from it any great or violent shock.[1]

---

1   The quotations in this paragraph are from *Hamlet* II.2.

Our three great novel-writers are Richardson, Fielding, and Smollet; and these, — to illustrate one art or profession by another, — we would compare with Reynolds, Le Brun, and Hogarth.[1] The first for truth and beauty of colouring, the second for a lively display of the passions, and the third for caricatura. We almost despair of seeing them equalled. It is, however, no little satisfaction to us to find, amid the multitude of "unfinished things," which are continually issuing from the press under the denomination of novels, or romances; and which we should really be at a loss to characterize, were it not the writers of them have kindly, and in imitation of the showman, set down in the title-pages of their respective performances — "*this is a novel*" — it is no little satisfaction to us, we say, to meet with a writer like the present, who to ease and correctness of expression unites that very essential requisite of a novelist, — a talent for nice and accurate delineation of character: who contrasts his several personages with considerable skill and ability: who gives to them their appropriate language, spirit, and manners; and who finally presents us with a fable or story, tolerably harmonious in all its parts.

The just and pertinent observations contained in the following extract will shew that our Author is something more than a novel-writer: he appears, indeed, in the honourable and amiable character of a philosopher, and friend of man, — for though in the dialogue we have here selected, a *quaker* and a *petit-maitre* compose the scene, it is very easy to discover that the quaker, the favourite character, speaks the sentiments of the Author's heart.

"My next excursion was to Philadelphia, to do my *baisemains* to that terrible congress, whose name is to be celebrated by future Livys as the ancient preserver of the only storehouse for liberty in the four quarters of the globe; where thirty generations of men, exclusive of accidents, may be furnished with what they want. I'll tell you a secret, my dear Count; I had it from a Quaker, one of the people who never swear, and very seldom lie.

"'The heads of the Kings and rulers of the old world are worm-eaten.' The man is a farmer, and though I have the honour to be the Marquis de St. Claur, and not to know wheat from barley in the blade, yet, as it is the fashion to visit him on account of his numerous improvements, I chose to be in the fashion. His conversation was so entertaining, his hospitality so warm, and his wife so pretty, that I stayed three days with him in the country, without becoming an *ennuyè*, except once, when the dissertation upon plants had been stretched out rather too long. I had the misfortune to gape. 'I tire thee,' says he. I was assuring him to the contrary. 'We study

---

1   Sir Joshua Reynolds (1723-92) was famed for his portraits; Charles Le Brun (1619-90) gave lectures on art that included advice on how to portray the passions; William Hogarth (1697-1764) was admired for his satiric paintings.

here the language of nature more than that of politeness,' says he; 'come, let us take a walk.'

"In a field, where many sheep were feeding, one of them very often, holding its head awry, staggered round and round, fell down, and soon rose again and eat. 'The brain of that poor animal,' says he, 'has worms in it; I must order it to the slaughter-house out of compassion. We call this disorder the turn; and I am apt to think, kings have it sometimes. Thou knowest the Americans are struggling for liberty. Thy King, and the King of Spain, who dote upon it so, that they keep it all to themselves, and tell their people it is not for common wear, help us forward in the obtaining it with all their might; and the King of England, who lives but to extend and secure this blessing to all his subjects, is labouring as lustily to deprive us of it. Much in the same manner acted thy fourteenth Louis, when he revoked the edict of Nantz, to destroy liberty of thinking at home, and sent millions to support it in Germany. — What thinkest thou? — Did it not denote worms?'

"'Possibly it might,' replies I; 'but this accusation brought against the present Kings of France and Spain, comes not well from the mouth of an American.'

"'Thou dost not imagine,' says he, 'that I think they can err on this side. But thou will not say they are consistent. Let them give their own people that liberty they endeavour to procure us, and they will be as high in my esteem, almost as William Penn.'

"'I should like to know what standard you measure merit by? It seems odd to compare the Kings of France and Spain with William Penn.'

"'Thou mistakest; I do not. I know of no point of comparison between them. One standard of merit is the *good* done to mankind. In reading the histories of thy country, one would be apt to conclude Kings thought themselves great in proportion to the *mischief* they did; and that their subjects were blind enough to sanctify the error.'

"'Surely mankind is much benefited by being well governed.'

"'I grant it. — Is thy country so?'

"'We think it is.'

"'Who dost thou mean by the term we?'

"'The public in general.'

"'The public in general then must be sunk low indeed in the scale of political freedom. Let us for conversation sake turn naturalists; and consider man by his inward as well as outward marks. The people of thy country, and ours, are doubtless classed under the name MAN as a GENUS; let us see if the SPECIES may not differ.

"'We will begin the comparison with the rank of peasants, that numerous class employed in raising subsistence for the whole community. In France, how poor they are! how abject! starving in the midst of those delicacies they are daily creating, as it were, for the use of others. See their rags, their black bread, and rancid bacon! If a man of the *Noblesse*, honours them with his commands, they are *abymès infiniment*, and ready to jump into a well, to shew their sense of the amazing condescension. View the same rank in America, and acknowledge the difference. It would be insulting thy understanding to point it out. Every man feels himself a MAN; claims his share of the common bounties of nature; and above all, of Liberty.

"'It is true, you have a vast superiority in your trinket men, your *taileurs, parfumeurs,* your *perruquiers,* and especially your *cuisiniers*; and may a thousand ages elapse, before America becomes your rival.'

"'St. Paul says, whatsoever you do, let it be to the praise and glory of God. A good Frenchman obeys the precept, but his God is the *grand Monarque.* If half a million are sent to Germany or Flanders, to die of the sword, disease or famine, the King's glory requires it, and we are content. If Versailles and Fontainbleau waste the treasures of a nation in useless magnificence, or childish splendor, it is for the King's glory, and we are content. In return, the *grand Monarque,* or the *grand Monarque's* mistresses take the trouble to govern these obsequious people according to their own good will and pleasure.'

"'At present, thou see'st America conceives it possible, though doubtless very afflicting, to subsist without this *species*; and when they had it, they said not with the French, We are thy servants, O King, do unto us as seemeth good unto thee. — But, thou art our servant, O King, execute our laws in righteousness. Dost thou perceive any difference?'

"'I do. But Frenchmen have a great deal to learn, and unlearn too, before they can enter into so licentious a course of thinking, and trample upon the sacred majesty of Kings.'

"'Sacred majesty of Kings! Lord's annointed! Delegates of heaven! Just less than gods! In my youth I also read tragedies, epic poems, romances, and divinity. Now, I read COMMON SENSE. And what pretty epithets hast thou adapted to the dignity of the sacred order? Wilt thou not think we are given over to all uncleanness of spirit, living, as we do, unsprinkled, dying ununctioned. Can there be salvation, thinkest thou, without a Bishop? Without that order of men so useful to a nation that chuses to think by proxy? But to tell thee a secret, and it may serve to confirm the difference in specie, American heads are so pertinaciously constructed, that rather than not take their own road to heaven, they will take none at all.'

"'The road to heaven, my dear Sir, has always been represented to us as a thorny path, and hard to find. Why then should we not take guides?'

"'I grant thee, to the people of thy world, the path is burthened with incumbrances; and prithee who put them there? I fancy it is the work of thy hierarchy only. They seem to me like pilots who tell of a thousand imaginary sand-banks obstructing the road into port, in order to be paid the pilotage. Scarce any thing to us is so safe, so easy, and so pleasant, as the way that conducts to heaven. Love God; love thy neighbour; and be just. This is our law and our prophets.'

"'In all the true holy catholic mother church, my dear Sir, there is not a priest who does not derive his descent, spiritually, from the twelve apostles. We believe they are called to the sacred work of salvation. We believe they know something of what they teach. We are sure we do not know. If they inform us right, we have all the advantage of it. If wrong, as we cannot guide ourselves better, we are no worse than we were.'

"'Thy plea is so good a one, that I promise thee whenever the men thou speakest of, prove their descent, *exclusively* — we will come over unto their faith. Till they do this, thou wilt excuse us, for not trusting wholly our estates to stewards, our consciences to confessors, or our souls to priests. We think all of importance enough to look to them ourselves.'

"'Well Sir, all that I know is, that you have sucked in one set of maxims with your mother's milk, and we another. Yours tends to establish reason, that damnable faculty according to our creed; ours faith; which whosoever has enough of, may remove your Apalachian mountains.'

"'Thou art right. Education is all in all.'"

Were it within the limits and compass of our Review, we would willingly follow this lively and ingenious writer through the several windings and meanderings of his work; but we must, however reluctantly, take leave of him, with recommending to our Readers, a performance in which instruction and entertainment are blended in a manner that is rarely to be found; and which, in the present state of novel writing, we cannot too much commend.

d. *James Wallace: Monthly Review*, vol. 80 (June 1789), 499–502.

When we reflect on the great diversity of characters among mankind, and when we consider that the volume of nature lies open to the inspection of all who may be inclined to study from it, it appears not a little surprising, that the writers who undertake to give a delineation of men and things, should yet so repeatedly and so strikingly fail in their attempts.

It has been observed of pastoral poets, that few of them, since the days of Theocritus, can be said to have succeeded in any great or eminent degree. They present us with smooth and polished verses, but rural images are rarely seen. The matter is, that they follow each other in *general description*, without adverting to *localities*, or to particular situations, which would be likely to interest us by reason of their novelty and of their *truth*. Now the censure which has been passed on these poets with regard to their *sameness*, is generally applicable to the writers of romances. The regular round of incident which so continually comes before us; the insipidity and tameness of the characters to whose dull and laboured conversations we are obliged to give attention; the scheme of the rake for the seduction of innocence; the whining of Miss for the loss of a lover, or for the *cruelty* of a father in hindering her from playing the fool: — All this, we say, is become so truly disgustful, that when an author, like the novelist whose production we are now to consider, presents himself to our *admiring eyes*, we bid him welcome! in a kind of transport, and "wish him health and wish it long." We, at the same time, would not be understood as insinuating that the writer whom we thus commend is without a fault. No such exemption! There is much eccentricity about him. It may be remarked, moreover, that he paints with boldness; but sometimes, and more especially in the present instance, rather too coarsely. — In a word, there is evidently more of *genius* in his compositions than of *taste*. But, notwithstanding the objection which we have started, as to the *finishing* of this performance, the story of it is not uninteresting, and it is conducted with no little degree of art.

Grouping, and, at the same time, a nice preservation of character, is particularly difficult; and we much more frequently meet with an artist who presents us with separate portraits in an agreeable style, than with one who can fill his canvas with a variety of personages, exhibiting *a perfect and regular whole*. To follow this author in his fable, would be tedious; we will, therefore, attend, in the first place, to some of his *observations*, and afterward to some of his *persons* — that is, to such of them as may appear to be most deserving of regard.

With respect to the *reasoning*: "Covering is a want of nature; and she has given us wool, and flax, and skins: but, merciful heaven! into what a variety of fantastic forms must these be twined and twisted before the animal can be covered? Not to be able to eat without formulas from cooks: not to defend ourselves from the blasts of winter without formulas from taylors and milliners: not to be able to love without formulas from fools; these, James Wallace, these are the causes of nine-tenths, by a very accurate calculation, of those mighty evils for which we arraign Providence, and insult Heaven with clamour." This is sufficiently pertinent and just: though with some, perhaps, it may be thought to look a little *cynically*.

"I like to treat things philosophically, James Wallace; and I say nature created no other evil for man but pain: all things else which we call evil, spring from — *improvement*. Man wants food. Nature has given him an accommodating appetite. Almost any thing is sufficient for its gratification; and he has *improved* it, till almost nothing will suffice." "*Almost nothing*," does not here convey the sense. It should be — *till scarcely any thing will suffice*.

We will now transcribe a part of one of the letters, in which the pretenders to philosophy and science are exposed with some degree of pleasantry:

"My father, that he may be well informed of what passes in the world of science, takes in the *Star*, by a paragraph of which he was told, that in France, Monsieur A — had electrified certain fruit-trees in his garden, and that the success was astonishing! The fruit was larger, more early ripe, and had a superior flavour! Monsieur B — had extended the idea to the cultivation of arable and pasture, and was preparing a machine, by which ten acres might be electrified almost in an instant! Now, my father's land wanted improvement as much as most arable and pasture in France, but the hacknied mode of manure was not for a man of genius. He caught the new idea, and cherished it till it served him as favourites do a King, occupying his royal mind to the exclusion of every other. Oh! could he be the first to introduce it into England, how would it immortalize his fame! an idea of which my father was very fond. But the *Star* was silent as to the *quo modo*; and no other method occurring to my father but of rubbing up, and conducting down, the necessary mass of electric fluid, he turned his attention to the proper manner of procuring an apparatus sufficient for the purpose. The machine was in all respects a common one, except in the bulk, which was to be enormous. Half a ton of iron wire and small iron chain was the least that could be wanted to diffuse the fluid with sufficient dispatch and regularity. But this ingenious and immortal scheme was ruined by the want of philosophic comprehension in the under labourers. The glass cylinder, three feet diameter and six high, was smashed to atoms: much mischief was done among glass legs and sticks of sealing-wax, and my father found at once his scheme ruined, and himself involved in a new debt of seventy pounds. Do not imagine, dear Wallace, that in speaking thus of my father, I intend any contempt of science, especially chemical, which I adore. But of the hasty conclusions of one or few experiments, of the eternal adoption of system, consequently of its eternal variation, I have seen so much in my father, that I consider it as the weakness of philosophy. There was a time when my father knew the nerves to be cylindric tubes filled with an invisible fluid. There was a time he was perfectly satisfied they were elastic chords, vibrating like fiddle-strings. A year had not passed away, but they became slender filaments admirably adapted to convey sensation by a something like vermicular motion: the nervous fluid became nervous influence: this influence was soon known to be the electric fluid, and the filaments the best of all possible conductors. At this instant, however, he is rather of opinion that the nerves are not concerned in the business of sensation any way whatever. But was this all, Wallace: had my father nothing worse than a feeble judgment and capricious imagination, how thankfully could I overlook his vanities and his hobby-horses. Oh! had he but the social affections, the common charities of life, or, was he adorned with integrity — all might be forgiven. But, dear James, this is too tender and delicate a subject, even for the ear of friendship. — Enough of philosophy."

With regard to the *persons*. The sketch of the character of Scovel, bears evident marks of the master's hand. The portrait is natural, bold, and animated. — Mr. Gamidge, the Justice; his Lady, and Thomas their son, are depicted in a truly laughable style. — Squire Thurl may also be noticed as a diverting character, though bearing too near a resemblance to *Tony Lumpkin* in the play.[1] — The Army Lieutenant and the Glasgow Rider are

---

1 The play is *She Stoops to Conquer* (1773) by Oliver Goldsmith.

drawn much in the manner of Smollet. The dialogue which passes between them contains some smart and humorous strokes: it is of too great length for us to transcribe, and to mutilate it would be unjust. The other personages are not without their merits. But after all, the author will not be thought by many, who remember his former performances, to have greatly *advanced* his fame by the present publication. The fact is, that he writes not with sufficient care. Let him not forget that — *Qui non proficit, deficit*: that is an actual *verity*: and not, as some may be inclined to imagine, merely a sophism of the schools.

e. *Man as he Is: Monthly Review*, n.s., vol. 10 (March 1793), 297– 302. [By Thomas Holcroft]

When we consider the influence that novels have over the manners, sentiments, and passions, of the rising generation, — instead of holding them in the contempt which, as reviewers, we are without exception said to do, — we may esteem them, on the contrary, as forming a very essential branch of literature. That the majority of novels merit our contempt, is but too true; and, for the reason above given, it is a truth of a serious and painful nature. The very end of a novel is to produce interest in the reader, for the characters of whom he reads: — but, in order to produce this interest, it is necessary that the novel writer should be well acquainted with the human heart, should minutely understand its motives, and should possess the art, without being either tedious or trifling, of minutely bringing them to view. This art is so little understood by the young ladies who at present write novels, which none but young ladies and we, luckless reviewers, read, that it is not wonderful that they should have incurred a considerable share of neglect from us: — but when a novel has the power of playing on the fancy, interesting the affections, and teaching moral political truth, we imagine that we are capable of feeling these beauties, and that we have liberality enough to announce them to the world.

Of this superior kind, is the novel now before us; which, though far from being without faults, gave us great pleasure, and is such as we can warmly recommend to readers of taste, science, and sentiment. In narrating his fabulous adventures, the author frequently leads us through the regions of metaphysics, politics, and even theology; in which, however, he seldom remains long enough to fatigue the attention, or to pall the appetite, or his reader. These flights have, in general, the additional merit of being adapted to character: they are managed with that happy art which raises associations, and which, by giving a sketch, incites and animates the mind to complete the picture.

Amid this well-deserved praise, however, there is one grand defect, which could scarcely have been expected from an author of so much taste, acuteness, and knowledge: — we allude to the want of unity. His hero, and heroine, are frequently neglected, and almost lost, in his digressive excursions, and delineations of character, that have little connexion with the furtherance of the plot. His power of making these eccentricities pleasing, sometimes, indeed, captivating, only adds to the injury. In splendor of ornament, unity of design is lost; and while we gaze at the beautiful columns, we almost forget the building. We are not, as in Tom Jones, continually interested by each new incident, because the state and well being of the persons concerned are changed. Nor are we impatient, as in Clarissa Harlowe, to know what must be the result of passions, which become more and more complicated, active, and violent: — not that this novel is without interest: — but our complaint is, that this part, which ought to constitute the ligaments and sinews of the whole, is comparatively languid and inadequate. The expedient of making Sir George Paradyne, the hero, fall sick at last, (without which, it is apparent, he knew not how to overcome the well-founded scruples of Miss Coleraine, the heroine,) is one which unfits Sir George for his post, and degrades Miss Coleraine.

The author, however, has written a novel which, we have no doubt, the world will read; and when he writes again, it will be worthy of his talents to exert them with their full force, and to emulate writers whose equal, we are persuaded, it only depends on himself to become. As a specimen of his discussive powers, we shall cite the following dialogue; only premising, that Miss Haubert, who begins it with Sir George Paradyne, is a rich, arrogant, old maid; Mr. Holford is a clergyman; and Miss Carlill is a quaker.

"You have probably been at Oxford Sir George, or Cambridge?

"At Oxford, madam.

"I presume the sciences there are in a very flourishing state?

"I hope they are always so there, madam.

"Has any able metaphysician arisen, or is likely to arise, capable of confuting Mr. Hume's system of universal non-existence?

"Dr. Reid, madam.

"Oh, no — I have read him; he does not go to the bottom..

"I have often admired, madam, says Mr. Holford, that a lady of your profound science, should think any thing worth notice which comes from the pen of such a man, so great an enemy to religion and piety.

"A man may be wrong in one thing and right in another, Mr. Holford, answered the lady. Every man who wants religion, may not want knowledge.

"It is pity but he did, replied Mr. Holford.

"You are certainly right, madam, says Mrs. Holford. Many of our most celebrated novels have characters tainted with infidelity, in other respects very learned and amiable. As Mr. Wolmar in Rousseau's Eloisa, the elegant Sir Charles Seymour in Cornelia Sedley, and many others.

"Very true, Mrs. Holford; I don't read many novels except yours; but I believe it is allowable to draw all sorts of characters as they are, and since it does happen that there are ingenuous people infidels, to be sure they may be drawn."

"I wish, says Mr. Holford, they were all drawn upon hurdles to the stake.

"Miss Coleraine absolutely gave a little start, and was upon the point of an exclamation, but corrected herself, and only said, with a smile — no, Mr. Holford, I must beg leave to refuse you credit on this head; your theory is cruel, your practice would be merciful.

"I have no mercy for the enemies of God, answered Mr. Holford. The lady, says Miss Haubert with a scornful toss of her head, chooses to shew her sensibility."

"I hope, says Miss Carlill, if the occasion was real, thou would'st shew thine. Miss Haubert replied with another toss. Then you don't approve of zeal in the cause of God, Miss Carlill? asked Mr. Holford.

"Yea — answered she — if it is of the spirit.

"Oh ma'm, replies Mr. Holford, we cannot boast of so plentiful a communication with the spirit, as your people.

"Thy spirit seems not to be our sort; we persecute no one.

"Nor would Mr. Holford, I am well convinced, says Miss Coleraine.

"Why not? says Miss Haubert; very great and good men have thought it right to persecute heresy.

"They would have been better employed, perhaps, in praying for it, says Miss Coleraine.

"You may think so madam, answered Miss Haubert, but without zeal what is religion?

"We also approve zeal, Miss Haubert, when it tends to improve our own faith; not when it condemns others, says Miss Carlill.

"Ay, says Mr. Holford, this is the modern doctrine of toleration, by which all unity of christianity is cut off from the face of the earth; and men are led astray by pretended spiritual guides, or permitted to wander without any.

"Thou knowest that in heaven there are many mansions. Why should there not be many roads? says Miss Carlill.

"There can be but one road, madam, answered Mr. Holford, the road of truth.

"And few there be that find it, replied Miss Carlill.

"It is because they shut their eyes, says Mr. Holford, and harden their hearts, and God gives them up to their own perverseness, and to all unquietness of mind. Here are the presbyterians again, I am told, up in arms, about the repeal of the test act, that bulwark of the church and constitution. Had there been any understanding among them, they must have acknowledged the superior force of our arguments.

"If the arguments of thy people, replied Miss Carlill, had been as strong as their motives, the dissenters must have found them irresistible long ago.

"Blindness, wilful blindness, says Mr. Holford.

"Nay, now friend Holford, replied Miss Carlill, thou must excuse me;

it is so important to see the truth, if they could, that I should rather impute it to their not being able to find good oculists.

"They envy us, says Mr. Holford, the very bread we eat, and would snatch it out of our mouths.

"I fancy, replies Miss Carlill, it will take them a great many pulls. Thy church is indeed built upon a rock, if it holds its faith with as firm a hand as its emoluments.

"Have we not a right to them? asked Mr. Holford.

"Yea, two rights, replied Miss Carlill; power and possession: neither of these, have the dissenters.

"I say, says the parson, the dissenters have no rights whatever.

"They were born, answers Miss Carlill, with as many as other people. What is become of them?

"They incapacitate themselves, by maintaining religious tenets which government chooses should not be maintained.

"So, says Miss Carlill, it was in the time of Dioclesian. Ye know the law, said the emperor; all christians are to be hanged. But ye need not incur the penalty; ye have nothing to do in order to avoid it, but return to Jupiter, the god of your fathers. Did Dioclesian reason well, thinkest thou?

"How can you ask such a question, madam? says Mr. Holford.

"Nay — answered Miss Carlill — I know not; if it were not that I thought the reasoning of Dioclesian and thy people, something similar.

"I assure you, madam, says Mr. Holford, you never were more mistaken; and you impute motives to us which never entered our pure hearts. All we want is to bring the community into one faith, and thereby avoid the confusion of sects, and the nonsense of sectaries.

"Thou need'st not tell me this. It is, they say, the distinguishing garb of the priesthood. If a man, in matters of faith, incline to tolerate any nonsense but his own, he hath not on a wedding garment; he is not a true brother.

"You are smart, Miss Carlill, says Mr. Holford, but smartness is not argument. Let us come to the point. There must be a national religion. Grant that.

"I pray thee, Miss Carlill asked, which is the national religion of America?

"Pshaw! says the parson, rather angrily; they'll come to nothing for the want of it.

"When they do the argument will be in thy favour, answered Miss Carlill.

"But if they flourish, says Mr. Holford, they must have one; they must have a chief magistrate; one or many. This chief must have a religion; he must prefer his own, and the very preference will soon give a decided majority; and a national religion follows of course.

"I do not at present see the justness of thy premises, or of thy conclusion, answered the lady. A Frenchman of great consequence, was once at Amsterdam, and being desirous to see every thing, was attended by a burgomaster, who noticed, as they passed along, many small places of worship. This, says he, belongs to the Anabaptists, very industrious people and good subjects; this to the Moravians, very diligent, quiet, good, orderly people; so he went on to twenty different sects, giving each its due praise of industry and obedience to the laws. And pray sir, says the count, what religion are you of? Me, answers the magistrate, — my lord, I am burgomaster of Amsterdam. Dost thou not think it a wise answer?

"It would not do in England, Mr. Holford said. The constitution was founded upon the inseparable connection of church and state.

"Pray of what nature may this connection be? How may it differ from the general connection betwixt crown and people? asked Miss Carlill.

"In being more close and intimate, answered Mr. Holford, in mutual assistance, when assistance is wanted.

"I believe I understand thee, replied Miss Carlill. If the crown gets into a scrape, the clergy will kindly help it out. If the crown has something to do the people don't like, the clergy is ready with its aid.

"What right have you to suppose this, Madam? asked Mr. Holford.

"Why, replied Miss Carlill, when the crown is doing that which the people does approve, it will necessarily have its support — the best of all supports, I think — surely, when it has the whole it cannot want a part.

"There is no reasoning, says Mr. Holford, with people whose prejudices are so inveterate, they will hear nothing which contradicts them. To me, there is not a problem of Euclid, which is more clear, than that the test act, and subscription to articles, are the bulwarks of the church; and that the church is the best bulwark of the state."

"I have heard of that Euclid, replied Miss Carlill; pray thee, how came it to pass that his problems were so clear, as to pass almost into a proverb. Did he demonstrate after thy manner?

"That — let me tell you ma'm is a very ignorant question, and shews you do not distinguish betwixt mathematical and speculative science; says Miss Haubert, with much dignity of aspect.

"I own my ignorance, says Miss Carlill, still addressing herself to Mr. Holford, without noticing the rudeness of Miss Haubert — wilt thou instruct me in the nature of those articles thou hast just mentioned?

"Mr. Holford did not seem to relish the employment, and only said, read, read, madam, and understand.

"Alas! says Miss Carlill, I have read, and do not understand.

"You read, madam, with the prejudice of a sectary.

"Possibly so. Considering however the very important part they were to act upon this stage of ours, one might have expected they would have exhibited the collected wisdom of ages. At least one should not have found them incomprehensible.

"There is no necessity, ma'm, says Miss Haubert, who never opened her lips to-day, but to express scorn or dislike — there is no necessity that your comprehension should be the measure of other people's.

"I grant that, replies Miss Carlill; but do not many of thy communion, learned divines, nay, prelates, acknowledge the same difficulty? have the faculties of mankind degenerated?

"No, madam, answered Mr. Holford; God has given to man his wonted capacity; but how does he now apply it? In the luxuries and vanities of this world; and in opposing his own vain imaginations to the mysteries of faith."

Of this, as of most other novels, we have to complain that the errors of printing are numerous, and highly reprehensible. The author, who could bestow the labour of writing these four volumes, ought surely to have been capable of the additional fatigue that was necessary to convey his own ideas accurately.

2. Selected responses to *Hermsprong*

a. *Monthly Review*, vol. 21, n.s. (Sept. 1796), 21-24. [By William Taylor]

Man as he is, a former publication of this uncommon writer, was reviewed in our xth vol. N.S. p. 297. We then thought fit to mingle, with our general and warm approbation of that novel, the remark that sufficient attention had not been paid to unity of design in the plan of the composition. The same opinion might be advanced, without injustice, respecting the production before us. The episode of Miss Sumelin is too long, and has too little influence on the proper story: — Gregory Glen appears at the beginning intended for the hero, but the level of his importance subsides with the continuation of the narrative, and at last evaporates into air — into "thin air."

We feel, however, disposed to ascribe a higher rank of excellence to this than to the former novel: it wanders less from its main purpose; there are equal beauties of detail; and the elevated soul of Hermsprong is a prominent and fine delineation of the accomplished, firm, frank, and generous man, worthy to be impressed as a model for imitation. This noble character has much originality: but its features may be traced back partly to the native openness and resources of the ingenuous *Huron* of Voltaire, and partly to the systematic sincerity and philosophic courage of *Frank Henley* in Holcroft's *Anna St. Ives*.

The story is that of an American Incognito, who settles in Cornwall, discovers estimable qualities in a Peer's only daughter, whom he convinces of the wisdom of putting herself under his protection in spite of every prejudice of wealth and family; and to whom, at the approach of their marriage, he reveals a relationship which renders the union acceptable on all sides.

Of the author's style, which has great excellencies, but which sometimes wants accuracy, a specimen or two may be given:

[Quotes from "'Grant,' said Glen" to "sugar, treble refined" (pp. 158-

60) and from "The time of dinner" to "Miss Fluart made the lawyer blush" (pp. 287-89).]

We hope for frequent entertainment from the pen of this amusing, instructive, and singular genius.

b. *Analytical Review*, vol. 24 (Dec. 1796), 608-09. [By Mary Wollstonecraft; she was also the author of the review of *Man as he Is* mentioned in the first sentence.]

In our last number we testified our respect for the talents of the author of *Man as he is*; observing, however, that it was rather the manner of telling the story, than the combination of the incidents, which claimed our admiration. The present novel presents a more complete plot; and is, on that account, entitled to a greater degree of popularity, not to dwell on the excellence of making a character, such as the hero's, so comparatively perfect, and interesting.

Hermsprong, the man of nature, educated in the back settlements of America, brought unavoidably the recollection of Voltaire's *Huron* strongly in our mind. That justly celebrated work may indeed have suggested the idea of this noble character to the author; yet warming, without fettering his imagination, we are only reminded of the original conception to admire the invention exhibited in the skilful deviations from it.

Hermsprong has a sensible father, who did not allow his mind to lie fallow while he acquired the practical virtues of savage life; and he returns to Europe early enough to polish his manners by cultivating his understanding; yet with a character sufficiently fixed to prevent any sacrifice of principles.

The strength of mind, and frankness of heart, which we praised, shaded as it was in the former production of this able writer, are in this the principal features, though a few harsh lines, of something like savage vengeance, in the hero's behaviour to his uncle, shows the paw of the wild hunter, in the forest.

> "Far from the milder joys which stray
> In life's more cultured path, and mark the way."[1]

A sprightly female character is well supported, difficult as it is to reflect such bright, ever changing, still the same colours, and the author has a happy mode of recommending mental improvement to a sex he loves, which the *dear creatures* can scarcely find displeasing.

Various conversations are introduced to display the hero's agility, sin-

---

1 Presumably a misquotation of Oliver Goldsmith's "The Traveller" (1765):
"But all the gentler morals such as play / Through life's more cultured walks and charm the way / These far dispers'd, on timorous pinions fly" (236-38).

cerity, presence of mind, and love of truth, in which the sentiments are pointedly expressed.

c. *The British Critic*, vol. 7 (April 1796), 430.

Notwithstanding there are many principles in these volumes with which we not only cannot agree, but even think them capable of a pernicious operation, yet we willingly confess that it is far superior to most publications of the kind, and has in its perusal afforded us much amusement. The character of Hermsprong is exceedingly well drawn, though occasionally somewhat overcharged. Miss Campinet is not made to excite sufficient interest, and is rather a foil to the sprightly and most agreeable Miss Fluart. The author evidently is a friend to many principles which, having been tried, have been found destructive of the end they proposed to accomplish, and to generate, not a greater equality of human comfort, but confusion and misery to thousands. We must however do him the justice to say, that he obtrudes his sentiments with no intemperate warmth, and we are much more frequently pleased with his ingenuity, than either tired or offended by his narrative; and should certainly think ourselves bound to reverence such a character as he has here delineated, if such could any where be found.

d. *The Critical Review*, vol. 23 s.2 (June 1798), 234.

This novel must be distinguished from the common sort. The author displays an intimate acquaintance with human nature, and delineates it with the pen of a master. His characters are drawn with just discrimination, and placed in situations where their actions strictly correspond with the original sketch. There is occasionally a little tincture of the new philosophy, as it is called, and a shade of gloom is thrown upon human life; but the writer is not unsuccessful in his humourous attempts; and, upon the whole, the reader has a chance of becoming wiser and better by a perusal of this work, if his taste has not been vitiated by the trifling productions of the age.

e. Anna Laetitia Barbauld, [*Hermsprong* versus *Man as he Is*], from *The British Novelists, with an Essay, and Prefaces biographical and critical ... A new Edition.* 50 vols. London, 1820. 48: ii–iii.

[Robert Bage] gave to the world *Mount Henneth; Barham Downs; The Fair Syrian; James Wallace; Hermsprong, or Man as He Is Not; and Man as He Is.*

Of these, *Hermsprong* is democratical in its tendency. It was published at a time when sentiments of that nature were prevalent with a large class of people, and it was much read. It has some strength of thought, but it is far from being a regular work, or exhibiting a consistent character. *Man as He Is* has more of a story, and more variety of character. Sir George Paradyne, the hero, is a young man of fortune, with noble and generous feelings and of a philosophical turn; but, being Man as he is, he is not able entirely to resist the temptations of fortune and gay company, by which he is drawn for a time into a course of dissipation: from this he is rescued by the representations of his tutor and the influence of honourable love; his mistress, who is a young lady of the most delicate feelings, refusing him her hand, though much his inferior in fortune, till he is brought to a more sober way of thinking. The character of Lady Paradyne, his mother, a vain, selfish, fine lady, fond of her son, but teasing him with lectures, is drawn with some humour. But the best sustained character is that of Miss Carlill, a quaker, in which the author has exceedingly well hit off the acuteness and presence of mind, and coolness in argument, by which the society she is supposed to belong are so much distinguished. In her dialogue with a high-church clergyman, she is made to have as much the better of the argument as the late Mrs. Knowles was said to have had in a debate with Dr. Johnson. It is easy to see how much the author delights himself in the dry humour and poignant retorts by which she is made to support her argument. One of the most affecting incidents in these volumes is the sudden discovery of Mr. Mowbray's insanity. The whole is the work of a man who knows the world, and has reflected upon what he has seen; of a man whose mind has more strength than elegance; and whose opinion, often just, sometimes striking, are marked with traits of singularity, and not unfrequently run counter to received notions and established usages.

f. Sir Walter Scott, [on the character of Hermsprong], from *Lives of the Novelists*. 1826. Ed. George Saintsbury. London: J.M. Dent, 1910. 287–88.

Having adverted to this prominent error [the treatment of female sexuality] in Mr. Bage's theory of morals, we are compelled to remark that his ideas respecting the male sex are not less inaccurate, considered as rules of mental government, than the over-indulgence with which he seems to regard female frailty. Hermsprong, whom he produces as the ideal perfection of humanity, is paraded as a man who, freed from all the nurse and the priest has taught, steps forward on his path without any religious or political restraint, as one who derives his own rules of conduct from his own breast, and avoids or resists all temptations of evil passions, because his reason teaches him that they are attended with evil consequences. In the expressive words of our moral poet, Wordsworth, he is

"A reasoning self-sufficient thing,
An intellectual all-in-all."[1]

But did such a man ever exist? or are we, in the fair construction of humanity, with all its temptations, it passions, and its frailties, entitled to expect such perfection from the mere force of practical philosophy? Let each reader ask his own bosom, whether it were possible for him to hold an unaltered tenor of moral and virtuous conduct, did he suppose that to himself alone he was responsible, and that his own reason, a judge so peculiarly subject to be bribed, blinded, and imposed upon by the sophistry with which the human mind can gloss over those actions to which human passions so strongly impel us, was the ultimate judge of his actions? Let each reader ask the question at his own conscience, and if he can honestly and conscientiously answer in the affirmative, he is either that faultless monster which the world never saw,[2] or he deceives himself as grossly as the poor devotee, who, referring his course of conduct to the action of some supposed internal inspiration, conceives himself, upon a different ground, incapable of crime, even when he is in the very act of committing it.

3. Robert Bage on novel-writing

a. Preface to *Mount Henneth* (2nd ed, 1788; 1: iii–vii).

A novel, according to the present usages, may be sent into the world with a preface, or without. I chuse the former, not with any intention to pre-instruct the reader in the nature of the work, for novels have all one nature, but to soften the severity of his criticism, by information of the reasons which drew me in to write.

It is very easy to say, I wrote it for my own amusement, and published it to satisfy the importunity of some very judicious friends, who could not bear that so many beauties should lie concealed in the drawer of a cabinet. But as I intend to be upon honour with my reader, in point of veracity, I have been determined by far different motives. In short, my three daughters assure me, that I write in a very tasty manner; and that it is two years, bating two months, since I made each of them a present of a new silk gown.

Now you must know, my dear Readers, that I live a great way from

---

1 "A Poet's Epitaph," 31–32, slightly misquoted.
2 This line appears in "An Essay Upon Poetry" (1862) by the Duke of Buckingham (line 235); it would, however, probably be more immediately familiar to Scott's readers from Frances Burney's *Evelina* (1778), in which it is quoted in the preface.

London, and have a pretty mechanical way of doing certain things, which has procured me some reputation; and, till lately, as much wealth as any man who thinks of the snug and quiet comforts of life, only, would desire.

But I don't know how it is, people are oftener dunning me for money than usual; and to be sure, I do not pay the ready for raw materials, as I was wont. The proximate cause of this, I am unable to discover; but the predisposing and occasional causes, I once presumed to think, lay hid in the heads or tails of the female part of my family, which, within a few years, have suffered an amazing expansion.

This, my daughters assure me, is an error of the first concoction. It is true, they say, ladies, in their stile of life, must conform to the fashion, and people who don't understand things, are apt to imagine that this must be attended with a great deal of expence; but people who know life, like my daughters, know how to make a little go a great way. In short, I am now convinced I have injured the dear creatures by my suspicions, and to make them amends, have laid the whole burden to the account of the American war.

But my daughters must have new silk gowns.

Now Messieurs, the Reviewers, will kindly inform the world, that in their opinion, I might have been better, and quite as profitably employed in getting up a few more of my mechanical matters. But, with submission to their better judgements, a man cannot be always making ———.

These gentlemen, I believe, are generally, and may they be always, better employed than in reading such books as mine. I have been indebted to their salutary admonitions for many a crown, which fair title pages would otherwise have drawn out of my pocket.

Willingly would I, in gratitude, do them any kindness that lies within the compass of my small abilities. Willingly will I review these books myself, and save their heads the many necessary aches which must otherwise ensue.

MOUNT HENNETH, &c. &c. &c.

"If readers expect to find, in these volumes, any thing like wit, humour, plot, character, or keeping, they will be much disappointed. The work puts us in mind of Doctor Johnson's sarcasm on Macklin's conversation. A perpetual renovation of hope, with perpetual disappointment. To say the least we can of it, it is bad in the beginning, worse and worse in its progress, but the end is heaven."

Into what egregious folly does gratitude sometimes betray simple minded people!

Books of this class are printed, published, bought, read, and deposited in the lumber garret, three months before the Reviewers say a syllable of the matter.

What a dunderhead!

If, after all, the WORLD will deny me its confidence, will buy, read, and judge for itself; do not, dear gentlemen, do not, for gallantry's, for pity's sake, do not *go out of your way* for the sake of establishing my veracity.

But if your book be bad as you say, it is incumbent on us to give the earliest notice, in order to save the WORLD its money, as we have heretofore done yours.

Oh! — that you had seen my daughters!

b. Preface to *Man as he Is*. London, 1792. 1: i–vii.

To a refined and sensible people, — says Mr. Rousseau, — instruction can only be offered in form of a novel. The English are a refined and sensible people; and I desire to instruct them in the best manner possible. Indeed, the mode of instruction by novels, is become as prevalent as Mr. Rousseau himself could have wished; and, to all who think in his elegant manner, will be irrefragable proof of my beloved country being, whatsoever may become of our politics, the first of nations, for refinement and sensibility.

Whether reviewers are graver than the rest of mankind; whether they do not accord to the abovementioned sentiment of John James; or whether they do not think us yet sufficiently refined and sensible; it is certain the whole corps, una voce, exclaim against this favor'd species of composition. Some, I believe, because they think, les Sages, les Marivaux, the Fieldings, the Smollets, are dead and buried, and will not rise again; others, because novels, as novels, do poison the minds of young ladies; and young ladies do poison young gentlemen; and so there is danger of an universal manies, from this corrupted and corrupting cause. But I humbly opine, that boarding schools, where young ladies go to learn to dress and behave, and where they do learn to dress with vanity, and behave with pride, may at least claim an equal share in this business of corruption.

It is true, and it is pity; but it must be owned, there are books called novels, and it is probable I am increasing the number, which would weary the patience of German or Dutch reviewers. Our gentlemen, might with reason complain of their tristes calendoe, those sad days when they were obliged to labour through them, if they were obliged; but surely, here, if any where, it may be allowed them to catch the eel of science, by the tail.

It is not now — as in the days of good Queen Ann — when none read, but those who could read. Except the wives and daughters of country labourers, all women read now, or seem to read. Whether fairy tales or novels, be the mental food most meet for a moiety of our reading ladies, I do not determine; but since, as I presume by the demand, their choice falls upon the latter — I remember what the great king of Prussia said upon a sort of similar occasion: — If my loving subjects chuse to be damned, I give them my permission. — So, if my pretty country women will read nonsense, I am not a man to bar them so reasonable a liberty; and I hope the reviewers will henceforward, grant them the same indulgence.

Upon a serious consideration of the foregoing premises, smit with the love of fame, and having weighed my own abilities in the accurate balance, which authors generally use upon such occasions, I ventured to assume the pen. For fame is fame; whither it arise from the delicate whisper of the well judging few, or the loud roar of the many. Kings have been known to prefer the latter. So has John Wesley. Why not I?

When I had gotten together a competent aggregate, I submitted it to the inspection of a lady of taste, who reads all novels, and has more to say in their praise, than reviewers. She returned my manuscript with this compliment: I thank you, sir, for the perusal; but it by no means answers my expectation.

"Pray ma'am," said I, with an odd sort of trepidation; for authors have delicate nervous systems, and I felt mine rather deranged; "pray ma'am — what a — are your — objections?"

"You call it a novel," answered she. "No, sir — it is not a novel. A novel should have plot. You have no plot. Character — but character is not your forte. Incident — you have indeed a few small incidents, but weak, and by no means of the right sort. Of the marvellous — nothing. Of distress — why you have absolutely no distress that deserves the name. And for love! — oh, I promise you, your twenty thousand fair readers will not thank you for the lessons you have given them on that subject."

"Pray, madam," said I, humbled to the dust, "if it is not a novel, what is it?"

"Really," answered she, "it is totally out of my power to solve that enigma. It is, I believe, what naturalists call a non-descript. However, if you will print, don't mind the title. Leave it to the reviewers to give your book a name; they will do it — depend upon it."

To the reviewers then, with all humiliation of spirit, I commit it; hoping they will condescend to tell us, as soon as may be convenient —

WHAT IT IS.

Appendix C: America and Eighteenth-Century Literature

1. Europeans observing Americans

a. From Pierre de Charlevoix, *Journal of a Voyage to North-America*, 2 vols. London, 1761, 2: 26, 29-31.

[Charlevoix travelled in French North America in 1721 and published an account of his travels in the form of letters to the Duchess de Lesdiguieres. His account of the Native Americans was generally admiring and influenced later writing on the "noble savage."]

It must be acknowledged, that proceedings are carried on in these assemblies with a wisdom and a coolness, and a knowledge of affairs, and I may add generally with a probity, which would have done honour to the areopagus of Athens, or to the senate of Rome, in the most glorious days of those republics: the reason of this is, that nothing is resolved upon with precipitation; and that those violent passions, which have so much disgraced the politics even of Christians, have never prevailed amongst the Indians over the public good. Interested persons fail not, however, to set many springs in motion, and apply an address in the execution of their designs, we could hardly believe barbarians capable of ...

... generally speaking, persons in any degree of credit, are entirely taken up about the public business. A single affair of however little importance, is long under deliberation; every thing being conducted with much coolness and phlegm, and nothing being decided till all who are desirous have been acquainted with it. If a present has been given underhand to any of the elders, to make sure of his suffrage, you are sure to obtain it, if the present has been accepted of. It has scarce ever been known, that an Indian has failed in an engagement of this sort; but it is no easy matter to bring them to accept of it, nor does he ever receive with both hands. Young persons enter early into the knowledge of affairs, which naturally renders them grave and ripe, at an age in which we are still children; this interests them, from their tenderest infancy, in the public weal, and inspires them with an emulation which is fomented with great care, and from which there is nothing that might not be hoped for.

The greatest defect in this government is, that they have scarce the shadow of criminal justice among them; though, to say truth, it is far from being attended with the same bad effects it would be amongst us: the great spring of our passions, and the chief source of those disorders which are the most pernicious to civil society, to wit, private interest, having scarce any power over men who never think of hoarding, and give themselves very little concern about tomorrow.

We may also justly reproach them with the way in which they bring up their children: they do not so much as know what it is to correct them. Whilst they are little, they say they have no reason; and it never enters into the head of an Indian, to think that the judgment is improved by punishment; when they are come to years of discretion, they pretend to be masters of their own actions, and therefore accountable to none. They carry these maxims to such a height, as to suffer themselves to be maltreated by intoxicated persons, without so much as defending themselves for fear of hurting them. Why should we do them any evil, say they, when you talk to them of the ridiculousness of this behaviour; they know not what they do?

In a word, these Indians are perfectly convinced, that man is born free, and that no power on earth has a right to infringe his liberty, and that nothing can compensate the loss of it: and it has been found a very difficult matter to undeceive even the Christians among them, and to make them understand how, by a natural consequence of the corruption of our nature, which is the effect of sin, an unbridled liberty of doing mischief differs very little from obliging them to commit it, because of the strength of the byass which draws us to it; and that the law which restrains us, causes us to approach nearer to our original state of liberty, whilst it appears to take it from us. Happy for them, experience has not made them feel in many things all the power of this tendency which produces so many crimes elsewhere. Their understandings being narrower than ours, their desires are still more so: reduced to desire what is necessary only, for which providence has sufficiently provided, they have scarce so much as the notion of superfluities.

b. From Benjamin Franklin, "Remarks concerning the Savages of North America" (in *Works*, 2 vols, London, 1793), 1: 181-82, 186-90.

[This essay is the probable source of Bage's episode featuring the unsuccessful attempt by Hermsprong's mother to convert Lontac.]

Savages we call them, because their manners differ from ours, which we think the perfection of civility; they think the same of theirs.

Perhaps, if we could examine the manner of different nations with impartiality, we should find no people so rude as to be without any rules of politeness; nor any so polite as not to have some remains of rudeness.

The Indian men, when young, are hunters and warriors; when old, counsellors; for all their government is by the counsel or advice of the sages; there is no force, there are no prisons, no officers to compel obedience, or inflict punishment. Hence they generally study oratory; the best speaker having the most influence....

The politeness of these savages in conversation, is, indeed, carried to excess; since it does not permit them to contradict or deny the truth of what is asserted in their presence. By this means they indeed avoid disputes; but then it becomes difficult to know their minds, or what impression you make upon them. The missionaries who have attempted to convert them to Christianity, all complain of this as one of the great difficulties of their mission. The Indians hear with patience the truths of the gospel explained to them, and give their usual tokens of assent and approbation: you would think they were convinced. No such matter. It is mere civility.

A Swedish minister having assembled the chiefs of the Sasquehannah Indians, made a sermon to them, acquainting them with the principal historical facts on which our religion is founded; such as the fall of our first parents by eating an apple; the coming of Christ to repair the mischief; his miracles and suffering, &c. —— When he had finished, an Indian orator stood up to thank him. "What you have told us," says he, "is all very good. It is indeed bad to eat apples. It is better to make them all into cyder. We are much obliged by your kindness in coming so far, to tell us those things which you have heard from your mothers. In return, I will tell you some of those we have heard from ours.

"In the beginning, our fathers had only the flesh of animals to subsist on; and if their hunting was unsuccessful, they were starving. Two of our young hunters having killed a deer, made a fire in the woods to broil some parts of it. When they were about to satisfy their hunger, they beheld a beautiful young woman descend from the clouds, and seat herself on that hill which you see yonder among the Blue Mountains. They said to each other, it is a spirit that perhaps has smelt our broiling venison, and wishes to eat of it: let us offer some to her. They presented her with the tongue: she was pleased with the taste of it, and said, Your kindness shall be rewarded. Come to this place after thirteen moons, and you shall find something that will be of great benefit in nourishing you and your children to the latest generations. They did so, and to their surprise, found plants they had never seen before; but which, from that ancient time, have been constantly cultivated among us, to our great advantage. Where her right hand had touched the ground, they found maize; where her left hand had touched it they found kidney-beans; and where her backside had sat on it, they found tobacco." The good missionary, disgusted with this idle tale, said, "What I delivered to you were sacred truths; but what you tell me is mere fable, fiction, and falsehood." The Indian, offended, replied, "My brother, it seems your friends have not done you justice in your education; they have not well instructed you in the rules of common civility. You saw that we, who understand and practice those rules believed all your stories, why do you refuse to believe ours?"

c. From John Shebbeare, *Lydia, or Filial Duty*. 4 vols. London, 1755. 1: 2–4.

[This passage is representative of the idealized figure of the "noble savage" in popular fiction of the day; the description of Hermsprong's moral and physical perfection owes something to such figures. The passage opens with Shebbeare's general description of the Onondagas and Cayugas.]

Their Names pronounced with Terror by the Nations round, their Valour recognized beyond all other People; the Tributes annually received from different Kingdoms, evince the Superiority of their military Fame; nor in the milder Parts of legislative Knowledge, are their Souls deficient. Elocution, Reason, Truth, and Probity, are not less the Characteristics of this People's Genius.

In all the oral History of this ancient Race delivered down from Sire to Son, no Instance is to be found of broken Faith with other Nations, no Anecdote of Friends betrayed, or Allies deserted in the Hour of Danger and Distress; their Words are sacredly preserved, their Lives offered up in Battle the Proof of it.

Amongst these Nations, so superior to the other *Indians*, shone forth two Natives eminently superior to their Fellow-Countrymen. *Cannassatego* blest the *Onnondagans* with his Virtues; the *Cayugans* rejoiced in those of *Decanessora*. Rivals in Glory, Friends in military Action, unenvying and unenvied, that Fiend-like Passion had not touched their Breasts, each to the other's Arm and Valour stood indebted for his Life, snatched from the Hands of their implacable Enemies alternately by mutual Prowess.

Cannassatego had now reached his thirtieth Year, in all the Bloom of Manhood; *Decanessora* but two Years elder, warmed with equal Vigour; no human Form was ever seen more graceful, than that of *Cannassatego*, his Person was as strait as the Arrow which his Hands directed from his fatal Bow, his Stature six Foot, the most perfect Height in Human Nature; on his large Neck his Head stood erect and bold, his Face was animated with Features that spoke Sensibility of Soul, high and open was his Forehead, from his Eyes flashed forth the Beams of Courage and Compassion, as each Passion at different Moments animated his Bosom, within which his Heart beat with honest Throbbing for his Country's Service; ample were his Shoulders, yet falling off with easy Grace, his Body all distinctly muscular, his Hips united his upper and lower Parts with perfect Symmetry, his Thighs and Legs completely formed for Strength and Agility. The Air, Attitude and Expression of the beauteous Statue of *Apollo*, which adorns the *Belvedera* Palace at *Rome*, were seen animated in this *American* the Instant he had discharged his deadly Shaft; and tho' the fair Complexion of the *European* Natives was not to be found in this Warrior, yet his Shape and Countenance hindered you from perceiving the Deficiency: the Perfection of his Form, and Expression of his Visage was such, the *Grecian* Sculptors of the famed Statue of *Laocoon*, or the fighting Gladiator, might have studied him with Instruction and Delight; such was the Figure of *Cannassatego*.

d. From William Smith, *An Historical Account of the Expedition against the Ohio Indians, in the Year 1764.* Philadelphia, 1765. (Ann Arbor: University Microfilms), 26–29.

[Smith is describing a release of white prisoners, arranged during General Henry Bouquet's frontier campaign. While Smith clearly disapproves of Europeans "going native," the passage is fairly representative in its account of white captives who have assimilated Native values.]

And here I am to enter on a scene, reserved on purpose for this place, that the thread of the foregoing narrative might not be interrupted — a scene, which language indeed can but weakly describe; and to which the Poet or Painter might have repaired to enrich their highest colorings of the variety of human passions; the Philosopher to find ample subject for his most serious reflections; and the Man to exercise all the tender and sympathetic feelings of the soul.

The scene, I mean, was the arrival of the prisoners in the camp; where were to be seen fathers and mothers recognizing and clasping their once-lost babes; husbands hanging round the necks of their newly-recovered wives; sisters and brothers unexpectedly meeting together after long separation, scarce able to speak the same language, or, for some time, to be sure that they were children of the same parents! In all these interviews, joy and rapture inexpressible were seen, while feelings of a very different nature were painted in the looks of others; — flying from place to place in eager enquiries after relatives not found! trembling to receive an answer to their questions! distracted with doubts, hopes and fears, on obtaining no account of those they sought for! or stiffened into living monuments of horror and woe, on learning their unhappy fate!

The Indians too, as if wholly forgetting their usual savageness, bore a capital part in heightning this most affecting scene. They delivered up their beloved captives with the utmost reluctance; shed torrents of tears over them, recommending them to the care and protection of the commanding officer. Their regard to them continued all the time they remained in camp. They visited them from day to day; and brought them what corn, skins, horses, and other matters, they had bestowed on them, while in their families; accompanied with other presents, and all the marks of the most sincere and tender affection. Nay, they did not stop here, but, when the army marched, some of the Indians sollicited and obtained leave to accompany their former captives all the way to Fort-Pitt, and employed themselves in hunting and bringing provisions for them on the road. A young Mingo carried this still further, and gave an instance of love which would make a figure even in romance. A young woman of Virginia was among the captives, to whom he had form'd so strong an attachment, as to call her his wife. Against all remonstrances of the imminent danger to which he exposed himself by approaching the frontiers, he persisted in following her, at the risk of being killed by the surviving relations of many unfortunate persons, who had been captivated or scalped by those of his nation.

Those qualities in savages challenge our just esteem. They should make us charitably consider their barbarities as the effects of wrong education, and false notions of bravery and heroism; while we should look on their virtues as sure marks that nature has made them fit subjects of cultivation as well as us; and that we are called by our superior advantages to yield them all the helps we can in this way. Cruel and unmerciful as they are, by habit and long example in war, yet whenever they come to give way to the native dictates of humanity, they exercise virtues which Christians need not blush to imitate. When they once determine to give life, they give every thing with it, which, in their apprehension, belongs to it. From every enquiry that has been made, it appears — that no woman thus saved is preserved from base motives, or need fear the violation of her honor. No child is otherwise treated by the persons adopting it than the children of their own body. The perpetual slavery of those captivated in war, is a notion which even their barbarity has not yet suggested to them. Every captive whom their affection, their caprice, or whatever else, leads them to save, is soon incorporated with them, and fares alike with themselves.

These instances of Indian tenderness and humanity were thought worthy of particular notice....

Among the children who had been carried off young, and had long lived with the Indians, it is not to be expected that any marks of joy would appear on being restored to their parents or relatives. Having been accustomed to look upon the Indians as the only connexions they had, having been tenderly treated by them, and speaking their language, it is no wonder that they considered their new state in the light of a captivity, and parted from the savages with tears.

But it must not be denied that there were even some grown persons who shewed an unwillingness to return. The Shawanese were obliged to bind several of their prisoners and force them along to the camp; and some women, who had been delivered up, afterwards found means to escape and run back to the Indian towns. Some, who could not make their escape, clung to their savage acquaintance at parting, and continued many days in bitter lamentations, even refusing sustenance.

For the honor of humanity, we would suppose those persons to have been of the lowest rank, either bred up in ignorance and distressing penury, or who had lived so long with the Indians as to forget all their former connexions. For, easy and unconstrained as the savage life is, certainly it could never be put in competition with the blessings of improved life and the light of religion, by any persons who have had the happiness of enjoying, and the capacity of discerning, them.

2. "Americans" observing Europeans

a. From Baron de Lahontan, *New Voyages to North America*. 2 vols. 1703. Ed. Reuben Gold Thwaites. Chicago, 1905. 2: 535–38.

[This excerpt is taken from a dialogue in which Lahontan discusses European values and institutions with Adario, a Huron who has supposedly "been in France, New York, and Quebec; where [he] Study'd the Customs and Doctrines of the English and French" (2: 519). Lahontan satirizes European hypocrisy through Adario, who here points out the gulf between French religious belief and practice.]

... pray, how comes it about that the *French* believe the Gospel and yet make a jest of its Precepts. This I take to be a manifest Contradiction: For, in the first place, as to the Adoration of the Great Spirit, I see no sign of it in your Actions, so that your Worship consists only in Words, and seems to be Calculated to cheat us. To give you an instance; do not you see every day that your Merchants when they bargain with us for Beaver-Skins, do commonly say, my Goods cost me so much, 'tis true as I Adore the Almighty; I lose so much by you, 'tis true as that God is in Heaven. But I do not find that they offer him the Sacrifice of their most valuable Goods, as we do after we have bought 'em from them, when we burn 'em before their faces. In the next place, as for Working on the days set apart for Worship, I do not find that you make any difference between Holy-Days and Work-Days; for I have frequently seen the *French* bargain for Skins on your Holy-Days, as well as make Nets, Game, Quarrel, beat one another, get Drunk, and commit a hundred extravagant Actions. In a third place, touching the Veneration we have for our Fathers or Ancestours, 'tis but seldom that you follow their Counsel; you suffer 'em to die for Hunger, you leave 'em and take up separate Habitations; you are always ready to ask something of 'em, but never to give 'em any thing; and if you expect any thing from 'em, you wish for their death; or at least you expect it with impatience. In the fourth place, as for Continence with respect to the tender Sex; who is it among you (abating the Jesuits) that has ever acted up to it; do not we see every day that your Youths pursue our Daughters and our Wives, even to the very Fields, with a design to inveigle 'em by presents? Do not they Roll every Night from Hutt to Hutt in our Village, in order to debauch 'em? And dost not thee know how many such adventure there are among thy own Soldiers? In the fifth place, to touch upon the head of Murder; 'tis such a common thing among you, that upon the least accident, you clap your Hands to your Swords and Butcher one another. I remember when I was at *Paris*, People were run thro' in the Streets every night; and upon the Road between *Paris* and *Rochel*, I was told that I was in danger of my life. Sixthly. Lying and Slandering your Brethren, is a thing that you can as little refrain as Eating and Drinking. I never heard four *French-Men* Converse together, without speaking ill of some body; and if you knew what I have heard 'em say publickly of the Viceroy, the Intendant, the Jesuits, and of a thousand People that you know, not excepting your Self, you would be convinc'd that the *French* are very well vers'd in Defamations. And as to the business of Lying, I affirm it for a truth that there is not one Merchant in this Country that will not tell you twenty Lies in selling the worth of a Beaver's Skin in Goods; not to mention the lies they invent in order to defame their Neighbours. In a seventh place, to adjust the Point of ingaging with Married Women, we need no other Proof than to hear your Discourses when you have got a little Drink in your Heads; then you'll entertain us with a great many fine Stories of your Adventures that way. But to go no farther, pray reckon up how many Children are got upon the Wives of the *Coureurs de Bois* during their Husbands absence. In the eighth place, to come to the Article of not encroaching upon our Neighbours Property, how many Thefts or Robberies have you seen committed among the *Coureurs de Bois* since you came to this Country? Have not the Thieves been taken in the Fact, and punish'd accordingly? Is not it such a common thing in your Towns, that one can't walk in the Streets in the Night time with safety, and that you dare not leave your Doors open? In the ninth place, as for going to your Mass to hear some Words spoke in an unknown Language; 'tis true the *French* go commonly to it, but their design in going is to think of other things than Praying. At *Quebec*, the Men go to Mass to pick up the Women, and the Women take the same Method to make Assignments with the Men. I have seen some of your Women call for Cushions, for fear of spoiling their Stockins and Petti-coats; then they sit down upon their Heels, and pull a Book out of a great Bag, which they open and hold in their hands, tho' at the same time, they look more at the Men they like, than at the Prayers contain'd in the Book. Most of your *French* People take Snuff when they're at Mass; they talk, and laugh; and sing rather for Diversion than out of Devotion. And, which is yet worse; I know that during the time of Mass, several Women and Girles take the opportunity of pursuing their Amours, by staying at home all alone. As for your Fasts, I must say they are very comical: You eat of all sorts of Fish till you burst again, you cram down Eggs and a thousand other things, and yet you call this fasting. In fine, my dear Brother, you *French* Folks do all of you make large Pretensions to Faith, and yet you are downright Infidels....

b. From Joseph Addison, *The Spectator* 50 (April 27, 1711). 4 vols. London: J.M. Dent, 1906. 1: 185-86.

[The editor has supposedly found a letter left by four "Indian Kings" — Iroquois leaders who visited London — and reprinted it in his periodical. The building described is St. Paul's Cathedral, which was built after the Great Fire of London in 1666.]

On the most rising Part of the Town there stands a huge House, big enough to contain the whole Nation of which I am King. Our good Brother *E Tow O Koam*, King of the *Rivers*, is of the Opinion it was made by the Hands of that great God to whom it is consecrated. The Kings of *Granajah*, and of the *Six Nations*, believe that it was created with the Earth, and produced on the same Day with the Sun and Moon. But, for my own Part, by the best Information that I could get of this Matter, I am apt to think, that this prodigious Pile was fashioned into the Shape it now bears by several Tools and Instruments, of which they have a wonderful Variety in this Country. It was probably at first an huge misshapen Rock that grew upon the Top of the Hill, which the Natives of the Country (after having cut it into a kind of regular Figure) bored and hollowed with incredible Pains and Industry, till they had wrought in it all those beautiful Vaults and Caverns into which it is divided at this Day. As soon as this Rock was thus curiously scooped to their Liking, a prodigious Number of Hands must have been employed in chipping the Outside of it, which is now as smooth as the Surface of a Pebble; and is in several Places hewn out into Pillars, that stand like the Trunks of so many Trees bound about the top with Garlands of Leaves. It is probable that when this great Work was begun, which must have been many Hundred Years ago, there was some Religion among this People, for they give it the Name of a Temple, and have a Tradition that it was designed for Men to pay their Devotion in. And, indeed, there are several Reasons which make us think, that the Natives of this Country had formerly among them some sort of Worship; for they set apart every seventh Day as sacred: But upon my going into one of these holy Houses on that Day, I could not observe any Circumstance of Devotion in their Behaviour: there was, indeed, a Man in Black who was mounted above the rest, and seemed to utter something with a great deal of Vehemence; but as for those underneath him, instead of paying their Worship to the Deity of the Place, they were most of them bowing and curtseying to one another, and a considerable Number of them fast asleep.

c. From Voltaire, *L'Ingenu; or, the Sincere Huron: A True History*. London, 1768, 25-28; 107-09, 112.

[In this novel, which seems to have strongly influenced Bage, a Huron lands in Brittany, where the Prior de Kerkabon finds evidence that convinces him that the young man is the son of his brother and sister-in-law, who died in Canada. After various adventures, including being converted to Christianity, beating off an attempted English invasion, and falling in love with the beautiful Mlle. St. Yves, the Huron is thrown into prison, where he meets and has long discussions with his fellow prisoner Gordon, a Jansonist.]

[from Chapter III: "The Huron Converted"] ...The prior at length resolved to make him read the New Testament; the Huron devoured it with great pleasure; but not knowing at what time, or in what country all the adventures related in this book had happened, he did not in the least doubt that the scene of action had been in Lower Brittany; and he swore, that he would cut off Caiphas and Pontius Pilate's ears, if ever he met those scoundrels.

His uncle, charmed with these good dispositions, soon brought him to the point; he applauded his zeal, but at the same time acquainted him, that it was needless, as these people had been dead upwards of 1690 years. The Huron soon got the whole book by heart. He sometimes proposed difficulties that greatly embarrassed the prior. He was often obliged to consult the abbé of St. Yves, who not knowing what to answer, brought a Jesuit of Lower-Britany to perfect the conversion of the Huron.

Grace, at length operated; and the Huron promised to become a christian. He did not doubt but that the first step towards it was circumcision: "for," said he, "I do not find in the book that was put into my hands, a single person who was not circumcised; it is therefore evident, that I must make a sacrifice of my prepuce; and the sooner the better." He sent for the surgeon of the village, and desired him to perform the operation, thinking thereby greatly to rejoice Miss Kerkabon and all the company, when the thing was once done. The surgeon, who had never performed such an operation, acquainted the family, who screamed out. The good Kerkabon trembled lest her nephew, whom she knew to be resolute and expeditious, should perform the operation unskilfully himself; and that fatal consequences should ensue, in which the ladies, through the goodness of their hearts, are always concerned.

The prior rectified the Huron's mistake, representing to him, that circumcision was no longer in fashion; that baptism was much more gentle and salutary; that the law of grace was not like the law of rigour. The Huron, who had much good sense, and was well disposed, disputed, but soon acknowledged his error, which seldom happens in Europe among disputants; in a word, he promised to let himself be baptized, whenever they pleased.

It was necessary that he should go previously to confession; and this was the greatest difficulty to surmount. The Huron had constantly in his pocket the book his uncle gave him. He did not there find that a single apostle had ever been confessed, and this made him very restive. The prior silenced him, by shewing him, in the epistle of St. James the Minor, these words: *Confess your sins to one another.* The Huron was mute, and confessed his sins to a Recolet. When he had done, he dragged the Recolet from the confessional chair, and seizing him with a vigorous arm, placed himself in his seat, making the Recolet kneel before him; "Come, my friend, it is said, *we must confess our sins to one another;* I have related to you my sins, and you shall not stir till you recount yours." Whilst he said this, he fixed his great knee against his adversary's stomach. The Recolet roared and groaned, till he brought people to his assistance, who found the catechumen cuffing the monk in the name of St. James the Minor.

[Chapter XIV: "The Progress of the Huron's Intellects"] The ingenuous youth was making a rapid progress in the sciences, and particularly in the science of man. The cause of this sudden disclosure of his understanding, was as much owing to his savage education, as to the disposition of his soul; for having learned nothing in his infancy, he had not imbibed any prejudices. His mind having not been warped by error, had retained all its primitive rectitude. He saw things as they were; whereas the ideas that are communicated to us in our infancy, make us see them in a false light.

"Your persecutors are abominable wretches," said he to his friend Gordon. "I pity you for being oppressed, but I condemn you for being a Jansenist. All sects appear to me to be founded in error; tell me if there be any sectaries in geometry?" "No, my child," said the good old Gordon, heaving a deep sigh; "all men are agreed concerning truth, when demonstrated; but they are too much divided about latent truths." "If there were but one single hidden truth in your load of arguments, which have been so often sifted for such a number of ages, it would doubtless have been discovered, and the universe would certainly have been unanimous, at least, in that respect. If this truth had been necessary, as the sun is to the earth, it would have been as brilliant as that planet. It is an absurdity, an insult to human nature; it is an attack upon the Infinite and Supreme Being, to say there is a truth essential to the happiness of man, which God conceals."

All that this ignorant youth, instructed only by nature, said, made a very deep impression upon the mind of the old unhappy scholiast. "Is it really certain," he cried, "that I should have made myself truly miserable for mere chimeras? I am much more certain of my misery than of effectual grace. — I have spent my time in reasoning upon the liberty of God and human nature, but I have lost my own; neither St. Augustin nor St. Prosper will extricate me from my present misfortunes."

The ingenuous Huron, who gave way to his natural characteristic, at length said, "Will you give me leave to speak to you boldly and frankly? Those who bring upon themselves persecution for such idle disputes, seem to me to have very little sense; those who persecute, appear to me very monsters."

The two captives entirely coincided with respect to the injustice of their captivity. "I am a hundred times more to be pitied than you," said the Huron; "I am born free as the air: I had two lives, liberty and the object of my love; and I am deprived of both. We are both in fetters, without knowing who put them on us, or without being able to enquire. I lived a Huron for twenty years. It is said they are barbarians, because they avenge themselves of their enemies; but they never oppress their friends. I had scarce set foot in France, before I shed my blood for this country: I have, perhaps, preserved a whole province, and my recompence, is, being swallowed up in this sepulchre of the living, where I should have died with rage, had it not been for you. There must then be no laws in this country. Men are condemned without being heard! This is not the case in England. Alas! it was not against the English I should have fought." Thus his growing philosophy could not brook nature being insulted in the first of her rights, and he gave vent to his just choler.

His companion did not contradict him. Absence ever encreases ungratified love, and philosophy does not diminish it. He as frequently spoke of his dear Miss St. Yves, as he did of morality or metaphysics. The more he purified his sentiments, the more he loved. He read some new romances; but he met with few that depicted to him the real state of his soul. He always felt that his heart stretched beyond the bounds of his author. "Alas!" said he, "almost all these writers have nothing but wit and art." At length, the good Jansenist priest became, insensibly, the confidant of his tenderness. He was hitherto acquainted with love as a sin, with which a penitent accuses himself at confession. He now learned to know it as a sentiment equally noble and tender; which can elevate the soul as well as soften it, and can produce, sometimes, virtues. In fine, for the last miracle, a Huron converted a Jansenist.

3. Eighteenth-Century Michillimackinac

a. From Pierre de Charlevoix, *Journal of a Voyage to North-America*, 2 vols. London, 1761. 2: 42–43, 46–47.

[Charlevoix travelled through the Great Lakes region in the summer of 1721 and described Michillimackinac when it was a French mission and trading post.]

The fort is still kept up as well as the house of the missionaries, who at present are not distressed with business, having never found the Outawaies much disposed to receive their instructions, but the court judges their presence necessary in a place where we are often obliged to treat with our allies, in order to exercise their functions on the French, who repair hither in great numbers. I have been assured that since the settlement of the Narrows, and the dispersion of the Indians which has followed upon it, several northern nations that were wont to bring their Furs to this place, have since found the way to Hudson's bay by the river Bourbon where they trade with the English; but Monsieur de la Motte could not foresee this conveniency as we were then in possession of Hudson's bay.

The situation of Michillimakinac is most advantageous for traffic. This post stands between three great lakes; lake Michigan which is three hundred leagues in circuit, without mentioning the great bay which falls into it; lake Huron which is three hundred and fifty leagues in circumference, and is in form of a triangle; and lake Superior, which is five hundred leagues round; all three are navigable for the largest sort of boats, and the two first are separated only by a small strait, which has also water sufficient for the same vessels, which may also without any obstacle sail all over lake Erie as far as Niagara. It is true that there is no communication between lake Huron and lake Superior, but by a channel two and twenty leagues long, and very much incommoded with rapid currents, which do not hinder canoes from going to Michillimakinac, loaded with all the commodities which lake Superior and its shores afford....

The Michillimakinacs live entirely by fishing, and there is perhaps no place in the world where they are in greater plenty; the most common sorts of fish in the three lakes, and in the rivers which discharge themselves into them, are the herring, the carp, the gilt-fish, the pike, the sturgeon, the astikamegue or white-fish, and especially the trout. There are three sorts of these last taken; amongst which is one of a monstrous size, and in so great quantities, that an Indian with his sword will strike to the number of fifty sometimes in the space of three hours: but the most famous of all is the white-fish; it is nearly of the size and figure of a mackrel, and whether fresh or salted nothing of a fish-kind can exceed it. The Indians tell you that it was Michabou who taught their ancestors to fish, invented nets of which he took the idea from Arachne's, or the spider's web. Those people, as your Grace, very well sees, do their deity full as little honour as he deserves, by sending him to school to such a contemptible insect.

b. From John Long, *Voyages and Travels of an Indian Interpreter and Trader*. London, 1791, 39–41.

[After some years of living among and trading with Natives in Quebec, John Long set out to try fur trading along the Northwestern frontier. He left Montreal on 4 May 1777; in this passage he describes his journey west along the rivers, the most usual way of travelling from the settled eastern colonies to the frontier.]

[At Lachine] the Indian goods are put on board very carefully; the dry merchandise in bales about eighty pounds weight, the rum, powder, and shot, in small kegs. The voyage from Trois Rivières to La Chine is tedious and troublesome, as there is a strong current to combat; and without a fair wind, and occasionally a brisk gale to assist or relieve the constant use of the paddles, it would be impossible to make any way. Where the water is shallow, the canoes must be forced forward with long setting poles, while the men wade knee deep, and pull against the current with ropes; this is a labour and fatigue beyond what will be easily imagined. Custom has however made the Canadians very expert, and I must do them the justice to say they encounter these difficulties with uncommon chearfulness, though they sometimes exclaim, "C'est la misere, mon bourgeois."

From La Chine to Michillimakinac, there are thirty six portages; the distance by land and water is about nine hundred miles: in favourable weather the journey is frequently performed in about a month. Great care is necessary to steer the canoes up the strong rapids; to labour and care must also be added experience to keep them upright, and prevent their striking or rubbing against the stones, as they are very slight, and easily damaged. Whenever by accident they receive an injury, as they frequently do, the hole is stopped with gum, melted with a piece of charcoal; the gum by wetting immediately becomes hard, and is capable of resisting the impression of the water. When the hole is too large to be stopped by gum only, the inner bark of the birch tree, pounded and tempered like mortar, is put on the aperture, this is covered by a linen rag, and the edges firmly cemented with gum.

We continued our voyage to La Barriére, at the head of the Long Saut, or long water fall, a very dangerous current from the extreme rapidity of the fall. At the top of this fall there are some traders settled, but they are not of any consequence either for the extent of their commerce, or the profits arising from the peltry they collect. The Savages in those parts being too well acquainted with the value of furs and skins to be imposed upon, unless when they are intoxicated, an advantage I must confess too frequently taken.

From this fall we proceeded to the Lake of the two Mountains, where there is a village belonging to the Connecedaga Indians, already described. At this place I stayed a day among my old friends, which was all the time my engagements would allow, as it is of the most material consequence in this branch of trade to be early at the wintering ground.

We proceeded to the Uttawa, or Grand River, coasting all the way till we came to Lake Nipissin, from whence the River St. Laurence takes its rise. We then entered the French River, leading to Lake Huron, and proceeded with very favourable weather to Michillimakinac, where we arrived on the 17th of June.

The country every where abounds with wild animals, particularly bears, moose and other deer, beavers, beaver eaters, lynx, foxes, squirrels, fishers, otters, martins, minx, wood cats, racoons, wolves, musquashes, &c. — There are scarce any but savage inhabitants to be found, who rove from place to place for subsistance, feeding on the animals they kill, except the skunk, or pole cat, which they never eat, unless pressed by the most extreme hunger.

c. From Alexander Henry, *Travels and Adventures in Canada and the Indian Territories*. 1809. Edmonton: Hurtig, 1969, 40-41.

[Henry did not publish his memoirs until 1809, but his account of life as an Englishman in Michillimackinac in the 1760s is one of the most detailed available. He was repeatedly warned, when he first set out to trade at the fort in 1761, that the local Native Americans were hostile to the English but accepted the French (the area was still in French hands at the time). He disguised himself as a French Canadian, but he could not sustain the masquerade, and he barely escaped with his life when he returned in 1763, just before the capture of the Fort. After that, he lived with his Native rescuers for a year before returning to the English settlements. Here, he describes the fort as it was just before changing hands from the French to the English.]

Fort Michilimackinac was built by order of the governor-general of Canada, and garrisoned with a small number of militia, who, having families, soon became less soldiers than settlers. Most of those, whom I found in the fort, had originally served in the French army.

The fort stands on the south side of the strait which is between Lake Huron and Lake Michigan. It had an area of two acres and is enclosed with pickets of cedar-wood; and it is so near the water's edge, that, when the wind is in the west, the waves break against the stockade. On the bastions, are two small pieces of brass English cannon, taken some years since, by a party of Canadians, who went on a plundering expedition, against the posts of Hudson's Bay which they reached by the route of the river Churchill.

Within the stockade, are thirty houses, neat in their appearance, and tolerably commodious; and a church, in which mass is celebrated, by a jesuit missionary. The number of families may be nearly equal to that of the houses; and their subsistence is derived from the Indian traders, who assemble here, in their voyages to and from Montréal. Michilimackinac is the place of deposit, and point of departure, between the upper countries and the lower. Here, the outfits are prepared for the countries of Lake Michigan and the Missisipi, Lake Superior and the north-west; and here, the returns, in furs, are collected, and embarked for Montréal.

d. From Jonathan Carver, *Travels through the Interior Parts of North America*. London, 1778, 18-19.

[Carver, who spent time among the Nawdoessie Indians (he spelled the name "Naudowessie") and wrote extensively about them, would have been an accessible source for information about North America. It seems likely that Bage knew this book, but he made no attempt to incorporate the specific details of Carver's account of native life. Here, Carver gives an account of the capture of Michillimackinac from the English in the Pontiac uprising, which occurred three years before he arrived there.]

Michillimackinac, from whence I began my travels, is a Fort composed of a strong stockade, and is usually defended by a garrison of one hundred men. It contains about thirty houses, one of which belongs to the governor, and another to the commissary. Several traders also dwell within its fortifications, who find it a convenient situation to traffic with the neighbouring nations. Michillimackinac, in the language of the Chipéway Indians, signifies a Tortoise; and the place is supposed to receive its name from an Island, lying about six or seven miles to the north-east, within sight of the Fort, which has the appearance of that animal.

During the Indian war that followed soon after the Conquest of Canada in the year 1763, and which was carried on by an army of confederate nations composed of the Hurons, Miamies, Chipéways, Ottowaws, Pontowattimies, Mississauges, and some other tribes, under the direction of Pontiac a celebrated Indian warrior, who had always been in the French interest, it was taken by surprize in the following manner. The Indians having settled their plan, drew near the Fort, and began a game at Ball, a pastime much used among them and not unlike tennis. In the height of their game, at which some of the English officers not suspecting any deceit stood looking on, they struck the ball, as if by accident, over the stockade; this they repeated two or three times, to make the deception more complete, till at length, having by this means lulled every suspicion of the centry at the south gate, a party rushed by him; and the rest soon following, they took possession of the Fort, without meeting with any opposition. Having accomplished their design, the Indians had the humanity to spare the lives of the greatest part of the garrison and traders, but they made them all prisoners, and carried them off. However some time after they took them to Montreal, where they were redeemed at a good price. The Fort also was given up again to the English at the peace made with Pontiac by the commander of Detroit the year following.

Select Bibliography

Works by and Reviews of Robert Bage

Bage, Robert. *Barham Downs*. 2 vols. London, 1784.

—. *The Fair Syrian*. 2 vols. London, 1787.

—. *Hermsprong; or, Man as he is Not*. 3 vols. 1796.

—. *James Wallace*. 3 vols. London, 1788.

—. [Letters to William Hutton]. Birmingham Public Library, MS. 486802 IIR 29.

—. *Man as he Is*. 4 vols. London, 1792.

—. *Mount Henneth*. 2 vols. London, 1782.

Faulkner, Peter, ed. *Hermsprong*. 1796. Oxford: Oxford UP, 1985.

Holcroft, Thomas. Review of *Man as he Is*: *Monthly Review*. 10, n.s. (March 1793): 297-302.

Review of *Barham Downs*. *Monthly Review* 71 (Sept. 1784): 223-24.

Review of *The Fair Syrian*. *The Monthly Review* 76 (April 1787): 325-29

Review of *Hermsprong*. *The British Critic* 7 (1796): 430.

Review of *Hermsprong*. *The Critical Review*. 2nd series. 23 (1798): 234.

Review of *James Wallace*. *The Critical Review*. 67 (Jan. 1789): 76-77.

Review of *James Wallace*. *Monthly Review*. 80 (June 1789): 499-502.

Review of *Mount Henneth*. *Monthly Review* 66 (Feb. 1782): 129-31.

Tave, Stuart, ed. *Hermsprong*. Philadelphia: Pennsylvania State UP, 1982.

[Taylor, William]. Review of *Hermsprong*. *Monthly Review*. 21, n.s. (Sept. 1796): 21-24.

[Wollstonecraft, Mary]. Review of *Hermsprong*. *Analytical Review*. 24 (Dec. 1796): 608-09.

Other Primary Sources

Austen, Jane. *Novels of Jane Austen*. Ed. R.W. Chapman. 6 vols. Oxford: Oxford UP, 1933.

Barbauld, Anna Laetitia. "Preface, biographical and critical." *Hermsprong*. Vol 48 of *The British Novelists*. 50 vols. 1810. London, 1820: i-iii.

Beale, Catherine Hutton, ed. *Reminiscences of a Gentlewoman of the Last Century: Letters of Catherine Hutton*. Birmingham, 1891.

Boswell, James. *The Life of Johnson*. 1791. Ed. R.W. Chapman. London: Oxford UP, 1935.

Burke, Edmund. *Reflections on the Revolution in France*. 1790. Oxford: Oxford UP, 1993.

Chesterfield, Lord. *Letters*. Ed. David Roberts. Oxford: Oxford UP, 1992.

Crèvecoeur, J. Hector St. John de. *Letters of an American Farmer*. 1782. Ed. Susan Manning. Oxford: Oxford UP, 1998.

Extract of a letter from a gentleman in America to a friend in England, on the subject of emigration. London (?), 1792 (?).

Fletcher, Eliza. Letter to Allan Cunningham, 26 Sept. 1838. National Library of Scotland, ms. 2617.

[Hazlitt, William]. Review of *The Wanderer*. *The Edinburgh Review* 24 (1815): 320-38.

Holcroft, Thomas. *Anna St. Ives*. 1792. Ed. Peter Faulkner. Oxford: Oxford UP, 1970.

Hutton, William. "Memoirs of Mr. Bage." *The Monthly Magazine*. 13 (Jan. 1802): 478-80.

Imlay, Gilbert. *A Topographical Description of the Western Territory of North America*. London, 1792.

Jeremy, David John ed. *Henry Wansey and his American Journal*. Philadelphia: American Philosophical Society, 1970.

[Jacson, Frances]. *Disobedience*. 4 vols. London, 1797.

[Lockhart, John Gibson]. Review of Sir Walter Scott's *Lives of the Novelists*. *Quarterly Review* 34 (1826): 349-78.

[Marishall, Jean]. *A Series of Letters*. 2 vols in 1. Edinburgh, 1789.

Paul, C. Kegan. *William Godwin: His Friends and Contemporaries*. 2 vols. London, 1876.

Pye, Henry. *The Democrat*. 2 vols. London, 1796.

Scott, Walter. *The Lives of the Novelists*. London. 1826. London: J.M. Dent, 1928.

Smith, William. *An Historical Account of the Expedition against the Ohio Indians, in the Year 1764*. Philadelphia, 1765.

Wardle, Ralph, ed. *The Collected Letters of Mary Wollstonecraft*. Ithaca: Cornell UP, 1979.

Wollstonecraft, Mary. *A Vindication of the Rights of Woman*. 1792. Oxford: Oxford UP, 1994.

Secondary Sources

Blakey, Dorothy. *The Minerva Press, 1790-1820*. Oxford: The Bibliographical Society, 1939.

Booth, Wayne C. *The Rhetoric of Fiction*. Chicago: U of Chicago P, 1983.

Butler, Marilyn. *Jane Austen and the War of Ideas*. Oxford: Clarendon, 1975.

Copeland, Edward. *Women Writing about Money*. Cambridge: Cambridge UP, 1996.

Faulkner, Peter. *Robert Bage*. Boston: Twayne, 1979.

Fliegalman, Jay. *Pilgrims and Prodigal: The American Revolution against Patriarchal Authority, 1750-1800*. Cambridge: Cambridge UP, 1982.

Flint, Kate. *The Woman Reader 1837-1914*. Oxford: Clarendon, 1993.

Heilman, Robert. *America in English Fiction, 1760-1800*. 1937. New York: Octagon Books, 1968.

Holmes, Richard. *Coleridge: Early Visions*. London: Hodder & Stoughton, 1989.

Johnson, Claudia. *Equivocal Beings: Politics, Gender, and Sentimentality in the 1790s*. Chicago: U of Chicago P, 1995

Kelly, Gary. *The English Jacobin Novel 1780-1805*. Oxford: Clarendon, 1976.

Kiernan, V.G. *The Lords of Humankind: European Attitudes towards the Outside World in the Imperial Age*. London: Weidenfeld & Nicolson, 1969.

London, April. *Women and Property in the Eighteenth-Century English Novel*. Cambridge: Cambridge UP, 1999.

Manning, Susan. "Introduction." Hector St. John de Crèvecoeur, *Letters of an American Farmer*. 1782. Oxford: Oxford UP, 1998.

Newman, Gerald. *The Rise of English Nationalism: A Cultural History 1740-1830*. New York: St. Martin's Press, 1987.

Perkins, Pam. "Playfulness of the Pen: Robert Bage and the Politics of Comedy," *Journal of Narrative Technique*, Vol 26: 1 (Winter, 1996) 30-47.

Robbins, Caroline. "The Rage for Going to America." *Pennsylvania History*, Vol. 28: 3 (July, 1961) 231-253.

Said, Edward. *Culture and Imperialism*. London: Chatto and Windus, 1993.

Saintsbury, George, ed. Sir Walter Scott. *Lives of the Novelists*. London: J.M. Dent, 1928.

Scheuermann, Mona. *Social Protest in the Eighteenth-Century English Novel*. Columbus: U of Ohio P, 1985.

Schofield, R.E. *The Lunar Society of Birmingham*. Oxford: Clarendon, 1963.

Sekora, John. *Luxury: The Concept in Western Thought, Eden to Smollett*. Baltimore: Johns Hopkins UP, 1977.

Siskin, Clifford. *The Work of Writing: Literature and Social Change in Britain, 1700-1830*. Baltimore: Johns Hopkins UP, 1998.

Skinner, Gillian. *Sensibility and Economics in the Novel, 1740-1800: The Price of a Tear*. London: Macmillan, 1999.

Thale, Mary, ed. *Selections from the Papers of the London Corresponding Society, 1792-1799*. Cambridge: Cambridge UP, 1983.

Tompkins, J.M.S. *The Popular Novel in England, 1770-1800*. London, Constable, 1932.

Ty, Eleanor. *Unsex'd Revolutionaries: Five Women Novelists of the 1790s*. Toronto: U of Toronto P, 1993.

Joseph Priestley → tried to fuse science w/ religion.
→ Rationalism w/ Christian theism.
→ founder of Unitarianism
→ Rational Dissenter
→ Millenarian

Armenian & Baxterian theology?
Arianism!